DREAM
of the
DRAGON POOL

A DAOIST QUEST

ALBERT A. DALIA

PLEASURE BOAT STUDIO: A LITERARY PRESS

Dalia, Albert A.
Dream of the Dragon Pool: A Daoist Quest

First printing

ISBN: 978-1-929355-34-1

Library of Congress Control Number: 2006937239

Cover art copyright © Jing-hua Gao Dalia, *www.jhdalia.com*
Interior design by Susan Ramundo

Pleasure Boat Studio is a proud subscriber to the Green Press Initiative. This program encourages the use of 100% post-consumer recycled paper with environmentally friendly inks for all printing projects in an effort to reduce the book industry's economic and social impact. With the cooperation of our printing company, we are pleased to offer this book as a Green Press book.

Pleasure Boat Studio books are available through the following:
SPD (Small Press Distribution) Tel. 800-869-7553, Fax 510-524-0852
Partners/West Tel. 425-227-8486, Fax 425-204-2448
Baker & Taylor Tel. 800-775-1100, Fax 800-775-7480
Ingram Tel. 615-793-5000, Fax 615-287-5429

and through
PLEASURE BOAT STUDIO: A LITERARY PRESS
201 West 89 Street
New York, NY 10024

Contact **Jack Estes**
Fax: 888-810-5308
pleasboat@nyc.rr.com
www.pleasureboatstudio.com

—

To My Parents for Their Boundless Support,

To the Chinese People for Their Boundless Imagination.

—

AUTHOR'S STATEMENT

The adventure you are about to embark on is based upon an 8th-century Chinese understanding of reality. While many of the characters, incidents, and locations in the story appear in Chinese historical records, some are yet to be discovered, and others may never be. It is up to you to decide if any of this matters.

MOUNTAIN DIALOGUE

I've been asked the reason for dwelling in blue-green mountains.
I laugh without answering, heart at ease.
In the mountains, peach blossoms on flowing waters—
mysteriously vanish.
There is another Reality—not of the human realm.

Li Bo (701–762 C.E.)

DRAMATIS PERSONAE

Li Bo (pronounced, "lee bwo," he is also known as Li Bai, 701–762 C.E.)—China's most famous poet was said to be from its far distant Western Regions, possibly of Persian origins. A brilliant poet, wanderer, drinker, womanizer, and Daoist adept, his impulsiveness and reliance on the wine cup constantly complicated his life. Our story finds him in the mid-fifth decade of his life on the way to exile in the far southwestern region of the Chinese empire (present day southern border region of Yunnan province).

Wang Ah Wu (known as *Ah Wu*)—Li Bo's closest companion is of Turkish origins. He was a frontier guard in the imperial army, a legendary crossbowman known as the "Steel Talon." He is fiercely loyal to Li Bo.

Old Zhou—Li Bo's boatman for the last ten years. His knowledge of the rivers and lakes of China opened an inspiring world for Li's poetic gift.

Luo Jhu-yun—A young and powerful Chinese shamaness. She is Grand Shamaness to the Chinese Emperor Xuan-zong. After saving the emperor from an assassin, she has escaped the intrigues of the imperial court and now seeks the "purity" of Mount Wu's solitudes and the service of its Rain Goddess.

The Lady of the Purple Vault—A powerful Daoist Immortal. She is the spirit contact to the Shamaness Luo and the servant of Mount Wu's powerful Rain Goddess. Li Bo tends to refer to her as the "Purple Immortal."

Ma Ssu-ming—A "wandering blade." A young, expert swordsman who claims to be a musician and drinker by trade.

Lao-huang—A drunken monkey. Ma Ssu-ming's talented pet that he claims to be his teacher in the art of ghost catching.

The Blood Dragon—A creature of traditional Chinese legend along the Yangtze River, said to be the immature form of a dragon. Lacking a fully formed dragon's grace and beneficial spirit, it feeds on human blood and enslaves its victims as ghosts. In water, it has the appearance of an alligator. It is, however, on land among humans that it assumes its most horrific form.

Chen Shao-lin—An attractive golden-haired, green-eyed female ghost, originally from the Central Asian land of Sogdiana (present day Uzbekistan). Killed by the Blood Dragon and transformed into a ghost, she is used by the monster to lure men to their death and enslavement.

The Albino Swordsman—An assassin of unknown origins. A deadly and ruthless eunuch sent by the emperor's enemies to kill Grand Shamaness Luo. Using a magic Tibetan black pearl, he can will himself into his victims' dreams and kill them in their sleep.

Su-lu—the fierce *qughan* (khan or chief) and one of the greatest early leaders of the Tügi confederation of Turks in Central Asia; also known to the Arabs as Abû Muzâhim ("Father of the Competition"). He was Ah Wu's frequent rival in the wars of that region; and was murdered by his own tribesmen in 738 C.E.

Hsiang Goddess—the mythical female ruler of the Hsiang River, Lake Dong-ting, and the central region of the Yangtze River. One of the greatest water goddesses of Chinese culture.

Tang Dynasty—618–907 C.E., considered one of China's greatest golden ages. Chinese power controlled or influenced most of East and Central Asia during this period.

Chang'an—present day Xian, once the grand imperial capital of the Tang Dynasty.

Long River—Changjiang or Yangtze River is the longest river in Asia and third longest in the world.

Xia-zhou—pronounced "sha-joe," is the main Long River port before entering the Three Gorges on the way into Sichuan province.

Daoism/Dao—the native Chinese religion/philosophy that is frequently spelled "Taoism," as its central concept of the Way is frequently spelled "Tao," but pronounced "dao."

The Dragon Pool Sword—A mythical Chinese weapon reputed to possess awe-inspiring power. Its exact nature, however, is rightly the substance of conflicting legends.

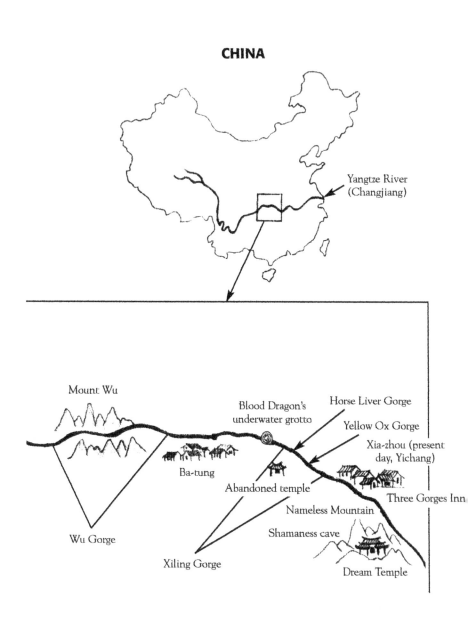

CHINA

Yangtze River
(Changjiang)

Mount Wu

Blood Dragon's
underwater grotto

Horse Liver Gorge

Yellow Ox Gorge

Xia-zhou (present
day, Yichang)

Ba-tung

Abandoned temple

Three Gorges Inn

Wu Gorge

Nameless Mountain

Shamaness cave

Xiling Gorge

Dream Temple

THE LONG RIVER JOURNEY OF LI BO

PROLOGUE

Mountains (*shan*) in ancient China existed in various shades of mystery and awe. There were the verified homes of respectable spirits, like *Tai shan*, where the Sons of Heaven, the Emperors of China, worshiped the mysterious powers of the natural world. There were those where the spirits of China's great religions held forth, like *Emei shan* in the west, home of the great Buddhist Bodhisattva Amitabha, or the equally famous *Wu-Dang shan*, home to some of the Daoist pantheon.

Then there were the homes of the popular spirits, like the famous *Wu shan* with its twelve peaks in the middle of the famous Three Gorges in the western province of Sichuan. It was the abode of the legendary Rain Goddess. Her story dates back to early antiquity, when she is said to have seduced the King of Chu. She left him heartbroken, however, when she returned to her natural form as the dawn clouds and evening rain. The howl of the gibbon is said to be the king's eternal cry for his lost love.

Our story involves that glorious peak, but starts with an earlier adventure on a much lesser known mountain on the upper reaches of the Long River near the famed Three Gorges region. The local people refused to name this mountain because they feared it so much and felt it was better left anonymous. Normally, the mountain spirit would be displeased by such an obvious lack of respect, but since he was killed by a much more malevolent spirit it did not matter.

According to the earliest gazetteers, Blood Dragons were destructive by nature. Thus, it was not unusual that the one in residence at the foot of this nameless mountain killed the local mountain spirit. Nor was it unusual that this Blood Dragon also enjoyed feasting on the blood of the local inhabitants, for that behavior was the basis of their name. As immature Dragons, although such creatures were powerful, they were neither wise nor compassionate. They were opportunists, seizing whatever suited their advantage. Like politicians, they abused the weak and schemed to increase their power at the expense of others.

These creatures were difficult to thwart. According to ancient records, it took the combination of a heroic spirit with an invincible weapon to vanquish them. While finding a hero was difficult enough, even such status did not guarantee an easy time with an invincible weapon.

PART ONE

THE SHORE

— 1 —

"Run faster, run! They're catching up!" said the boy running behind his younger brother along the forested path. The smaller boy, tripping over his shabby brown robe, landed on the dirt track and began crying aloud. "Don't let them catch me, please!"

"Get up and run," urged his brother. It was too late. The two men who had been chasing them, bracketed them, blocking access to either end of the trail. They smiled. Their pale thin hands drew their swords.

"Now, my noisy little pests, you will meet our leader, one way or the other," said the taller one in a half-whisper, his eye twitching in anticipation of the kill.

The little boy, clinging to the arms of his brother, sobbed uncontrollably. "I want to go home; no more games, please take me home."

"Calm down. I won't let them hurt you," said his older brother, drawing a short vegetable knife from inside his tunic.

"One step closer and . . ."

The gaunt swordsman smiled and made a killing thrust at the boy. The gleaming sword tip rushed toward his unprotected chest.

Krack! A crossbow bolt shatterred the tip of the sword it in mid-attack. The rest of the sword flew out of the man's bleeding hand. His partner, ready to strike at the children, wheeled around and received the second crossbow bolt through his forehead. His eyes widened. A colorless fluid gushed out of his head and ran down his nose. He vanished.

The swordless swordsman turned and ran back down the path. A bolt ripped into his back, flinging him forward into some other realm, and he too disappeared.

"I didn't realize you could reload that thing so fast," said a thin man dressed in a faded blue robe. He had stepped out of a clump of flame-shaped junipers on the side of the dirt path. Above average height for a Chinese, but the roundish shape of his eyes and long red-tipped nose marked him as someone whose family origins were far to the west of the ancient centers of Chinese civilization. His unruly white hair was pulled to the back of his oblong skull and barely held in place by a lacquered wooden hairpin. It was carved in the shape of a dragon after the style of the Daoist sages. The slight breeze flowing up from the Long River animated the thin white strains of his goatee and moustache.

"Made some changes to the drawing mechanism just before we left Yangzhou," said the large man. He was dressed in an ample black tunic trimmed in white, with loose white pants tucked into calf-high leather boots. His thick black hair was covered and restrained by a large black bandana. His great beak-like nose, flourishing bushy brown beard and eyebrows, round eyes, and foreign accent clearly indicated that his ancestors were also not from the Chinese heartland. The jagged pale scar that ran diagonally right to left across his face, like the Grand Canal across the heart of the Middle Kingdom, indicated he was a veteran warrior. His lack of a right ear was further testimony to the unpleasantness of such experience. He set two more bolts into his double-shot crossbow and pulled on the mechanism that set the two short double reflex bows. A large leather-sheathed broadsword dangled off his left hip.

"Are you two all right?" asked the blue-robed man blocking the path of the frightened boys.

They cringed together more tightly, the older boy still holding his pathetic vegetable-cutting blade high.

"Who are you? What do you want around here?"

"Oh don't worry, he's not as foreign as he looks," said the bear-like crossbow man with a hearty laugh. He limped toward them.

"Please, get up. We'll take you home. We need directions," said the thin man.

The older boy stood up slowly. The thin man's eyes seemed to have a hypnotic effect on him. The boy blinked vigorously and shook his head. "What do you want here? No one comes here." He lowered his knife only enough to help his brother stand.

"But we are crazy," said the big man. He continued to scan the forest that pressed in on both sides of the path.

"Enough, Ah Wu. Sorry, boys. We are seeking the Dream Temple and are in need of directions," said the thin man. He pointed to the dark forested mass that towered before them.

"Dream Temple? Never heard of it," said the older boy.

"Knew it," said Ah Wu, not taking his eyes off the forest.

"I am Li Bo, a professional traveler. Please take us to your village elders."

"No one knows this Dream Temple . . .," said the older boy, but his brother blurted out, "It's the Blood Dragon's realm!"

"Quiet," said the older boy. "That mountain is haunted. It is an evil place. Not a place for humans."

Li looked at the boys intently. In an instant, his eyes flashed and the Persian dagger, sheathed under his left forearm, hidden by the sleeves of his robe, was free. The older boy gasped.

Li smiled, his round eyes softening. "Go, quickly."

Just as the boys vanished, two crossbow bolts hissed into the beaten dirt of the path, exactly where they had been cowering.

"Camel's ass," said Ah Wu. "You let them escape!"

Li Bo looked away down the path. He noticed how it rose up into the somber forest. "I saw my sixteen-year-old son in the elder."

Ah Wu's red scar changed to a softer white. He looked down at his spent crossbow; briefly the thought of his two sons, both lost in the Western Region wars, gave him pause. "This side trip, it's dangerous. We should get on with this exile and be patient. These political cases, they soon blow over. In no time, the Court will issue a reprieve, and you'll be back with your family. It happens all the time."

"I think the Dream Temple will give me a better chance of making something positive out of this . . . this wrongful judgment."

"Camel piss! A stupid idea! You heard what that kid . . . what that thing said. Even the ghosts of this region never heard of your precious Dream Temple."

"You believe a ghost?"

"Why not? Do you really believe that drunken dancing girl we met in the inn can tell your future? 'Find the Dream Temple,' she says, 'a place where dreams bring peace to troubled hearts.' Camel turds! One minute you're cursing the Court and all the spirits and the next . . . you're like some pious grandmother ready to burn incense and offer scented paper money to the mere hint of a spirit."

"The path back down to the boat and the river will only lead to my death in exile. They'll never call me back. But the Dream Temple . . . to dream . . . in dreams all things are possible. Dreams are opportunities. Maybe there's even a way to be reinstated to Court and to see my family again. I must try this path."

"The Court! That Court has ordered your death exile! Maybe you should become a Buddhist, since you seem intent on trying everything. Then you could be reborn as an aristocrat. It's the only way for people like us to get into that Chinese mausoleum of a Court. Of course, you've never been much help in keeping a position at Court either."

"What do you mean?"

"The 'old wine genius,' 'wine makes its own rules'? How many times can you use those lines and appear before the Emperor drunk? The first few times it's amusing, but then, no matter how great your wit, your affair with the wine cup is bound to defeat you."

Li smiled.

Ah Wu's scar reddened. "It's no longer a joke. This is not a dream. Look where we are!"

Li turned away from Ah Wu and looked up the path. The narrow dirt track moved up into a dense pine forest. Its twisted forms appeared as dark grotesque outlines in the gathering mist. Li picked up his bamboo frame backpack and untied his reed rain cape. The movement jarred out of the pack a small vermilion scroll tied with yellow imperial ribbons and seals; both men stared at it as if some rare and terrible creature had made a sudden appearance.

The Imperial order of Li's exile to far Ye-lang in Yunnan province was like a meteor ordered by Heaven to take direct aim on his life. It had destroyed his family, his career, and, most painfully, his poetic voice.

There was little doubt now that Li had misjudged the Prince of Yung's intentions when, having been forced out of his Court position, he joined the young man's voyage down the Long River. He was unaware of the Prince's intention to revolt and set up his own kingdom in the region south of the Long River delta. When the plans for the rebellion were discovered, the Prince executed, and all those associated with him sentenced to execution, Li Bo's friends came to his rescue. The initial death sentence was commuted to exile, but now, in his fifties, Li still thought of himself as dead—a man without his family, an immortal without his wine, a poet without his voice.

Li picked up the small scroll, which he called his "travel pass to hell," and stuffed it back into his pack. He looked up at Ah Wu, who turned away and began to reload his crossbow. When Li was released from prison, Ah Wu retired from his duties as captain of the Imperial Guard. Only Ah Wu greeted Li at the prison gate and joined him on his trip into exile; there was no question of his loyalty. Yet, there were those at Court who questioned Ah Wu's loyalties to the Emperor when he requested retirement to join a "criminal" in exile. The Emperor, however, was not one of them as he was indebted to Ah Wu for saving his life.

The Emperor was also indebted to his Grand Shamaness Luo Jhu-yun for exposing the assassination plot in time to alert Ah Wu and his guard. She, however, was not granted her request to leave the Court for religious cultivation on distant Mount Wu. Ah Wu was of the opinion that while there was enough military skill to protect the Emperor, spiritual connections such as Shamaness Luo's were extremely rare. He also felt that the Emperor simply liked to surround himself with beauty. Although he had never met her, hidden away as she was in the recesses of the Imperial family quarters, Ah Wu had frequently heard of the shamaness's virginal beauty and of the Emperor's desire to partake of it. On their way up river, Li and Ah Wu heard stories claiming that the shamaness escaped from the capital. If the stories were true, it was common belief that only divine intervention could save her from the Emperor's reach.

This was now all history, thought Li Bo. Now, the long road into exile lay before them. Ah Wu was right, of course; his addiction to the wine cup had landed him in this situation. While wine had opened his heart to the grandest poetic inspirations, it had also clouded his judgment and loosened the constraints on his behavior. In a place like the Imperial Court, where jealousies abounded, his position as an outsider, a non-Chinese without aristocratic pedigree, made him a natural target. Adding wine to his uninhibited, impulsive nature only quickened the gathering of his enemies at Court. His brief interlude with the rebel Prince was all that they needed to strike and have him eliminated once and for all. Court politics was a deadly game that in the end filled his wine cup with tears of blood. Yet, and this frightened him, he could not let go of his dream to succeed at that game, to again experience the honor of the Imperial hand seasoning his soup as had once happened when the Emperor requested his presence at dinner.

Li's mind was filled with memories. He threw the reed rain cape over his shoulders. The thought of wine still made him thirsty, but he and Ah Wu carried only water to this nameless mountain. Perhaps the Dream Temple would be better stocked— yet, he secretly wondered if it really existed.

Ah Wu finished loading the two bolts into his crossbow. His scar was red, but not from the effort. He turned back to Li. "Dreams can also turn out to be nightmares!"

A thin, tired smile crossed Li's pale face. So can memories, thought Li. He moved off up the trail and Ah Wu stood there for a moment watching him. He knew there was no way to change Li's mind. No matter, thought Au Wu, I will be at his side. After all, I would not be standing here if not for the lightning wit of Li's poetic powers. Yet it was a wit, once more powerful than the Imperial Guard, that had now fallen silent. Ah Wu limped on behind his friend. He wondered if the loss of a poet's inspiration was like the loss of a warrior's fighting spirit.

***

The sun was on the downside of its arc before the two men spoke again. The nameless mountain wasn't high, but the western slope followed a long, gradual rise to its summit. It was a thickly forested mountain, mostly scraggly pine, blue-berried juniper, and scattered clumps of blue-green bamboo. Even in broad sunlight, it would have been a gloomy trip. However, a heavy fog settled over the mountain and the light gave way to deep gray shadows. As the sun continued on the downside of its arc, grays turned to charcoal, then toward a starless night.

The narrow dirt file path above the river turned inward and disappeared into a formless rust-colored pine needle bed. Ah Wu studied the land before them: rocks and boulders broke the soft pine floor as if haplessly tossed by forest spirits at play. Here and there, clumps of thick bamboo sprouted. Ah Wu could see no path through the dense, fragrant pine forest that populated the mountain's gentle flank.

Li Bo had stopped. Ah Wu limped along next to him and said, "There's no path from this side, and the other sides can't be reached from the river. Old Zhou will have to move the boat off shore when the tide goes out. That could strand us here."

"Then we have till tomorrow morning. Old Zhou will manage," said Li, thinking, another good friend that I am blessed with. Old Zhou, his boatman, had been with them for the last ten years. His skill with sail and tiller matched Li's with brush and verse. They had sailed the Long River, its tributaries and lakes, together. Old Zhou had been his guide to the wonders of the great waterway. In turn, Li's verse had given expression to Old Zhou's love for the river. Li was fond of singing his poems aloud, and after Old Zhou had heard a few he refused to take money from Li. He told Li that he could never take pay from the River Spirit, to which the poet must certainly be related. And even though Old Zhou was illiterate, the two were like brothers—Old Zhou provided the inspiration and Li the voice. And now, Li thought, even though the voice is silenced, Old Zhou has continued to offer inspiration in hope of rekindling the poetry.

The mist, flowing around Li's feet, distracted his thoughts. It passed them, streamed toward a large boulder, and disappeared. Li ran over to the smooth-faced dark stone. He turned to Ah Wu, smiled, and waved him over.

Catching up to Li, Ah Wu saw behind the boulder an opening that led to a path worn along the pine needle floor.

"How's your foot?" asked Li.

"It's aching. We shouldn't be here."

Li led the way. They followed the mist and were able to weave in and out, around and through stands of pine, bamboo, and scattered boulders the size of a man. The mist seemed to guide them.

But where were they being led? thought Ah Wu. Could it be a trap? Hadn't one of the boys said something about a Blood Dragon's realm? He froze. *Thump, thump*, a dull but clear sound shook the forest. Something was pounding along the pine needle bed—*thud, thud, thud*—it hopped, as if on one leg, toward them.

Li noticed Ah Wu had gone motionless. "What?"

"Listen."

Li could hear it bound toward them. "What is it?"

Ah Wu raised his crossbow. "A single legged being . . . a mountain spirit."

A crisp frenzied laugh broke the stillness of the mountain forest.

Ah Wu tried to track the movement. "A mountain spirit has spotted us. They laugh when they sight humans. Arm yourself and strike for its throat, if you can find it. Its lips will cover its head just before it strikes."

Li pulled out his dagger and listened. The dull "*thud, thud, thud*" somewhere out in the forest was moving away.

Ah Wu lowered his crossbow. "Probably going to get its friends, share the catch."

Li looked at him. "Hope they choke on my bones, for that's all they'll get from me."

The wind suddenly gusted from below. The pines briefly sang and the bamboos knocked. It was as if something had passed by them, higher up in the tree and bamboo tops.

"That's not wind," said Ah Wu.

"Perhaps they've come to guide us . . . ."

Ah Wu watched the tree tops. ". . . to hell."

The flowing mist that had guided them over the forest floor stopped, as if blocked directly ahead.

"I know how to deal with this," said Ah Wu. He stepped in front of Li, leveled his crossbow and fired a two-shot volley.

There was a shout, "*Ahee!*" The wind grew agitated and dissipated. The mist resumed its flow upward along the forest floor.

"That'll give them something to think about," said Ah Wu. He reloaded quickly.

"Was that the one-legged mountain spirit?"

Ah Wu looked around at the pine trees that seemed to press in from all sides. "No, only a ghost. We'll hear that one-legged imp when he returns with his friends."

Li Bo watched the mist moving along the forest floor. "I only need one night in the Dream Temple, one night in that place. It could be true . . . no ordinary dreams . . . not in the Dream Temple. No, I'm sure the dream will at least be a portent, a clue, some direction, allow me to see clear the meaning of all this . . . show me the way to reclaim my poetry, my family, my life. If this is granted, I'll stay close to my family, no more of this wandering life. I swear!" Li looked up through the green pines at the overcast sky.

"I pray Heaven will grant you that dream, but this path . . . I don't know," said Ah Wu. He watched the mist flow up ahead, twisting and turning in between the pines and the boulders. And he wondered if it was Heaven or the gates of Hell drawing the mist through the forest.

Li moved ahead, speaking to himself. "That woman was telling the truth; there was something about her." The relaxing scent of damp pine permeated the air. Li Bo breathed in the mist-laden mountain fragrances that he loved so dearly. He was transported to another realm.

"Bah! You were so drunk," Ah Wu broke the spell. "Amazing you can even remember that night. Up comes this dancing girl with green eyes and golden hair and there go your brains. The story of your life—lost in dreams. Where has it gotten you? I know you. You still want to be accepted by the Court. We're outsiders. We can fight their wars and entertain them, but we'll never be accepted as one of them." Ah Wu's large callused hand brushed the mist out of his dark beard. His right hand lifted the crossbow. He made use of its weight to lend a rhythm to his movement.

But Li Bo would not leave his dream so easily. "If I find the right patron, I can get a position. It doesn't have to be at Court; a small post. At least, there would be a steady income. Then, maybe, with time, the poetry would come back."

"Ha! With your drinking, you'd either run out of money or be thrown out of office."

Li stopped and looked at the ground mist for a long time. His deep eyes lacked the flash of his youth and reflected the surrounding gloom. "What else can I do?"

Ah Wu's dark round eyes brightened, "We'll double back, rescue your family, then just melt away in the distant areas of the Western Regions. I was raised there, have friends there."

"And be hunted down like the Grand Shamaness, if she really was foolish enough to try an escape?"

"Even if we find this temple and you have a dream, will you be able to interpret it correctly?" asked Ah Wu. He scanned the area around them. Dusk was beginning to fall, and the fog that had brooded in the treetops all day began to filter farther down through the pines. The last thing Ah Wu wanted was to camp out in this forest at night. Darkness favored whatever creatures lurked on this mountain, and his old foot wound was never wrong.

Li remained silent.

"Take it from someone older than you: Life doesn't amount to anything, so why be concerned? Ha! Once you're dead, you'll never know life didn't have any meaning. Kick 'em in the teeth and don't look back," said Ah Wu. He grasped his crossbow as if he was about to shoot some beast.

"I've been kicking all my life, Ah Wu, but they kick back . . . harder," said Li.

Ah Wu saw that his friend looked tired and worn. And then he noticed the bamboo clump beside him. "Ahh! Look!"

Li Bo moved over and saw the small white cuts in the green bamboo shaft. They were characters, someone's name and a date. Each shoot had a name and date engraved upon it.

Ah Wu stepped back and raised his crossbow. "They're grave markers."

Li Bo recognized them—markers for the unburied dead.

Now they heard the "*thump, thump, thump*" of what Ah Wu had identified as a mountain spirit—reputed to be a one-legged creature with the heel turned backward, three toed with three fingers on each hand and long, sharp teeth.

Looking at the marked bamboo, Ah Wu said, "It's the souls of the unburied dead that are the source of such specters."

Li pulled his dagger from his sleeve. "We don't have time to find them and give them a proper burial, so let's see if we can give our host some serious indigestion."

Ah Wu frowned. Although he always enjoyed a fight where the odds were against him, creatures of the *Yin* realm made him uneasy.

"Who knows?" Li continued. "The temple might serve some great wine, and that's really the answer. Three cups to fathom the Great Principle. One gallon to flow with Nature's Way! Right, old friend?" He gave Ah Wu a slap on the back.

"You're crazy. We don't even know if your temple exists. Even the ghosts warned us away from here. And to make matters more interesting, I believe we are as lost as a sand flea in a Gobi sandstorm."

"But the dancing girl . . . ," protested Li.

"The man's got donkey fever." Ah Wu threw up his free hand as if to ask Heaven to come to his aid and enlighten his friend—or, perhaps, just to get him out of there. He searched the forest for further signs of the mountain spirit, but there was no longer a sound, not even a bird or insect. That was always a sign of trouble.

"All right, we are lost. So going back is just as good as going up," Li argued, then realized that Ah Wu had left the conversation and was listening to something. The ghosts, remembered Li; then he too noticed how quiet the forest had become. "It's gone," he whispered. "Trust me, old friend, if there is wine on this mountain, I'll find it. With wine, there is no fear!"

"Could use a drink, a whole jug," muttered Ah Wu. He continued to look out into the forest. The view was the same: pine, rock, and some bamboo; but now the shadows had drawn longer. He limped on with Li Bo.

Li laughed. The mist was on the move again, and Li followed, skirting the boulders, rocks, fallen trees, and other assorted objects that an ancient forest deposits in the course of its life. He didn't know where they were in relation to where they had left the river. Yet he sensed that the mist was not random, that it was following a definite course and that it would lead to his goal—the Dream Temple, where dreams gave visitors the answers to their deepest questions.

At least, that's what the dancing girl at the inn last night had told him. Li Bo, unlike Ah Wu, believed that life was purposeful, that so-called "chance" meetings were not in the least coincidence, that there was meaning to everything that happened in life. That the Great Dao was not some chaotic, blind, whirling mass. Rather that life was the purposeful, working out of the Way's mysterious path, a path that the Immortals and the Perfected Ones had found and that humans, once versed in the ways of the Immortals, could share and understand.

It made perfect sense to Li Bo, that the dancing girl was part of the path. That she appeared in his time of need to place him on the right track. That once he reached the Dream Temple, his dream there would guide him toward a fuller understanding of the Way. And with that, he could restore order to this chaotic period in his life. However, he did not speak of his feelings to Ah Wu, for he knew that his friend doubted that even the Immortals could deal with the disorder of Li's life.

Ah Wu shifted the weight of the crossbow in his right hand; he had a bad feeling about this place. The mist, the light, his throbbing foot—everything here was a warning. Darkness was coming on too fast, almost as if a trap was being drawn about them. They had seen no birds, no animals, only the trees and this thick mist flowing along the forest floor.

Li pointed. "An opening in the tree line, the only one. That is the path. The mist is the Way, it guides us . . . and without even a drink. Ahh, this is truly an amazing place!" He headed toward the dim break up ahead.

Ah Wu only shook his head. He took another look around, but couldn't see much beyond the spot where they were standing. Anyone or anything could be within sword strike, not to mention bow or spear shot of them, and they would never see it coming.

They moved ahead, always upward—though there were some moments when Ah Wu wasn't even sure they were moving up. Boulders sometimes loomed out of the gloom; at other times twisted tree limbs seemed to threaten. Ah Wu raised his crossbow again—the safety catches were off both triggers. He needed to focus on his hearing. Sight was an almost useless defense here. There were no sounds, not even as they moved. The ground was covered with a soft, thick bed of pine needles—moistened by the mist, they did not snap when stepped upon, so their footsteps were as silent as the rest of this shrouded world. There was only the pine scent. Not even a breeze. He wondered how the mist could move without a breeze. Nothing made sense here, thought Ah Wu.

He felt defenseless and turned to his energy skill, focusing his inner vital force (*chi*) down to its center—the *dan-tien* or "fields of cinnabar" as the Daoists refer to it—directing his *chi* to his senses. He was able "to hear what is not heard, see what cannot be seen, feel what is beyond touch"—and it was here, in that mysterious tactile sense, that he refined the feelings that his old wound had first sensed. An unseen presence was hovering just outside their perceptions, watching them. He felt it.

Ah Wu refocused his energy. Where was this presence—in front, behind, to the side, or perhaps, as the nomads in the forest regions out west had once done to his troops, hiding above in the trees? He stopped and peered above him: nothing but the darkening gloom. The stars would be out soon but there would be no way to read them down here. They were lost.

The wind picked up for a moment and swirled the mist around the two men—almost as if the wind was reacting to Ah Wu's sensing. Wait, thought Ah Wu, it is not the wind swirling around us. It's a ghost. How to deal with it? He stopped moving and watched the pines around them, trying to find a pattern, some repetition of movement that he could follow and shoot. He saw it among the bamboos, which seemed to swirl round and round in one spot. He shot. The bolt tore into the bamboo stand.

"Aow!" It sounded like a child. The bamboos stopped moving. The wind was gone. Ah Wu ran forward, ready with a second shot.

"What happened?" shouted Li. He rushed over to Ah Wu, his knife already unsheathed.

"A visitor gone home with a memento," smiled Ah Wu. Then they saw it. At their feet, a pool of clear thick liquid was evaporating on the rocky ground. The two friends looked at each other. For a moment, both had the sense that, like the bamboo and rocks around them, they seemed to be mere illusions in an illusive frosty white world. The pines behind the bamboos moaned slightly and knocked as a gentle breeze passed over them.

"More company?" Li said, not taking his eyes off the pine trees surrounding them. The fog had moved halfway down the trees.

"Camel piss, they're everywhere"

"Quick, hurry before night falls and we are left out here in this gloom."

"Hurry? Where? Don't you understand? Without the stars, we are lost. This is not your beloved Chang'an with its broad boulevards clearly marked. This is some strange forest . . . on some strange mountain . . . and we are lost. This is not a good place to be lost in."

"You sensed that we were being followed?" asked Li with a wry smile.

"You sensed it, too?"

"No, of course not, my martial skills have long gone the way of the wine jar."

"We are not alone." Ah Wu pointed to his left foot as he continued to search among the fog-draped bamboo and pine for anything that moved. The "wind" was no longer air in movement, but nothing stirred, not a slender branch, not a leaf.

Li Bo smiled. "I didn't expect we would be, after that mess we left down below. The Blood Dragon should be quite unhappy with its new visitors."

Ah Wu returned his smile. He thought, that perhaps time in prison hadn't broken Li after all. He hoped so—Li Bo used to be the most irreverent of all those at Court. How many times had he shown up drunk in the presence of the Son of Heaven? It made even Ah Wu shudder. Each time when the eunuchs, those dickless bastards, thought they could embarrass Li, he was able to evade certain defeat, possibly even death, by scratching out a brilliant verse or two. Some at Court began to believe Li's line that he was a fallen Immortal, condemned to roam the earth spouting off inspired, otherworldly verse.

Then the failed rebellion, another one of Li Bo's "dreams" gone wrong . . . and prison, thought Ah Wu. He had seen what prison could do to a man. He and his men had been captured and imprisoned while fighting in the Western Regions. Warriors with far greater strength and experience than Li Bo, a poet, broke.

He remembered the day they released Li. Ah Wu had traveled from the Court to greet his old friend. That day, a ghost left that cell, a ghost of the former brilliance that had been Li Bo. He looked well beyond his age of fifty-odd springs and autumns; the hair on his head had turned white.

That was six months ago. The trip revitalized Li and he seemed, at moments, more like his old self. However, the poetry had stopped. Ah Wu hadn't dared ask why, but he was worried. It was like a seasoned warrior who no longer knew how to wield his weapons. Ah Wu had seen this too, and it usually led into the darkness of the *Yin* realm. He wondered if this mountain was not the entrance to that realm.

They continued to walk, threading past the rocks and the twisted pine limbs. Always upward, always managing to find a break in the pines or the bamboo stands that seemed to suddenly loom and then melt away as they drew closer.

They had one bamboo torch, but unless they could find dry kindling, they would have to pass the night in darkness. That didn't matter much, thought Ah Wu. He feared nothing that possessed a beating heart; rather he worried about certain heartless beings that fed on the blood of beating hearts. The air was growing cooler. They continued their ascent and night began to close in.

"Exile is no dream, but it doesn't have to be the end of your life. You could still write . . . ." Ah Wu stopped. He refocused his energy and projected it out around them—nothing. Whatever it was had left with that last gust of wind.

"Here, here it is. Look!" Li Bo stood pointing to the ground.

Ah Wu searched in front of him and, at first, saw nothing but the matted pine needle bed of the forest floor. Then he noticed that the ground in front of Li was darker. It wasn't ground, but stone, stone cut into the form of a step. They had come to a sharp rise in the forest floor, a hill or mound of some sort. He pulled the torch out of his knapsack and struck the stones that sparked the torch to life. Steps cut out of the mountain rock led upward into the fog, which had descended all around them.

"We must be careful. This is an excellent spot for an ambush," said Ah Wu. He passed the torch to Li and took up his crossbow with both hands. He reached back over his shoulder to see if the other crossbow bolts on the leather back strap were in easy reach. He began to mount the stairs.

"Who would want to kill a poet, or what is left of a poet?" said Li. He took the torch and climbed upward with Ah Wu by his side. They moved slowly, not so much out of caution as out of necessity. It had been a long climb and Li Bo was obviously tired. Ah Wu let his friend set the pace.

"My enemies at Court prefer to see me die a slow death. It is like them to send someone to protect me and make sure I reach the tropical malarial mists of Yunnan in one piece. That way the scorpions, centipedes, and vipers can take little poisonous pieces out of me as I lie dying of some horrid fever," said Li.

Ah Wu smirked. "That's a relief. Unless your courtly friends really aren't human, it wasn't them that I sensed back there."

"Ghosts. Perhaps that's better than humans. But just wait until we are farther up the Long River near, say perhaps, the Three Gorges home of the legendary Rain Goddess. Now that's a place to find creatures from the other realms. This place is second rate."

"I have bolts for them, too," said Ah Wu, swinging his crossbow upward, watching the forest on either side of them.

The wind moved up from below and stirred the bushes and trees on either side of the steps. The mist swirled around them and the torch flickered wildly. Li tried to shield it from the brunt of the wind's force. He turned and twisted away from its direction. The wind seemed to respond, trying to put out the flame, and for a moment, it looked as if Li was dancing. Ah Wu couldn't help but laugh out loud. The wind stopped. Ah Wu sensed movement. He swiveled around and tried to bring his crossbow to bear on that which was not there.

He gestured with his weapon. "There, up ahead."

Li looked up and saw a warm glow in the mist. "It must be from the temple gate—quick!"

The two friends hurried up the remaining stone steps. Soon they smelled a fragrance unlike that of the forest.

Li Bo stopped.

"Smell that? We must be near the temple."

"Incense. Seems familiar."

"Frankincense, brought from the Western Regions, perhaps India. The temple must have a wealthy benefactor."

The aroma grew strong. It overwhelmed the earth's scent and flooded Li Bo's mind with memories. He inhaled slowly and deeply:

The dimly lit altar room in our family home back in Shu; that scent was the same. My father called the room, "the realm of remembrance." Our family's ancestor tablets were there, written in that mystical language. The foolish Chinese called it a "barbarian" tongue, stupid. What is not their own is "barbarian." My family's roots extend far across time and space. Perhaps it is true that we reach back to the distant lands of Persia—no one knows. But, like this fragrance, I am not of this land and perhaps it is for this difference that I am climbing these steps. Why does Heaven no longer favor me? Why has the poetry left me? And of my son who has hardly known his wandering father.

— 2 —

The steps ended at a level area of earth. The two friends stood before a main gate that was part of a wooden-walled enclosure. Two large oblong lanterns hung on either side of the gate. Li Bo read aloud the single character on each, "*Dream*," "*Realm*," and then the signboard over the gate, "*Dream Realm Terrace*."

Li Bo smiled. "We made it . . . on the pathless path no less, and with no wine. I could use a drink."

Ah Wu's smile was more one of relief than of delight. At least the temple exists, he thought, but his fingers remained on the triggers of his crossbow. He surveyed the temple and its surroundings. "We were out on patrol in the Western Regions. Found a place like this. It was a trap. Lost many fine friends that day."

Something had tracked them up the mountain. Ah Wu was sure of that, but it was peaceful here. Maybe what had followed them was waiting, watching their next move; perhaps it was scared of what was inside the temple. Perhaps they should be too.

Li laughed. "Ah Wu, we are safe! This is the Dream Temple. As for the source of our information, singing girls can be trusted if they are drunk enough."

"My foot needs no drink."

"But I do!" Li's eyes were sparkling.

Li, however, knew that what was to come next would be no laughing matter. What would he do if his dream turned out to be a nightmare, as his life had become? Perhaps he was just an old fool for coming here, but what was his alternative? If he did not go through with the banishment, his family would be executed. He missed them, especially his son. And if the snakes, insects, and fevers of distant Yunnan attacked him—how would he die, as a poet or as a man already dead, unrecognized by the Court?

"In we go," urged Ah Wu, who knew that his friend was already immersed in the doubts that now seemed the only certainty of his life.

"Yes, yes, of course," Li Bo laughed and pulled off his reed rain cape. He pushed the dark wooden gate open. It was old and weathered, but moved as if it were gliding on air. He found himself in a small narrow courtyard. In front was the main entrance to a covered walkway that ran the width of the enclosure. Beyond the entrance was the only building, a simple single-story wooden structure.

Li Bo crossed the courtyard and entered the small reception hall. There was an altar against the wall. In front of the altar, two cushions were drawn up to a low lacquer table. The narrow ends of its rectangular shape sloping down to the ground formed its exquisitely carved supports. Two sticks of fresh incense smoldered on the altar. In front of it, the table's dark lacquered luster reflected a meal for two. A large iron tripod cauldron with a magnificent meat *geng* (stew) sent clouds of steam toward the visitors. Li's mouth watered.

Ah Wu ignored the meal and kept his crossbow at the ready. He turned 'round in circles "feeling" into the shadowy recesses of the room.

Li moved closer to the table. There were two large elegant porcelain gray-blue wine cups and a fat brown ceramic wine pot, a white glass plate of steaming rice, a light-green jade bowl of red fruit—they looked like litchi—and a silver plate of sliced roasted meat that smelled like venison. Li's stomach was screaming for him to sit. Ah Wu eyed him and just shook his head. They moved back out to the courtyard.

Li called out. "Hello, is anyone around? We are travelers seeking the wisdom of your dreams. Anyone here?" He moved around the courtyard, breaking the quiet spell that seemed to have been cast at the main gate. But there wasn't much more to the enclosure, and obviously the kitchens weren't in it, nor were there any other people. As they returned to the reception hall, they noticed that the wooden front portion of the building ended in a great wall of stone.

"The front of the building is only an edifice built into this stone wall," said Li.

Ah Wu gestured with his crossbow. "There are two rooms to either side of the altar." His large hand slid over the smooth surface. "They are cut into the rock."

"Yes, cut into the mountain," said Li. He examined each one. The rooms, not in plain sight, were simply furnished: a low bamboo-framed sleeping pallet with a peculiar stone pillow, an amber colored lamp, a water clock, incense sticks and holder, a metal water pot with one white cup, a yellow ceramic chamber pot, and a white candle that gave off a soft golden glow. The difference was that only one room had a painting hanging over the sleeping pallet. It was an ink-on-paper sketch of a mountain scene. Li looked closer; the mountain seemed to have many peaks. Most peculiar were the murals that decorated the arched ceilings.

Li pointed to the artwork on the ceiling. "These paintings are done in an ancient style. See the entwining snakes and dragons. And over there the two tigers and two black-headed horses."

Au Wu gawked upward at the patterns that ran all over the arched ceiling.

"I've seen most of the horses in the Middle Kingdom. None were black-headed, but I did hear some fairy stories about such animals," mused Ah Wu, who was carried away by the sight of the horses.

"Don't like it," he continued. "Not a proper sleeping chamber . . . that shade of purple that everything is covered in . . . would keep me up all night . . . at least, with fleas you can kill 'em."

"Yes, this is a bit odd." Li stroked his white chin whiskers.

"I'll take the room with the painting; I enjoy mountains." He threw his reed raincoat next to the pallet, opened the leather flap of the waterproof bag held in the bamboo frame of his backpack, and began digging through it.

"I'm going to dress for dinner. I'll be with you in a moment," said Li.

Ah Wu rolled his eyes up toward Heaven and left. As he walked out, he shot back. "Are you sure the food is safe?"

There was no answer and Ah Wu limped over to the low lacquered dinner table. Li Bo emerged from the sleeping chamber transformed by the magnificent court robes that he had donned. The long-flowing blue silk outer robe had sleeves cut in the courtly fashion that almost touched the wooden floor when Li Bo's hands were folded at his chest—the respectful posture of humility in the presence of the Son of Heaven. The inner robe was cut from light brown, earth-colored silk. Both robes were finely trimmed in a red-and-gold embroidered flower pattern. Li's fashion status was out of sorts with his haggard, disheveled appearance.

"Not again," said Ah Wu, wondering if his friend's despair was becoming tinged with madness.

"Granted it did look a bit silly sailing up the Long River the last few days, but in this region only the fish noticed that. For all we know there could be noble spirits of the Dao in this temple. We must show some sense of respect."

"Bah! More aristocratic nonsense."

"They are as real as that ghost wind out there waiting for us."

Ah Wu looked around and noticed how tranquil the world had become.

Li moved over to the end of the low lacquered table where the host would normally sit.

"Ah Wu, what do I have to lose? I am banished to the most dreaded part of the empire. At my age, how could I survive? However, dying here with a delicious meal, good wine, and a trusted friend . . . ." He held up the wine pot and noticed the purple sun and moon symbols that made up the pot's design motif. He stopped speaking for a moment.

Ah Wu noticed his friend's sudden interest. "What?"

Li was still studying the wine pot. "Interesting, isn't it?"

"The robes are making you light headed. At your age . . . . Bah! Nonsense, I'm older than you and no exile is going to stop me. It'll take a stout crossbow bolt, or two, for that!"

The wine pot, however, still engaged Li Bo's attention. "This pot and those sleeping chambers all have the same ancient motif—they all represent the heavenly afterworld."

His remarks jolted Ah Wu back to the dinner table. "What! What kind of decoration is that for a bedroom?"

"Ah Wu, this is, after all, a temple,"

"Yes, but isn't the Dream Temple supposed to be concerned with the future, not the afterlife?"

"Exactly! All of us will eventually experience the future in our afterlife. Ha! Sit, my friend, and drink. Certainly passing on through this gateway to the afterlife would be better than in Yunnan from the bite of some poisonous viper or insect."

Li Bo dropped down on the seating cushion before the table without the customary arranging of robes before seating. Picking up his chopsticks, he smiled. Several strands of white hair tumbled into his face and he blew them away.

"Now show me what good company you can be. Let's eat! I have much dreaming to do."

Ah Wu, hesitated and moved closer to the table. "Strange, the food is hot . . . ."

"And delicious, here try some *geng*." Li ladled the perfectly cut squares of beef and sections of scallions into Ah Wu's black-and-tan lacquered bowl.

Ah Wu found himself a reluctant guest at a strange table on

a strange mountain. "Thank you. Let me serve." He poured wine into Li's cup and tried to act as if this meal was like any other in their ten-year friendship, but he could not convince himself. "There is no one around, no kitchen. Where did the food come from? How did they know to set the table for two?"

Li Bo smiled. "Ah Wu, don't spoil an excellent meal with details. I have no answer except that this wine is truly marvelous. Your favorite, grape wine from the Western Regions. Marvelous! Drink up, and if you must worry, worry about what we will do when the wine runs out."

Li Bo closed his eyes and concentrated on his sense of taste, thereby heightening the wonderful sensations on his tongue.

"Now all we need is the moon," said Li. He got up and wobbled over to the door, pushed it open, and peered up at the mist-shrouded heavens—a gray-black void stared back. "Ahh, it doesn't matter. There's still a moon in my heart, somewhere, and a moon or two on this wine pot. That will have to do for tonight."

And probably for a long time to come, he thought. He staggered back to his place at the table and reflected that since his last month in prison, he had been unable to compose a coherent line about that moon—something that he used to do as easily as breathing, especially when intoxicated. The poetry had stopped and he didn't know how to bring it back. He hoped the Dream Temple would offer a clue. Without his divine poetry skill, he would have nothing to offer the Court.

Sitting in his official robes, he remembered the three years he spent at Court. Well, as much as he could remember, since he had to admit he was drunk most of the time. He did remember the delicious wines and the wonderful times at the taverns in the capital with his group of poet friends. All night long, they wildly made verse after verse, sampling the various wines and the exotic female bouquets of the capital's singsong girls. And he remembered the Emperor's hand reaching over and gracefully shaking salt into his soup. The Emperor had attended him . . . .

He had convinced himself that the Dream Temple was his last hope of a return to Court. He would drink deeply tonight to insure a sound sleep, and with it dreams.

He looked up at Ah Wu. "You are right . . . as usual. I drink too much. Once upon a time, it was my way to accord with the poetry, the Way. Now . . . I follow a lost path. I drink, but no longer pass into the realm of poetry . . . . Rather, I pass into oblivion, as does my life . . . ." Tears were rolling down Li Bo's thin cheeks.

Ah Wu felt his friend's pain. He felt a deep bitterness toward Heaven for visiting this suffering on Li Bo. He wished his bolts could reach Heaven, to sting it into realizing that it had silenced one of its greatest champions. The Way of Heaven is as stupid as the Way of men, reflected Ah Wu. He wondered if Li would regain his poetic voice. For the last six months, ever since his release from prison, Li had been trying to compose, but failed every time. How often had he been drunk, trying to recapture the almost unearthly brilliance of his rhyme? Ah Wu believed it was the prison experience. Sometimes men were able to come back from such humiliations, but the odds were against it. He looked up at his old friend and smiled. Of course, Li Bo was no ordinary man.

Ah Wu pushed aside the porcelain wine cup and pulled out his cup, made of rhinoceros horn to counteract poison. He filled it with the grape wine and drank. Sometimes, he thought, wine was really the only Way. Memories flooded his mind, of the good times with his troops in the Western Regions when they traveled far beyond the web spun by officials and their politics. But this could be a trick. Were evil spirits using those memories to distract him? There were also many bad memories, very bad memories. His fingers brushed the right side of his head where his ear once hung. So what? The wine would deal with these.

After several more cups, he began, like Li Bo, to enjoy the

meal, for they began to forget. So subtly did the wine work its way that they were unaware that toast-by-toast, swallow-by-swallow, their memories were fading.

Li smoothed his whiskers. "That was a wonderful meal. Though the *geng* was peculiar in that it seemed to lack flavor, almost as if it was prepared as an offering. Yet, if this was my last meal, it was a delicious way to end it all."

"I'm not afraid to face him before I go. I'd . . . ," roared Ah Wu, his face and its jagged scar reddened by the grape wine.

"But the strangest dish of all," Li continued to himself, "was the litchi. We are quite a distance from their source in the South—beyond the one-day range of any earthly horse—and yet they were so fresh, as if picked today. Truly delicious, and yet so mysterious—in all a great mea. I wish I could personally thank our host." Li smiled a drowsy smile and raised his cup in toast to whatever unseen host might be present.

A scream cut through the quiet forest, then another. Ah Wu's crossbow was at the ready. If not for the safeties being set, he would have let loose a volley in the room.

"How do you do it? With all that wine your *chi* still has not settled down!" thundered Li Bo. "It's only a gibbon. Certainly the man who defeated five nomad swordsmen at once, bare-handed no less, can't be afraid of a poor lonely gibbon."

Ah Wu let his weapon sink to the ground. His hand involuntarily groped for his missing ear. "In other places, it might just be a gibbon, but here . . . I don't like this mountain. You sleep. I'll stand watch. For me, there are no problems that need dreams. Death's face has been my constant companion . . . even a source of comfort."

The wine and growing anger showed in Ah Wu's face; the scar glowed like the desert sun of the Western Regions. He stood up, his left foot aching. "Come old Su-lu, I'm ready! Come from wherever your kind hides. Let's make it to the death, for I'm still standing here cursing you, you camel-turd bastard Turk!"

"He's dead, a Turk killed by his own tribesman! Why raise the dead? Have it your way, a warrior to the end, but I *am* in need of the dreams," said Li Bo trying to wave down Ah Wu, who was staggering around the altar room after his invisible nemesis, the Tügis *qughan* Su-lu—the Turkish leader who disfigured him.

"I'll take the room with the painting," Li Bo mumbled. "I like mountains; they bring you closer to Heaven and farther from the world of men . . . ." As sleep overtook him, he stumbled into the bedroom and flopped onto the bed mat, lost in his courtly attire.

"Perhaps a warrior to the end, an old warrior who is weary, but this whole mountain has become his hiding place . . . the mist, the forest, this incense, the meal, crying gibbons, or whatever they were . . . . I know you're here . . . ." Ah Wu sat and stared out into the night with his back to the altar, facing the entrance. He placed the crossbow on his lap and unsheathed his broadsword.

The rest of the night was quiet—no gibbons, no wind, and no lights beyond those that burnt on the altar. The candles flickered in the stillness, but gave a constant light. Ah Wu was now only aware of light; he no longer remembered its source . . . and from that forgetting a dream arose and through it a face and memories of war in a distant place . . . a war that scarred his spirit and his flesh.

Swathed in a yellow and red turban, a dark face—Turkish— eyes ablaze with anger arose before Ah Wu. The lips parted in a smile. White teeth flashed against a black beard. The man's hand rose to his mouth and, when it lowered, a bloody ear was left clenched in those white teeth.

～ 3 ～

Far on the other side of the same nameless mountain in a hidden cave, a woman slept and dreamed:

The flaring of the spirit lamps on the altar has awakened me. I will not open my eyes. I'll only lie here and listen to the lamps crackle. I can feel my long black hair sprayed around me on the sleeping mat and imagine the light reflecting off it like the lightning off the clouds that I soar over on my visits to the Lady of the Purple Vault.

I can sense nothing else, just the light. If I lie quiet, perhaps the world will finally vanish into the Void. Could it be that between me and the altar there is now only the icy darkness of the Void? I dare not open my eyes. Two more loud crackles have forced my eyelids to flutter, but not open. The next eruption has briefly lit the apartments. I can feel the light trying to work its way through my closed eyelids and into my mind.

Now, I feel an overpowering urge to know if the world still exists. My eyes meet the dim light of my sleeping chamber. The long silk window curtains are billowing across the room. Listen. The wind is rising out of the West. Is this not a warning, a west wind at this late watch? I part the gauze drapes on the side of my bed and peer into the gloom. A dark figure casts against the wall. It glides past the shrine room down the hall and moves toward my room.

My mind is acutely alert, senses straining to catch anything out of the ordinary. The wind came in gusts, throwing the curtains into greater contortions. The spirit lamps erupt, the wind whips their flames, and their surging light barely reaches the room. Was this a warning from Heaven? I must move, get out of here. This realization burns in my mind, but my muscles refuse to respond. I am sinking deeper into the bed mat. Some force pulls me down, holds me here— for what?

A black figure appears before me. A sword flashes. I remember . . . the burning . . . the pain . . . my chest on fire . . . the light . . . my consciousness ablaze . . . searing white light fills the Void . . . I am consumed . . . .

She awoke to hear herself screaming and—with great difficulty—regained control. Her body was bathed in cold sweat. The west wind blew a frosty mist into the cave. She felt a chill and tossed more twigs on the dying fire. Her fingers pressed against the welt of flesh on her chest directly over the heart. The lump throbbed.

She knew the reality of dreams, but this was more than just an omen. He was closing in on her, reaching out for her mind again. She wasn't sure of her pursuer's powers, but after the incident that night in her palace apartments, she knew he wasn't an ordinary assassin. She wondered if he were human, for his powers crossed the realms of *Yin* and *Yang*. He could enter her dreams and wield a sword that touched the physical reality of the *Yang* realm. She bore the proof on her breast. If it weren't for the Lady of the Purple Vault, she would be dead, slain from within her dream.

She knew that the mysterious assassin had been sent by the Court eunuchs to silence her. It was their still-unexposed plot to assassinate the Emperor that, with the assistance of her spiritual mentor, the Lady of the Purple Vault, she had foiled. The assassin would not be the only one intent upon finding her.

Certainly, the Emperor would send his own men to retrieve her. She knew that he was deeply attracted to her graceful feminine form. As the poets liked to write, her jade-white skin, teeth, and swan-like neck, lustrous black eyes, and raven, cloud-like long hair framed her with a classic Chinese elegance. She despised the cliché-ridden Court poets and all they stood for. She was not seeking worldly attractiveness or worldly honors and wealth. Her grandmother had shown her another way—the Way of Lord Lao, the Daoist deity who illuminated Nature's supreme Way.

Her goal was Mount Wu, a Daoist sanctuary. She would be safe there, but it was still far upriver. She had to reach it before those courtly avengers caught her. Out of a red silk bag, she pulled paper and scissors. Within seconds, the shape of a horse took form. Then she prepared a bowl of water and, over it, set the paper horse on fire.

She stirred the ashes in the water and, over the bowl, intoned, "Lady of the Purple Vault, my spirit guardian, the Grand Shamaness Luo Jhu-yun pledges that the vow is her life." Then she took a mouthful of the mixture and sprayed it out over the fire. A flame exploded, painting the cave with the light of a thousand suns, only to be consumed by the darkness.

A neigh echoed from within the cave. The fire flickered back to life. A saddled horse stood there bathed in the firelight. Its head was black.

She gathered up her bedroll, several scrolls, and a water gourd. Slinging the red silk pouch over her head and across her chest, she jumped up on the black-headed horse and rode out of the cave. The thickening mist swallowed horse and rider.

— 4 —

Li Bo rolled over on his sleeping pallet and suddenly:

From the hilltop clearing, I can see mountain peaks surrounding me. There are twelve. I am far from that nameless peak that hid the Dream Temple. My dream is unfolding.

For all my traveling in the Yang realm, I cannot recall a mountaintop with twelve peaks. Yet, I feel as if I should know this place well, but Ah Wu is nowhere to ask. Off to the west, white mist foams; it devours each peak. I should leave this spot before that storm strikes. Just below is the protection of the forest.

What is that? A clearing up ahead. Peculiar, the mist is being drawn from all over the forest . . . . It gathers at the center of that clearing. It congeals into a form . . . an old woman. I must speak to her.

Excuse me, auntie, but do you know where I might be? But Heaven! What is this creature, with one eye askew and a pimply, pus-ridden complexion? Her gray-streaked hair is long, falling in disarray around her short, fat neck. Perhaps it is better that I leave; there should be others about.

I cannot leave! What is this thought that shoots through my mind with such force!

Who said that?

"I did, foolish poet. Nice robes, were you expecting the Emperor?"

Who? I can see no one. Wait! The old woman is smiling at me. Oh, those rotten teeth—a smile full of worms. What a contrast to those strange dark brocaded robes she wears, as if she has just stepped from the palace of some long forgotten dynasty . . . .

"You are such a gossip; now stop that and come here. Did you not come to this temple to learn of your future?"

Yes, yes, but who is to guide me in this endeavor? It is the old woman. She communicates without words. Her thoughts speak directly to mine—as the Immortals are said to speak.

"Enough of this nonsense! What do you know of Immortals, Li Bo! Still your mind and heed what I have to say!"

What is going on here? Perhaps I should try my most formal bow and show some respect.

"That's better. I've had a long wait for you and have not been amused by your companion's remarks about my mountain home."

I must be careful. I have spent most of my life in hopes of communing with the Immortals and now I am faced with one. But why is she not beautiful? I don't even know what to ask her. Perhaps this is my fate, to meet the Immortals and with all my supposed eloquence have nothing to say.

"For as long as you have been able to avail yourself of your poetry gift, you have been claiming to be an Immortal banished from Heaven condemned to roam the Earth."

Ahh . . . well . . . I just . . . .

"Heaven has been moved by the clarity and power of your poetic visions."

It has?

"It would like to see them restored and has decided upon a quest for you so that you may regain your vision. If you accept this quest and are successful, the path to the highest teachings of the Way available to humans, those of the Heavens of Upper Clarity, will be granted, as you will have proved your right to a place among the Perfected."

I am overwhelmed by Heaven's blessing and respectfully request the honor of this quest.

The old woman reaches down and picks up a sword in its scabbard, "Good. This is the famous Dragon Pool Sword. Your quest is to deliver it to the Rain Goddess on this twelve-peaked mountain where we are meeting. I must, however, warn you, that in addition to those residents from both the *Yin* and *Yang* realms who will seek the sword once it reappears in the *Yang* realm, this task is also fraught with unseen dangers. The Dragon Pool Sword embodies immense power; only the purest hearts are capable of wielding it."

And if I fail?

"Ha, you are not so sure of yourself! If you fail, not only will you never attain Immortality, you will live to see this dynasty collapse and untold suffering visited on the inhabitants of this empire. For if pure evil gains the sword, a thousand years of suffering will visit this land. Do you still accept this quest?" *She held out the sheathed sword.*

As I no longer possess my poetic vision, I stand before the sword crippled in spirit. At least if I go away without the sword, only I am doomed and the rest of humanity is assured a future.

"Do not underestimate the power of your verse, Poet. It has reached Heaven and Heaven is moved to offer you this boon."

Like a line of new verse spontaneously flashing into my mind, my hand reaches out for the sword and grasps it. But she does not let it go.

"Before I can release the Dragon Pool Sword, you must know its origins, for this is no mere scrap of iron formed by human sinew and bone, cooled by blood or other putrid liquid, and scraped sharp. The Dragon Pool Sword is the material emanation of an adept whose cultivation is so pure, so refined that you may only know her name once you have proved yourself equal to this quest."

I am awe-struck that such an instrument be entrusted to me.

"You will be struck dumb when you hear how this great adept refined her human form into that of a perfected astral being. Listen closely, Li Bo, few humans have had the privilege to know the history of the Dragon Pool Sword. The adept who formed the sword had desired from birth to attain the refinement of the Perfected. She hid among distant mountains, advancing in the various purifications, gradually mastering the art of ingesting light and drinking auroras."

Breathing light! Can this be?

"Ha! How little you know, Li Bo. The teachings of the Upper Clarity Heavens are beyond those of the gross world, where the refinement of breath is the highest practice. In the Upper Heavens, light is the substance of refinement. The Perfected have mastered the techniques of refining themselves into pure beings of light, astral light—they ingest sun, moon, and starlight. And so our adept continued her quest, until the Sage Lords of the Upper Heavens took notice of her shining white jade form and arrived on earth to further instruct her. They provided her with the teachings, talismans, secret names, and seals that would allow her to travel into the Heavens. Her goal was to gain audience with the Sage Lord of the Grand Pivot."

My eyes are being drawn upward, as if I were taking this trip with the adept. Look! Directly above this spot, the diamond lights of the Dipper's seven stars, and at the handle's end the radiant Pole Star, the Grand Pivot! As I rise, the starlight is changing. I can hear it! A heavenly melody; and smell it: such a fragrance! I am bathed in a purple glow. Light flows into my mouth.

"Yes, Li Bo, the goal of her quest is to have her accomplishment, her transformation into a star being, confirmed by the Sage Lord who resides in the Grand Pivot, around which the universe turns. As the handle of the Dipper sweeps through space, the four seasons change, *Yin* and *Yang* cycle, and the Elemental Forces of earth, fire, metal, wood, and water pass through their transformations. Good and evil are distinguished by the sweep of the Dipper's handle as it dispenses happiness and hardship."

Can such a force be mastered by mere mortals?

"Mortals have within them the potential of the Perfected. Our adept knew this and, armed with her cultivation and teachings from the Sage Lords, mounted the Heavens and approached the Dipper seeking audiences with its nine star lords."

Nine? But there are only seven . . .

"To mortal eyes on earth, there are only seven stars; but to the refined vision of the Perfected, they see the two secret soul stars that orbit the Dipper and protect it. However, our adept must first confront the Nine Empresses of the Great *Yin*, the female star beings who protect the Dipper with a field of black *Yin* light. If the adept does not have the proper dragon talismans, tiger insignias, special incantations, mystic seals, and adequate levels of attainment, these star ladies will imprison the mortal adept and make her lose her reason by exposing her to the paradoxes of a universe in reverse."

I am approaching the Dipper! Below me lies the earth!

"Have no fear, Li Bo, our adept's cultivation is well grounded, and she is welcomed by the nine ladies and escorted to each of the star palaces of the nine Dipper stars. She meets with their Sage Lords and receives further instructions. Finally, she stands at Heaven's Gate ready to make the jump to the Heavenly Pivot and the audience with the Sage Lord of the Pole Star."

Before me looms a great glowing gate, bathed in the most radiant purple starlight. Around me is the black void of space.

"She is met by the Sage Lord's attendants and ushered into his most august presence. They commune and her attainment as one of the Perfected is confirmed, upon which, a splendent beam of purple starlight issues forth from her forehead and shoots down to Mount Mao, the earthly home of the Upper Clarity teachings. There it burrows deep into the mountain summit, where a glowing stone is later brought to the surface. On that night, the stars of the Dipper do not shine forth. On the radiant stone are the words *Dragon Pool Sword*, and within it lay this sword that I now release to you."

A blinding purple light has surged throughout my body; the universe pivots around me!

"To seal our exchange, I must have something in return."

I have nothing. She is smiling and raises her finger.

"I will take your fan in return for this sword."

My fan flies out of my waistband and into her hand!

Ai-yah! That fan has the Emperor's calligraphy on it, a special gift to me . . . . I have only that from my years at Court and now even this token is gone!

"You still do not understand what you have been granted. Perhaps the quest will advance your understanding. Nevertheless, you will not need a silly fan if you fail. Heed my words well: Though you now possess the Dragon Pool Sword, only a pure heart can use it."

Surely, she can see the future. Will I succeed? What if I change my mind? Perhaps I have been too hasty . . . . And this pure heart she speaks about? She is gone . . . only the mist, which now has a purple tinge to it, lingers . . . .

***

"Li Bo, Li Bo, get up! Something has happened! We must get out of this place!"

Li Bo opened his eyes. It was dawn and Ah Wu was shaking him. The fog had lifted and only shreds of mist lingered here and there. The blue sky arched over him and sparkled in the sunlight.

"What, what's the matter? Ooh, my head! That wine must have been more delicious than I realized, much more so than that dream."

Li realized he was lying on cold stone. He rolled over and saw the characters carved on the tomb. Ah Wu helped him up, they jumped off the grave. The temple had vanished.

"What happened? The Dream Temple . . . where are we?"

"We are on a tomb, Ah Wu. I can't make out the characters. Get my paper and ink . . . and my fan from your backpack."

"Your fan?"

"Quick, no time for questions."

Ah Wu found the backpack and brought paper and ink to Li Bo.

"The fan?"

"There is no fan in the pack. What is that?"

Li Bo saw the sheathed sword lying up against the tomb and tried to remember where it came from. Ah Wu reached it first. The ornate hilt protruded from an even more elaborate scabbard that had fine filigreed and precious stone-inlaid hangers just below the small hand guard in the middle of the scabbard, from which ornate cords hung. The scabbard tip was also capped with fine filigreed metal work. The small hand guard between the blade and the hilt was finely engraved in what Ah Wu recognized as an ancient style.

"The hilt is rather unusual," said Li Bo, breaking in on Ah Wu's mounting concern. "Certainly its filigreed pommel cap is striking, with that red stone set in the center. This green dragon-eyed stone set in filigree near the hand guard is remarkable." He reached for the sword.

Ah Wu moved his hand forward. "Don't!"

"Why? Is it not real?"

"That is the Dragon Pool Sword; there is none other like it."

"Yes, yes, that's what the old woman told me when she gave me the sword. What do you know about it?"

"Keep away from it. The Dragon Pool Sword carries a curse. Whoever owns it carries death."

Li Bo brushed Ah Wu's arm aside. "Naturally, swords are meant for killing. But this one . . . I can't remember, an old hag told me a story about it, but I don't remember the words, only fantastic images of a journey among the stars."

Li Bo looked upward, and could see, even in the morning sky, the seven stars of the Dipper. They seemed to be winking at him.

He turned back to Ah Wu. "Nonetheless, Heaven has granted me a quest. I must bring the sword to a mountain with twelve peaks."

"Mount Wu," Ah Wu blurted out, regretting it the instant he spoke.

"Yes, of course, home of the Rain Goddess. How fortunate, we are traveling upriver, right past it."

"I don't like the idea of carrying that thing around with us. It doesn't have to come out of its sheath to cause death."

"I have accepted this task as granted to me by Heaven. If I am successful, Heavenly recognition will follow."

"I don't trust the spirits either, especially on this mountain. Look!" Ah Wu waved his hand toward the tomb, "Where's the Dream Temple? Nothing but tricks."

"What's this?" Li Bo pointed to a freshly cut inscription on the stone next to where the sword lay.

> Only a mind as pure as the Dragon Pool,
> Will be its master.
> When such purity wields this blade,
> What resistance can there be?

"Then it is the Dragon Pool Sword," said Ah Wu, stepping back. Li Bo grasped the hilt. The sharkskin wrapping was still abrasive. He tried unsheathing the sword to admire the beauty of its legendary blade, but it wouldn't move. Li examined every detail. "It's real and so light. Come on, Ah Wu, there is nothing to worry about."

Ah Wu's face was contorted with dread. "Put it down; it's cursed. Don't touch it. It carries with it the *Yin chi* of all the dead slain by its diamond blade. Anyone who wields it dies an early and painful death. The curse extends for nine generations!"

"Your foot wound . . . fine, I believe that it can detect . . . whatever it detects. But this, where did you get that grandmother's tale?"

Ah Wu moved away from the sword.

"It was given to me in my dream. What would be the point of a curse? I'll take care of it. We must make a rubbing of this tomb inscription. Its owner must have been the woman in the dream. I must find out who she was. Quickly now, there is not much time." Li looked in the direction of the sun, and put down the sword. "The currents will soon force Old Zhou to move out into the river and leave us behind."

Li and Ah Wu spread the paper over the tomb's inscribed surface, wetting it with water from their gourd. Li took a small cloth bag containing cotton and let it absorb the ink Ah Wu had prepared, then patted the ink-soaked bag, section by section, over the damp paper, sliding it over the top of the carved characters. The sheet blackened; this allowed the characters to stand out as unstained sections of the white paper.

"Quick, Ah Wu, my fan. I need to dry the paper faster."

"The fan is nowhere to be found. Please, we should go. This is not a good place to be."

"Ah Wu, hurry, cut me a length of bamboo to roll this paper around."

Two broadsword flashes later, and Ah Wu handed Li a length of bamboo that fit perfectly the paper Li had peeled from the tombstone. Ah Wu began to clean the equipment, but Li said, "Leave it, we must return to the boat. The scroll is all I need." He moved down the steps, then remembered, "The sword!"

Ah Wu's foot began aching. He looked up at the tomb. The wind was now swirling around. It could be dangerous.

"No! I'll go."

Li Bo stopped. "But . . . ."

"It's not safe up there. It doesn't matter anymore." Ah Wu limped up the steps. He picked up the sword as if it were a venomous reptile, then he grabbed Li Bo's *jheng* (zither), which always traveled with them so that Li could compose his verse.

Ah Wu headed to the steps. The wind stirred and he felt the back of his neck prickle. A strange scent—sweet, almost lavender—filled the air and his mind began to cloud. He knew this martial art trick and responded by sending his vital force downward and outward, surrounding him with a field of heightened sensory perception. Focusing his mind, he sensed something behind him. He was ready. Again directing his *chi* force, he blocked out the scent and fixed on his *dan-tien*, the center of his vital energy.

Few humans could have resisted his speed. In one flowing movement, he swiveled and fired the crossbow. It looked like a wild shot. Ah Wu dropped to the ground and gulped in the fresh air that had remained unscented.

"*Aah!*" a cry from the bamboo stand behind the tomb. The slender stalks swayed in the wind. Ah Wu fingered the second trigger and followed the familiar pattern. Just as he was ready to fire, the movement stopped. The wind rose upward, and a bright white column of mist reached up to catch it. For a moment, there might have been a form—but whatever it was broke apart in the wind that moved the mist downhill away from the tomb. Ah Wu was ready to leave the sword and *jheng* to fire a second shot, but he thought perhaps this is a trick to get me into the bamboo where the crossbow would be at a disadvantage and, of course, have me leave the sword behind. Someone, or something, is after the sword. Perhaps Li Bo was right and the stories he himself had heard about the Dragon Pool Sword were nonsense. It didn't matter, Ah Wu decided. Li Bo needed it and that was enough.

Ah Wu waited—he knew patience was the mark of true skill. The wind rustled the pines and bushes. The mist was gone, but the sky remained bright and cool. He shivered, and reloaded the crossbow. Looking around, he moved into the bushes behind him and knelt. He opened the end of Li Bo's *jheng* and slid in the sword. It was a close fit, but the sword's extraordinary lightness would hardly add any weight, and with the end closed who would be the wiser? Then he rewrapped the *jheng* in its waterproof traveling cloth and slung it over his shoulder. He moved through the dense undergrowth as if gliding over water until he reached the stairs.

Li Bo was lying face down at the bottom of the steps. Ah Wu rushed to him.

"What happened?"

Li Bo sat up and began to take off his elaborate court robes. "In some ways, these robes are quite useless."

"It is the Court that is quite useless. A bunch of egotists who never get enough of themselves."

"Am I like that?"

"As long as the Court is your goal in life."

Li Bo smiled. "The Chinese say a lot of things about the Turks, but a lack of frankness is not one. I don't know. Right now, my goal is to get that sword to Mount Wu."

"This whole mountain is haunted. The Dream Temple, the food we ate, the wine we drank, even the incense we breathed were all ghostly illusions. Why that drunken singing girl must have been one of them. Camel piss!" His great forest of eyebrows and the red streak that ran across his face distorted his eyes as if he still suspected ghosts nearby, listening.

"Ah Wu, the spirits of this place have already spoken with me regarding your impolite remarks about their abode."

Ah Wu's scar reddened.

Li Bo packed away his silk robes. Dressed in his faded blue cotton robe, he looked almost like any other starving scholar, thought Ah Wu. Of course, the gleam in his almost round eyes and his red pointy nose set him off from the typical Chinese scholar.

"Well then, no more should be said. Let's get to the boat and leave them their mountain," said Ah Wu. He lifted the zither and his own backpack and plunged ahead down the stone steps.

Li Bo followed and called out. "So what was your dream like?"

Ah Wu froze.

"I do not need dreams. They are for poets! I kept watch," he shouted back over his shoulder.

"Some watchman. The whole temple is stolen and replaced with a thousand-year-old tomb and you didn't notice a thing."

"What? A thousand years old!"

The old warrior turned and moved back up to Li.

"Though the characters are archaic, I could make out the reign date; that is a Western Han tomb," said Li. He gazed back up the steps.

"Western Han?" A puzzled look spread over Ah Wu's face. "A thousand years old! This is not good; those ancient bastards are not easy to deal with, been around too long. Maybe we should move quicker."

"No, pace yourself. It's still a long way. The spirit I met was not hostile." Li Bo took a steady sideways glance at his friend. "You had a dream, too, didn't you?"

Ah Wu kept walking and his face turned stony. After a long silence he spoke. "Yes. But it does not mean anything; it answers no question, for I have nothing that needs answering."

Li smiled. "We all need answers, Ah Wu. Perhaps the dream was the answer to a question you haven't formed yet, or don't want to ask."

Looking back up at where the tomb now lay, Ah Wu said, "Let's get to the boat. I would not enjoy being stranded here."

~ 5 ~

The wind coursed down the nameless mountain toward the Long River. Nearing the shore, the mist that scattered at Ah Wu's crossbow shot congealed. In a cove surrounded by thick bamboo, it reached earth, and Chen Shao-lin, a golden-haired young woman in a dark green robe, stumbled to the ground. She held her wrist in pain; a clear fluid seeped around her hand. Her fair complexion was lightly freckled; her deep round green eyes and high nose indicated an ancestry drawn from near the western rim of the Chinese empire.

In the cove, a pair of eyes, yellow with black vertical slits, broke the surface of the water and watched the descent of the mist-maiden. The eyes glided closer to the shore. As they moved, the rough scaly body propelling them rose to the surface. The water creature had flowing swept-back ears and a long ugly snout with a high-set pair of nostrils. Its powerful tail moved back and forth quietly until it reached the shore. It crawled up the stone-strewn beach, its mouth opened to reveal a slender red forked tongue flashing out between rows of sharp white teeth. Its clawed, webbed feet raised its long body and moved it noiselessly up behind the girl.

Chen turned to the creature, but tried not to look at its face, for now it stood upright in the form of a human male. "Oh, uncle, why does it hurt so? And why do I still bleed?"

"I am not your uncle and if you don't remember, I will treat you as he did," said a female voice.

A middle-aged Uzbek man of average height in a dirty white funeral robe stood over the young woman. His eyes were obviously not human; they emitted a red glow.

He spoke with a female voice, "How many months has it been since you entered the *Yin* realm? Humans are so stupid. This is the last time that I explain this. While my form takes on the appearance of your worst *Yang* realm memory, I am a Blood Dragon, your master, not your uncle, and you will refer to me respectfully, as a slave does to its master. Understood?" His eyes flared red.

"Yes, master."

"What were you doing? So careless. How many times have I warned you that even in your present form you are still vulnerable?"

Chen didn't respond. She continued to examine her wrist and wondered why the Blood Dragon didn't appear in its water form. After all, she reflected, jumping off the ship and being killed by the monster was really her worst *Yang* realm memory.

"I have fools for attendants. These two humans that have stumbled upon the Dream Temple are very troublesome. You are the third to come back injured along with two others so scared they are useless. Must I deal with these humans myself?" The creature's eyes glowed. It reached out and grabbed Chen's wrist, "Let me see!"

"Aaaoow, it hurts! Don't do that!" Chen cried out. The hatred she reined back almost broke through when the creature slapped her across the face.

"How dare you speak that way to me! I'll give you a hundred more pains, each worse than that simple scratch."

Focused on only the pain, Chen regained her composure. The creature examined the wound and pushed Chen's arm away.

"How did you get this?" it growled in an almost male-human voice.

"I followed those two men up to the Dream Temple and I saw it."

"Saw what?" the creature snarled.

"The sword, the sword you once described to me. I know it has to be it. I was going to take it for you, but . . . ."

"What sword? What are you talking about?" The creature's eyes smoldered.

"Please, master, don't be angry with me. I . . . I only meant to serve you. I saw the Dragon Pool Sword . . . ."

The creature's eyes were engulfed in flame. It struck Chen again, sending her sprawled to the ground. A thin trickle of clear fluid formed where her lip was cut. Again, she concentrated on the pain. It cleared her mind. She must not despair—despair would destroy whatever remained of her human spirit; she had seen what happened to the others. There was hope, there had to be hope. Her human form was gone, but it wasn't the end. Hope could transcend. She knew it was so. The others had given up and they had become shadows, empty of substance, controlled by the Blood Dragon. Was this not a fate worse than death? Funny, that idea. Once upon a time, she thought that there was no fate worse than death. Now she knew better. Think of the poetry— the poetry—it has the power to transcend.

"Don't fool with me about that sword! It hasn't been seen for the last thousand years!" The Blood Dragon's rant brought Chen back to the monster's presence. She sat up on the rocky shore. She had to remain alert. Tears formed in her eyes, her wrist burned, and now her whole head ached. She knew the monster was obsessed with the sword.

"Master, I saw it. I heard them refer to it by that name. It came to the scholar in a dream . . . ."

"It must be true! That sword can only be transmitted through dreams. I knew this mountain was the key to finding the sword."

A blue-green radiance shone from the Blood Dragon's "human" eyes. "With that sword, I could control the Long River, and whoever controls it rivals the power of the Son of Heaven. Wouldn't that be interesting—a Blood Dragon soaring beyond the Rain Dragons? With control of the river, there would be tributes, temples, and even my own palace. And revenge for the centuries of abuse I've endured from the other spirits. Quick, what happened up there?"

"The scholar's attendant shot me before I could trick him into leaving the sword," Chen said. Her tears stopped. She imagined the devastation to human life along the river if the Blood Dragon was able to control it—thousands would die and be enslaved as she had been.

"How do you know one's a scholar?"

The monster's impatient question brought her back. "I followed them up to the temple. The thin, white-haired one is a very careful, thoughtful man. You can see it in the way he moves and talks, and in his simple dress. I knew this type of man when I worked in the wine halls of the capital. It was he who sought the Dream Temple. The other fellow is his bodyguard or attendant. Scholars don't arm themselves with crossbows," she said bitterly and rubbed her wrist.

"A scholar—one of the most worthless forms of a most worthless species." The creature scowled. "A scholar and his bodyguard . . . why would a scholar receive the Dragon Pool Sword? Perhaps the mistress of the Dream Temple is playing a joke on him . . . . She has made a big mistake this time, entrusting such a powerful weapon to a mere human, to the weakest of a weak species no less. I might have her now! Where are these humans?" said Chen's master, in a milder, thoughtful, almost soothing, voice.

"On the way down the mountain toward their boat."

"Here take this." The creature handed Chen a small box. "Smear the salve over your wound and the bleeding will stop. You're lucky the bolt he fired wasn't poisoned, or coated with some other human concoction to do us harm."

The creature thought for a moment, then continued: "Make your way upriver to their boat and appear to them as a stranded woman. Male humans, especially scholars, are so easily beguiled by soft, helpless females of your species. Once you have their confidence, which is easy with scholars—just act sincere; they are very gullible—then find out where the sword is. Report to me as soon as you can. And remember," the creature's eyes glowed, "I will be nearby."

Chen bowed. The creature turned and walked to the water. There was a loud splash and ripples spread from two eyes that moved away from the shore.

Chen remained for a while, holding her arm. Another task for the monster. How painful this new existence is, she thought. Will it ever end? And if it does, what form of existence lies ahead? Tears softly fell from her eyes. She once again remembered what her uncle had done to her. Could hell be much worse?

***

The Long River moved impassively toward the east. Cool air, mist, and splashes of bright sunlight had beguiled it into indifference. Due to the presence of the "nameless mountain" and its horrific lore, this stretch of the river was deserted. Even without the presence of a Blood Dragon, the region was inhospitable to human habitation due to the cliffs that lined the river from the mountain to Xia-zhou, the next port of call. It is said that these cliffs prepared the traveler for the Three Gorges, but they are not half as high as those in the gorges.

Various types of water birds built nests along the cliff walls. During the spring, there was much flitting back and forth and general merriment, for the birds could fly high above the sorrows brought by the Blood Dragon's presence down below. While the river was wide enough for ship traffic in both directions at once, the currents were difficult; some say that Blood Dragons enjoy living in dangerous waters, for there were greater chances of shipwreck and human misfortune in such waters.

The rocky shoreline made landing a boat difficult and the shore was too narrow for any type of permanent habitation. The widest area was created by the nameless mountain's northern slope, which leveled off before it met the river shore. A few trees and high grass grew back from the stony shore.

Li Bo's boatman, Old Zhou, however, was like one of the water birds. The river was his lifelong friend. It had charmed him from childhood. He watched the waves lap up on the gray stones. For centuries this great course of water has witnessed humankind's puny attempts to master it, he thought. The river spoke of pain and suffering and of joy and peace. Yet, it spoke most eloquently through master Li's songs. There is no doubt that all Nature found voice through him. Now the river reflected the sadness of his banishment. Surely there will be a sign from Heaven at the unfairness of his punishment, he thought. The boatman then prayed, as boatmen do, to the river spirit—the Hsiang Goddess—that she would guide Li Bo on his difficult journey.

The hooves of an approaching horseman intruded upon his prayer. A lone rider wearing a cap and dressed in a green tunic and tan pants rode up to the boatman. Old Zhou noticed the rider's unusual black-headed horse. Placing the boat hook between him and the stranger, the old man moved forward and spoke, "Not for hire."

"I need your boat," a rugged voice demanded.

The boatman raised the hook, "Back off. This is a private boat. Move along or I'll feed you to the fish." The boatman was old, but he knew how to handle a boat hook.

"Ha! I'm tired from riding all night and seek only your boat. I will pay well." A small leather sack of coins fell at the boatman's feet.

He raised his hook higher, "No!"

Almost before the last word was spoken, the rider raised a small golden bell pulled from the red silk pouch slung across her body. The brilliant light from the bell startled the boatman. He had no time to react. The sound of the bell paralyzed him. With his boat hook raised to strike, his frozen posture only threatened the wind.

Shamaness Luo smiled. She removed her cap, letting her long black hair fall free around her jade-white neck and face. She replaced the bell in the pouch.

"A fair trade for this boat," she said in a voice as smooth as the finest silk from Shu. The boatman watched helplessly. She untied the mooring line and pushed the thirty-foot wooden boat into the Long River's sleepy current. She thought, this should put some distance between the assassin and me. She poled farther into the current. Somewhere down the beach, the black-headed horse vanished while grazing on the shoreline mists.

***

As the morning wore on, the river took on a silver sheen and the low-lying fog melted away. Here and there, waves broke the mirrored surface. Another rider appeared. He was completely dressed in black, except for a wide brimmed straw hat with a hole in the center for his top-knotted yellow-white hair to flow out. He wore a short sword strapped to his back; its worn hilt protruded above his shoulder to the right of his neck. Dismounting in front of the immobilized boatman, he moved behind him and directed a series of fingertip blows to pressure points along the old man's spine. The boatman's rigid form went limp and collapsed.

The swordsman sat on the ground next to Old Zhou. He pushed back his straw hat revealing his bone-white skin. His pink eyes peered closely at the boatman. He poured a rationed amount of liquid from a small red gourd down the old man's throat. The boatman stirred and fell into a deep sleep.

The albino swordsman took up a seated meditation posture. He reached into his robe and pulled out a metal case suspended by a leather thong around his neck. As he opened the case, the light around him began to dim. In the case lay a black pearl-like orb. Its luster increased as it absorbed the light around the swordsman. The air stirred; white-caps appeared on the river. The swordsman entered a trance state that carried him into the sleeping boatman's memories, where he could see a lone rider approaching and then the boatman being paralyzed by the sound of a bell. It was the shamaness. She said something and left with the boat.

The swordsman leaned close to the boatman's ear. "She will not get far. Her fate will be the same as yours, old man. And someday, the Emperor, while he is dreaming of his plump concubines, will also feel the steel of my nightmare blade. For now, however, I must be content with taking the Shamaness Luo's life. She has interfered for the last time with our plans to assassinate the Emperor. I share this secret with you and the Long River, old man, for the Long River keeps its secrets, as do the dead."

The boatman was aware of his dreams. He now saw a black shadow moving toward him. He tried to relax, for this was simply some sort of nightmare, he thought. However, the gleaming sword that struck him in the heart did not wake him.

The swordsman came out of his trance and sheathed his sword. He closed the metal box and returned it into the folds of his robe. The light brightened and the air calmed; a mirror-like sheen returned to the river. He reached down in front of him and picked up a leather coin pouch. A smile formed on his soft white face. He mounted up and rode off down the shore. Behind him, the bright morning light reflected in the blank eyes of the boatman. The river's waves peacefully lapped upon the shore.

6

"Ah Wu, were you frightened by your dream?"

"The Dream Temple is just a trick. It's that cursed Dragon Pool Sword that bothers me."

"Bah! The tales of Turkish wet nurses. Why send me on a quest with a cursed sword? They could have killed us as we slept."

Ah Wu didn't answer. He carefully made his way down the rocky path away from the Dream Temple and toward the Long River.

"The wine was good," said Li. "You didn't see any more of it around when you went back?"

"That was a tomb, not a temple up there," said Ah Wu, pointing back up in the direction they had come from. "Who knows what the hell we were drinking? Could have been camel's piss for all we know."

"Have you ever drunk . . . ," Li started to ask, but was cut off by the sight that greeted them when they rounded a large boulder: the Long River in all its silvery glory lay below. They were on a different path down the mountain to the river shore. Much as the Dream Temple had disappeared and been replaced by the tomb, so had the pine forest been replaced by a stony path and high grass and shrubs with a few trees and boulders scattered on either side.

Ah Wu ran up to the edge of the ridge and peered down, waiting for a break in the misty cloud that obscured the view. Chunks of white frosty nothingness alternated with incredibly clear images of the Long River moving impassively on its way to the sea. It took several gaps in the strands of mist, until he saw clearly.

"I knew it. I knew it!" yelled Ah Wu motioning wildly with his crossbow.

"What?"

"The boat's gone!"

"Are you sure?" Li said, searching the mist for the shoreline.

"I think I see someone lying on the shore . . . wait, mist rolling in from the river . . . I can't make it out . . . one or maybe two figures . . . ." Ah Wu's eyebrows were tired, but they shot up again, "Look! Up the river, that bright light . . . ."

"Where?"

"Just for a brief moment, a speck of pure golden light shone from the river. This whole region is haunted," said Ah Wu. He scanned the grasses and undergrowth that now seemed to press in closer around them.

"Let's get to the shore. Old Zhou could be injured," Li Bo said. He led the way down the damp stony trail toward the river.

"It's that accursed sword," grumbled Ah Wu limping behind him.

***

Shamaness Luo returned the golden bell, which she had just held high in the bright morning light, into her pouch. She continued to chant, and the wind answered her beckoning by filling the sail. She reached up and undid her hair, letting it fall in stormy black disarray cascading over her shoulders. The skiff was under sail and moving up the river. Her eyelids half closed while she swayed back and forth, sitting cross-legged on the aft deck. The fragrance from the incenser in front of her rose through the air, unaffected by the winds, and wove a protective enclosure about her. She chanted. "Oh Lady of the Purple Vault, your disciple Luo Jhu-yun, former Ministry of Rites, Grand Shamaness to the Emperor Xuan-zong, Son of Heaven, awaits your pleasure."

She began to quiver and her whole body shook violently. Her mouth moved, as if she were trying to force sounds out of it. A voice from deep within her welled up and escaped from her soft, full red lips, "Jhu-yun, you have done well." The voice pulsed through her body but it was not her voice.

Deep and lush, it continued. "We will meet later. I must warn you, there are three who pursue you: a talented swordsman, sent by the Son of Heaven himself; a black-hearted albino, sent by those who would dare to take the Emperor's life and who has already struck at you; and a most foul creature that crawls out of the darkest recesses of the Yin realm—it represents your greatest danger. Be alert! These threats to your vow are dangerous and must be faced."

The voice ceased and Luo collapsed, unconscious, on the deck of Li Bo's skiff. The wind steadily pushed the boat upriver. The incense smoke, ignoring the wind, moved to caress the young woman's sweat-soaked form. She lay in a sweet exhausted sleep.

***

The sun had climbed closer to its zenith before they were on the shore running toward the two figures lying there. Ah Wu, who even with his limp was in better shape, reached them first. He froze.

Li Bo finally caught up. "What is it?"

Ah Wu approached the fallen form of a woman dressed in an orchid-print deep-blue robe.

"Golden hair . . . keep back," said Ah Wu. His crossbow was leveled at the girl's form, a golden-haired form that called back painful memories of his family and their destruction during the Western Region wars.

Chen kept still, hoping the giant ape, as she thought of him, wouldn't shoot first and then examine her condition.

"Don't be the camel's ass that you're constantly invoking. Come here. Old Zhou is hurt!"

They ran over to the boatman. Blood drenched his chest. Ah Wu took over. He pushed away the pain of the past, knelt down and took the old man's arm in his hands, carefully placing three fingers over his wrist. Li Bo cradled his friend's head in his hands. Ah Wu concentrated, trying to feel for the triple pulse beat. At the same time, he examined the Old Zhou's chest wound by observing its depth, angle of penetration, and flow of blood. It didn't take long, "He is with his river now. The sword blow was powerful, one clean blow through Old Zhou's heart."

Li's eyes glistened. He continued to hold the aged boatman's head; he felt its warmth dissipate. Old Zhou had been in his employ for almost ten years now. He was a loyal and faithful companion. On land, he appeared clumsy and oafish, but on the water, few could read the river as he did. The Long River was a part of him, and he transported Li Bo to some of its most beautiful visions. Li owed the inspiration for much of his water poetry to Old Zhou's knowledge of the ancient waterway. Tears fell freely from Li Bo's eyes.

Ah Wu got up and moved to the girl. He backed away again for as soon as he approached there was that scent—almost, but not quite lavender; the same as he smelled near the Dream Temple, rather, the tomb. And her golden hair—this time anger arose in his heart to push away the pain. Clearly, she wasn't Chinese, but, more important to Ah Wu: was she human?

"It's that cursed Dragon Pool Sword," said Ah Wu. "We should have left it at the tomb, where it belongs." He put down Li's *jheng* and limped away from it as if it were some dangerous animal ready to strike out at any moment.

"Ah Wu," Li called. He rose and moved toward Chen. "What's the matter? Is she dead too?"

Ah Wu approached Li. "Keep back! She has golden hair!" He felt trapped with her on one side and the *jheng* containing the Dragon Pool Sword on the other.

"Yes. Golden, like the girls in the taverns at the capital . . . Chang'an girls from Sogdiana or Tukhäristän. And maybe even green eyes and a high nose . . . she's one of us!"

"This isn't the capital, and at least we are human! She's a ghost, another trap! We should have left the sword on the mountain. It's bad luck," said Ah Wu. He looked for footprints—they were everywhere. Yet, he put his arm out and stopped Li from moving forward.

"Smell that? The same as on the mountain—be careful! That fragrance will cloak your mind, I . . . ."

"Enough! Humans are more fearful than any ghost. It is the Chinese who have condemned me to death, not any creatures of the *Yin* realm . . . or any swords," Li's voice boomed out. He brushed Ah Wu's large arm aside and moved to the girl. He gently turned her over. Her round eyes and high nose confirmed that she was from the Western Regions and not Chinese. He noticed the light freckling along the top of her cheeks and nose. It reminded him of the great river of stars that flowed above on clear nights when he drifted on the river currents with Old Zhou.

"Ah Wu," Li commanded, trying to control his grief over the loss of his old friend, "don't stand there chewing grass like some camel; bring the medicine bag!"

Ah Wu snapped out of his stupor and went to their backpacks.

"Ah Wu, bring water . . . she is still alive!" Li held his finger under her nose.

Ah Wu was trying to understand how Old Zhou had died. It didn't make sense. He handed Li the water gourd. Focusing on Old Zhou's death cleared his mind. Now he was thinking like a warrior not like some frightened peasant. He noticed the girl's wrist wound. No other injuries were visible.

"Ooh, what happened, where am I," said Chen, with an unmistakable Chang'an capital accent, and then she fainted again. Her eyes had flickered open briefly. They were, to Li's great anticipation and Ah Wu's great dread, as hauntingly green as any bamboo grove.

Ah Wu was troubled. Such golden hair and green eyes were common enough in the far Western Regions and in the taverns of the capital. Near this mountain, however, she could be a fox spirit or, perhaps, one of the Blood Dragon's ghosts that had been threatening them. They weren't free of the mountain yet.

"Ah Wu, Ah Wu, she's fainted again. Get the medicine bag. We must give her something to revive her properly." Li Bo had to call out again before he could get Ah Wu's attention.

"Yes, yes . . . reviving ghosts, I'd rather kiss a camel's . . . ," mumbled Ah Wu rummaging around in the brown leather medicine bag. He came up with some salve from Yunnan and smiled at the thought—Yunnan, that's where they were traveling to die. He applied it under the girl's nose. Her bamboo-colored eyes popped open and then closed against the light. She opened them bit-by-bit and moaned. "Oh, my head. A mountain has fallen on it."

"Young lady, what happened here? Are you all right?" asked Li.

"I . . . I'm not sure. I was talking with the boatman. I'm traveling up river. I was struck from behind," said Chen.

"And on the wrist . . . ," interjected Ah Wu. He pointed to the fresh scar on her arm.

"Oh that, I don't know . . . . I can't remember where I came from . . . only that I must go upriver," Chen said, looking around at Li and then Ah Wu. Her golden hair, once piled up on top of her head in a familiar capital style, had half fallen down on her shoulders. The sunlight played off it in a most fascinating way. Ah Wu could see that it had certainly caught Li's attention, as had her lilting capital accent. Her golden hair had even brought back painful memories of Ah Wu's wife, now long dead.

"Why?" asked Ah Wu, trying to focus on the situation at hand.

"Don't know. I can't remember . . . just that it is urgent," said Chen.

"Hmm," said Ah Wu, not impressed with her answers. But he could see that Li was succumbing to her charms. Understandable for any man who just spent time in prison expecting to be executed, thought Ah Wu, but for Li, given his attachment to the capital's party life, this could be unsettling.

Chen was also worried, but not about Li Bo. That other ape of a man had shot her. She wondered if he suspected her of being his previous target.

"Oh, don't mind him," interrupted Li Bo. He stood over the girl with an ashen smile, "We've had a difficult time on that mountain, and now our boatman has been killed."

Realizing that his eyes were still wet, he blotted them with the sleeves of his worn pale-blue robe. She noticed this and for a moment remembered her own former humanity—the caring of one person for another. How long ago had that been?

"And our boat, stolen," said Ah Wu in a hushed tone. He continued to eye the girl and keep a close grip on his crossbow.

Li didn't respond. He looked down at the ground only half-aware of the girl. Old Zhou's memory returned. It was strong. The lines of verse that he composed under the old man's steady sail, the images that ignited the inspiration for them played in his head:

An egret stands alone in golden water, its shape distorted by the waves; hidden waterfalls suspended from the skies, warm mists that came softly down mountains; gibbons playing with the moon in the water: all this and more Old Zhou's tiller and sail brought to me. How can one repay such gifts? He refused my offers of payment, saying that my poetry was far greater a reward. Are these songs so valuable? Now both my ability and the one who provided the materials that fed that ability are lost. What is the point of traveling to my death when I lie doubly slain on this shore?

Li Bo looked up and noticed some scrolls that had poked out of the girl's cloth traveling bag. The characters on one seemed so familiar that he couldn't resist reaching over and pulling at the sheet.

"Sir, what are you doing? Those are my personal belongings!" Chen's voice rose. She sat up and grabbed at the paper in Li Bo's hand.

It was easy for him to recognize the characters of his own poems. Chen pulled the scroll from him, and stuffed it back into her bag.

Li looked at her. What does she find so valuable in that dried ink? She's young, he thought, doesn't understand the foolish pain and suffering that formed those characters.

"Why are you carrying those poems?" he asked.

"Sir, are you a government official?"

"No."

"It's none of your business."

"Do you like poetry?"

"Everyone likes poetry."

"Ah Wu can't stand it."

"He's only a servant. What would he know of the great poet, Li Bo?"

The scar on Ah Wu's face reddened. He moved forward to speak, but stopped short when he felt Li's icy stare.

"Ah Wu is my traveling companion," said Li with a strained smile, "and he is also one of the greatest warriors in the empire."

"Men who kill others don't interest me. Men, like Li Bo, whose words move Emperors, whose poems can make gods and ghosts cry . . . ." She hesitated, willing her tears back. "These are admirable men. They succeed with words where 10,000 swords fail. You know, they call him the 'banished Immortal,' a brilliance exiled from Heaven." The wistful look in her eyes added to Li's feeling that she was sincere, but naive.

"Another dreamer," scowled Ah Wu, who winced at the mention of the "banished Immortal," a subject that Li Bo had loved to harp on whenever he felt melancholy—as he frequently did after his Court dismissal. Ah Wu turned back to examine the ground around Old Zhou's body.

"You have a great respect for poets, but I must confess that I tend to share Ah Wu's sentiments. Poets are fools who couldn't even turn over a furrow of land to feed themselves."

Ah Wu's bushy eyebrows were all tied in knots. His scar lit up. He was fast forming the opinion that the girl must be a ghost who had already enchanted his old friend. Normally at this point in a conversation with a beautiful woman, Li would have launched into his speech. How he was indeed a banished Immortal, condemned to roam the empire without recognition for his brilliant talent. It was the first time Ah Wu had actually heard him agree with his assessment that poets were indeed help-less fools. It must have really been bad in that prison, or that girl's bewitching powers were very formidable, thought Ah Wu.

"You both should read Li Bo before forming such opinions. He is no fool. He sees deeper than any man alive today," she said.

The blood raced through Li's neck and into his thin cheeks; his nose reddened more than its normal glow. "Well, if this is so, then where is this great poet now? Is he at the side of the Emperor passing on his great insights? Does he still sit in the Han-lin Academy with the empire's greatest minds and enlighten the Son of Heaven?"

"I think he's left the capital . . . ," Chen said. "I've heard he chose to wander somewhere in the South, free from the worries and trivialities of Court life."

Li almost lost his composure. "Chose! Your great poet has been banished to die in the malarial mists of Yunnan!"

Ah Wu was growing more certain that either the mists of this region or the girl had affected his friend's mind. This all went to prove his favorite opinion, that the world was mad and it didn't matter what happened, for it was all madness anyway.

"How could that be? Certainly the Emperor or, at least, Heaven could not be so blind!" Her fair cheeks reddened at a faster pace than Li's did.

Li was surprised by the intensity of her feelings. Tears fell from her green eyes. Li grew quiet. He watched the Long River as it flowed impassively eastward. For thousands of years, he thought, the river has undergone change, yet it also remained the same. He wondered if he would ever attain that state, and then he said, "He made a mistake. Perhaps even Immortals can make mistakes."

Ah Wu watched him.

Chen sat quietly, her tears still falling.

"Why do you weep; he is just another poet." Li tried to comfort her.

She wiped her eyes with her sleeves. "You don't understand. Poets are special. They have a sensitivity that most humans lack . . . . They are all that is worthwhile in our . . . in the human species."

Li smiled. "Do you know how this *sensitive* Li Bo discovered his so-called poetic talents? One night, lying totally drunk and naked in a field, he watched the moon climb into the heavens. He toasted it and felt sad that it could not share his wine, so he wrote it a letter to cheer it up. The next morning, his friends found him still lying in that field with the letter covering his private parts. He gained notoriety, at first, because it was claimed that he wrote his first poem with his, ah, male member. It was only later that people noticed the skill of the poem. Poets!"

Her eyes, softened by her tears, now hardened. "Do you think most humans, obsessed with taking advantage of each other, even notice the moon, much less, when drunk, write a poem of cheer to it? How do you know so much about this poet, a man whose poetry you claim not to know?"

Li Bo's face reddened. She has strong opinions, he thought, and so did he. "I don't know poetry, but in the capital, where we have just come from, its taverns are full of gossip about such excessive people. One cannot but overhear such conversations. They mock him."

"They, like the Court and all those who aspire to join its ranks, are fools." Chen's voice trailed off in her tears. She was aware that the Blood Dragon was out there in the river somewhere. Perhaps, she thought, glancing out at the river, it will think this is part of my act to ensnare the scholar. I am lucky that it doesn't really understand humans.

Li Bo rose and turned to Ah Wu. "We must do something for Old Zhou. This Li Bo fellow is beyond help."

The two men went about finding a suitable burial site for their friend among the trees that were scattered along the rocky coast. Chen looked at their baggage, then caught sight of the red eyes floating in the river, watching her. She had to get up and look around, if only for a moment. Each man had a backpack, and there was a longer case, probably the *jheng*; no sign of the sword. If the monster got impatient, it would rise out of the river, look for the sword, and kill these men.

But the sight of the *jheng* caused her to recall the scholars who used to frequent the pubs of Chang'an, how they enjoyed singing poems. Her tears continued to fall. She remembered the first time she heard someone chanting Li Bo's poems. Moving over to her things, she sat down. Let the monster come, she thought. The sword is not here and there is nothing I can do about it.

After Old Zhou was buried—with Li Bo tearfully reciting some of the boatman's favrite rier poems over te grave—Li Bo and Ah Wu walked back toward the shore.

"Between the mists of this land and your conversation with that . . . that woman or whatever she may be, I am lost," said Ah Wu.

"Sorry about what I said back there, but it just flew out of my mouth, and I'm completely sober; that's what scares me. I can't go back to her now and introduce myself as Li Bo. How about this: I am Jiang Wei-lin, a merchant specializing in exotic items from the Western regions. We are on our way back to those regions from the capital . . . . Business has not been good. Understand? We'll catch a ship and at the next port never see her again."

Ah Wu threw his hands up, shrugging his large shoulders. "Who can make sense of a mad world, but I enjoyed your first poem story. You still have a lively imagination."

Li smiled. "Imagination?" And moved off toward the shore where Chen was still sitting.

Chen was still weeping. She sat alone reading the poetry. "How could they banish him? No matter what, I have his words—they are my hope, and as long as I can cling to them . . ." Some of her favorite lines caught her tear-filled eyes—the lines that gave her the most courage, the most hope of keeping her imagination—the one thing that still made her human:

> . . . his body astride a soaring dragon,
> the wind rose in his ears.
> Crossing rivers, passing over seas,
> and reaching Heaven, I know on this trip,
> his heart will never be extinguished!

"Never be extinguished!" She chanted the phrase again and again, smiling. Then she felt a chill run through her body. Those eyes were out there, somewhere. Chen carefully scanned the river along the shoreline and spotted the two red orbs floating with the current. The monster was still watching. She rolled the scroll and returned it carefully into her bag, trying not to glance toward the river.

She was cornered. Here in the *Yang* realm was this ape of a human who had shot her. He was suspicious and thus dangerous. Behind her lay the *Yin* realm and the monster that held her in its terrible grip. Where was her refuge?

"How are you?" Li's question so startled her that she almost lost control and turned into mist.

"Oh, you frightened me." Chen stood up and faced the two men with her back to the river.

"I would like to apologize for our lack of manners in not properly introducing ourselves," Li said in a formal tone. "I am Jiang Wei-lin from the Shu region, a merchant of western exotics, and this is my companion, Wang Ah Wu. He has assisted me for the last ten years. We are returning to the west from a recent trip to the capital."

Chen rose and bowed in the capital manner. "Pleased to make your acquaintances. I am Chen Shao-lin, originally of Sogdiana, but raised in the capital by my master who is Chinese. I cannot remember what happened to him or why I am here. My head still hurts terribly." It was a only small lie, she thought. She didn't know what happened to the old bastard once she jumped overboard to escape his advances. Certainly, he didn't try to rescue her. Instead, she awoke as a slave of the Blood Dragon.

"Ah Wu will give you something to ease the pain and help return your memory," Li said and paused. "Miss Chen, I'm afraid we have a problem. Our boat has been stolen and the shore is impassable from this point."

"What shall I do?"

"Don't worry, we will help you to the next port, but for now a good meal takes priority."

The sun slipped away behind the mountains and the river darkened. Ah Wu was restless.

"I'll get some wood, so we can have a strong fire for the night. Maybe it will keep away some of the other beings in this region," said Ah Wu, looking at Chen. She smiled and politely cast her eyes away.

Ah Wu moved to the woods that reached the edge of the clearing where the boat had been drawn up and began to cut dead branches with his broadsword. Li and the girl gathered what food was left from the travel bags and set about making dinner. The *Yin* realm of ghosts and spirits preoccupied the minds of all three travelers while they prepared for darkness on a strange shore.

***

Farther up the same shore, the albino swordsman, Old Zhou's killer, had built up his fire so it could be easily visible to passing ships. The shore had turned too rocky for travel on horseback, so he had camped. Moving back from the fire, the swordsman sat cross-legged on the rocks. Opening the metal box hanging from his neck, he exposed the shining black orb to the firelight. Its blackness grew in intensity dimming the fire. He closed his pink eyes and began to chant the mantra. A dream-net was cast over those sailing through the region.

— 7 —

The man rolled back and forth with difficulty in his small bunk. His flesh sagged like soft dough around his waist and on his face. He was asleep and dreaming:

It was night and he was on the deck of his imperial salt-hauling river ship. Off to the port he saw a fire on the shore. A voice out of the dark called to him: "I will make a brief stop worth your time."

The captain ordered his men to pull close to shore and pick up the stranger at the campfire. The stranger, whose face was hidden by the dark, tossed the captain a small pouch when he came aboard. Its weight told him that the stop was indeed worth the effort.

The captain awoke to the sound of excited voices outside his cabin.

"This is a haunted region. Fire or no fire, we're not going near the shore . . . ."

"Just last week I heard that three bodies had been found here. The blood drained from all of them!"

"Blood Dragons—they roam this stretch of the river taking the unwary . . . ."

"It's crazy to pass this region at night . . . ."

The door flung open, and the captain loomed out on deck. "What's this nonsense about a fire? This region is deserted . . . ." Then he saw the fire. It passed to port and he remembered his dream.

His voice boomed out over the deck. "Pull to, we're stopping here to investigate."

The order startled the crew. However, they had seen how he handled dissent among his men—usually a tow through the river at the end of a bamboo cable 'til the captain finished a jar of wine. If he passed out, as he sometimes did, the sailor had little chance of survival.

The bamboo rattan sails flew down the three masts and the crew prepared the anchor. The captain, with his armed mate, was in the small boat, which was towed behind the imperial salt hauler, with his armed mates. Upon reaching the shore, they fanned out making directly for the campfire.

"Halt! Another step and you wear a crossbow bolt," commanded a voice from the darkness.

"We've come to help. I'm Wei Shu-li, captain of an imperial salt hauler on the way to Xia-zhou. Can I render assistance?"

"Come! Hands away from your weapons! No tricks or you, Captain, meet your ancestors first!" yelled the voice out of the darkness.

"Men, you heard the gentleman, no tricks."

Of course, "tricks" were the last thing on the crews' mind. They were all petrified with fear just stepping on the shore. The group entered the light of the campfire to find two men and a girl.

"I've arrived," said the captain, breaking into a broad smile, expecting his bag of coins.

"So what?" said Ah Wu, still leveling the crossbow at Wei.

"Oh," was all that Captain Wei could say. What a fool I am, he thought, acting like some temple woman expecting every dream to come true—never again!

"Captain," said Li Bo. He moved forward pushing Ah Wu's crossbow downward. "It is very kind of you to stop. Our boatman was killed and our boat stolen. We are stranded here. Could we possibly ride with you to the next port, where we are to pick up a gorge runner to Shu?"

"There are no passenger accommodations. We haul salt from the coast of Wu," the captain remarked in a disappointed tone.

"Deck space would be sufficient, for the next port, Xia-zhou, is just overnight from here."

"Yes, that's true . . . . What's your business? Maybe you have some talent that could make the trip a little more pleasant," the captain said. He wiped the sweat from his forehead and ample jowls. He checked to see that Ah Wu's crossbow remained pointed at the ground.

"I am Jiang Wei-lin, a merchant dealing in exotics from the Western Regions, and one of the best drinkers you'll ever meet."

The captain's eyes lit up. Ah Wu's eyes rolled toward heaven. Chen ignored most of the conversation.

"Come, you're welcome on my ship. None of my crew can even hold a cup properly," he laughed.

On board the ship, Ah Wu, Li Bo, and Chen were given mats on the forward deck, the only space available since the ship was loaded with salt for transshipment through the narrow gorges upriver to Shu.

The night was cool and comfortable. Chen fell asleep immediately. Ah Wu, however, was in no mood for sleep; he had something on his mind. Standing at the deck rails, he took his friend aside.

"Old Zhou's death"—Ah Wu spoke in whispers even though that forward section of the ship was deserted, the crew having all gone back to their bunks or their duties. "He was murdered by an extremely skilled swordsman. The motive is unclear."

Li Bo looked at the steadily passing water. He enjoyed the sense of the ship's slow, steady movement upriver. After a few moments he answered. "The theft of our boat?"

"No. A killer with such sword skills does not rob."

Li turned toward Ah Wu.

"Few men can strike a blow like that . . . . With those skills, their living is assured."

"An assassin?" said Li Bo. "It makes no sense. Who would hire an assassin to kill a boatman?"

"No one. That's what troubles me. That sword cut takes the highest skill to achieve, and the blade is just as exceptional. This assassin is expensive."

"The Court?"

"Someone of means, but why Old Zhou?"

"Perhaps the target was not Old Zhou, but someone reaching through Old Zhou at another target."

Li Bo's eyes tightened. He looked out at the whitecaps moving past the ship. Are the eunuchs, my former Court enemies, behind this, he wondered? He smiled to himself—certainly making the chief eunuch pull off Li's muddy shoes when he was lying in a drunken stupor wasn't an ingratiating move. What could he do? Wine makes its own rules!

Ah Wu interrupted Li's speculation. "The only tracks were made by a horse with a rider on it. The rider dismounted, moved behind Old Zhou, who then fell to the ground. The rider sat next to him—that was when Old Zhou died. The rider remounted and rode off."

"Then he was with Old Zhou when he died?"

"The footprints are those of the killer and his horse, but there are no tracks of the sword stance that struck that blow." Ah Wu watched the whitecaps breaking on the bow.

"And our boat?"

"That's what's so peculiar," said Ah Wu, and he moved closer. "The impressions left by the boat launch are older than the killer's tracks."

"If he didn't take the boat, then why kill Old Zhou? And even if the Court eunuchs are out to make me suffer further on this trip, they wouldn't need to hire a skilled swordsman to kill an old boatman."

Looking out at the dark shadow of the mountain, Ah Wu said, "This place is haunted; who knows what spirits are loose. None of this makes human sense, and that sword you dreamed up doesn't help."

"You're wrong about the Dragon Pool Sword. We just don't understand it. So, it was this horseman who killed Old Zhou?"

"Perhaps, but there are no footprints that show such a sword stance." Ah Wu paused, and glanced quickly around the deck. "A seated horseman could not have struck that death blow. I cannot see from where he could have stabbed Old Zhou." Ah Wu gazed off into the darkness; he found himself wondering what creatures were watching them. He turned back to Li Bo. "That's not all."

Li didn't want to hear more, but he had a responsibility to Old Zhou. "Go on."

"The girl," his head nodded in the general direction of Chen on the deck, "I can find none of her footprints."

Well, thought Li, at least Ah Wu doesn't suspect her of the murder. "You think she's a ghost?" he asked with a smile.

"The shore is rocky and hard to read. I don't believe her story. She is up to something," said Ah Wu. He glanced back at her sleeping figure.

Li didn't respond. Mention of the girl had recalled her passionate defense of his poetry. Why? His poetry was popular, but her passion was unusual. He didn't quite know how to describe it, not at all the usual type of enthusiasm. Perhaps that had made him conceal his identity. He needed more time to understand this girl and her strange passion for his works and, of course, this new situation—the great Li Bo, no longer able to compose verse. The white water breaking past the side of the ship distracted this train of thought. He was soon lost in the Long River's eloquence. Memories of Old Zhou rose.

Ah Wu understood that Li was upset by both the death of Old Zhou and the banishment order. It wasn't clear if the dream at the temple had helped Li Bo or not, but Ah Wu didn't like carrying around the Dragon Pool Sword. He was sure it was bad luck. He was sorry, however, that he had gone on about the girl; surely, that would be the last thing on his friend's mind. Sensing that the conversation had run its course, Ah Wu moved away to the other side of the deck and lay down to sleep.

"Merchant Jiang!" The captain's booming voice shook Li Bo out of his melancholy trance.

"Yes, captain," said Li Bo, turning to meet a large, fleshy hand on his shoulder.

"The cook has heated the wine. Would you like to come to the mid-deck?" The captain smiled. "I have a drinking platform there, a good place to enjoy the Heavens."

"Of course, please," Li held out his hand inviting the captain to lead the way. The captain made a similar gesture. The two men stood for a moment being polite, until the captain took the lead and moved toward the mid-deck.

***

When Chen heard Li and the captain leave the bow deck, she opened one eye, then the other. She saw them disappear down the passageway. Pretending that she was still asleep, she rolled over so she could observe Ah Wu. The ship's warning lanterns strung on the deck provided enough light for her to see his chest following the rhythmic motions of deep sleep. Her eyes continued to search the bow area for other signs of human movement. Convinced no one was watching, she closed her eyes and reappeared at the stern of the ship.

There was no one on watch, the tiller had been tied off and the ship was making its way by itself. She glided over the deck to the railing at the end of the ship. A half moon had risen to the surface of the lightly clouded sky. With one glance, she found the dark shadow following the ship. Two reddish points of light gleamed back at her. A cold breeze swept up from the river. Chen shuddered.

"You must take better care of yourself, my dear," the deep voice whispered. "You could catch your death."

Chen turned. Her uncle stood beside her, smiling his lecherous grin.

"Yes, master, thank you," Chen said, trying not to look at the painful memory that was talking back to her.

"Let me see the sword."

"There hasn't been a moment to be alone with their things. Once we reach the next port, I will act."

For a moment, the creature's eyes flashed red. "The sword, I want that sword. After so many centuries, it is now this close. I could walk in and take it from them—if I knew where it was."

"Yes, master, I will . . ."

"Hey, what's going on here!" said a large sailor armed with a spear, returning to his post. Leveling his weapon, he moved toward them, then froze. "Mother! It can't be you!" he said, frightened and confused; his mother had died many years ago under suspicious circumstances.

"Evil," the creature hissed back in a deep male human voice. Its eyes glowed. Before the sailor could retreat, his spear pulled him forward.

***

"Fire off the port!" The lookout's cry woke the ship. Li Bo followed the captain out to the open deck.

"Pull to," he bellowed. The sail clattered down and the anchor plunged overboard. It bit into the riverbed and the old salt hauler creaked in protest.

"Do you follow your dreams, merchant Jiang?"

Li Bo smiled. "Sometimes people seek dreams only to find they are living one."

The captain's face lit up. "Excuse me, I have to live one right now."

Li nodded raising his hand. "Please. Thank you for the wine and pleasant company."

The captain acknowledged the compliment and then made for the small boat that the crew had drawn up alongside the ship. Landing on the shore, the albino swordsman, dressed in black wearing a broad-brimmed straw hat that covered his face, approached them. He handed the captain the small leather pouch left by the shamaness.

"Thank you for your assistance. A small token of my appreciation. I'm a traveler whose boat sank in the fog several days ago off this forsaken shore. I would appreciate passage to your next port." The man's voice was high and very soft.

The captain felt the weight of the small leather bag in his hand. He knew it was a tidy sum, easily worth the trouble of picking up this man and the other three. Nevertheless, the dream was what the captain found most remarkable.

"Please, we are only a humble salt hauler, but I have a wine platform that could provide you with some comfort."

"Not necessary, only hot water. I am not well and require certain medicines frequently," the swordsman said, without revealing his white face.

"You shall be left undisturbed, with a constant supply of hot water. Please . . . ." The captain gestured with his corpulent hand toward the small boat.

The traveler had a carrying bag and a short thin object wrapped in cloth and tied with silk cord at both ends. He slung the object over his left shoulder and walked slowly to the boat.

"Captain, captain," the mate yelled as the captain's boat pulled alongside of the salt hauler.

"Now what has you scared?" the captain yelled back, feeling that he had lost face in front of his new patron.

"A Blood Dragon has attacked the ship!" The mate was frantic. As soon as the captain boarded his ship, he cuffed the mate, knocking him to the ground.

"Take me to the scene of this so-called attack, you old woman."

Springing to his feet, the mate wondered if it would be easier to serve a Blood Dragon. He led the way to the stern of the ship. The crew and even the passengers they had picked up earlier were crowded around a dark outline lying on the deck. As the captain broke through the crowd, he saw a shriveled form wearing the uniform of the imperial salt hauler—it was steeped in a foamy yellowish liquid that gave forth the stench of death. What used to be a man, one of his crew no less, was now only a damp, shrunken pile of cloth, skin, and bone.

"He was bled clean from a wound under the left armpit."

The captain recognized Li Bo's accented Chinese.

"Ah, merchant Jiang. Do you have enough wits about you to figure out what's going on here?"

Li Bo bowed to the captain.

"To the wine platform . . . ah, wait, someone is occupying it now. Then to my small compartment. We can do little for that poor fellow here. Mate," the captain turned to the sailor who had led him to the stern, "organize a cleanup detail, hoist the sails, and get us back underway."

In his quarters, seated at a low table, the captain leaned forward, a cup of steaming wine in his hand. "What do you make of this death?" He hoped that Li Bo could come up with a rational explanation. There had been, of course, murders on his ships before. Sailors got drunk, angry, in a bad mood, or whatever, and they killed each other. That was not strange, but a Blood Dragon? Of course, that lore was part of the river culture, but such a thing had never struck one of his commands.

"From what Ah Wu and I have seen tonight, the wound is highly unusual. Certainly not that made by a human hand."

The captain's face in the harsh lantern light seemed more tired. As was his custom, hot wine was served as soon as he entered his quarters. He finished another cup of the steaming liquid and listened to Li Bo.

"Ah Wu has seen enough war wounds to make a good judgment. Further than that, he cannot go. We've heard of the Blood Dragon traditions but are not acquainted with any first-hand encounters of such a fabulous beast," said Li, who then turned his attention to the steaming wine cup before him.

"Anything else?" the captain asked. He rubbed his thick sweaty jowls.

"Yes, just as strange," Li paused, "the dead crewman's spear had a hand print burned into the shaft."

"What?" the captain's eyes grew wide.

"It is as if someone grabbed the spear and pulled the victim like a fly toward his death."

"What kind of power is this?"

"We don't know, Captain, but he didn't have a chance."

"None of us would have a chance . . . ." The captain's big hand rubbed the sweat on his cheek. "I can only leave this for the port authorities. Could you assist me in writing out what you know and I'll sign and seal it? My writing skills . . . well, let's say . . . are limited."

Li bowed his head in assent, understanding the captain to mean that he couldn't write much more than his name. Li paid his respects and took leave. He returned to the forward deck where Ah Wu and Chen were waiting.

"Nothing we can do now but get some sleep," said Li Bo.

"It must have been a Blood Dragon, but why kill a sailor? Why did Old Zhou die? The bodies are beginning to pile up," said Ah Wu. He looked at the *jheng* case. How many would die before

Li Bo got rid of the Dragon Pool Sword? Everywhere it went, death followed.

Chen said nothing. Li noticed that she seemed pale. He took some strong powders from the medicine pack and made her inhale. The scents took effect and her face became contorted. She started to cry. Li tried to comfort her and managed to get her back to sleep.

Ah Wu lay down again with his crossbow close at hand. While he didn't know what to expect from a Blood Dragon, he knew what his crossbow could do. The uncertainty of the Blood Dragon bothered him less than what had happened earlier, just before the sailor was killed. He didn't know if Chen had been missing or if his suspicions of her were getting the better of him, making his imagination provide the proof she was a ghost. Had he dozed off or had he really seen that her bedding was empty? It irritated him. I must be getting old, he thought. Years ago there would have been no doubt.

High above, the scattered stars appeared and disappeared; his perceptions flickered as they did. As he thought of the girl, the shadow reappeared, then it was the girl again. Did the trip to the Dream Temple call forth the ghost of that Turkish turd, Su-lu? If the return of his old nemesis was the answer to a question, as Li suggested dreams were, then what was the question? That name-less mountain, thought Ah Wu, has bent the world out of shape.

As the ship plowed through the Long River, its timbers creaked and groaned. The wind was steady now and the sails were full, straining against the masts. Ah Wu again saw the stars and then Su-lu's shadow. He knew the meaning. All the people of the Western Regions did—his old nemesis had returned to draw him into the Yin realm.

Ah Wu was not afraid of death—it was a constant com-panion in the Western Region wars. He had faced Su-lu, the qaghan of the Tügis confederation of Turks, many times before on the battlefield. The first time they met, the ear that Su-lu liked to hold in his teeth, had adorned the right side of Ah Wu's skull. The next time they met, Su-lu had marked Ah Wu's face. And their last meeting resulted in Ah Wu's limp—Su-lu's spear driven through his foot. Ah Wu, however, didn't have the pleasure of killing him. That was granted to his own men who finally turned on him.

Ah Wu felt he had nothing to cling to in this dusty world except his friendship with Li Bo. He feared for Li left alone to follow his own "path." It was when Ah Wu was called to the frontier to plan an attack against Rokhshan's rebels and left Li Bo alone for a few months that his old friend had decided to join the Prince of Yung's entourage. Sleep finally overcame Ah Wu's reminiscences and drew him away from his newly misshapen world.

It was the third watch, just past midnight, when Li lay down on his bedroll. He was feeling the effects of his drinking and the long day that had begun on the top of an ancient tomb. He knew what Ah Wu thought. It didn't make sense. Why would the lady of the Dream Temple give him the sword to guide him, only to have it kill those around him? Besides, the deaths were too random. If the Dragon Pool Sword was cursed then why hadn't Ah Wu, Chen, and the salt hauler captain died? But Old Zhou was dead, and there seemed to be no rational explanation of it.

The dream of Mount Wu's twelve peaks, the Dragon Pool Sword, the disappearance of the temple, the identity of the grave, the death of Old Zhou, and Chen's appearance—it all kept working at his mind. Most of all, he wasn't certain of the Dream Temple dream. Was it a Heavenly quest or a hellish curse? He recalled Ah Wu's warning that dreams could also turn out to be nightmares.

And what could be the significance of Chen's obsession with his poetry. As much as Ah Wu distrusted her, Li Bo could see that they shared the same opinion when it came to his poetry. They both preferred Li Bo the "divine poet" to Li Bo the Court jester.

He knew what the Chinese aristocrats thought of him, the commoner from the barbarian far West who had mastered their own language far beyond their wildest imaginations. He couldn't help smile at that thought. They hated him.

Yet, the Court was the source of prestige within the Chinese empire. There had to be some way to regain his status there. Perhaps that was Heaven's intention in entrusting him with the Dragon Pool quest. Perhaps the sword was the path back to the capital. Certainly, it was of little use to a poet. Are swords not power symbols? Is the Court not the center of the Empire's power? The two must belong together. He just had to figure out the connection.

The winds kept the sails full, driving the salt hauler against the Long River's eastern flow. The stars of the great River of Heaven shone brightly, distracting Li from his courtly concerns and allowing sleep to dissolve his considerations.

Neither Ah Wu nor Li Bo, however, could have noticed that the red gemstone in the Dragon Pool's hilt had been lit with a blood red glow ever since they left the tomb on top of that nameless mountain.

— 8 —

Lowering the small bamboo mat sail, Shamaness Luo worked the
tiller and guided Li Bo's boat into a mooring under the Zhi-xi
Pavilion. Dawn was at hand when she reached the small river
port of Xia-zhou. From here she planned to take a special gorge
boat designed to cross the Three Gorges—the most dangerous
stretch of the Long River as it plunges through cragged, towering
limestone and sandstone mountain crevasses that rise straight up,
in some places, for three thousand feet from the river, blocking
out the sky. That stretch of the Long River is filled with treach-
erous rapids, sink holes, shifting currents, the constant threat of
landslides, and strange mists and vapors.

The first gorge, the Xi-ling Gorge, zigzagging for forty-seven
miles, is the longest, with the most dangerous waters of the Three
Gorges. Along its towering, broken cliffs, only the occasional
coffin set high above the river on wooden poles by the mysterious
Ba tribesmen is sometimes seen. If a boat is lucky and makes it
through, the traveler enters Shaman Gorge, the darkest and most
somber section of the Long River's entire 3,900 miles. There the
cliffs soar high enough to blot out the sun. Only groups of monkeys dare to visit its misty heights where, down below, river travelers report hearing strange music after the frequent rainstorms
that sweep its peaks. Most people dread the passage through
Shaman Gorge, believing it to be under the supernatural influence of the powerful Rain Goddess. She is said to inhabit Rain
Goddess Peak, one of Mount Wu's twelve peaks, and Shamaness
Luo's destination.

The trip upriver through the two gorges from Xia-zhou to Mount Wu, depending on the currents and weather, takes two weeks, so there was much for her to prepare. She planned to settle into a cave above the town to hide from those who were pursuing her. Stepping onto the shore, she made a change of clothes, packing away her flowing robes for a riding outfit. She gathered wood and made a small fire. Out of her red silk pouch came scissors and fine paper. After the horse figure was dropped into the fire, she took a swig of water from her gourd and sprayed the burning figure. Her mind blazed with the chant to her spirit protectress. "Lady of the Purple Vault, Lady of the Purple Vault, Lady of the Purple Vault . . . ."

A burst of flame and on the smoky landing a saddled black-headed horse neighed softly. Moving quietly in the early morning dimness, Luo paused for a moment. She heard the faint echo of a musical instrument playing a sad tune—a friend's parting. How well she knew that feeling. Luo strapped her gear on the horse and rode off toward the highlands behind the town.

***

A little farther upriver at another mooring place, the young swordsman Ma Ssu-ming was softly singing and accompanying himself on his three-string lute in his boat. He sat in its open nine-foot-long bow compartment with his back against the mast. His long trip overland from the capital had been tiring. He made only a few stops at government post stations for a change of horse, a quick meal, and a few hours sleep. After considering the reports about the fugitive shamaness and studying her background, Ma had concluded that she would head for the Long River. His conclusion was not shared by the rest of the Imperial Agents, whose analysis of the same information had convinced them she would flee to the eastern seacoast. From that point, their opinion was evenly divided among those who felt that she would seek passage on a seagoing merchant junk to the far southern regions around Guangzhou and those who felt she intended to flee north to the Korean kingdom. In either direction, central government control was always weakest in the empire's extreme border areas.

Ma, as usual, had a very different basis for reaching his conclusion. He had an advantage that the other agents lacked—a small, yellow monkey named Lao-huang. This was, of course, no ordinary monkey. Lao-huang, according to Ma, was able to detect ghosts. It was after a particularly refreshing round of wine drinking that Ma began to speculate about Lao-huang's possible other hidden talents. He placed a map of the empire in front of the monkey and asked, "If you were a powerful shamaness and wanted to escape the utter boredom of this capital, would you go east?"

Lao-huang looked at Ma, took another sip of wine from his cup, and pissed on the map.

"Good. I didn't think much of that idea either. After all, once you get to the coast you have to go either north or south, so we're just as lost as when starting back at the capital."

Lao-huang drank more wine and began to stagger around the table where the map was laid open.

"Not east? Well, that leaves north . . . ."

The monkey grabbed Ma's short blade that was lying on the table, threw it down at the map, and began to chatter. Ma looked at where the blade had pierced the map: Xia-zhou.

"West! Up the Long River? What's up there? The Three Gorges, perhaps Mount Wu . . . ."

Lao-huang fell over, sprawling on the map, and was fast asleep.

Ma smiled now at the memory and huddled closer to the boat's brazier. An early morning chill swept over the river. If she doesn't show up here, he thought, at least he could look forward to a pleasant return journey down the Long River. After that, well, why worry? The music he played was mournful and spoke of the frequent parting of old friends, of a longing for better times when they could all be together again.

Lao-huang broke into the melancholy. He ran up to the bow compartment, threw down his wine cup, and chattered madly. Something behind Ma had caught his attention. The musician turned around, leaned back over the side just as the fireball was subsiding, but even so, he had seen her. It had to be—his little friend was seldom wrong. He cut the mooring rope with a quick graceful stroke from his sword and poled the skiff downstream to where the fire had erupted.

The air was damp and fog began to roll across the water. Ma's skiff glided silently over the river's still surface, gently pushing through the veils of fog. Only the sliding of the staff into the water broke the spell. Lanterns dotted the shoreline, throwing their reflections across the rippling waters. The monkey had quieted down in seeming anticipation of what was to come. There was a landing ahead. Ma made out the dim shape of the Zhi-xi Pavilion. The first grays of dawn pierced the river's misty cloak.

He heard the muffled beat of a horse's hooves against the damp earth. It moved upward and away from the river. Then a small boat took form through the fog. The two boats bumped, but Ma kept his balance. He pulled adroitly alongside the moored boat and, with his double-edged sword glinting in the early dawn grayness, jumped aboard. Lao-huang had boarded at the other end of the boat, cutting off the other line of escape.

Once aboard, Ma remained motionless. He listened and watched—only the gentle lapping of the river against the wooden hulls. Whatever was aboard, human or otherwise, Lao-huang would alert him.

Ma found a small lamp in the open stern area and lit it. The boat, like his, had an eight-foot-long sheltered area with wooden sides and a tightly woven arched bamboo thatch roof in its center. After going over the scrolls and other items in the sheltered area, he realized the boat belonged to the famous poet, Li Bo. He remembered that Li had been banished and reasoned that somewhere along his trip into exile his boat had been stolen.

It was the Grand Shamaness Luo. He had just seen her leaving this boat. Lao-huang's reaction was clear. The little monkey was right—she had turned west. But what was she doing in Xia-zhou? Was she planning to head upriver or has she come here to turn inland? Inland, at this point, made little sense. Since Xia-zhou was the main jumping off port for those going through the Gorges, she must be planning to go farther upriver. Ma wondered, what would attract her upriver?

As he considered these questions, the birds began to chirp. Dawn was upon him. The fog gathered itself up and rose off the river. He shivered and became aware that his hand rested on the scrolls of Li Bo's poetry that surrounded him in the shelter. Of course, he thought, the scrolls. Could she be going to the Precious Sword Gorge with the imperial scrolls she stole from the Emperor's collection? The ledges high above that gorge were legendary hiding places for secret writings and fabulous weapons. Though he doubted the truth of those legends, she might not and could be heading there to hide the stolen scrolls. The stop at Xia-zhou then would make sense, as she would have to change ships here for a gorge-runner that could make the dangerous trip through the Xi-ling Gorge rapids to reach that hiding place.

He wondered which the Emperor wanted to retrieve more, his precious scrolls or his shamaness. Even though the government ministers wouldn't let on, Ma had figured out the scrolls were the imperial calendar calculations, which in the wrong hands could give their owner the authority to predict an end to the current Tang dynasty, and the rise of a new one.

Ma Ssu-ming and Lao-huang returned to their boat. Ma poled back to their original mooring spot. Adding more charcoal to the brazier, Ma warmed himself and placed a small flagon of wine on it. He would toast and sing a tune to the morning—one morning closer to completing his mission, he hoped. Lao-huang scrambled for the wine cup he had earlier thrown down and joined in the toast. Waiting in Xia-zhou for the shamaness to return was a gamble, for she could be heading inland, but he had been gambling all his life. Anyway, he smiled to himself, Lao-huang agreed. The young musician toasted his monkey and it returned for another cup of wine.

"If we do this right, old friend, we won't be laughed at any more and should have enough for all the wine we could ever drink," he said to the monkey. Lao-huang chattered away and held out his empty cup.

***

Shamaness Luo continued to ride up into the highlands behind Xia-zhou to a cave that her spirit-guide, the Lady of the Purple Vault, had chosen for her escape. After settling in, she found it was stocked with ample firewood and food supplies. The region was in a seldom-frequented area of the mountains outside of Xia-zhou, yet provided her with a good view of the port area. She had arranged herself according to ritual law, seated cross-legged on a small meditation cushion. A jade-white incense burner was positioned before her. A special fragrance appropriate for the ritual smoked restlessly.

Luo's long raven-b lack locks spilled over her shoulders, reaching almost to her waist. She began to hum an ancient tune. After a few curls of incense had reached the top of the cave, the tune changed into a chant. Her eyelids dropped and she slid easily into the trance state. Her body began to shake, sweat poured forth. A strange voice, deep and strong, welled up from inside her. "The Lady of the Purple Vault is present and commands a mirror body of the Grand Shamaness Luo Jhu-yun to appear."

The incense burner poured forth smoke. It swirled into a column. A form took shape within the smoke . . . a naked female doppelganger. As the smoke dissipated, her double stood before Luo. The shamaness opened her eyes and for an instant seemed to stare into a dark mirror.

Luo got up and went to one of her saddlebags. She handed the doppelganger some clothing. "Passage on the first gorge runner out of Xia-zhou. Stay to the shadows. Don't let anyone follow you back."

The form bowed, dressed, and left the cave. Later that day, it appeared in Xia-zhou and headed for the ship booking wharves along the river. However, shop after shop turned it away.

"We're sorry madam, but the rebellion destroyed many gorge runners and those still afloat are fully booked."

The image spent most of the afternoon searching for a passage upriver. Finally, in a small shop off the main wharf it found an opening.

The booking agent's wife hesitated. "There's not much room and I'm not sure if this is the proper ship for a lady like yourself."

"A small space is fine. You need not worry about the rest," the doppelganger said in a dusky voice. She placed cash in the woman's hand. It was more than necessary, and the booking agent's wife understood there was no need to make change.

"Fine, as you wish," she said. She wrote out a receipt and sealed it with her husband's red agent seal.

"The gorge boat sails three nights from now on the midnight tide, with or without you." She placed the receipt in the doppelganger's hand and explained where the boat was moored. A few minutes after the customer left, the booking agent's wife noticed a peculiar fragrance in the office, but made nothing of it and returned to her work.

— 9 —

As dawn paled the sky over the imperial salt hauler, Chen moved to the side of the ship and disappeared behind a cabin. From its roof, she surveyed the deck below. Li Bo was on the port side. His only bag, a backpack, was on his right side. It was not long enough for the sword she had seen near the tomb. On the starboard side, Ah Wu lay sleeping with his arm over a long rectangular shaped cloth sack and his backpack near his side. The long sack, she figured, must be Li Bo's *jheng*. His backpack was also too small for a sword. Where was it? Did they leave it behind on the mountain? Or have they hidden it on the ship? She had to remain with them till she could figure it out. The monster, however, was becoming more impatient. If angered, Chen knew it would kill, and its rage could consume her, too.

***

The morning had worn on for several hours when the imperial salt hauler came in sight of Xia-zhou, a port city that first entered the historical record in 278 B.C.E. when it was destroyed in a battle between the states of Chu and Qin. Six hundred years later, it was again attacked, this time in a battle between the states of Wu and Shu. Because of its geographical position, however, at the eastern entrance of the Three Gorges, it managed to revive and thrive on the constant flow of shipping along the Long River.

The port occupies a small bend along the eastern shore of the Long River where it swings north into the Xiling Gorge, the first of the Three Gorges. On either side of the river, a series of wharfs was constructed for the transferral of cargo: down the river to Yangzhou on larger merchant junks or up the river to Shu in small, fast gorge runners. The port existed to facilitate these transfers. There were shops for ship repairs, outfitters who crafted various ship parts and equipment, and crew and ship hauling contractors. Near the inland area of the port, up against the mountains that limited its expansion, there was a shantytown where the families of sailors and haulers lived.

Xia-zhou, however, boasted only one inn for travelers. The others had closed due to the rebellion, which had contributed to a serious decline in the number of "river travelers"—these were mostly government officials traveling to or from government postings. Down on the shore, there was also a government customhouse for tax collecting and police duties.

Although the port was small, ships lined both sides of the river with constant activity. Along with the transfer of cargoes, tales of the strange and marvelous events that crews had witnessed traveling through the Three Gorges were also passed along. As were warnings about newly discovered currents and shifting rapids when frequent landslides reconfigured that boulder-strewn stretch of the Long River.

Li Bo and his party were the guests of the captain for a simple breakfast of rice gruel, rancid dou-fu, salted peanuts, pickled vegetables, and steaming bean curd milk.

"Captain," asked Li, "your other guest from the shore last night?"

"He's not well. Dines alone." Leaning forward, the captain added, "He's a strange one. Yet not afraid to spread his cash around." A large grin covered his fleshy face. Li returned the smile and he picked at a salted peanut, knowing what the captain was driving at.

"The girl? Golden-haired beauties . . . rare out here on the river. How's the capital? We rarely get back. You hiding her?" the captain asked, still grinning.

Ah Wu's eyes narrowed with suspicion at the mention of her.

"She's not comfortable," said Li. "These foreign women aren't accustomed to ships. And she's probably still upset by that dreadful incident last night."

The captain's grin disappeared and he directed his full attention to a piece of rancid dou-fu. His awkward attempts to pick the grayish cube of fermented bean curd off the plate resulted in its crumbling into smaller pieces.

Li wanted to leave the ship as quickly as possible. He needed to identify the occupant of the tomb where he had received the Dragon Pool Sword. Perhaps that way he could be certain that the quest he had accepted was legitimate. As there had been another death, Ah Wu's concern about the sword being cursed had made Li more cautious about the trip to Mount Wu.

"When we dock, leave the ship quickly. The authorities in these small ports are very troublesome when murder is involved," said the captain, interrupting Li's concerns. By this point, the piece of dou-fu had completely disintegrated, and the captain had moved onto the destruction of another.

"Just being on the ship makes you a suspect in their little minds. They'll hold the whole crew up for ransom, the greedy bastards. But we are central government. It gives us our own leverage. You and your friend, just ordinary folk. Prime targets."

He gave up on the dou-fu and went after the peanuts.

"I have connections," he continued. "For a small sum, you leave the city without the attention of local officials."

"Why do you think we need leave the city under those conditions?" said Li, puzzled by the captain's suspicions.

"You're no merchant. Twenty years on this river, I know. And your companion, the Steel Talon, does not travel with merchants."

A broad smile crossed Ah Wu's face. His eyes sparkled and he raised his crossbow. The captain's eyes widened.

"Captain, I commend your excellent discernment. I am the poet, Li Bo," said Li with obvious pride. His hand pushed down Ah Wu's crossbow.

"Oh." The captain seemed disappointed. "A poet . . . certainly, not a merchant."

"Yes," mumbled Li, "just a poet, Captain. A former poet would be more accurate."

Ah Wu's smirk fed Li Bo's irritation. The captain paid little attention to Li's qualification.

"So, Captain, there is no need to worry about the authorities. There is little they could want with a poet."

"Why false name and occupation?" said the captain, obviously relieved that the crossbow of the famed Steel Talon was no longer aimed at his digestive organs.

Li paused for a moment; there were several reasons he could give the captain. He chose the easiest. "I have been banished to Yunnan by the Emperor for offenses concocted against me by the palace's cockless wonders . . . ."

There was a muffled bump against the back wall of the cabin. A crossbow bolt tore past the startled captain and through his wall. A metallic *ping*, and another bolt smashed through the wall six inches to the right of the first one. Ah Wu, his face scar bright red, was reloading. He raced out the door and around the back of the cabin. His first bolt lay on the deck and the second was wedged into the passageway behind the captain's cabin. No one was around—only the wind lingered.

When Ah Wu returned to the cabin, Li Bo was upset. "Was that mountain too much? You could have killed the captain or whoever was in the passage way."

"I hit what I shoot at."

The captain was examining the hole in his morning cape made by one of the flying bolts.

"Well?" Li asked angrily.

"Someone was listening."

"So you try to kill them?"

"They are dangerous. Not a common sailor."

"How do you know that?" The captain couldn't refrain any longer.

"Deflected my first shot, anticipated the second one. A skilled warrior."

Both of Ah Wu's interrogators were silent. They had seen the ferocity of his flying bolts and understood the difficulty of avoiding them.

Li spoke first. "Old Zhou's killer? On this ship?"

Ah Wu didn't answer. He knew he was jumpy. That strange mountain, the return of Su-lu's ghost, and that sword had all unnerved him. Yet, his instincts were still true—he shot to kill an evil. Perhaps it could have been Old Zhou's killer; they certainly had similar levels of skill. Or perhaps Su-lu was now haunting him in broad daylight. There was no sense in explaining to Li— he couldn't.

"Sir," a mate entered the cabin. "Ready to dock."

"Good," said the captain. "I must go."

"Thank you, Captain. I apologize for the holes in your wall," Li bowed and saluted with both hands clasped.

Ah Wu performed a token bow and left the cabin with Li.

As the ship pulled into the dock, the gangplank was lowered. The albino swordsman was the first one down. He stopped to talk with the officials on shore for a moment, revealing something within his cloak that made them all bow, then moved away into the city. Several officers moved up the gangplank while others took up posts on the dock, blocking any land exit from the ship.

Li and Ah Wu walked back to the forward deck where they had left their belongings with Chen. When they arrived, she was nowhere in sight. A deck hand ran up to them. "The captain asks you to follow me; he dictated this note to you."

Li glanced over the note. The local officials were looking for them. Someone had accused them of the murder. The captain, however, was offering Li and his party a way off the ship, avoiding contact with the government.

"Lead the way," said Li, "but first we must find Chen."

"She's gone; we've searched the ship. There is little time," said the crewman.

The local government officials had boarded the ship and were making their way toward the forward deck where Li and Ah Wu had gathered their bags.

— 10 —

After disappearing from the ship, Chen made her way along the shore and entered a dense stand of dark-green bamboo outside of Xia-zhou. Rays of morning light sifted through the mist and high-lighted the different shades of green—at the top of the long, slender bamboos there was a cool, light-green diffusion. The darkness increased farther down where the throng of thick green trunks took on a gloomy, more ominous presence.

Chen threaded her way through the closely spaced bamboos. Though it was difficult to see far in any direction, she sensed the monster before she actually sighted it. A damp chill ran through her.

"Well, my child, you carry the sword?" an icy voice asked from behind. Chen turned around and beheld her uncle's emaciated form. Shadows cast across his face enhanced the ghostliness of his figure. In his eyes, fire danced whenever the sword was mentioned.

Chen prostrated herself before the creature to ease the pain she expected. "Your worthless disciple has failed to locate the sword."

She could see the ground around her flash red with the rage burning forth from the monster's eyes.

"Only two men, two men on foot," it growled in a deep male voice. "How much can they carry?"

"My master, I searched their few bags early this morning, but I found nothing."

The early morning air began to stir. A slight breeze knocked the bamboos against each other. It was as if Nature was drumming its fingers on the earth, impatient for the Dragon Pool Sword to be brought forth. Chen waited with her head bent down. Someday, she thought, somehow she would escape from the monster's clutches. Her life as a ghost had begun with this monster, and until she could understand the powers that held her prisoner, she dared not oppose its commands. It would not be her first escape from overwhelming odds.

"They know the value of the sword. It is hidden," her master said in low tones. "It must be either with them or hidden nearby. There is only one place in the empire where its full power can be released. And they are heading toward it."

"Where?" Chen blurted out.

"You just bring the sword to me. Don't get any other ideas. Understand?"

"Yes, Master." Chen bent her head lower, in response to the monster's increasing anger. The sword must be very important to the Blood Dragon, she thought. It was at this point Chen realized that the sword might be the key to her freedom. It was a very dangerous gamble. She needed to know more about the powers of this famous Dragon Pool Sword, then . . . . The Blood Dragon interrupted. "But I think these men are more than a match for your wiles. Bring them to me."

"Both?" she asked and thought, this is no good. I will lose my chance to get the sword first.

"No, just the warrior. You said he last held the sword before he chased you off?"

"Yes, Master," Chen, answered apprehensively; perhaps the monster could read her thoughts. She wasn't sure of its powers.

"Your clumsiness alerted him to protect the sword," her master said with contempt. "He knows where the sword is, and he damaged my other slaves. Bring him here! Lure him with whatever charms you can devise."

The bamboo stirred and a few dead leaves fluttered to the ground. The creature was gone—only the dull "*knock-knock*" of the bamboos recorded the passage. A tear streaked Chen's soft pale cheek. Another death . . . . She was sinking deeper into the nightmare.

The crewman reached down and pulled open a hidden deck hatch.

"Quick, follow me down here."

Li and Ah Wu followed the crewman through the belly of the salt hauler to a door. After their strenuous joint effort, the door creaked open over the river on the other side of the ship.

The crewman smiled. "You'll have to swim for it."

Li and Ah Wu were holding their baggage and looking at each other. The shouts of the local officials were now below deck.

Just then, a young man asleep in the open stern compartment of his boat, his leg draped over the tiller, drifted by and bumped into the salt hauler. The jolt woke the man, but the small yellow monkey, sprawled in front of him, didn't move.

"Sir! Sir!" called out Li Bo.

The man—a Chinese of approximately Li's height, well built, neatly trimmed black moustache and goatee: overall, thought Li Bo, a rather good-looking young man by capital standards— looked around and then upward.

Li smiled back. "May we join you in some poetry and drink?"

Ma Ssu-ming reached for his wine cup, lifting it in a toast to Li. "One should never be surprised when wine is the transportation. Please, join me in a toast to the morning!"

Li and Ah Wu eased themselves and their baggage down into the boat and took shelter in the enclosed area just behind the mast in the center of the thirty-foot boat. The young man poled away to his previous mooring under the shade trees that lined the shore and retied his loose mooring cable. Peering out of a small rectangular opening in the wooden side of the sheltered area, Li could see a group of men gathered at the salt hauler's hull door. They watched the river traffic for a few moments and then resealed the door. Li smiled.

Before they could introduce themselves, Ma's yellow monkey awoke and screeched at them. He beat his paws against his head.

"Ah! Lao-huang, these are guests, not ghosts. Have you forgotten your manners?" Ma cajoled the monkey. Lao-huang ran back into the shelter and came out with a wine cup in its hand. Everyone laughed.

"I am Ma Ssu-ming from Ding-zhou, a musician and drinker by trade. And this is my master, Lao-huang from Mount O-mei, a ghost catcher and drinker by birth."

Li Bo broke out laughing. "Your master?"

"Yes, I am studying with Lao-huang to master the art of ghost-catching. His fees are quite reasonable—all the wine he can drink and all the music he can dance to."

"How can a monkey catch ghosts?" sneered Ah Wu, who had already decided that Ma was a lunatic and therefore had much in common with Li Bo.

Lao-huang went crazy. He ran up to Ah Wu and screamed at him. Ah Wu raised his crossbow, flipped off the trigger locks, and brought his finger into contact with the triggers. The monkey screeched louder and ran off to the bow of the boat. He began to undo the woven bamboo mooring cable. Ma laughed, smoothed his moustache, and made an appeal to his furry teacher. "Oh, master, forgive our guest, for he does not yet have the gift of wine-vision."

Lao-huang ran back into the boat's sheltered area. Once inside, he began to hurl things out in the general direction of Ah Wu.

Ma gestured with the warm wine flagon. "Master, the wine is cooling off and we are losing the proper perspective on all this. Quick, come and join us."

"Please?" Ma then said in a low voice to Li and Ah Wu, "When he returns, never in his presence call him a 'monkey.' He considers himself an Immortal who has taken this form to live amongst us stupid humans."

Ah Wu was at first dumbfounded, but he smiled when he realized that both the monkey and Li Bo were making similar claims—that they were exiled Immortals. Did this crazy musician, like Li Bo, really believe what he was saying, wondered Ah Wu? The crossbow remained aimed at the shelter. I'll show them my "respect" for the Immortals, thought Ah Wu—may a herd of camels piss on them!

Li Bo moved his hand to Ah Wu's crossbow and pushed it downward.

"Lately, you have been too quick to resort to this as a first response. I would prefer you use your mind instead of your trigger finger." The strength of Li's voice told Ah Wu that his friend was giving him a "polite" order. He placed the crossbow on the floor of the boat. Yet he moved his hand, as discreetly as he could, to the hilt of his broadsword.

Li laughed. "Oh, master Lao-huang, please we desire your brilliance at our wine table. To the morning!" Li raised his wine cup and downed it. The small yellow monkey came scrambling out, wine cup in hand, and joined their toast.

"I am Li Bo from realms beyond this earthly dust, also a dreamer and drinker by trade!" he said, raising his cup. He drank it dry and then remembered he was the merchant Jiang—or something.

"This," he continued, as Ma refilled his cup, "is my loyal but headstrong friend Ah Wu."

"Ah, yes, the Steel Talon," Ma smiled and saluted Ah Wu with his cup. "An honor, Sir."

Ah Wu's eyes brightened. He acknowledged Ma's recognition by raising his personal rhino horn wine cup. Li Bo had refused to use such a cup, considering it an insult to the host and preferring, so he claimed, to die drinking when his time to enter the *Yin* realm had arrived.

Turning his cup to Li, Ma saluted him. "To the honorable Li Bo. I know your poems."

Ma chanted several of Li's better-known verses.

"If you permit, Sir," said Ma, "let us put them to music."

Li nodded and Ma played a few verses dedicating them to the morning mist.

"Delightful," beamed Li. "Your playing is superb; I would be honored. Did you learn your present style while you were at the capital?"

Ma's smile froze for the shortest moment. Ah Wu missed it, but Li didn't. Ma's lute style was the most recent vogue in the capital and Li was familiar with it.

"Well . . . ," Ma smiled in a more relaxed manner, "yes, in fact I did. After passing the government exams, I was stationed in the capital for several years until my present posting."

"Ah, then we are graced by the presence of a high government official?" inquired Li. Ah Wu's scar reddened at the mention of "government official."

Ma's face took on a serious demeanor. He turned over some of the coals in the brazier. "Hardly. I've been assigned, more like exiled, to some far off spot in Sichuan. Seems I offended some eunuch with a song I made up about his missing member."

"A brother! I have also been banished, but beyond Sichuan to the land of Yunnan, no doubt for offending the same dickless bastards. Since we share so much already, why not band together and travel up through the Three Gorges?"

Ma hesitated for a moment. What if Shamaness Luo did not travel upriver and went inland? He decided to put off a final decision until he had clear evidence of her travel plans.

"I need to take care of some business here; then I will happily join you."

"Wonderful," said Li, raising his cup again. "Now, let us see if we can do some more damage to those courtly dickless wonders," he laughed. "Please sing your song for us."

Ah Wu wasn't delighted about joining up with this "musician," but a change seemed to come over Li while in the company of Ma. He was no longer referring to himself as "merchant Jiang" and he was interested in singing his own poetry again. Perhaps, thought Ah Wu, some good could come of this after all.

The banter and song went on until Ma's boat, set adrift by Lao-huang, bumped into a boat moored downstream, sending the brazier and wine flask tumbling onto the deck.

Ma smiled, "Oh, I forgot to tell you that I have located your missing boat."

Li and Ah Wu both stopped smiling and lowered their wine cups.

"Here it is," said Ma, pointing to the boat they had just bumped. He explained that he had seen a glow in the night and went to investigate. After searching the boat, he found some unfinished poems by Li and concluded that this was his boat.

"But how did you know it was missing?" asked Li. Ah Wu put down his cup and closely watched Ma. He already had his suspicions about this "musician" who recognized him by his martial sobriquet. It was Ah Wu's opinion that most musicians would be lucky to recognize the difference between a camel's nose and its ass, much less know Ah Wu's prowess by name. When they first met, something in the way the young man moved had alerted Ah Wu.

"Easy," answered Ma. "I saw a woman running off and knew the famous Li Bo was certainly not of the same gender."

"A woman?" puzzled Li.

"A woman?" questioned Ah Wu, who thought of the golden-haired Chen, but that made no sense. She had just traveled with them to Xia-zhou. Ever since they had visited that mountain, and picked up that sword, thought Ah Wu, the world has made no sense.

Li turned to Ah Wu, "Could it be possible that the killer sold the boat to this woman?"

Ah Wu shrugged his shoulders, his scar was changing color.

"Killer?" asked Ma.

Li explained to him what had happened. Ma said nothing. He was reviewing in his mind what he knew of Shamaness Luo's past behavior. There was nothing to classify her as a killer. This, of course, he did not explain to Li or Ah Wu, for his mission was an imperial secret. He had been sent by the Emperor to bring back his favorite shamaness who had run away from Court.

"It was still quite dark and I could only make out her female form," Ma lied. "Sorry I can't be of much help in identifying her."

Li thought for a moment and then responded, "Well, our immediate problem is not the killer, for that seems impossible to solve at this time. There is another pressing problem. We need to find someone acquainted with ancient scripts."

Ma had restored the brazier and replaced the spilt wine with a fresh flagon. Lao-huang was wobbling all over the boat.

"I have a passing interest in ancient scripts," Ma said. "I would at least enjoy looking at your text."

Li motioned Ah Wu to get the stone rubbing from their baggage.

"It is not a text, but a rubbing we took of a grave we . . . how should I put it . . . stumbled across," Li said in an amused tone. He laid the rubbing across Ma's lap and watched the young man's expression change to that of complete sobriety.

"This is an Eastern Han tomb, but the characters are much earlier than that," Ma said. His fingers played with one end of his black moustache; Li noticed that he seemed to favor the left side, constantly twirling the end. Ma continued intently studying the rubbing. A smile played across Li's face. He admired the young man's scholarship and thought: *The Chinese . . . they have wronged my family and me in so many ways. Yet, I sit here admiring this young man's mastery of the very culture that has caused my downfall . . . and perhaps in the near future my death. My heart says we are friends, for obviously, we share a love of verse and drink, but can I trust this as the basis of friendship? Has not my drinking caused me intolerable suffering? Has my verse been a faithful companion or an easy betrayer?*

Ma broke in on Li's thoughts. "Although archaic, I can read them, but they make no sense. They are just individual characters . . . ."

Lao-huang had fallen asleep on the deck, and Ah Wu was busy on Li's boat making sure everything was still intact. Li continued to observe Ma and drink the excellent wine he offered.

"It's the code of some Daoist school. The eminent one buried in that tomb is of very high status in the Daoist spiritual hierarchy," Ma said, then looked up at Li. "But I cannot identify the person. The code is beyond my capabilities and I fear there are few, if any, scholars alive today who can still understand it."

"You have done well. Your scholarship is most impressive," said Li, who then lifted a cup of wine. "I toast it and pay my respects to your learning." He downed the wine.

Ma smiled for a moment, responded with his cup of wine, and returned to the rubbing. "Possibly if we could identify the particular school and if it continues down to the present, we might find one of its learned practitioners who could read it."

"But," pointed out Li, "they might not want their secret revealed."

"It's near noon," said Ah Wu, returning to Ma's boat, "shouldn't we . . . ?"

"Yes of course, good of you to remind me," replied Li. "Scholar Ma, I insist you and your 'master' join us for dinner. It is the very least I can do to repay your kindness in rescuing us, finding our boat, and indulging my silly fancy for tomb rubbings."

"Oh, but how could I intrude upon your urgent business?"

"Please, good friends can always do without the nonsense of courtly courtesies. Is there a place in this desolate river port that sets a table worthy of a scholar and a gentleman such as yourself?"

"Please, no need for such courtesies. The finest place in town is easy to find, since it is also the only place to board travelers," said Ma and broke out in laughter.

They moored their boats together, gathered their things, and headed into the town of Xia-zhou.

~ 12 ~

The Three Gorges Inn offered typical small-river-port lodgings. There was a two-storied restaurant with a walled compound of sleeping quarters off to the side. Within the sleeping compound, there were smaller compounds. Each had its own courtyard that led to a greeting hall. Off either side of the greeting hall were separate sleeping quarters. The buildings in Xia-zhou were all constructed from wood hauled down from the same mountains that limited the port's expansion and from the same stone that silted its port. The river's dampness permeated all the buildings.

Ah Wu, following Li's instructions, arranged for a small compound for all of them. Ma and his "teacher" would occupy the western sleeping wing and Ah Wu and Li Bo the eastern quarters. In the morning, they planned to arrange for the trip up the Three Gorges. Li and Ma agreed that the evening would bring more enjoyment, no matter what the food was like. Everyone went to rest up for the festivities. Yet once alone, they discovered that their problems resurfaced—powerful problems that demanded action not rest.

Images flickered through Li Bo's mind,

Green eyes and golden hair, why do they haunt me? Is your face calling me back to my ancestors' homeland in the West? Or do you haunt me because of your certainty that this Li Bo is such a great man—a confidence that he now lacks? Is his poetry really so powerful? Or are you really so naive? What has happened to you? How can you suddenly appear, offer such sincerity, and then just vanish? As my daughter . . . and my son have . . . how tall, Son, six years the younger, are you—have you reached your sister's shoulder? My wife, do you still cry for me each night? You are also left behind as I travel west . . . to my death? Will I never see any of you again? The Dream Temple haunts me—Is this Dragon Pool Sword a boon from Heaven, as the Immortal claims, or a cursed joke, as Ah Wu has warned?

In his lodgings, Ma Ssu-ming listened to his monkey's breathing as he lay on the bunk across from Lao-huang. He stared at the rough log ceiling with its intricate cross and balance beams, but the monkey was not on his mind.

It was she . . . Lao-huang knows . . . not a mirror body this time . . . Lao-huang . . . . Ha! None suspects his true worth . . . . I must not fail . . . a new life awaits . . . . With the return of this shamaness . . . my family's duty to the Emperor will be fulfilled . . . . Perhaps, then, my father's spirit will accept me and forgive me for not being able to follow in his footsteps as a civil official. The Way of the sword is the only path that I can follow.

Back in Li Bo's quarters, Ah Wu faced the cold, damp stone wall next to his bunk.

Su-lu, you have finally caught up with me . . . . Good, for I have yet to avenge the deaths of my family and long to meet you again. But what is the meaning of this cursed Dragon Pool Sword? Has it brought with it the death of Old Zhou? The return of my old nemesis, Su-lu? Who else will die? And this golden-haired woman, is she after the sword? Is she a reminder of my deepest regrets? Did she kill Old Zhou? Perhaps soon I'll meet with Old Zhou and then we can settle all of this. Li Bo is in danger, I must be aware for him . . . .

***

Chen, the golden-haired ghost, had taken a room at the same inn as Li Bo and the others. She spent the late afternoon in her room reading the poetry of the same man she hoped to see at dinner that night, although she didn't realize these were his words. As usual, tears stained her lightly freckled cheeks as she softly sang the familiar lines:

> In the morning, he drank from River Yang's pure surge.
> In the evening, he returned to Mount Sung's purple vapors.
> Long did he travel around its thirty-six peaks, around and
> around and . . .

The volume of her tears doubled. Were these dreams only for the Immortals or, she softly cried, for humans, also? Soon she had to stop reading, for her stomach was knotting up from the pain. A few minutes later, as usual, she was asleep.

***

The sun, covered by gray clouds all day, set. Activity on the river had ceased except for an occasional skiff darting among the larger ships. On the wharves the work of transferring cargo from the large riverboats to the small gorge-runners continued. At the Three Gorges Inn, Ah Wu was the first to appear at the table his friend had him reserve for tonight's dinner.

"Innkeeper!" yelled Ah Wu in a voice he once used as a commander in the Imperial Guards. A small round man wearing an innkeeper's hat and carrying a hand towel scrambled up the stairs to the Li party table. Ah Wu had selected a table from which he could keep an eye on as much of the restaurant as possible. From here, he could survey the second floor, the staircase, and most of the ground floor. Yet, he didn't know what he was guarding against. Like everything else on this trip, he reflected, nothing was what it seemed . . . not even himself.

"Is the feast ready?"

"Yes sir, all ready, all ready. We've never had such a wonderful meal organized like this. Your companion is a true genius . . . ."

"Yes, yes, just make sure the wine is served properly or else this feast will turn out to be a nightmare for you." Ah Wu wished he hadn't used that word; there were already enough nightmares for everyone.

"Of course, of course, our greatest efforts will be expended to make sure all goes smoothly."

When Ah Wu saw Li Bo enter the restaurant, he waved away the innkeeper.

Li Bo was seated and the innkeeper returned to pour the heated amber wine in his cup. Ah Wu's hand covered his cup as the innkeeper moved toward him.

"You are not drinking?" inquired Li Bo.

"No, I had enough dreaming."

"Ah Wu, there will be little chance to drink and eat like this where we are going. I politely suggest you throw caution to the river and enjoy what life we have left."

"Innkeeper, wine!" Ah Wu called out.

"That's the spirit," said Li, raising his cup to toast Ah Wu.

"Not quite—your honored guest has arrived," said Ah Wu, his head nodding toward the main door as he began to fill his rhinoceros horn cup.

"We haven't had a chance to speak about this, but what is you impression of master Ma?" Li asked as he waved and smiled at Ma, who was being received by an attendant on the first floor.

"He is no simple musician, but I'm not sure yet what he is up to," said Ah Wu, who toyed with his lined drinking cup, watching the steaming amber liquid move from side to side.

Ma had some sort of bag slung over his shoulder. Li wondered what the young musician was carrying to dinner. Ah Wu saw the blue bag and reached back to make sure his crossbow was in easy grasp. He was still concerned that Li's enemies at Court would prefer to see Li die an earlier death than the one the Emperor had decreed for him.

Ah Wu knew a skilled swordsman when he saw one, no matter what instrument he was handling. Those of us who have dedicated our lives to the martial arts cannot easily hide what we have accomplished, he thought. This was most obvious to Ah Wu in the way Ma moved up the stairs to their table. Though not especially muscular, Ma's movements were like those of a cat in the sun—its grace masks its speed and power.

Ah Wu could imagine a sword in the musician's hand. Could he be Old Zhou's killer? The thought had occurred to Ah Wu, but why would Ma need two boats? And why lead them back to their boat? Nevertheless, Ah Wu remained cautious because Ma was covering his identity and the reason for his deception was unclear.

When Ma had reached the table, Ah Wu noticed the golden furry leg that dangled out of the shoulder bag.

"Welcome, master Ma, savior of river travelers in distress." Li broke out laughing. He and Ma exchanged toasts. Ah Wu went through some polite motions.

"I see Lao-huang has not yet recovered," Li gestured toward the blue shoulder bag.

"Ha! The rascal doesn't drink that well. He can consume it, but he can't handle it. He will wake soon and be irritable. Don't be surprised if I toss him out the window," Ma said and laughed.

Li laughed and raised his cup. "To Lao-huang and a safe landing."

Ma returned the salute and caught the glint in Ah Wu's eyes. Something was troubling Ah Wu. Ma followed Ah Wu's line of sight and saw a beautiful golden-haired woman in turquoise robes trimmed with cream color borders. Her golden hair was arranged in Chang'an style with a large loop on the center of her forehead and down on either side like a cap. A red dot adorned her forehead just above the bridge of her nose. Two brush-tip black dots on either side of her mouth accentuated her small red lips. She was heading toward the table. Ah Wu's hand moved back to the crossbow, and his movement alerted Ma, who was also ready to act if necessary.

Li had finished his drink and set the thin blue ceramic cup down on the table with such force that it shattered. He was staring at the woman. It was also obvious to Ma that Li was as much taken with her as Ah Wu was distrustful.

"Why, Miss Chen, you are all right!" Li had reached her before she got to the table. He escorted her to a seat and called the innkeeper to set a place for her.

"Master Ma, may I present Chen Shao-lin, a fellow river traveler."

Ma rose, and for the first time noticed her green eyes. He stood transfixed. For a moment, his wine cup floated in midair.

"Ah, excuse me for staring . . . but I was just transported back to the cafés of the capital. I am Ma Ssu-ming—musician and imbiber of fine wines," he said with a smile and bowed his head. Li was pouring wine for her. She responded with several polite toasts in the capital fashion and settled in at the table.

Ma noticed the change that had come over Li Bo. His features seemed to soften, releasing the tension that had tightened the lines around his eyes and the corners of his mouth. He was as relaxed as when he drank too much. Why such a reaction, wondered Ma?

The tension, however, was transferred to Ah Wu, who was clearly uncomfortable with this woman around. How interesting, thought Ma. Is the friend becoming too defensive about his companion's choice of attractions? There is no doubt this woman is unusually attractive, especially with her golden hair and wine-green eyes. Yet this was common in the capital, and Ah Wu must have spent many years there with Li Bo. Why react this way, Ma wondered?

While these introductions and toasts were going on, the inn staff was flitting around filling the table with the dishes that Li Bo had ordered. Because the port of Xia-zhou was on the greatest river in the Middle Kingdom, it had access to the huge diversity of food products available in the lush rice- and fish-raising lands to its east and south, and up river to the great fertile region of Shu in the west.

The condiments were first spread out: fishmeal pickle, salted black beans, and ant-egg relish all in brown glass bowls. Next, steaming white aromatic rice in ceramic ice-blue bowls, one set at each person's place and a large white serving bowl with a cover set in the center of the table. The vegetables were laid out around the table: tender blue-green eggplant, black mushrooms from the trunks of the mulberry tree, toasted turnips, yams and cabbage, with soft spotted bamboo sprouts from Hunan. Then one of the main dishes made its appearance.

"Oh, the fish," Li said, moving over, interrupting Ma's thoughts, and making room for the innkeeper to deliver a large blue-green ceramic plate to the center of the table.

"A golden carp, sir. Fresh from Lake Dong-ting, chilled exactly to your orders." The innkeeper bowed and prepared to serve the fish. He fumbled with the cutting knife, trying to figure out how to best approach the difficult task of slicing the fresh carp thinly as officials from the capital region preferred. The success or failure of this dish depended on the server's slicing skill. Ma went over to the innkeeper and gently relieved him of the knife.

"Let me have a try," he said with a smile, and he inspected the knife. "I'm afraid this thing is not up to the task." He bowed to Li Bo. "If you will permit me to use my own," he said, reaching around to the small of his back under his tunic and drawing forth a knife. Its blade was pure frost—icy blue. This confirmed Ah Wu's suspicion that Ma was a skilled swordsman; this was not an ordinary blade.

Ma proceeded to slice the fish—his blade strokes were like the wings of a hummingbird. Snowflake-thin slices of raw carp—slivers so thin that some seemed to float in the air before they fell back into the plate. Li toasted the young musician.

"Incredible skill, incredible skill, Master Ma. A toast to the master of the snowflake blade!"

They all raised a cup in salute. Ah Wu was trying to figure out why Ma was being so obvious about his blade-wielding skills.

At the other end of the room, another patron was also taking note of Ma's exhibition. The albino swordsman dressed in simple black cotton clothes and wearing a large straw hat smiled and went back to his simple meal of noodles and boiled vegetables.

"Master Jiang, I really shouldn't be intruding here. This is obviously a special occasion," said Miss Chen.

Ma looked at Li. He had heard the girl call Li by a different surname. Li returned his glance and smiled his now familiar mischievous smile. Ma understood; Li was playing some sort of game with the woman and he lifted his wine cup in a toast.

"To Master Jiang and his wonderful choice of dishes for tonight's feast and to the exquisite Lady Chen, who adds grace and beauty to our dinner," said Ma, and drained his cup.

Li returned the toast. He was delighted with Ma's compliments to Chen and happy that Ma's wit was as quick as he had judged it to be.

Ah Wu sat in stony silence; he stared at the fish's gaping mouth. He had almost stood and toasted the fish's "elegant" mouth, but managed to restrain himself. Instead, he offered to serve the fish. Li consented.

The innkeeper delivered the other main dish to the enthusiastic praise of the guests.

"My dear friends, barbecued elephant trunk," said Li, proudly beaming over his big surprise.

"Master Jiang, how did you manage this?" asked Ma.

"Oh, I do have a bit of a reputation here. It wasn't hard. I failed, however, to find Ah Wu's favorite: spit-roasted camel humps. I'm afraid we are a bit too far south for such delicacies. Eat up, dear friends. It is unlikely that we'll again be together to enjoy such fare . . . considering where we are headed."

Ah Wu made a polite bow to acknowledge Li's comments and went back to nursing his wine. The innkeeper then placed a leaf-shaped dish with sliced python in vinegar next to the elephant trunk, bowed, and left.

"Miss Chen," said Li, "we were worried about your disappearance from the ship when we made port."

Chen was still blushing from the attention that had been lavished upon her. She picked at her fish for a moment and then responded. "I had already caused you and your companion too much trouble, so I left the ship when it docked, after you went to breakfast with the captain."

"Then your stomach complaint was just a ruse to stay behind so you could escape, ah, leave the ship without us?" asked Ah Wu, who was staring at the red dot on her forehead. It reminded him of the red gemstone on the hilt of the Dragon Pool Sword, which furthered his apprehension.

"Oh, no . . . ," Chen started to say, when Li Bo, first glaring at Ah Wu, turned to her and said, "Quite the contrary, your presence has added grace and elegance to a trip totally devoid of those noble qualities."

Chen's cheeks flushed. Her chopsticks dropped to her plate.

"What's in there?" she said, pointing to the blue bag next to Ma, which was moving.

"Oh," laughed Ma, "it's just Lao-huang, my master."

"Your master is in that bag . . . with hairy yellow legs . . . and a tail!"

Ma leaned forward. "Well he's actually a . . ." Ma used his fingernail to draw the character for monkey on the tablecloth.

Before Chen could repeat the character aloud, Ma's hand was hovering near her mouth.

"Shhh, don't say that word. He thinks he's an Immortal and not a . . ." Ma was pointing to the impression of the character he had drawn on the tablecloth.

"He becomes very upset when he hears that word used about him. Right now he's sleeping off a drunk."

Chen moved a little closer to inspect the blue bag. She had seen many things in her capital career, but never a drunken monkey.

"What is he a master of?" she asked.

"He catches ghosts," said Ah Wu. A smile wrinkled his scar.

"What?" Chen was startled and quickly moved farther away from the stretching form. She had made a mistake.

They all laughed, except Ah Wu, who was now studying Chen's reactions. She could feel his scrutiny, and tried to relax.

"Just how does Lao-huang go about catching ghosts?" asked Li.

Chen was having trouble picking up the tender flakes of golden carp with her chopsticks. Her concern was not for the fish. She waited for their attention to be distracted by a waiter, pursed her lips, and gently blew in the direction of the incensor set up on a nearby low stool to add the proper fragrance to their meal. Ah Wu was the first to notice the change. The sandalwood fragrance had changed to a strange scent—sweet, almost lavender . . . the same as at Dream Temple! He looked around for its source.

"He doesn't actually capture them," said Ma. A sly smile spread over his lips. "He identifies them. Once he finds one he begins howling, and then someone must arrive with the proper ghost-trapping or killing equipment."

One of Chen's chopsticks clattered onto the plate. Her cheeks reddened as she quietly apologized for the interruption. Li and Ma paid little attention as they were fully engaged in their conversation.

"But how does he identify a ghost?" Li persisted.

Chen kept staring at the prostrate form wrapped in blue. Ah Wu had been distracted by the change in fragrance and called over a waiter.

"What is wrong with the incensor?" he asked, his scar reddening. The quite frightened boy answered. "Ah, nothing, sir. I think."

"Change the incense."

"Yes, sir," said the boy, who scrambled off with the incensor.

This brief distraction gave Chen the opportunity to regain control of her breathing, which had become much too rapid for someone who is supposedly dining at ease.

"It seems he can smell them. At least, that's the only way I can explain it," said Ma.

"Ghosts have odors?" Li asked, absent-mindedly stroking his gray chin whiskers. Neither he nor Ma had paid much attention to Ah Wu's interlude with the waiter and the incensor.

"Of course they do!" interjected Miss Chen, who, distracted with her own question of scent, seemed just as surprised as the rest of them that she had joined the conversation on such an eso-teric topic.

The innkeeper returned with a freshly provisioned incensor. He looked to see if he could collect some of the emptied dishes. As he picked up a few, he listened to Chen and then added his own comments. "I don't know about ghost smells, but I do know the shores in this region are dangerous. We—" he stopped for a moment and looked around. "We have," he began again in a lower tone of voice, "Blood Dragons in this region. Several fish-ermen have washed up on the shore near Xia-zhou, drained white of all their blood. Terrible! The Prefect is helpless. Beware of the river and its shoreline, kind guests, beware!"

He shuffled away, his arms filled with dirty dishes.

The table was silent. Chen, not wanting them to dwell on the innkeeper's warning, resumed, "Aren't they like humans? Doesn't it follow that each ghost, just as they retain their physical appearance and personality in the *Yin* realm, also retain their individual scent in that realm?"

"Perhaps, but who really knows?" said Li. "While some of us have encountered beings from the *Yin* realm, few have had the opportunity to smell them."

Except for Chen and Ah Wu, they all laughed. Ah Wu continued picking at his food and watching her. He noticed that the sandalwood incense helped sooth his nerves and thought that the innkeeper had probably skimped on the first round of incense. Either that, or Li Bo had been right, their recent mountain experience had been more unpleasant than he realized.

"But we do know that they bleed when wounded and can be sent back to their cold world with a good crossbow shot to the head," said Ah Wu, staring at Chen.

"Humans lack compassion," Chen blurted out, staring right back at Ah Wu. She wanted to blow at the incensor again, but all eyes were upon her.

The wine was hindering her control; without control, she could completely disappear right before them. Her identity as a ghost confirmed, the Blood Dragon would have no use for her, like the others that these humans identified on the path to the Dream Temple.

"How's that?" asked Ma.

Li was giving Ah Wu another icy stare.

Chen hesitated for a moment, making sure her present state in the *Yang* realm was secure. Emboldened by the wine, she answered. "People immediately consider everything associated with the *Yin* realm to be evil and everything in the *Yang* realm of humans to be good. But can we, especially with the terror that Rokhshan's rebellion has spread, say that the *Yang* realm and its inhabitants live in paradise?" Chen stopped to sip some more wine and looked relaxed as she continued her reply. "I would not be surprised to find that some ghosts are better than humans in their moral behavior." She blushed again and drew her handkerchief across her face. Had she gone too far, she wondered?

"Yes, miss," said Ma, "your point is well taken. Ghosts do inevitably set off many irrational fears within the hearts of men. Yet, can humans be blamed for being so frightened? The common man fears death, and ghosts are emanations from the cold *Yin* realm of death."

Ma reached over and refilled Chen's cup with wine, then helped himself to some of the finely sliced python in vinegar. The wine pot was empty, and Li was already in the process of flagging the innkeeper down.

"Yes, sir," the attendant said, with a bow.

"Bring on the dark green wine."

"Ah, yes sir, excellent choice. Shall I serve the desserts?"

Li surveyed the table. The main courses had been laid bare, the vegetables well picked over, and the rice exhausted.

"Yes. I believe it was crabapples steeped in honey and cinnabar and perhaps some sweet rice cakes for our large friend." Li smiled at Ah Wu, who continued to ponder Chen's reactions. Ah Wu didn't blink. The innkeeper scurried away, counting in his head the profit he was going to make on all these luxuries.

"But there is the realm of the truly fantastic, beyond *Yin* and *Yang*," Li returned to the conversation as if the interlude with the innkeeper had not transpired.

"It is the realm of the Immortals," he continued, "the realm that has fascinated me for most of my life. At the age of fifteen, I began to seek them out. For dessert tonight we will taste some of that tradition as the crabapples I have ordered are done to a recipe passed on to me by my Daoist sword master."

"Yes, brother Li, er, Jiang." Ma smiled. "Those beings who can fly up beyond the mundane worlds of the human and ghost. But how many of us can partake of such a rarefied atmosphere? On the other hand, all of us will experience both the *Yin* and *Yang* realms," Ma said and laughed aloud. He downed another cup of wine.

The bamboo green wine arrived, and Li wasted no time in breaking open the blue-black ceramic jar's red paper seal and filling everyone's cups.

"Certainly," Li said, raising his cup high, "as a musician and experienced drinker, you must have already reached those regions far beyond these commonplace cares of the living and the dead. Wine is the path, the Way; it makes its own rules and ignores the follies of men and ghosts!"

"Excellent! And excellent wine, brother Jiang." Ma laughed aloud as he helped himself to another cup and returned Li's courtesy by filling his cup. Neither Chen nor Ah Wu had touched theirs. Ma went on, "Elder brother, those realms are so esoteric that one can spend lifetimes wandering among them and end up losing all sense of reality. I frequently wonder if, like the great sage Chuang-tze, I am already an Immortal who is merely dreaming of these various earthly encounters and will awake to find myself in a realm beyond life and death."

"Or perhaps you will simply awake with a headache in the Three Gorges Inn," said Ah Wu, who never had much patience for the "higher levels of thought," as Li Bo liked to call it.

"Younger brother Ma," Li's voice broke the short silence, "have you ever succeeded in capturing a ghost or even seeing one?"

"I am a beginner. Lao-huang is instructing me."

Ah Wu was becoming increasingly restive; he picked at the sweet rice cakes that had arrived and sipped some wine.

"Has this monke . . . excuse me, 'Immortal,'" Ah Wu scornfully pronounced the character, "ever captured anything besides a wine cup?"

"Not exactly, but he has helped me find the spirit manifestation of a shamaness that I have been trying to locate." Ma explained his earlier encounter with Luo Jhu-yun's manifestation.

"Who is this shamaness?" asked Li.

"Ah, a very accomplished master with whom I hope to study some of the more esoteric aspects of spirit contact." Ma picked at the steeped crabapple and then continued. "She, however, has set many obstacles in the path of those who wish to contact her."

"Yes, the best masters are this way. One has to earn their respect first before they will teach," said Li.

"There is certainly that aspect to deal with, but beyond that she has recently begun to eschew all contact with humans."

"Why?"

"No one really knows."

"Ah, perhaps she has actually contacted beings in the *Yin* realm and prefers their company," Chen blurted out. The wine was continuing to have its effect and loosen her inhibition to participate in the conversation, a conversation that could turn extremely dangerous for her if she slipped. As a human, she vaguely remembered, she had a reputation for being able to drink men under the table; but now, in this existence, only a few cups and she was losing control. How could she ever escape the monster's control when she couldn't even control the effects of a few drinks?

Li laughed and then mused. "The role of a shaman is to act as a conduit between the *Yin* and *Yang* realms. If she cuts herself off from the mundane world then her powers will atrophy."

Ma thought for a while as he picked at some more of the crabapple and sipped some hot wine. The wine was extremely pleasant, and he admired Li's excellent taste.

"That's a good point," Ma rejoined the conversation. "I don't know what to make of her recent behavior. But I must continue to pursue her, for her skills are quite extraordinary and could be of great benefit to society."

"Is your presence in Xia-zhou then linked to the pursuit of this woman?" asked Ah Wu, seeking to figure out Ma's "real" identity. Li Bo was at first surprised by his friend's interest, but he too found himself curious about what Ma was doing in Xia-zhou.

"Yes, I have tracked her here and suspect she was the one who stole your boat."

Li dropped his chopsticks. Ah Wu was on his feet. His eyes burned. Chen's eyes widened. A powerful shamaness could be very dangerous, she thought, and she glanced at the monkey. Things were not going to be as easy as she hoped.

"Why didn't you mention this when we first met?" blurted out Ah Wu. Just then, Lao-huang began to stir. Miss Chen grew apprehensive and inched farther away from the blue bag.

"Sit down!" Li commanded. "Everyone will notice you. This is no way to conduct a murder investigation."

Li then turned to Ma, speaking in a lowered tone. "Tell me younger brother, would this shamaness kill for a boat?"

The monkey's arms popped out of the bag and stretched, then its head. Its eyes were still closed but its mouth opened, to Chen it seemed forever, in a large yawn.

"Brother Ah Wu, I didn't know either of you that well when we first met and chose to be discreet. But we have become friends, I hope, and between friends there should be no secrets," said Ma. He gave Ah Wu the two-handed, open-palm-and-closed-fist, wandering-blade salute that Ah Wu immediately returned, thereby acknowledging a mutual pledge of brotherhood.

"As much as I know about her, which isn't a lot," continued Ma, directing his comments to Li Bo, "she has never taken a life. The most specific case that I know about involved her saving a life at great risk to her own."

Ah Wu was still uncomfortable, but with all that had recently occurred he did not associate this report of a shamaness with the rumors of Shamaness Luo's flight from the capital.

Neither did Li Bo, for he was focused on Old Zhou's death. He concluded, "Then it is unlikely that she would kill simply to steal a boat."

"She is powerful and can easily incapacitate a man with her skills; there would be no need to kill," Ma said in agreement.

The monkey did not awaken. It closed its mouth and curled back in the bag.

"Then if it was not she, and she did take our boat . . . ," mused Li aloud.

Ah Wu looked at Chen. Li noticed his friend's gaze and knew what Ah Wu was thinking.

"Miss Chen," asked Li, "do you have any esoteric skills that could subdue a man, or for that matter are you skilled in some form of martial art?" As he finished the sentence, he flicked a chopstick at her and then at Ah Wu.

So quickly had Li Bo moved that it seemed both chopsticks were sent flying at the same moment. Chen let out a yell as the chopstick glanced off her shoulder. In a flash, Ah Wu flicked the missile directed at him with one finger and broke it in half.

Ma and Li both laughed. Chen was so startled she thought she was going to completely dissolve into mist right in front of them.

"Good, now we know it must have been the horse rider who found Old Zhou disabled and then killed him. That explains the tracks we found around his body," said Li.

Ah Wu thought about the impressions in the dirt around Old Zhou's body; Li was right, but he remained uncomfortable in Chen's presence—there was still the unexplained attempt on the Dragon Pool Sword by some ghost-like being and then Chen's sudden appearance on the shore. Even more unsettling, thought Ah Wu, was the appearance of that sword. He tried not to dwell on their experiences at the Dream Temple, but it was futile—the anxiety was too strong.

"Interesting," said Ma, who was picking at the remains of the thinly sliced python meat.

"But if the boat had already been stolen, why would this rider need to kill your boatman? And how did the shamaness get hold of it? Was anything stolen?" asked Ma.

"No. It is a very strange incident. Unfortunately, Old Zhou's death still makes no sense," said Li. He picked up a cup of the dark green wine. The glint of the green wine reminded him of cool summer days spent in a verdant cove somewhere along the southern waterways that Old Zhou loved so much. That was all gone now, he thought. He drained the cup.

"I'm sorry," said Chen, who was struggling to appear composed—Lao-huang's snoring had buoyed her spirits. "I cannot add any more. The confusion in my mind about the events on that shore has not cleared up. At some moments, I'm not even sure if I really did speak with your boatman or if it was merely a dream."

Then she turned to Ah Wu and said, with a smile, "As a warrior, you must certainly know how that feels. I would guess that in the heat of battle, with all that confusion and danger, there must be times when reality seems to slip from your grasp."

Ah Wu felt a chill go through him; there was nothing in the human realm that he could not deal with. He was even confident when meeting the Emperor face to face, but this woman—there was something in her manner of speech. It was almost as if she were teasing or taunting him. Ah Wu knew that Li and Ma were watching him. He smiled.

"Yes, but one doesn't need to be in battle to feel that way."

He had said too much, recalling last night on the imperial salt hauler when he wondered if Chen had disappeared or not. His attention retreated to the sweet rice cakes and then to pouring wine for everyone.

Chen turned her attention to Li and Ma. "But regarding my esoteric skills, I must confess that I have none, especially in the field of subduing men." She blushed. "I have, however, devoted many years to the study of ancient scripts and although not very accomplished do have some knowledge in that area."

Li and Ma exchanged glances—both knew exactly what the other was thinking. Li spoke first. "There is a tomb rubbing from a Western Han tomb that we made just before we descended the mountain and found you on the shore. Younger brother Ma and I have tried to decipher it but cannot completely understand it."

"Why?" asked Chen. Her green eyes sparkled, as the wine and Lao-huang's sleep provided a greater sense of security.

"It seems written in a coded manner that belongs to some esoteric Daoist sect dating from that period."

"It's our conclusion," said Ma, "that someone who has continued the traditions of that sect probably can read it."

"I have a friend in Xia-zhou who is a Daoist hermit. I am sure he could read this script for you," Chen said. Her eyes avoided direct contact with either man—she was going about the monster's business.

"Fine, fine," said Li enthusiastically. "Could we show it to him tonight after dinner?"

"Yes, that would be no problem. I am supposed to meet him tonight for tea to see if he could help me regain my memory, and I could bring the rubbing."

"A toast! To a charming and resourceful lady," said Ma.

Li and Ma lifted their cups. Ah Wu tried to ignore them, but he felt Li's eyes boring into him and raised his cup. The after-dinner period was spent making poems about the river, the suffering of ghosts and humans, and the imagined joys of life as an Immortal. And, of course, consuming more wine.

⌐ 13 ⌐

The midnight sky was overcast. A soft, moist breeze wafted up from the river, but there was a chill in the air; spring had almost displaced winter.

A shadow glided between the buildings that lined Jie-hua Street where The Three Gorges Inn was located. It filled a dark recess between the herbal medicine shop and a rice store. Passing within hearing distance was a group of merrymakers that had just come out of the inn. They were heading into the inn's sleeping compound.

"Let's get the rubbing and go to tea with your friend," suggested Li to Chen.

"Yes of course, Master Jiang."

"Listen, elder Brother Jiang," said Ma, who was trying to keep his wits about him after all their drinking. "There is no need for all of us to run in there for a scroll. You and Miss Chen best go," Ma staggered closer to Li and winked. Li returned the wink with a smile.

"Right, Ah Wu, stay with younger brother Ma. We'll be right back," said Li as he turned and led Chen to his quarters.

Ah Wu didn't like the idea of leaving Li alone with Chen and felt he should accompany him. However, before he could follow, Ma had hold of him and invited him to try some of his own specially brewed wine. Ah Wu was tired. It did not take much to persuade him to drink with Ma. The shadow waited in the recess between the herbal medicine shop and the rice store.

Li led Chen through the dimly lit alleys to his compound. He asked her to wait in the guest hall and staggered into his sleeping quarters. After rummaging around in the room for a moment, he came across his backpack with the rubbing in it. He pulled it out and made a quick check. Re-rolling it, he turned to leave and almost touched lips with Chen, who was standing right behind him.

"Ahh!" shouted Li as his right arm moved instinctively for his left sleeve. Recognizing her face, he stopped.

"Chen!" said Li, his voice rising. "What are you doing in here?"

"Oh, I'm sorry, but I heard a sound outside and was frightened, so I . . . ." She was trembling.

Li realized how frightened she was and responded more soothingly. "Don't worry. I'm here and I have the rubbing . . . ."

As Li looked down at the scroll, trying to focus his eyes, Chen exhaled a pale-blue-colored mist from her mouth toward Li's turned face. He passed out immediately, and she caught the scroll as he went down onto the bed mat. Chen pulled his legs up onto the mat, draped a quilt over him, and disappeared.

***

Lao-huang awoke with a howl. Ah Wu jumped up from the street bench where they had all fallen asleep and flicked the safeties off his crossbow triggers. Ma was startled into consciousness. Lao-huang was up and out of the bag, running off down the street. Ma saw a female figure moving away in the same direction. He got up and ran.

Ah Wu didn't move. Since Li Bo hadn't returned with that woman, he could not leave.

"Master Jiang has been overcome with drink," the voice behind Ah Wu said.

He whirled around aiming the deadly bolts at her heart, before he realized it was Chen. He relaxed the pressure on the triggers. She screamed—remembering last time he had done that. In all the excitement, neither noticed a dark figure that glided down the street after Ma and Lao-huang.

"Sorry, please calm down. Sorry, but two screaming—" he almost said *monkeys*, "—ah . . . two screaming lunatics in one night are enough to make one want to . . . ."

"What on earth are you talking about? You just tried to drill two holes through my heart," Chen retorted, greatly "vitalized" from the dinner drinking.

Ah Wu gave a quick glance at Chen. "It's that crazy monkey. No way to wake up." Staring off into the darkness, he continued. "What a night. Now Ma and the monkey have run off chasing some woman." Ah Wu stopped, noticing that Chen was eyeing the crossbow that was still aimed at her heart. He lowered the weapon. "And then you appear out of nowhere. Has the whole empire got camel fever?"

"I don't know or care about camels, but master Jiang has been overcome by the wine and is fast asleep. He asked if you would be so kind as to escort me to my Daoist friend's hut to go over this rubbing with him."

Ah Wu's suspicions answered first. "I must go see my friend. He can usually handle much more drink than this evening."

"But I thought the two of you spent the whole day drinking with master Ma?"

"Yes, but even that would not stop Li, ah, ah, Jiang, the merchant Jiang."

Chen thought Ah Wu was acting a bit odd, but she knew he didn't trust her and she had to bring him, not Jiang, to the monster.

"Please hurry then, for my Daoist friend is a wanderer and could have already left our meeting spot."

Ah Wu nodded and headed to his compound. When she was alone, her tears fell. Again, she was being forced to lead someone to certain death. What could she do? To disobey would mean being sold into Hell, an unimaginable suffering. That would probably break her and then she would truly become an empty spirit—She feared that more than anything else.

***

Ma followed Lao-huang down the street and then off through several alleys. The alleys grew narrower and darker. He wondered if this could be a trap. At times, during the chase, he thought he heard footsteps behind him. He stopped and checked once, but the sound also stopped. He wasn't sure, until a few minutes later.

He rounded a corner and saw that Lao-huang had boxed the stranger in a blind lane. Ma ran up to the dark figure with his double-edged sword drawn.

"Who are you?"

The figure didn't answer. Ma quickly looked over the trapped runner; there were no visible weapons and only a purse slung over the left shoulder. The straw hat, however, blocked the dim house lights from revealing the person's face.

Ma leveled his sword at the dark figure.

"Shall I loosen your tongue for you?" As he spoke, a shadow gently eased behind him. Lao-huang was too busy chattering to notice. A black-gloved hand quietly grasped the hilt of the short killing sword belted onto the shadow's back. The albino swordsman was within sword-striking distance of Ma.

***

Chen and Ah Wu had been walking for about half an hour when they reached the bamboo grove by the shoreline. It was dark except for a lantern lit within the grove. They entered.

A strange fragrance—sweet, almost lavender—was the first sensation that Ah Wu experienced. He thought he was back at the Dream Temple. The grove was cold, much colder than the air outside it. Bamboos were knocking against themselves, but the wind seemed to flow around the grove, for the air within was still. Then he heard the music of a *jheng*. The thick sounds of its silk strings seeped through the stillness and surrounded him. He felt his senses being gauzed over as the pluck of each string spilled waves of brooding sound around him.

He made out a dim red lantern hung on a bamboo. It cast a dark light over a seated figure playing the long wooden *jheng*. Ah Wu raised his crossbow and Chen carried the rubbing scroll. They entered the clearing where the *jheng* player was seated in shadows. He could make out the player's hands; they were the large hands of a man. Ah Wu felt even more ill at ease not being able to see the player's face.

The *jheng* music stopped and Ah Wu stood before the shadowed player. Chen was paying her respects. The figure remained seated and, in a high-pitched voice, invited them to sit on cushions in front of them. Ah Wu placed his crossbow on his lap and sat to the right of the shadow. Chen sat directly in front.

"Please have some tea, sir," the shadow said. Ah Wu looked down and a teacup was sitting before him on a low table. He wasn't sure if it had been there when he sat down. That sweet, almost lavender scent was strong now. The bamboos had quieted. Ah Wu tried to focus on the shadow, to catch some hint of a face. He sensed the danger, but the fragrance kept distracting his concentration.

"Sir, I have the rubbing that I spoke to you about," said Chen in a very deferential tone. She was frightened and hoped that neither Ah Wu nor the Blood Dragon noticed.

Ah Wu thought he sensed a hint of fear in Chen's voice, maybe terror. This perplexed him. Again, he renewed his concentration.

The figure need only make the slightest threatening move and he would have two bolts in it before its next heartbeat, Daoist master or not. Then the thought that it might not have a heart beat rose. He quickly refocused his energy, searching out in front of him, but the sweet fragrance interfered with his concentration.

Chen laid out the rubbing for the shadow to read.

"Yes, I know this group. This is the tomb of the *Yang* remains of the Mount Mao Immortal known as the Lady of the Purple Vault. She transmitted many of the earliest revelations from the Lord of the Highest Purity to the Mount Mao masters. While the characters and style of the tomb are Eastern Han, it is of a much more recent construction," said the shadowy presence. Its thin, high voice seemed to float out of the darkness where Ah Wu imagined its mouth.

The information meant nothing to Ah Wu. He memorized what the shadow said and thanked it. He started to rise.

"Ahhh, but wait. I have a favor to ask of you," it whispered.

"Please, forgive my lack of manners," said Ah Wu, his finger tightening on the crossbow triggers.

"At the location of this tomb, did you or your master come across any . . . ancient . . . objects?"

"I'm sorry, your holiness, what are you talking about?" Ah Wu knew it was after the Dragon Pool Sword. That damn sword, thought Ah Wu. I must convince Li to get rid of it.

"There is a legend that the Lady of the Purple Vault was given a famous sword, an ancient religious object, by the Lord of the Highest Purity for her services. Many have searched for her mortal tomb, but none have found it, until you and your companion," the shadow interrupted his thoughts.

"Sword? What does this sword look like?" Ah Wu was trying to figure the best escape. The shadow was dangerous—the moment he entered this grove, all Ah Wu's senses were signaling him to get out. However, Li Bo's need to know the tomb's occupant had prevented him from just walking away.

"Do not play games with me, human! I know that the famous Dragon Pool Sword is in your hands! Tell me where it is or meet your ancestors, tonight!" Its voice changed into an inhuman growl, and as it leaned forward, Ah Wu caught sight of the red and yellow turban.

***

Meanwhile, in front of Ma Ssu-ming, the trapped runner pulled back its hat and revealed the face of the Grand Shamaness, Luo Jhu-yun. Ma stepped back. The doppelganger smiled. Before anyone could react, Lao-huang attacked the form and flew right through her neck into the wall behind. He bounced off and landed on the ground. The startled figure tried to cover up the hole that the monkey's body had broken in her form.

Ma understood and slashed out with his sword. It was parried. The glint of another blade flashed before him. Ma turned to face a dark-clad swordsman wearing a large round-brimmed straw hat with a hole in the center for the man's topknot.

Before he could say anything, the hiss of his opponent's blade ripped the night air. Ma parried and struck back. The mysterious swordsman was certainly worth his full attention, and the fight was engaged. Strike and parry as the two expert swordsman exchanged maneuvers without directly hitting each other's frosted razor-sharp blades. Their strikes were always oblique, using just enough force and deflection to give each attacker position for a follow-up strike.

Whenever Ma's blade made contact with the swordsman's, he sought to gauge the power of his opponent's *chi*, which he could feel through the contact of the two swords. This swordsman is highly skilled, thought Ma. He is able to hide the full extent of his *chi* power. Ma, naturally, did likewise. The albino swordsman, just as naturally, also picked up on this and remained cautious in his thrust and parry with Ma.

***

Su-lu caught Ah Wu's first bolt in his hand just before it would have ripped through the fabric of its robe right above its heart. The second bolt flew through the vapor that had been its form and smashed into a bamboo.

"Ha! Stupid human!" Su-lu's form bellowed as it appeared behind Ah Wu, who flipped forward crashing through the *jheng*. Ah Wu rose with his broadsword drawn and struck with all his power. The startled figure stepped back. A jagged line of white liquid formed at the base of its neck. Su-lu smiled as his head fell off.

"For my sons and my wife, may you rot in Hell!" yelled Ah Wu.

Chen watched in utter amazement. Had he really killed the Blood Dragon, she wondered. Am I free?

Ah Wu stepped back and retrieved his crossbow. Chen screamed. Ah Wu turned, shocked to see that the form before him had reached down and grabbed its head by the beard. It flopped the head back on its shoulders, and Su-lu's eyes snapped open. The creature, thought Ah Wu, was not human—smiled at him. Ah Wu threw down his spent crossbow and attacked with his broadsword. The monster caught his upraised arm and went for his armpit with its mouth.

Chen screamed. "No, no, don't kill him!" And she lunged forward to push the monster away. A touch from her uncle's form sent Chen crashing into the bamboos. Within seconds Ah Wu lost consciousness. The red lamp in the bamboo grove was extinguished.

***

Back in the alley, while the two swordsmen stabbed, sliced, and parried, Lao-huang attacked the shamaness's doppelganger, this time making a hole in her left leg. The figure was laughing. Ma noticed, parried the swordsman's blow, took a quick turn back, and directed a sidekick at her face. He connected and literally wiped the grin off her face. When the albino swordsman saw what happened, he realized it was another of the shamaness's tricks and disengaged, disappearing as fast as he had appeared.

The phantom shamaness then turned and dissolved into the wall. Ma flopped down in the dust at the base of the wall. The swordsman was unusually good, thought Ma. Lao-huang limped over to him.

"Yes, you have taught me well. Next time we will not chase an illusion. Now where are we? And who was that swordsman? Was he trying to protect the shamaness?" Then Ma laughed, "At least until he got a look at how I rearranged her face!" Lao-huang screeched wildly as he also enjoyed the joke.

Ma's face grew serious, "Lao-huang, do you smell that?"

The little yellow monkey sat up and began sniffing the air. He ran over to the wall that the form had just passed through. Ma followed. Pulling a cloth from his inner sleeve, Ma wiped the wall with it.

"Is this what you smell?" giving the cloth to Lao-huang. He jumped up and down screeching.

"At least we have one clue," Ma said glumly as he folded the cloth and stored it back inside his sleeve.

"I think we need a drink. Shall we?"

Lao-huang did a flip and jumped up on Ma's shoulder. They left the alley.

— 14 —

A gibbon's cry shattered the night. Li Bo briefly awoke to an oppressive sense of sorrow. The anguish of the cry—he had never heard it so sorrowful. His face was wet. Had he been crying in his sleep? Then the strong sense of dread that had been following him up the river broke through, flooding his consciousness. The dread was now sharp like the frosty sheen of a newly honed blade—his life was beyond his control. The events surrounding the Court and his banishment, the river, the dream and that sword: all were taking him where they willed. He was powerless . . . powerless . . . . His eyelids closed. If he could only will it all away, but, like the gibbon's cry that still rang in his mind, he could not—he no longer had the poetry to transcend his earthly worries. He felt he had become mortal, and he was afraid.

***

Down at the shore in his boat, Ma and Lao-huang stopped their drinking. A shiver went through them as they heard the gibbon's sharp painful cry. Cold rain poured down on the river. Successive waves of thunder shook the boat. Ma moved into the boat's shelter, but Lao-huang remained in the rain and began to howl. Ma had never seen his pet act this way, and a vague sense of dread rose in him. Something along this river was badly out of alignment with the Way.

***

The cold rain on her face and the rumbling of dark clouds brought Chen around. She bolted upright and surveyed the area. It was pitch dark. Large drops of rain had broken through the bamboo vault of the grove and were beginning to form puddles in the soft earth around her. She heard a gibbon wailing and remembered . . .

"Ah Wu, Ah Wu," she called out. Only the rain answered, splashing in the puddles and falling on the bamboo. She stumbled in the direction of the *jheng* and managed to relight the lamp. The ground in front of her ran red with blood mingling with the pouring rain. Then the fight did happen, she thought. She looked around—no body.

She searched the immediate area. Through the green shafts, she could make out another light. It seemed to bob as it moved toward her. Frightened, Chen turned and flew up into the night. Just as she cleared the bamboo grove, a flash of lightning illuminated the sky. A fisherman, who was beaching his boat, looked up and saw a woman in white sail above the bamboo grove.

"Ahh, ahh! A ghost!" he screamed and fell into the bottom of his boat, hiding under the ropes and other fishing gear.

It was almost dawn. The rain continued to speckle the river.

***

Huddled in his boat's shelter, watching the rain stream down, Ma thought back to the encounter with the shamaness's doppelganger.

"The way I figure it, she was coming from the docks, probably trying to get passage on a boat. From this port there is only one direction that makes any sense—the Three Gorges."

Lao-huang, who had calmed down, jumped up and down in agreement. Ma continued, "If we use the scent we picked up from the shamaness's phantom we might be able to trace her." He shifted his position in the boat's covered area. "I still can't figure out who that swordsman was or what he was up to." Ma smiled and patted Lao-huang, "Well, no use in worrying about our new friend, eh Lao-huang? We need to get some rest." The pouring rain on the river lulled them both into a deep slumber.

***

When the Shamaness Luo returned to her cave, just before dawn, she found a scrap of paper on her fox-hide mat. It was a receipt for a gorge boat reservation in three nights time. Someone must be on to her, she thought, for her shadow image had not returned intact. The Lady of the Purple Vault had warned that she was being tracked.

Her hand touched the small bronze mirror in her pocket; carefully she made sure not to disturb its cover. Feeling through the cover, she ran her fingers over the elaborate celestial markings on its back. With this gift, she thought, it didn't matter even if the Emperor was at the docks. No one would recognize her when she boarded the gorge boat; she was again indebted to the Lady of the Purple Vault. She carefully slid the mirror back into her pocket and lay back, falling into a deep exhausted sleep.

～ 15 ～

Li Bo awoke at dawn. The rain continued as he dressed. It was a hard, cold rain. A small leak had begun in the roof, and the water was beginning to pool at the foot of Ah Wu's bed, but Ah Wu had not returned. Li figured that with the tomb rubbing gone, Ah Wu and Chen must have gone to the Daoist to decipher it. Why was it taking so long? Once dressed, he walked over to Ma's quarters.

Empty. Could they have gone with Ah Wu and Chen? That would make the most sense, thought Li, but why would it take the whole night? His memory of last night, after dinner, was confused. One moment he was talking with Chen in his room and the next it was dawn. He had no memory of what happened in between.

Entering Chen's compound, he heard someone wailing. Li rushed to her door and knocked, "Chen, Chen, is that you, are you back?"

There was only the sorrowful sound of steady crying, punctured by shrieks of anguish. Li pushed through the rough wooden doors. Chen was sprawled on the cold stone floor. Her golden hair was wet and knotted, her clothing torn and bloody, and her hands, crimson fists, were pounding on the floor. On her sleeping mat were pages of writing that spilt onto the ground.

Li quickly picked her up, scattered the paper off the bed mat with a sweep of his arm, and set her down.

"Aaaah! Keep away! Don't touch those papers! Don't touch them! The only beauty, the only thing untouched by the filth . . . keep away!" she screamed hysterically and then fainted.

Li gathered the papers from her mat and placed them on a nearby low wooden table. Making more room for her on the sleeping pallet, he moved her into a comfortable position. He tried cleaning up her face. It was caked with mud and what seemed to be splattered blood. He placed a quilt over her and went about removing her wet clothing, making sure he kept her covered from his sight.

The fire was going for a while before she came to. Li had some strong soup from the inn kitchen ready for her when she opened her eyes. However, when she saw him, she began crying again and couldn't talk.

"Please, you're safe now. Don't worry. Tell me what happened. Where is Ah Wu?"

That seemed to make things worse, and she began shrieking again. Li gave her some powders from his travel kit that calmed her. She slept.

A knock at the door and Li admitted Ma and Lao-huang.

"Oh, I'm intruding . . . . I thought you were all out and was just checking to make sure," he said, seeing Li sitting on Chen's bed mat.

"Don't be silly, brother Ma. It's not what you think. Something dreadful has happened. The poor girl is scared to death."

Lao-huang started yelling and jumping around. Li's nerves were worn. "Get that monkey out of here!" he yelled. Neither Ma nor Lao-huang had heard Li at full fury. Lao-huang was so frightened that he didn't have time to get angry at being called a monkey. He fled in panic out into the rain and stayed there.

"Elder brother, forgive my thoughtlessness . . . ." apologized Ma, realizing how upset Li was.

"No, forgive my outburst, but Ah Wu must have gone with her and he is still unaccounted for. She returned covered with blood, but I cannot calm her enough to find out what happened."

"Yes, they must have gone together."

"You did not accompany them?"

"No, Lao-huang and I had our own adventure last night." Ma quickly related the encounter with Luo's "phantom." But Li's heart wasn't into listening. His concern for Ah Wu's fate overrode everything else. Just as Ma finished his tale, Chen came around again.

"Here, let me try this," said Ma, as he moved over Chen and, using his fingertips, lightly struck her at several pressure points on her neck and wrists. Her eyes opened and she seemed calm.

"Oh, master Jiang, it was terrible. Ah Wu never had a chance. It was my fault for asking him to come along. I will forever be haunted by that terrible night."

Li was shocked. "What are you talking about?" his voice boomed.

Chen sat up, struggling to keep the covers over her. "I'm sorry. But the attack was so horrible."

Ma gave her some soup and she drank deeply. Her cheeks flushed and color began returning to her lips.

"We went to a bamboo grove to meet my Daoist friend and while we were discussing the tomb rubbing . . . ." Tears formed along the lower lids of her round eyes, but she fought back and continued. "It must have been what they refer to as the Blood Dragon . . . but its form was that of a man." Chen used the blanket to blot her eyes. "The Daoist master tried to save us but was killed instantly. Ah Wu fired at the monster but it avoided the shots and grabbed him. The monster demanded to know where some sword was."

She pushed back golden hair that had fallen into her face. "Ah Wu refused to tell and it killed him," she sobbed. "I tried to stop the creature, but it brushed me aside like a paper doll. When I awoke, it was dark and raining. No one was around. I searched for Ah Wu and the Daoist . . . but it was so dark in there. I don't remember how I made it back, I could only think of the poetry . . . the poetry, the only comfort I have . . . ." She started crying again.

Ma fed her more soup. Li sat on the bed watching her. He blinked back the tears that were beginning to gather in the corners of his eyes.

"Chen, none of this is your fault. If anyone is to blame, it is I." Li glanced down at the dark stone floor and shifted his weight on the pallet.

"That sword! Ah Wu is right, it is cursed! It fell into our hands because I insisted on going to the Dream Temple to find out my fate after my banishment. Perhaps fate should be left to the wind and stars, and one should just live life as it unfolds." Li looked away from them and then turned back. "The sword is very famous and, cursed or not, I should have known that eventually it would bring us misfortune. Such objects arouse the greedy nature of sentient beings and bring sorrow."

"No, you only did what was normal for any person under such terrifying circumstances. I'm sorry, I didn't realize you had been banished. Just like Li Bo: only the kindest and most honest are banished while the hateful, evil ones are free to work their terror. Why do things work out that way?" Chen's eyes earnestly sought an answer.

Ma watched Li to see how he would respond.

"Yes, it seems that is the way for those of us caught in the red dust of the everyday world, like your poet. But what can we do? Go to Dream Temples, seek soothsayers, Daoist and Buddhist masters? To what avail? In the end, we must each face our misfortunes alone. And now, if what you're saying is correct, I am more alone than ever," said Li. Tears streaked his cheeks.

"We must make a search of that place. Ah Wu is possibly lying wounded," said Ma.

"Of course, I pity myself too much these days," said Li. "Miss Chen, give us good directions and we will go quickly to check out the area. Ah Wu has survived many impossible situations."

"Master Jiang, I insist that I accompany you . . . ," said Chen.

"Out of the question. You are too weak and too distraught to be of any positive help now. Rest up, for we all face difficult times ahead," Li said. His voice was forceful and filled with conviction. Chen knew the search would be fruitless, for the monster never showed mercy and it would not hesitate to kill again to obtain the sword. Yet she could not bring herself to warn them.

***

Ma and Li hurried to the bamboo grove. The rain continued and turned all of Xia-zhou's roads into muddy streams. It took them some time before they reached their destination. Ma sent Lao-huang into the bamboo grove and told him to report anything, human or otherwise.

They drew their weapons and entered. The ground was littered with dead and newly fallen bamboo leaves. A fine mist hung throughout the rain-soaked grove. In the gray morning light, bamboo stalks loomed around them. Up ahead they could hear Lao-huang chattering as he moved among the bamboo.

The chattering turned to sharp screeches and the two men came running. A clearing seemed to appear miraculously before them. Lao-huang passed the shattered *jheng*, table and lamp. Lodged in the bamboo behind them, Li found one of Ah Wu's crossbow bolts. And across from the *jheng*, he found the second bolt with a handprint burned into it—broken in half.

"I fear for Ah Wu; no human could catch his bolts. Whatever creature this was not only side-stepped one, but also caught the other."

Li held the broken bolt in his hand and rolled it in his fingers. His thoughts of their times together were interrupted by Ma.

"It was a Blood Dragon. That's what I heard on the river last night."

"What?"

"The gibbon's cry was not only for Ah Wu's death, but for the vengefulness of that monster on the loose."

"I too heard the gibbon and felt the pain . . . ," Li said, holding the bolt. "I must avenge him."

"You have an advantage."

"Yes!" Li laughed. "My hatred and desolation are so much more powerful than any Blood Dragon!"

"Possibly, but even more tangible, you have the sword that it fancies."

"You're right. The monster must come to me now. Quick, let us return for it is not safe here."

Lao-huang let out a shriek and ran toward a clump of bamboo. The thin stalks moved and Ma was upon them, his sword drawn.

"Please don't kill me. Please, I'm only a poor fisherman. I mean you no harm."

As Li entered the stand of bamboo, he saw Ma with his sword point at the throat of a kneeling figure.

"What are you doing here?" Li yelled at the man, aiming his Persian dagger at him.

"Don't harm me, please. Last night strange sounds and lights came from here. My father was landing on the shore and in a flash of lightning saw . . . saw . . . ," the man was trembling, "a ghost soar above the grove and off into the darkness."

"Take us to your father," commanded Ma.

"He has become deranged . . . . We cannot make any more sense of what he has been saying," sobbed the man.

"What did he see last night?" asked Li in a more soothing tone. The man said his father saw a woman in white robes fly out of the grove and head back toward town. Li and Ma let him go and headed back to their quarters.

"Could this be the Blood Dragon?" asked Ma.

"I know little of such things, but it sounds more like a ghost to me. I haven't heard of Blood Dragons flying like that," Li said, his brows furrowed. "Blood Dragons, so I've heard, usually travel by water and might jump into the air to reach water when frightened. But this monster certainly was not frightened, and I've never heard of ghosts being so fierce. We must ask Chen about this." Ma nodded in agreement.

"Until I touch his body, I will not believe Ah Wu to be dead. He's too tough, even for a Blood Dragon," said Li. Tears filled his eyes.

***

When she was sure Li and Ma were out of the compound and that infernal monkey gone, Chen appeared in Li's quarters. She began a careful search of his and Ah Wu's luggage. Nothing. Could Ah Wu have left it behind on the mountain? That made little sense, she continued to reason, especially if Jiang was granted the sword to solve the dream he was given at the Dream Temple.

As she opened the last compartment in Li Bo's backpack, scrolls came spilling out. Quickly gathering them up, she tried to get them in the right order to return them in the backpack. She couldn't help, however, but read one that had opened. The more she read, the slower she moved. It was poetry. It was poetry in the process of being written—not just copying like hers. She stopped. She read a few lines at first:

> Among the flowers, a pot of wine. Alone I pour, without a friend.

Raising my cup, I invite the radiant moon.
Facing my shadow, we become three friends.
The moon doesn't know how to drink, and my shadow only
follows my body.
Yet, while I accompany the moon and escort my shadow, this
merrymaking must last till spring . . .

She grabbed more scrolls and read them all in great haste. Tears poured out of her eyes. She knew! This was the work of the poet Li Bo, not copies of poems but the real thing in the process of being formed—she had met Li Bo.

Quickly returning the scrolls to the backpack, Chen ran out of Li's room into the rain and out the courtyard gate. She ran toward the river, staggering through the muddy streets, fighting on until she reached a deserted section of the shore. She ran into the Long River, screaming wildly as the rain never touched her, "I'll kill you! I'll kill you! You monster! You monster . . . ."

The water closed over her head. The rain continued to pour down as the river erased all traces of her wild rage.

— 16 —

Li and Ma returned to find that Chen had disappeared. They searched the whole compound, door to door. No one had seen her and there was no trace of where she might have gone. Ma and Li ended up resting in Li's room, trying to coax some heat out of the small charcoal brazier that was placed in each chamber.

"We can join forces and help each other," suggested Ma, "I have a clue to find the shamaness and, while we are searching, we also can make inquiries about Ah Wu and Chen."

Li thought for a moment. He had lost Old Zhou, his boatman; then Ah Wu, his companion for the last ten years, went missing—he refused to believe Ah Wu was dead; and now they were searching for Chen. He was complying with the imperial order for his exile, yet he was losing those closest to him. Would his family be safe? How would he even know? Ah Wu was right: the Dragon Pool Sword was cursed.

"Yes. I could not bear to carry out this search alone. I have lost two friends in the past few days, and now Chen. What else can Heaven take from me? If it would only relieve me of that damned sword."

"Elder brother, can you tell me about this sword?"

"As a swordsman," began Li Bo—Ma moved to raise his hand in objection, but Li Bo gently pushed it down and continued—"you have certainly heard of the famed Dragon Pool."

"But of course, even commoners know of its legendary might," said Ma, suddenly realizing what Li was about to say. "*You have it?*"

Li went on to explain what happened at the Dream Temple, the quest that the supposed "Immortal" had offered him, his acceptance, and his receipt of the sword.

"Ah Wu had immediate doubts and warned me of the sword's curse," said Li. He blinked back his tears. "But being my usual egotistical self, I waved aside his misgivings and kept the sword."

"May I . . . ," said Ma.

"You're not worried about the curse?"

"My religion is the Way of the Sword," Ma said and smiled.

"Yes, when I was your age, I was the same way. Life changes, however . . . . The sword . . . I don't think it's too hard to figure out where Ah Wu put it as he built a removable hidden section into my instrument for our trip," said Li and turned to their baggage. The sight of Ah Wu's pack brought more tears to his eyes. He didn't bother trying to wipe them away or hide them from Ma as he unwrapped his *jheng*. He pulled out the thirteen silk-stringed instrument made from polished paulownia wood. Li fumbled with the end cap for a moment and pulled it off. A red glow spread out of the *jheng*.

"What is this? It glows?" Li hesitated and then reached inside and drew out the sword.

Handing it to Ma, he said, "This is strange, the red gemstone is glowing. The sword cannot be drawn from its scabbard."

Ma took it with the great reverence. "How light, how exquisite, as if truly forged in Heaven. Imagine what the blade must be like." He noticed the red gemstone and handed the sword back to Li.

"You know what that means, don't you?" said Li.

Ma laughed. "There are many stories about such fabulous weapons. It's difficult to tell which to believe. I choose to base my opinions on fact. Yet, there is a story—or is it a poem—that claims when the Dragon Pool glows red, blood will flow. But that can hardly be if it cannot be drawn from its scabbard." Ma hesitated for a moment. "The story continues that when its green gem glows, a pure mind is its owner and it can be released from its scabbard."

"Well, things don't look so good for me," said Li.

"That's if you believe such fairy tales. There are those that do and place a high value on such objects."

"What?" said Li, still distracted by the sight of Ah Wu's backpack.

"I can't tell you what to believe about that Heavenly quest. You certainly have the Dragon Pool Sword, but I know that the Court, no, the Emperor would be greatly impressed with such a gift. It might even be a way to get your banishment rescinded."

Li looked at the sword. Its red gemstone gave off a steady glow— the color of blood, he thought. What would Ah Wu counsel?

"I accepted the quest to deliver it to Mount Wu," said Li.

"Then this involves the Rain Goddess who is said to inhabit its twelve peaks?"

"Yes, she is supposed to be the recipient, but you don't believe in such spirits."

"Once I would have told you that Blood Dragons are only in fairy tales, but I know better, now. Perhaps there is a Rain Goddess and perhaps you have been chosen for a Heavenly quest. Only you can decide."

"Yes," said Li. He carefully replaced the sword in its hiding place and rewrapped the *jheng* in its waterproof covering. "And I am also prepared for a Court appearance," he added, pulling out part of his Court robe from his backpack to show Ma.

Ma leaned forward and placed his hand on Li's forearm. "While I must admit things don't look too good for Ah Wu, I agree with you that he is not dead until we touch his stone cold body. And for Chen, there is nothing to fear. The Blood Dragon is only interested in that sword. Harming Chen will not bring it the sword."

"It is good that I met you, younger brother. Your youthful energy and clear thinking are very much lacking in this old pile of bones," Li said, offering a weak smile.

"Then join me in my search and we can also make inquiries about Ah Wu and Chen. It could be that he is wounded and is holed up someplace to get clear of that monster before he returns to us."

Li smiled. He appreciated Ma's good heartedness in trying to comfort him, but he knew the mourning for the loss of his oldest friend had already begun. Perhaps, Ma was right. To hell with the spirits and their fantastic quests, present the sword to the Emperor and beg for reinstatement.

***

Li, Ma, and Lao-huang spent two rain-soaked days searching Xia-zhou for a scent of the shamaness's phantom figure and for sightings of Ah Wu and Chen. All the while, they were being followed. It was the afternoon of the second day before Ma realized what was irritating Lao-huang.

"Lao-huang, someone following us? Is that what's bothering you?"

Lao-huang twittered away, covering his eyes with his paws.

"Elder brother Li, don't look back. Lao-huang, are they human?" The little monkey jumped down from Ma's arm, ran over to a tree, urinated, jumped back up and chattered.

"Human. I've had a feeling for the last two days that we have company."

"Why?" asked Li, who found himself amused at Lao-huang's associations.

"I think it's the swordsman that intervened when I caught the phantom. I can't figure why. He could be trying to protect her. But that is very out of character for her to have a male bodyguard."

"Why?"

"Well," Ma seemed embarrassed. "She distrusts men and would never have any man around her, much less one to protect her."

"Oh, one of those headstrong types," said Li, trying to smile.

"Yes, I guess you could put it that way, but you can't imagine exactly how headstrong this one is."

Li realized that Ma had not told him everything about the shamaness. However, the loss of Ah Wu and his concern for Chen left little emotional energy for involvement in the affairs of others, even such a good companion as Ma Ssu-ming. He didn't pursue his initial curiosity. This was unusual and Li Bo noticed it in himself. He realized how deeply the loss of Ah Wu had affected him. Certainly, regaining his position at Court could never be worth the loss of Ah Wu. He continued in silence to walk on with Ma.

Lao-huang stood up on Ma's arm. With the constant rain, Xia-zhou's streets were awash in mud, so Ma had decided to carry Lao-huang. His pet was now shaking Ma's lacquered paper umbrella in the direction of an alley off the main wharf.

"Let's take a stroll down here," said Ma. Li nodded and followed. Lao-huang couldn't wait. He jumped out off of Ma's arm and splashed into the doorway of a shop.

"Aaaah! An animal has just jumped through the door!" screamed the shop owner.

"Lao-huang, come back up here. Don't worry, madam, he is quite harmless," said Ma. He tried to coax the little master back to his perch. Once Lao-huang was settled down, Ma approached the woman. He described the shamaness's phantom figure and asked the woman if she had been in the shop.

"Many people come in here. At least, before the rebellion when there were ships to go upriver. Anyway, I can't recall them all."

"Then maybe this scent might help your memory," said Ma as he held out the cloth that had captured some of the phantom's residues from the wall. The woman sniffed and then thought a while. Li, who was getting impatient, reached into his robe and plunked down a piece of silver cash.

"It's known to have wonderful powers for renewing memories and bringing forth the most amazing recollections." He scowled at the woman.

"Yes, I remember," the woman's face brightened. Li ignored her and went about brushing water from his thin blue robe.

"Two or three days ago. She bought space on the gorge boat that leaves ar midnight tonight."

"Are you sure?" Ma jumped in.

"Why yes, that smell . . . who could forget it?"

"We'd like two more places on that boat for tonight," said Ma. He looked at Li to see if he would join him.

Li was adrift. The Dream Temple had given him a sword and pointed him toward Mount Wu, upriver in the second of the Three Gorges. But it also put him on a path that led to the death of Old Zhou and Ah Wu—he would have returned by now if he was alive, Li had concluded—and the disappearance of Chen. He said nothing and did not interfere with Ma's purchase. He had concluded that now was the time to drift with the Way, even if it meant death in the jaws of the Blood Dragon. He had no energy to resist.

"Well that might be difficult," the woman's voice broke in on Li's thoughts. Eyeing the silver piece that Li had shoved under her nose, she continued, "There are only two deck cabins and they cost . . . ."

"We'll take them," said Ma.

The woman smiled and made out the bill as she figured out the fat commission she had just made. Ma paid and they moved back out into the rain.

"Sorry about dragging you along on this. Of course, if you want to remain here . . . . I only feel that it would be better for you to keep on traveling. Possibly our companionship could assist in the renewal of your spirits."

Li knew then that Ma had indeed read his poetry closely, for Li's deepest feelings were always reserved for matters of friendship.

"Yes, I think you are right . . . . Anyway, even if I decide to offer the sword to the Emperor, it is useless locked in its scabbard. The dream I had at that temple directed me to Mount Wu; perhaps it will be released there . . . ." Li's voice trailed off.

"Good, then we are both headed in the right direction. Friends should always help each other. Let's go back to the inn." Ma extended his arm inviting Li to go first.

The shadow that had been following them for two days slipped into the shop they had just left. The woman never heard him approach her desk.

"Madam," he said in a soft, high voice.

"Ahh! Oh, Heaven! You startled me. Must be the racket of the rain. Can't hear a thing . . . ."

She was tense. The black-robed figure that stood before her wore a straw rain hat that covered most of his face, but she could see that he was an albino. The discovery increased her discomfort.

"A ticket on the same boat as the gentlemen who just preceded me."

"Yes, but we . . . we seem now to be fully booked . . . ." She nervously opened the booking log to show him. He slid it out of her hand and glanced over the page.

"Does this boat require identity papers to board?"

"Oh no, Sir, nothing like that. Since the rebellion we've been lucky to have any service at all much less follow full imperial regulations." She smiled tensely, realizing she might have said the wrong thing. If this person was a government official . . . .

"You've been a great help," he said. His hand moved back from the counter exposing a small silver ingot. He left before she could respond.

Many strange ones have come in here recently, she thought. The rebellion flushes them all out. No matter, as long as they keep tipping like the last ones. She wondered where she could hide the ingot left by the last stranger so that her husband wouldn't find it.

Later that evening, there was a murder outside the Three Gorges Inn. A sword thrust to the heart killed a merchant named Wang Shen-gung. The authorities found it strange that none of his money was taken.

Rain continued to fall that evening. It seemed to further wash away Li's emotions, leaving him numb—numb to his inner world and numb to the outside world. Perhaps, he reflected, the numbness will permanently replace my feelings. Almost as soon as it arose, he lost interest in pursuing that line of thought, preferring the numbness to any form of thought. Ma's consideration of their next moves gained Li's fleeting attention—at least as much as he could muster as they sat in the Three Gorges Inn drinking.

"You have the advantage over the Blood Dragon. Now that we know it is desperate for the sword, it must come to you. When dealing with an enemy that is more powerful than you are, this is one of the best offenses. Draw it to you and meet it on your terms."

"Yes, of course. But then maybe I should wait for it here?"

"The old hag in the dream gave you the sword to take to Mount Wu. Right now, the sword can't even be withdrawn from its scabbard. What use is it? It must have some special powers that are activated on Mount Wu. Once activated, the gift of such a powerful weapon will surely find you acceptance at Court," Ma said. He munched some of the peanuts that were served with their wine and continued. "We should get to that mountain as fast as possible. Fulfill the dream, and then deal with the Blood Dragon. It must follow you to get the sword and it is better that the two of us face it than only yourself."

"Younger brother Ma, you cannot get involved here. This is dangerous business and only concerns my debt to Ah Wu . . . ."

"Please, we are friends and friends share each other's burdens. And don't forget, Ah Wu was also my friend. We exchanged salutes as brother wandering blades. I cannot allow the outrage of his death to go unavenged. That is, of course, if he is dead."

Ah Wu, dead? Could this have really happened, thought Li Bo? For ten years we have shared adventures together. No matter how strange or how hopeless things got, Ah Wu was always there with his trusty crossbow and unshakeable loyalty—the swordsman's code. Ah Wu lived by it, and, perhaps, now has died by it.

Li Bo let out a loud laugh. "Spoken like a true wandering blade! Yes, I too was once a wandering blade and remain true to our code of honor. We both will avenge our brother's murder!"

The zest for life seemed to return to Li the more he partook of Ma's excellent wine and stellar company. He overfilled his cup and toasted his friendship with Ma, then the honor of swordsmen everywhere, then courage, then loyalty, then justice, then . . . by that point they realized if they didn't hurry up and pack, they would miss the ship. Anyway, they had run out of wine.

***

"That was without a doubt, the most stupid thing I have ever witnessed in all my centuries!" the Blood Dragon raged in a deep male voice that for once suited its appearance as Chen's degenerate uncle. It paced the room, eyes aflame. "Don't you understand?" it seemed to plead. "You are dead! You killed yourself when you jumped off that transport a year ago. Running into the river to drown yourself is a useless gesture. If you want to hurt yourself or give yourself some pain, then I will accommodate you!"

Without warning, the monster wielded a thin bamboo pole striking Chen on the back. Again and again the Blood Dragon struck her. Chen fell to the ground and writhed in pain.

"That's to teach you never to interfere with me. If you ever fail to carry out my orders or dare turn against me, I will inflict real pain on you, then sell you to one of the Lords of Hell who would love to have a golden-haired mistress."

Chen did not answer. She sobbed softly on the wooden plank floor of a two-masted junk as it rolled gently at anchor outside of Xia-zhou.

"What's got into you? Why were you trying to destroy yourself? What is the matter with the world these days? I can no longer get competent help. They are either a bunch of bungling idiots who get themselves shot up or a sniveling bitch who is still all too human for the tasks I have at hand," the Blood Dragon roared.

"I . . . I . . . I was upset over the death of Ah Wu. You know I have never gotten used to the killing," she wept.

"Fool, you are still too human. Your stupid emotions are fouling your thinking. What a miserable catch for an assistant," the beast grumbled. "Unfortunately, I still need you to get that sword from this human. I cannot deal with your species; they are so stupid that I lose my temper and desire to crush them much as they treat annoying insects."

Chen held back her tears. She knew that with control, she could do some good in this terrible affair, and that thought alone gave her comfort that she was still human.

"Yes, master I will do my best," she lied softly as she continued to fight back her tears.

"Good, that's a sensible girl." The Blood Dragon's voice had changed to a soothing female voice. "I'll explain what I want you to do."

When her master had finished, Chen bowed and left the cabin. A man on deck took her to a small boat and rowed her ashore. He directed her to the gorge boat that Li and Ma had booked for midnight.

"All right, come out now," said the Blood Dragon, when Chen had left. Out of the shadows a large figure edged forward, but remained in the darkness as the Blood Dragon spoke. "Go aboard that gorge boat and keep to the shadows. Follow Chen. I don't trust her. Make sure she does not betray me. Once the sword is revealed, send her to the Void with this ghost-killing pin." She handed the large figure a shiny steel pin the size of a small dagger. "And send Li Bo into the *Yin* realm with your own hands." The figure bowed and moved off through the wall. The Blood Dragon howled with laughter. Although the rain continued, it didn't wash the air clean of that horrid laugh.

***

By midnight, Ma and Li had boarded the boat. A few minutes before sailing, a woman appeared on the dock. Ma had been on deck waiting for the passengers to arrive. Although he had no way of seeing either Chen or the Blood Dragon's other henchman arrive, he watched a woman advance up the gangplank to have her ticket checked. Slowly he worked his way to the boarding gate and managed to get a close look at her. He had never seen the woman before.

Just as she moved off, she glanced up at him and he thought he saw, in the lamplight and through the rain, a faint smile on her lips and a twinkle in her eye. He couldn't be sure. Lao-huang had passed out from drinking and was useless. Ma was tired. He cursed his own drinking and went off to his cabin.

Just before the anchor was weighed, a man came running up the gangplank.

"Wait, wait, the rain delayed my carriage. I abandoned my luggage to get here on time."

The crew held the boat as the man, mud splattered and soaked with rain, boarded.

"I'm Wang Shen-gung, a merchant. Here are my papers."

"We don't need your papers. Only your ticket," ordered the mate.

"Oh, yes. Here," said the man, fumbling with his document bag.

"Fine. A deck hand will show you to your cabin," said the mate. He ordered one of the other sailors to show the man to his cabin. The merchant bowed and hurried off. All he had was a small carrying bag and a longer thin object wrapped in cloth tied with silk cord at both ends. He slung the long object over his shoulder and moved off with the deck mate. The dim light of the ship's lamps grayed his albino complexion.

The gorge runner pushed off the dock into the main channel. Its ear-shaped bamboo mat lugsail was hauled up the length of its eighty-foot single mast. When dawn broke, the captain wanted to be first in position to sail through the shoals at the mouth of the Xi-ling Gorge. He was anxious to proceed before the water level changed and favorable *shang-feng* (upward wind) abated. With a strong pushing wind, he could save on the expense of hiring trackers to pull his ship over the various rapids that dotted the course through the Gorges.

The captain of this gorge runner, a boat built from the finest cypress the region had to offer, had modified his ship to carry a mix of passengers and cargo. The deckhouse, just aft of the mast and running back to the stern, had been divided up so that there were two comfortable, and expensive, cabins for passengers. The rest of the structure housed the crew of six in hammocks, a small galley, the tiller room, and the captain's small cabin. Down below, several of the bulkheads had been walled off to create two additional passenger cabins. The rest of the space below was for cargo.

Li walked out onto the forty-foot flat foredeck, which lay between the bow and deckhouse, into the rain with an oiled-paper umbrella. He moved to the bow. The river was white foam churned up by the force of the rain that had not stopped since the night Ah Wu was killed. The only light came from the pale glow of the ship's lanterns and the channel markers out on the river. Li wondered if other ships could really see them. Would it matter? he thought. There was serenity in the wet darkness of this night—perhaps like death.

"Although this is only a brief moment in the flow of the universe, it can be a gateway for grasping the greater whole," a gentle voice said from behind. Li whirled around and came face to face with a woman dressed in a dark robe with white edges that covered her head and was drawn as a veil across her face. He thought of Ah Wu's black robe trimmed in white. When he refocused on the woman, he could barely make out her features in the dim flickering of the ships running lamps.

"What?" he answered, his face quite pale.

"You're bound through the Gorges?" she asked.

"Could be, I never know till I get where I'm going." He laughed, and the lightness of his head overcame his initial surprise.

She did not indicate it with her voice, but her eyes alerted him. He turned and looked out beyond the bow. His eyes adjusted to the dim light. The ship was now moving upriver and a white light was descending from the sky. It arched over the river, then moved downward toward the water—a white rainbow.

Li had heard of them among the tales of strange phenomena that circulated the capital wine halls, but he had never actually seen one. As soon as he saw it, it vanished. The river was dark again, foaming with the downpour of rain. Turning back to the woman, he noticed her eyes were tranquil. She understood the phenomenon. He waited.

"Yes, I know it. The white rainbow, an omen of death," she said calmly, looking out over the bow as if she could still see it—perhaps she could. "There are those who claim it represents the *Yin* essence at its worst, at a point where it overcomes the *Yang* essence. Blood will flow beneath it."

"The Blood Dragon," Li said under his breath.

She smiled. "Yet the Way always returns to perfect balance."

PART TWO

THE RIVER

~ 17 ~

The rain continued through the night. There were moments, however, when Li Bo awoke to stillness. Inside his small deck cabin, he would stare into the darkness. A darker form seemed to take shape, as if darkness itself had congealed to watch him. A scent, vaguely familiar, brushed his memory. Then the rain would return, the wine's influence would overcome him, and sleep's black currents drew him under. Or was it all just a dream? He hoped it all was a dream: the Dream Temple, the sword, Old Zhou, and Ah Wu. Li managed to smile at the thought, and he let himself be pulled under.

Chen felt his eyes boring into her as sharply as his poetry cut into her heart. However, she had made herself invisible and knew he couldn't see or hear her. She could not face him, not now. The pain of Ah Wu's death was bad enough. The discovery, however, that this man in front of her was the great poet Li Bo, not some merchant from Sichuan, had almost destroyed her. Her hatred for the Blood Dragon and her deep feelings for Li Bo's poetry had restored her.

The poetry had made the difference. It had been the only support as the dark whirlpools of the *Yin* realm and enslavement by the Blood Dragon had almost drowned her spirit. This man's poetry, she thought, had protected her and she was bound by her renewed human spirit to protect him.

She sat at the small writing table in his cabin and from memory filled a piece of pure white silk with one of his poems. Tears streamed from her eyes as Li Bo's verse flowed through her mind, out through her brush. She stood up from the table. Leaving the tear-stained silk behind, she turned and left the cabin.

The room was silent. The rain had begun again to churn the river into angry white foam. A shadow emerged from the wall of Li's cabin and moved over the writing table. It paused for a moment and then receded the way it came.

***

Ma Ssu-ming was dreaming. He saw a dark form enter his room and move toward him. A glint of polished steel bore down on him. He couldn't move. He strained to reach his sword. His arms were numb . . . thick. The shadow's sword struck as Lao-huang's screeching woke Ma. Tumbling to the hard-planked floor, he had dodged the blade, its movements strangely familiar.

Lao-huang continued to screech. Ma lay in the dark void. He felt as if he were floating through thick black ink, borne up by the dark currents swirling around him. As he slowly rose, a searing pain shot across his chest. He touched it. His tunic was ripped and wet with a sticky warm liquid. Ma crawled over to the nightstand and lit the lamp. Then fell back into his bunk to examine himself.

It was blood. Grazed across the chest, he was bleeding lightly. Yet, wasn't it a dream? he thought. The door and porthole were still firmly bolted. His level of skill should have alerted him to anyone physically entering the room, before they reached him. This must have been a dream, yet the wound made him wince.

***

That same night, in her small room below deck, the Shamaness Luo entered a trance. She began to shake and sweat, her eyes rolled upward, and her mouth went into convulsions.

The voice rose from within, "The mirror has done its work well. You have picked your mother's face and her face has changed you, hasn't it? But beware, the white rainbow—a sign of death. Both your human pursuers are onboard. Restrain your powers, lest they give you away. This could be difficult, for I also sense the presence of two ghosts. Their natures are confused and vengeful. Yet they are both controlled by an even greater evil. Be on guard. The vow is your life—you must protect it."

Luo collapsed onto the bed mat. The incense rose from the burner and curled around the lamp, smothering it. She slept dreamlessly in the Long River's darkness.

～ 18 ～

Li woke in the morning, expecting the day to be an extension of the night's lonely emptiness. The rain had stopped and the ship was motionless, except for the waves breaking on its bow. When he rose to dress, he noticed a square piece of white silk with black ink characters on the small writing table next to his sleeping pallet. Tears flew down his cheek as he recognized one of his own poems written in Chen's elegant hand. He lifted the silk to his nose, the familiar strange scent—sweet, almost lavender. He set the silk down, dressed, and went out on deck to find Ma.

The sky was overcast, but the view that met him, even though he had been through the Three Gorges before, stopped him. He paused for a moment, and then walked away from his cabin toward the bow. The ship was anchored in the mid-channel approach to the Hsi-ling Gorge, the eastern entrance to the narrow mountain passage of the Long River into Sichuan, the ancient kingdom of Shu. Either shore seemed within swimming distance of the ship. But veteran river travelers knew that the currents, eddies, cross-tides, and sharp rocks that lurked just below the smooth surface would make any such foolish swimmer an immediate sacrifice to the river spirits.

Wondrous hard gray sandstone cliffs rose from either side, dwarfing the ship and its puny human presence. The cliffs were spotted with blue-green juniper and stunted and twisted pine. Looking over the bow of the ship, he could see a huge dark form that rose in the gray upriver mist and seemed to block any passage. Li, however, knew that the river took a sharp turn at that point. Going west, as they were, against the great river's eastward flow was a much slower trip. He remembered the times he had returned eastward from Sichuan, his old home province, and the excitement of riding the river's downward rush through the Gorges. But that seemed to be in another lifetime. Loud voices broke him away from his memories of more pleasant times.

At the stern, Li could see the captain, a tall, thin, lightly mustached man dressed in a gray half-tunic with black pants. His large head sported a bright green bandana with a large gold-hooped earring in each ear. Like the rest of the crew, he was bare-foot. Gathered around him was the crew of six. They were all arguing with the captain. Li moved into hearing distance. The crew was obviously upset.

"We should wait. It's too dangerous to go without the pilot . . . ."

"With all the rain last night, he has probably been held up."

"Probably bailing out his boat right now . . ."

The captain smiled. "How many years have you sailed with me? I know the river's twists and turns better than those of my wife's. I don't need any drunken pilot for a guide."

"But you're not married," said the cook.

"How would you like a quick swim in the Long River!" shot back the captain. He looked up at the yellow pennant streaming from the top of the ship's single mast. It was blowing west.

"We don't need a pilot, or for that matter, your backs. Look!" he said, pointing up at the mast. "We have a *shang-feng* wind. For this time of year, it is good omen enough for our swift voyage through the Gorges. Now get back to your posts. Up anchor and raise the sail. We'll catch this gift from the river spirit. Quickly!" he bellowed. The crew ran into action. The captain smiled and poured himself another cup of hot wine from the flagon that the cook had been holding.

"Elder brother, you are up so early," said Ma, as he stepped out of his cabin. Li Bo, didn't respond. Ma gently touched his shoulder. Li turned quickly; his eyes were wide and, at first, he did not focus on Ma.

"Are you all right? Did anything happen to you last night in your cabin?"

"Yes, yes. How did you know?" Li said. He searched Ma's eyes for some sense of understanding, some fragment of knowledge that would allow him to explain to his young friend.

"Are you wounded?" asked Ma drawing closer.

It was then that Li noticed Ma's ashen hue and the few stains of crimson that were scattered across the front of his olive colored tunic.

"Younger brother," Li moved forward to support him, "you have been injured."

Ma moved back, slightly raising his hand. "Please, don't let on that you know."

Both men turned their backs to the cabin on the mid-deck and faced the boulder-strewn shore as they leaned on the railing over the river. Higher up on the jagged cliffs, birds flitted back and forth tending to their newly built nests. A mist settled over the tops of the cliffs and began to blot them out.

"Yes, I have been cut . . . ."

Li moved to grasp Ma by the shoulder, but the younger man deftly moved away.

"Please, no show of surprise. I'm not sure of the attacker and don't want to reveal that they succeeded."

"Younger brother, wouldn't the attacker know what happened?"

"I don't know."

Li's eyes opened wider, then he remembered Ma's warning to show no surprise and stared off into the river's swirling brown waters. For a moment, he could make out some rocks lurking just below the surface. Li hoped that the captain was competent.

Familiarity with the river at this point could get them only so far. Once they reached the New Rapids, they would have to have a native pilot. The New Rapids were so named because constant landsides frequently changed the configuration of those torrents. Ma's soft voice intruded on Li's ruminations. He explained how his dream had turned lethal.

"How can one cross from the dream realm into the *Yang* world?" asked Li.

"Perhaps an Immortal like at the Dream Temple. I would have said that it was impossible, but I bear the scar. Though I have heard of such swordsmen, nowadays there are so many tales it's hard to say what is possible. Lao-huang saved me by his screeching."

"Immortals aren't killers. Someone must have entered the room and set Lao-huang off."

Ma smiled. "Elder brother, I never boast about my skills, but let me assure you, the slightest sound—a key in the lock, a knife at the bolt, a door moving on its hinges, footsteps on the floor— would launch me into the teeth of the intruder."

Ma faced the streaked cliff walls for a moment where he saw the images of his dream. He continued, as if speaking to the cragged sandstone. "The intruder was not physically in that room last night, yet someone or something has the power to kill in dreams—to physically cross from *Yin* to *Yang*. Perhaps it wasn't human. A ghost?"

The only sounds that passed between the two men for some time were those of the water under the bow and an occasional cry or twitter from a bird or two high on the cliffs.

"If this is so, and I tend to believe in the impossible," said Li, "why attack you?"

Ma remained lost in his stony silence a while longer. Then he looked down at the water sliding past the ship before he spoke.

"I like sailing, to watch the water flow when the sails are full. It doesn't matter where it flows, past a ship, past a rock, wherever.

I guess it's the motion, the movement that I like. My life is that way. I'm always on the move. Like water, Heaven sends me forth to sweep the obstacles in its way."

He turned and stared into Li's eyes. Li understood. Ma was on an imperial mission. Although, at this moment in his life, Li did not have an especially high regard for the Emperor, Ma was his friend and that alone required loyalty. At that moment, Li made the connection—Ma is hunting the Grand Shamaness Luo. The stories about her escape must be true, thought Li. He decided not to mention any of this to Ma, for Li tended to sympathize with the shamaness's plight. He would have been in the same position if he had taken Ah Wu's advice and gone back for his family to escape to the Western Regions.

"Good," said Ma with a smile, "and in case you're wondering, I don't think it's the shamaness."

"She might be the natural choice."

"Her powers are life-affirming. Though she seems to shun human contact, she exists to ease contact between the Yin, Yang, and, maybe, the higher realms. And if she ever wanted to kill, she wouldn't need a sword."

"Is she on board?"

"At first I was not sure. The only woman who boarded last night had a slight resemblance, but the shamaness has an intense arrogance that was absent in this woman. I almost began to believe that she had tricked me again with another elaborate diversion, another false trail."

"Almost?"

"Yes, until last night's dream."

Li, again, wore a puzzled look. Ma smiled his gentle youthful smile and twirled his mustache tips. "I'm sure the attacker is the swordsman who intervened when I cornered the shamaness's phantom in Xia-zhou. He must be on board for her. She is here—somewhere."

"But why does this swordsman want to attack you?"

"Maybe he is trying to protect the shamaness and knows I'm after her."

"Does she have many enemies?" asked Li, thinking about his own situation when he was at Court. Ma's face went pale, almost matching the mist that was swirling over the craggy cliff tops.

There was activity on the ship as the captain had ordered the crew to clear the foredeck. The river was unpredictable and he wanted to make sure there was no delay when it was necessary to lower the sail and go to the oars for more control. The open foredeck, between the bow and the deckhouse, was designed for four long oars, two on each side, worked in a standing position. Li and Ma found their position less secluded and moved off the bow.

"Come to my cabin." Then Li hesitated. "But then I've also had a midnight visitor."

Ma's brow wrinkled.

"Upon first consideration, it seems that mine was gentler than yours." A faint smile played over Li's lips and then vanished. "But further thought might prove that its damage was greater."

"Come, we'll go to my cabin. Lao-huang can catch anything on two legs or not that might try to listen in on our conversation."

Ma, like Li, had one of the few deck cabins. Since ships that plied the upper reaches of the Long River had long flat foredecks to rig oars and cables for towing when the rapids in the Gorges got too low or too dangerous, this left limited space for the deckhouse.

Lao-huang greeted them as they entered Ma's cabin.

"Master, we need your help again," said Ma. Lao-huang chattered away.

"Elder brother Li and I must speak of very serious matters. We need you to stand on guard against any being that might want to overhear us." Lao-huang chattered and jumped up and down, then leaped to the only porthole in the cabin and sat in the middle of it. Ma and Li smiled.

"I think you have answered the question of the swordsman's identity." Ma's words startled Li. Ma offered him a seat cushion and positioned himself on the bed mat. He leaned closer to Li.

"I was pursuing the wrong direction, looking for her protectors. It's her enemy—a very deadly enemy."

Li remained silent.

"The Shamaness Luo saved the Emperor's life through the use of her powers to discover an assassination plot. But after the plot was revealed and foiled, she disappeared." Ma paused. He looked around the room, then continued. "Your remark on deck made me realize that she has another pursuer, that swordsman—he has no intentions to bring her back to Court for she is far too dangerous to his masters. Those who seek the blood of the Son of Heaven have sent him."

"And," continued Li as he picked up Ma's line of reasoning, "this group is very powerful and their chosen assassin is likewise a formidable opponent. It is just possible that this formidable opponent is capable of the 'impossible.'"

"This cut on my chest confirms your reasoning."

"This . . . this assassin, then, must be part swordsman and part sorcerer," Li wondered aloud. "And if he is traveling up the Long River on the trail of your shamaness, then perhaps he is the swordsman who killed my boatman," said Li, realizing the truth of this insight and the accuracy of Ah Wu's speculation about Old Zhou's murderer.

"It is a possibility. With my sword or my fists there are few within the Empire I fear. But I am no sorcerer. As you can see, without Lao-huang I could not track Luo nor could I have risen from my pallet to greet you this morning."

"Then we are bound even closer as we add together the death of Ah Wu, a fellow wandering blade, to that of my boatman, who was the victim of a hired assassin. And I am also no sorcerer," said Li.

Ma considered Li's words.

"Last night," Li continued, "my assailant was not the same. I woke up several times with the feeling of a presence in my cabin. But, of course, when I lit my lamp there was nothing. This morning, however, I found a piece of scented white silk on the writing table."

Ma watched Li closely as he spoke. The older man was deeply troubled. Ma could see the pain in those large luminous eyes.

"It is not an ordinary piece of silk," Li paused as he drew a cloud of pure whiteness from his sleeve. "It has one of my poems inscribed upon it."

He opened it and handed it to Ma.

"How can this be?" puzzled the young swordsman as he recognized the deft brush strokes of a woman's hand.

"She clung to 'Li Bo's' poetry. Has she now returned in spirit to identify me with these traces of ink?"

"This is uncanny, but I watched everyone who boarded last night. She was not among them."

"Even if she were, why play this game? And how could she have gained entrance to my cabin which was locked as securely as yours?"

Ma held the silk close to his nose.

"It is not her scent," said Li.

"Tonight, when they are all asleep," said Ma, standing and looking out the small cabin porthole, "I must search the ship and find out who is on board."

"The night will give this assassin the advantage."

"Yes, as it gave your visitor," said Ma.

Li smiled. How ironic—both of them haunted by "ghosts."

"We have little to lose. Either they get us in bed or we get them on our feet," said Ma with his sheathed sword raised in defiance.

～ 19 ～

"From now on we will dock in the evening. The river is too unpredictable to navigate on moonless nights. We are hoping to have a native pilot come aboard to guide us across the New Rapids section," the captain said. He shoveled more rice into his already full mouth.

The morning air was cool and fresh. The wind continued to blow steadily from the east. Li picked at a bean dish, and Ma drained his bowl of warm rice gruel. The galley was cramped, and it took two turns to get everyone fed since only five people could sit in it at once.

"Well, our other two passengers don't seem to need food. They didn't appear for breakfast," said the captain into his wine cup. He drained the amber liquid and offered a pot to his two passengers. Ma held out his cup and Li followed. "Ahh, a fresh cup of Floating Ants wine, just the thing on a chilly early spring day!" said Ma. His eyes twinkled.

The captain laughed, "Yes, nothing like fine wine and a full stomach." He poured the unfiltered amber wine, rice husks and all, into and over the sides of both men's cups. Li smiled as he thought that for a thin man the captain definitely had the manners of a glutton.

"I've been on the river many years now. I always find my passengers almost as interesting as the Long River itself."

"In what way, captain?" asked Ma, draining the last of his Floating Ants. Li watched Ma drink and tossed down the contents of his cup. He coughed as several pieces of rice husk lodged in his throat. The captain filled Li's cup.

"Drink, drink, it'll clear your passageway," he said as he gestured with his hands. "Our other two passengers are interesting," the captain continued. "The woman has the bearing of a man and the man that of a woman."

"Are they the only other passengers?" Li said between his coughing. He tried some rice gruel instead of more wine to clear his throat.

"Why yes. With the rebellion, passage up the river has declined. But I still find my passengers most interesting."

"Do you know what the other two passengers do for a living?" asked Ma. Li thought his question was a bit too obvious, but the captain, pouring more Floating Ants, was oblivious to all but his amber liquid.

"I have a game I play with myself. I try to guess the occupations of my passengers and their reasons for traveling the river."

"And what conclusion have you come to regarding our co-passengers?"

"The woman must be some sort of entertainer. Few women travel alone on this stretch of the Long River." He leaned closer to them. "Many tales about the Gorges . . . you know. Only a woman who is an entertainer has the courage to do it."

"How's that?" said Ma, who was having difficulty following the captain's "logic."

"Well, they just consider the risks to be part of the general entertainment of life—like their occupation. I had one that sat right out there on the end of the bow," the captain gestured vaguely in the direction of the bow, "when we went through the most dangerous rapids. Got my crew all worked up; thought she was some evil spirit—bunch of grandmothers. We almost lost the ship, my ship!"

"But you only saw our female passenger as she came on deck last night," said Li, quite amazed at the boatman's reasoning. "How could you tell so much?"

"Oh, I heard her last night in her cabin practicing her voices. She must be a singer."

"Practicing her voices?" wondered Ma aloud.

"Yes, first she starts in a young voice, almost sounds like a chant. Then a deep voice, coming up from nowhere."

"Then what?" asked Ma, surprised by the captain's knowledge of his guest after only one night.

"Then . . . ." the captain had to concentrate. "Oh, nothing, just silence. Guess she got tired and fell asleep. After all, what do I know? I don't go standing outside my passengers' doors at night." With that, he got up and staggered out of the galley.

Li and Ma finished their meal and returned to the foredeck. The work there was completed and the crew went off to other chores. A few, gathered at the stern, were fishing. The wind was still steady, the sail full, but the mist continued to edge its way down the cliffs toward the river. The cliffs seemed to be moving in on the river. The world, thought Li, is growing smaller; will it be any more manageable?

"An entertainer? Well, I guess he's close," laughed Ma.

"What about these two voices he heard?" asked Li, back in the world aboard ship.

"She has a spirit contact, a guardian spirit that she serves. No doubt she was calling the spirit and it was responding—she is, after all, a shamaness."

"Then our captain, without knowing it, has further confirmed her presence."

"Exactly," said Ma, with a smile. "I don't know who her guardian is, but it must be a powerful spirit."

"I wonder," said Li thinking aloud.

"What?"

"Would that spirit be the equal of the Blood Dragon?"

"It's an interesting idea, but putting that question to her would reveal that we know her identity," said Ma, closely watching Li's reaction.

"Yes, yes, of course. But if she is so powerful, how do you plan to get her back to the Court?"

Ma looked off to the boulder-choked shore, then up into the descending mist. He remained silent for a while, then observed, "The captain will have to slow down if those vapors continue to descend." He turned to Li, "Tonight, elder brother, we will get to the bottom of all this. Now let's go get some real wine and come back to enjoy this ever-changing world we are sailing through."

They started to move off when Ma paused a moment. "I'm not sure how I'm going to get her back. She could probably just vanish right in front of me when I confront her."

"Then you will need someone who has a way with women," smiled Li and walked off toward Ma's cabin. Ma followed with a grin on his lips. *Li seems to be coming to terms with his losses,* he thought.

A frosty, gray light continued to bathe the river as the world seemed to crowd in on their solitary ship. Ma and Li enjoyed an afternoon of drinking and verse rhyming. Ma put it all to music and Li accompanied him on his silk-stringed *jheng*. However, the first pluck of Li's *jheng* stopped Ma. Li continued through the first verse, lost in the music, before he noticed that Ma was not accompanying him.

"Younger brother," Li stopped, "I'm sorry. I'm not up to form, ever since . . . ."

"No," Ma cut in. "Your playing is fine. It's your instrument."

"This?" Li held up the rectangular *jheng*. "It's rather ordinary. The order for my banishment didn't leave us much time to pack. I was in prison and the next day out on the road. Ah Wu—" Li stopped for a moment and gazed at the wooden instrument, his heart saddened at the mention of his good friend. "Yes, Ah Wu hastily packed the old traveling *jheng* and not the better one given by a prince of the royal house. Ah Wu wasn't too well versed in the musical arts . . . ."

"I'm not making myself clear. The beauty of its tone has befuddled my mind."

Li's eyes opened wide. "The beauty of its tone," he seemed to repeat the words as if in a dream. "But this, this is just an average *jheng*. There is nothing at all special about it."

"Really, Brother Li you're being too modest. While it certainly looks ordinary, the wood must be of some very rare quality. I have never heard tones so Heavenly."

Li plucked at the strings. Yes, the tone was magnificent—he hadn't been paying attention. This was not the tone of his old *jheng*. Strange. Could it be the effect of the river and the moisture of the mist on the wood? thought Li. "Yes, the tone is quite marvelous. But I don't understand it; this is not its usual tone. Could it be the river?"

"It's possible. But perhaps it is the influence of what it contains," Ma said, clearly referring to the Dragon Pool Sword hidden within. "Whatever it is, let's take special pleasure in its voice while we have it." He laughed. "Who knows what tomorrow may bring."

Li lifted his wine cup, "Let's hope for even better wine and that this instrument ultimately lends itself to our successes!"

The two continued for the rest of the afternoon composing verses and setting them to the wonderful new tone of Li's *jheng*. Li avoided trying to create new poetry. He knew that would be fruitless, and instead, did variations on his older verses and those of poets he admired.

During the afternoon, the captain awoke and had the crew reef the sail to reduce their speed as the mist continued its descent to river level. Later, as the evening darkened the mist, they moved closer to the shore looking for suitable anchorage. After mooring in a small cove, they had their dinner. As usual, the two "strange" passengers did not appear for the group meal.

Ma, helped by Lao-huang, had engaged the captain in a round of drinking. At the end of the meal both men and the "Immortal" monkey, staggered out of the galley and went below decks. Ma was invited to inspect the ship from stem to stern.

Li smiled as he watched Ma get the captain's unwitting cooperation in his plan to search the ship. Soon they would know exactly who was aboard. Most of all, mused Li, the mystery of Chen's disappearance might be solved if they found her hiding. They had anchored far enough offshore that it was difficult to escape the ship. Therefore, thought Li, anyone who has been onboard should still be here when Ma and the captain made their rounds. Yet, Li realized that whoever or whatever could enter locked cabins and even dreams without a trace could easily traverse the distance to shore.

Another rice husk caught in his throat. It brought him out of his ruminations and back to his cup of Floating Ants. He spat the husk out and left the galley. Vile wine, he thought, fit only for river captains and their crews.

The crew turned in, leaving only a few lanterns lit. Li walked along the deck and settled in where he and Ma had been drinking in the afternoon. The charcoal brazier had died out. He set to work rekindling the fire. Night had veiled the ship. Reflecting off the thickening white mist, the glow of the bow lantern cast a soft light on Li and his wine-heating efforts. The insects chattered on the shore as the frogs sought out their meals. Occasionally an owl hooted from farther inland. Then a gibbon's cry broke the relative quiet. A sense of grief arose within Li, but before he could think of Ah Wu . . . .

"May I join you in a cup of wine?" a soft, clear voice asked from behind his back. He rose and beheld an ordinary looking woman in a light cream-colored robe. Trimmed in brown, the sleeve and neck borders were embroidered with small golden mountain flowers. Her radiant black hair was swept up from her face and held in back by a single auburn lacquered hairpin—certainly no courtly fashion but rather a simple country style. There was no doubt she was Chinese, with her gentle, delicate features, jade white complexion, long graceful neck, and almond-shaped eyes.

"Please, I would be delighted with such charming company. The night can be so lonely and so sad," Li said and bowed. He took her out held thin, elegant hand and helped her to Ma's cushion. The touch of her hand sent a surge of warm *chi* energy through him.

"The mist makes our hearts so much clearer, and the silence of the night can be so calming."

Li nodded as he thought of the gibbon and how its howl had broken the night's silence and so shaken Ah Wu at the Dream Temple. But that was so long ago, almost another life. He turned to attend to the brazier for a moment. This visit was a complete surprise to him. Ma was supposed to be snooping around her door and here she was in front of him.

"Sir, I could not but overhear you and your friend this afternoon, singing and playing."

"Oh, I apologize for disturbing you. It will not happen again."

"What a shame, for I dearly enjoyed your verses. And the music of your *jheng* was as if it came directly from Heaven. The verse seemed very familiar, and that is why I was so curious to meet you this evening."

"You've heard it before, or at least some of it before?"

"Yes, but I couldn't make out the words from my cabin below deck."

"Allow me." Li placed his *jheng* before him and played and sang some of his better-known poems; their themes were that of lost friendship. The night sounds from the shore ceased. Perhaps, Nature was also showing its appreciation. A gentle smile formed on the woman's lips, then a single tear. Li stopped and poured a cup of hot clear wine. They toasted the mist, then the night, then the river, before she interrupted. "You are the master poet, Li Bo."

Li smiled. He had always relished recognition from those deeply moved by his verse. Even now, having lost his boatman Old Zhou, his faithful companion Ah Wu, troubled by his banishment and the mystery of Miss Chen, he still found himself enjoying this brief recognition.

Yet, something had changed. Here, anchored offshore, surrounded by the mist and the night, and in the presence of this strange woman, he dimly felt a sense of completeness, something he seldom felt at Court or, for that matter, anywhere else. He sipped another cup of wine and smiled as he listened to her continue.

"I have long held a great respect for your poetry. It is an honor to meet you."

"But alas, under these circumstances it is hard for me to chant and sing," Li's mood had swung.

"Sir, why such deep despair?"

"You understand its depth?"

Compassion shone in her eyes, which were as black as the finest ink but sparkled like the brightest stars. Staring into her eyes was like roaming the universe—pacing the Void, out beyond the realm of human concerns and sufferings.

"I sense that you are an unusual woman," he said, shifting his gaze into the empty wine cup he held.

The hint of a smile, like the glimmer of the moon slipping out from the clouds, brightened her face just before she spoke. "There is little hidden from someone like you."

"Whether we converse with the Yin or Yang realms or those beyond, the perception required for such communication sets us apart from others. Yet, sometimes such perception can be a curse," said Li.

She smiled in agreement and in acknowledgement that Li Bo knew who she was.

"In the realms of pure perception, where both of us find refuge, there is no need for physical masks to hide behind," she said. Her smile continued to warm their conversation.

Reaching into her sleeve, she drew out a small brass mirror. As she looked into it, her face transformed back to its original form, like the difference between a barren, spent winter landscape and the fresh vitality of a spring pond. Her hair fell down along her shoulders, a gentle waterfall enfolding such beauty. Li found himself composing a poem to the spell cast by her presence. It was like old times, beauty spontaneously igniting the poetry within him. Had her presence transformed him? There was little doubt in Li's mind that she was a shamaness, one of unusual talent, power, and beauty.

"We are now truly face to face, master Li."

"Am I truly transformed by your presence?"

"Transformation is a natural occurrence. You must learn to appreciate change and thus return to Nature. We all pass through the great transformation. Yet look around at Nature; there is no hesitancy and no end."

"But I fear loss—the loss of my youth, my position, my poetry, and my family and friends."

"Yet that very fear is the root of your loss." As she spoke those words, Li's awareness of his fear seized the poetry and cut it off.

"Lose your fear and your poetry returns."

"How am I to address you?"

With a graceful lowering of her head, she said, "The Shamaness Luo Jhu-yun—indebted to your pure visions."

"Please, my so-called vision has led me to a death-sentence exile." Li refilled her cup.

"Why do you speak like this? This is not the great Li Bo that I have heard so much of in the capital."

Li's face lit up for a moment and he smiled. "So they still mention my name there?"

"Do you think, even in the capital, your genius is so easily forgotten?"

"They only remember me when it comes to revenge and hatred," Li said. He swallowed another cup of wine.

"The sentiments of men are small when compared to the grandeur of the Way. One learns to ignore them. Your present problems will pass."

"I am old and too much has recently occurred for me to reclaim the lofty position I once held."

"Should the meanness of courtly life really be your ambition? Master Li Bo, I owe you something for what your poetry has given me, for your understanding of a woman's feelings and position in this society. Let us take up this poem of yours regarding your trip in a dream to Mount Tian-mu. It is one of my favorites," she said and smiled. "Let us sing it together."

Li nodded. Not sure what her point was, he began playing a tune to accompany their chanting of the poem. The poem took the reader on a mystical journey through a mountain thunderstorm over a real mountain, but from Li's imagined perspective of a Daoist Immortal who could fly through and above the storm and over the mountain.

As they chanted the poem, however, Luo's pure, clear voice drew Li to a new level of realization. He realized that they were actually flying over Mount Tian-mu. He saw its sunlight, the clouds growing dark, the wind rising; and he felt the rain against his face. The thunder reverberated against his eardrums, and the flashes of lightning shocked his eyes! He looked down and saw the earth shake and crumble. The trees bent in the wind, and all the fabulous beasts he had imagined played and frolicked below.

The next minute, he seemed to blink and he found himself sitting across from the smiling shamaness.

"This then, Li Bo, is the power of the Way and the ability of your poetic vision to be in accord with it. Would you give all this up for some musty Court robes? Heed what I am to tell you."

She stopped. Li watched her, his mind still whirling from the journey they had just taken. Her eyes half closed, as if in a trance, she said, "I see two beings from the *Yin* realm that followed you here on this ship. They want something from you. I don't know what it is, for it is hidden from my vision, but their master must never get it. Otherwise, great calamity will befall this dynasty. Your true road transcends anything the Court could offer you. Consider clearly the path you follow." Her eyes opened and sparkled as she looked at him.

For a moment, Li could not say anything; thoughts continued to whirl and flash as if he were composing verse. The Dream Temple quest was legitimate. The Dragon Pool Sword must be delivered to Mount Wu.

"The Blood Dragon," he blurted out, "how do I deal with it? It has killed my faithful companion and driven off, or worse, a young woman whose only crime was her passion for my poetry. I have an ancient sword that the Blood Dragon wants and is willing to kill for."

"I have little knowledge of these things; my visions have limits, but I sense your danger. A Blood Dragon is a fearful monster. It is a dragon not yet fully formed and thus not a benevolent creature. Surviving on the blood of humans, it has the power to make slaves of its victims. These ghosts that are following you could possibly be its victims."

"How do I defeat the monster?"

"It is difficult for humans to defeat such a creature, but I can give you something to protect you from its ghosts." She drew a slip of yellow paper from her sleeve. "Do you have a brush?"

Li leaned over and got the brush that he and Ma were using to record verse. The evening remained calm with the mist and water caressing the boat. The warmth of the wine and brazier made Li relax for the first time since the grand dinner in Xia-zhou.

The shamaness crossed her legs in a meditation position and straightened her back. As she began to shake, she entered a trance state. Her eyes rolled back exposing the whites. She took the brush into her left hand and turned the paper sideways. In one continuous long flourish, she wrote in Daoist talisman style. The talisman could not be deciphered by humans, but held great consequence for all beings in the *Yin* realm.

"Your wine has assisted me in creating a very powerful charm." She smiled and handed him the slip. "While it will not destroy the ghosts, it will make them so uncomfortable that they will loathe frequenting your vicinity. Carry it with you always. But remember, it is not powerful enough to overcome their master, the Blood Dragon."

"Thank you, but I must ask what will destroy the Blood Dragon?" Li asked taking the yellow slip of paper carefully into his hands.

"I am greatly moved by your poetry and the sensitivity it shows my gender. Nevertheless, what you ask, the destruction of another being, is something I am pledged to forsake. I will defend myself when necessary, but no more. Remember, for all beings, death, the great transformation, is a renewal and not an end."

Li's first thought was to object, that such a hideous beast deserved to die, but he restrained himself. Impressed by the depth of her compassion, he accepted her refusal.

"I must ask a favor from you," said the shamaness.

"Please, whatever my meager ability can do to assist."

"The one you have recently befriended should not know of our meeting and friendship, as such knowledge will complicate all our relationships."

"You mean, Ma Ssu-ming?"

"The swordsman, whatever his name," she said, then smiled and took a sip of wine as if to savor Li's surprise.

"You know!" Li said with a start.

Her eyes sparkled. "He is an obvious fellow—most men are."

"Ma is a good friend and I must respect such relationships."

"Are we not also friends, Li Bo?" Although her mouth moved to form the question, Li only noticed her eyes—they were speaking directly to him. They were equal to the wonders of the night sky and they reminded him of her power to bring forth, if only for this moment, the poetic powers damned up deep within him.

Li smiled and raised his wine cup. "To the mountains, mists, and moon, the most steadfast of friends—never a demand, but constant in their companionship." He tossed back the full cup. The shamaness laughed and drained her cup.

"I must return to my cabin before your friend sees us. Accord with the Way, Li Bo."

Li reached for his refilled cup to toast her, but as he raised it found only the swirling frosty mist.

— 20 —

Ma, with Lao-huang clasped to his neck, and the captain moved as quietly as they could, given the amount of Floating Ants wine they had consumed.

"This is the entertainer's cabin," said the captain, bumping his head against the door. The ship's insides seemed to be moving back and forth as shadows and light moved over the network of beams and bulkheads that supported the hull. Lao-huang was close to passing out. Ma nudged him awake. Without Lao-huang's alarm, they would be easy targets for whatever might prowl below deck. Ma took the lantern from the captain's unsteady hand and brought the inside of the ship to an even keel.

"Let's see if she'll join us." The captain's voice was slurred as he attempted to knock at Luo's door. Ma intercepted the knock, which was nowhere near the door.

"Ah, not right now, we have just begun the tour," Ma said, trying to keep his wits about him. "Let's find a nice spot down here and invite her to join us. After all, it is impolite to join a woman in her quarters."

"Really? Well, I knew you were a gentleman. It's a pity that I never got to study the teachings of the great sages like Confucius and his kind."

"Ah, yes, Confucius. You've heard of him?" Ma asked with a smile.

"Well, I'm not an illiterate, you know."

"Oh, I would never imply such a thing. Confucius, as you know, always insisted on asking a woman, especially one as talented as this entertainer, to some nice, cozy, private spot to consider her various gifts," Ma said, unable to restrain his grin.

"Ah, it must be wonderful to be so well educated. Quickly then, forward. There are several choice spots I must show you."

"Make sure we see them all," Ma laughed.

The three moved down the passageway through the next bulkhead. A shadow moved forward toward the shamaness's door, but the sound of footsteps coming down the ladder from topside sent it back into the darkness.

The shamaness reached her door and unlocked it. As it swung open, she stepped carefully over the "well" character she had inscribed on the doorsill. The shadow was not so careful and as it rushed forward stepped squarely in the center of the character. A poison-tipped dart flew toward the shamaness as the shadow plummeted downward. It grazed her hand as she whirled around protecting her face. Blood outlined the thin cut.

She knew instinctively what to do. Kicking the door shut and bolting it, she sat on her meditation cushion and scrawled a talisman with her blood on the yellow paper in front of her. There were only heartbeats of consciousness left. Burning the paper over a cup of wine, she managed to drink most of the concoction before she fainted. There was no time, however, to seal the well. If the shadow was skillful enough—he might escape.

***

"The sword?" a gravelly voice growled at Chen, who just returned from her haunting of Li Bo's quarters.

"Not yet."

The tatami-floored room shone red as the Blood Dragon's eyes, peering through a man's pale face, turned to flame.

"You have a plan?"

"Yes. He must have hidden it. I will make him fall in love with me and get him to show it to me."

The tatami took on a more natural hue when the Blood Dragon paced back and forth considering her words. The room was simply furnished and clean, which made the unpleasant fish odor even more noticeable. The small house stood over the river, and the trap door behind the Blood Dragon led directly to its natural habitat.

"How long will this take?" the Blood Dragon demanded, snapping Chen back to their interview.

"Within the week we will have . . . ah . . . ," stuttered Chen, a blush suffusing her cheeks.

"Ha! A fast worker, eh? You think you have what it takes to lure this old poet into your bed?"

Chen did not answer. She tried to stifle the thoughts of hatred that were storming her consciousness. She had to be careful, for she still didn't know if the monster could read those thoughts.

"You have your week. But of course the alternative, since you have now provided me with a solution to this problem, is me." A hideous smile played over the monster's face. "If you fail, I will take your place in bed with this human . . . and I have never failed." The monster laughed in its horrible high-pitched voice.

Chen bowed and reappeared on Li's ship. As soon as she neared Li's cabin, she felt it. Something reached out and grabbed her stomach. She felt as if she were going to vomit. How could this be? she thought. Ghosts don't get sick, do they? By the time she was at his door, the feeling was overwhelming. She backed off and retreated to the deck. The wave of nausea dispersed. The light in Li's cabin went out, but she did not move. Sitting on the stern deck, she watched the mist reflect off the lantern and thought of his poetry. Her tears made quiet circles in the Long River.

***

"You heard?" Su-lu asked in a disconcerting, gentle female voice.

"Yes, master," the voice from the shadows responded.

"Well, hopefully, you still remember your friend—if nothing else. Does the plan have merit, or is it another example of stupid human emotionalism?"

"I believe it is an apt plan. He is vulnerable to such a woman—especially at this time."

"Oh, you think this woman is beautiful?" Su-lu asked in a mocking tone.

"Of course not, but to this poet she is attractive."

"Interesting." The voice had changed back to the gentle female tone. "Humans do amuse me so. What would I do without them?"

Ah Wu's dislike for Chen had changed to utter hatred. He used what little control that was available to him in his new circumstance to evaluate his course of action. Denouncing Chen's despicable plan to gain the immediate satisfaction of seeing her destroyed by Su-lu, risked an abrupt confrontation between Su-lu and Li Bo. If his own experience was any judge, Li was no match.

No, let Chen try. That would gain him at least a week, Ah Wu thought. In that time, he might be able to restore his strength enough to communicate with Li. Although his resistance to Su-lu's repeated attempts to learn the sword's hiding place, by feigning loss of memory, had succeeded, the effort had further seriously weakened his mental powers. In his new form, Ah Wu had only those mental powers to rely on. In many ways, it was a new experience for him. He was also perplexed by Su-lu's powers. They seemed far more profound than that of a "typical" ghost.

***

Air streamed up past the shadow as the albino swordsman continued to fall. He knew that he had fallen into the shamaness's Mystic Well and would continue to fall forever. If she had closed the well, there was no escape. He had to act fast. His fingers fumbled for the metal case around his neck. Pulling it out of his robe, he worked his finger into it and touched the orb.

"Cold-hearted orb, ruler of the darkness," he chanted as he fell, "cast your net. Find one to replace me in this endless rush through the Void."

The sailor's scream woke the whole ship. When the lantern in the crew's quarters was lit, they found him lying in his hammock eyes wide open. Aside from the blood trickling out of his nose, there were no marks on him. The crew was frightened. They were milling around outside the cabin when the captain stumbled onto the deck.

"What are you old women doing?"

"Captain, 'Big Nose' is dead! He screamed that he was falling before he died. Captain, what does this mean?" they shouted in unison.

The captain was drunk and began to laugh. The crew grew uneasier.

"Yes, I'm possessed too. The ghosts of myriads of floating ants are bobbing around in my mind, or is it my gut?"

He paused to consider exactly where the wine had gone in his body. If it went to his stomach, why was his head feeling the effects? Not able to solve this problem, he turned to the next one.

"My advice? Wrap him up nicely, with some heavy rocks, say a prayer, or better yet pour some Floating Ants over him." The captain sat on the railing and added, "No, that would be a waste of good wine. Better yet, drink a toast to a gallant sailor and dump him overboard. But check first to make sure it's deep enough."

With those words of sage advice, the captain passed out on deck. Thus with their conversation at an end, the crew wrapped the body, ignored a suggestion that they include the captain, and dumped it overboard. A pot of wine was opened, and they attempted to drown their fears among the Floating Ants. A little while later, they also passed out on deck.

About a half an hour earlier, Ma had emerged on deck after his tour with the captain. He stopped when he noticed Li rushing out on deck. He was throwing a long garment into the river. Ma stepped out of sight behind a piled stack of bamboo tracking cables. Li was getting rid of his Court robes. After looking around, Li returned to his cabin.

Ma nudged his sleeping monkey. "Hey, Lao-huang, wake up."

Lao-huang stretched and kept on sleeping.

"You're never there when I need you," scolded Ma. He wondered what Li was up to. It seems, Ma considered, something has turned him against the idea of returning to Court. Or, perhaps—he smiled, feeling the influence of the Floating Ants—perhaps, he felt those robes were out of style and decided to acquire a new wardrobe. Ma figured he should go and find out . . . after he rested a bit.

As Li entered his cabin, he passed Chen's ghostly form, which was invisible to those in the *Yang* realm. She was coming out of his room, after leaving another white silk poem. The encounter with Li brought her to her knees, paralyzed by a wave of nausea. Chen was barely able to make herself appear at the bow. She retched clear fluid, like that of her crossbow wound, over the side of the ship.

Ah Wu had just returned to the ship and remained in the shadows behind some bamboo lath piles on the foredeck, watching Chen. He could not figure out what had happened to her. Since he had only been a ghost for a short time, it did not strike him as strange to see a ghost sick. Rather, he thought, leave it to a woman to figure out ways for wasting time. He had half a notion to march right down to Li's cabin and try to talk with him. However, he still had no idea how to cross to the *Yang* realm and communicate with its inhabitants. He was also aware that if he prematurely gave away his intentions, there would be no second chance. Waiting until he was better acquainted with his ghostly situation and his adversary was a better tactic—he had always recognized patience as a powerful ally.

***

Near dawn, a light rain began to fall. The mist retreated to the tops of the craggy cliffs, which now were a mixture of sandstone and yellow and white streaked limestone. The crew had woken early, dragged the captain into his bunk, and got the ship underway. But the death of "Big Nose" Lin was the major topic of conversation.

"It's the river."

"We're too near shore."

"No, we're not close enough, probably anchored right over some river spirit's cave."

"This mist, it's not normal for this time of year."

"This following wind is unusually strong, I wonder if the captain really knows where we are. We could be much farther up the river than he thinks."

"Too much wind for this time of year."

"And the farther up we are, the closer to Mount Wu."

"Mount Wu?"

"The home of a powerful rain spirit. They say that for more than a thousand years the ghosts of her lovers have roamed this river valley searching for her. She hates the sight of men, you know."

"This is too early in the trip for a death. I think we are under the influence of some very evil spirit, right now! Perhaps from the very start of the trip."

"And these passengers we are carrying. One of the strangest lots I've seen in a long time."

The crew, reduced to five men, shook their heads in agreement.

"By the depths of Hell you're right! And that evil spirit is me, your captain!"

The men all scrambled to stand up and move toward the railing.

"I don't run the Three Gorges with a crew of old hags. If you ladies can't handle the river then please leave—NOW!"

Most of the men had shipped with the captain for several years. He was one of the few captains on the Three Gorges route that had not lost a ship. They had stayed with him because of that and because of the money to be made transporting cargo on the most dangerous section of the Long River.

"You have to admit, Captain, Big Nose's death was very strange. It was as if he were attacked right in his hammock."

"No," piped up the cook, "as if he were attacked right in his sleep, in his very dreams! It has to be some sort of evil spirit."

He just got the words out of his mouth when the captain grabbed him and flung him overboard. The crew reacted just as quickly—for this was not the first time that the captain had expressed his displeasure with his men—one of the long oars reached the cook just in time to pull him out.

"Like I said, I'm the evil spirit on this ship and will feed any one of you to the river if I hear old women's talk. I don't have time for such nonsense!"

He turned and walked toward the bow to take a sounding. The crew knew he was right. This stretch of the river was unforgiving. The constant shifting of its rapids made it a graveyard for any ship that wasn't fully alert.

The captain hoped his display of anger would at least scare the crew. He was far from convinced that their fears were for naught. Yes, Big Nose's death was strange and so was the trip through the bowels of his ship with that fellow Ma last night. Though only part of his drunkenness was faked, he still could see that Ma was looking for something or someone. It had to be either the fellow in the bow compartment or the woman in the stern compartment. Or, he thought, a stowaway.

Ma is obviously a swordsman of high skill on some sort of mission, thought the captain. But for whom? He definitely has an air of command about him, maybe that of an official. Dealing with Ma would require care. The captain certainly did not want to be involved in government business; that would be worse than evil spirits.

Li, the captain reflected, seems very much what he says he is, a foolish old poet who got involved in Court affairs and has received his reward—a slow death in the malarial mists of Yunnan. The captain smiled. The ancient philosopher Chuang-tze was right: it is certainly better to be a live turtle dragging one's tail through the mud of the Long River than a stuffed shell decorating the Emperor's throne room. He had to laugh aloud.

The sound of the water crashing on the rocks, somewhere ahead in the mist, abruptly brought him back to the river. They had reached the Yellow Ox Gorge.

"Rocks! Rocks dead ahead! Drop the sail! Rig the oars! Now! Or die!" he screamed.

The crew reacted. The sail crashed down as the blow from a broadsword cut its main line. The four oarsmen set their oars and were in position. They awaited the captain's orders. The rocks broke through a wall of mist that had dropped across the river. Directly ahead, the river raged spewed foaming white water.

"Oars! Helmsman, take her out to the middle!"

The crew blanched with fear. The middle! Who knows what's out there? He must still be drunk. We must pull for the shore.

"Oars!" the captain bellowed above the raging water.

Shocked, the men rowed for their lives. Slowly the rocks seemed to change course and slide to the starboard. The captain grabbed the tiller from the helmsman and pulled for all he was worth. His arm and neck muscles seemed ready to explode from his body. The helmsman, recovered from the shock, joined the effort along with the cook.

The whole ship changed direction—straight down! The crew yelled and the captain laughed wildly. Li Bo was thrown from his writing table where he was examining a new white silk poem. Lao-huang flew toward the ceiling, screeching all the way. Ma was jarred from his bed mat, but managed to catch Lao-huang as he came down. The Shamaness Luo, still unconscious, was thrown to the other side of her cabin. In the front compartment, the albino swordsman, thrown from his hammock, landed on his feet.

The ship pitched up and leveled off as the crew was still rowing frantically. The captain, clinging to the rudder, yelled to the crew. "Good! Now we'll take her back near the shore, slowly. Keep rowing. Watch and listen for rocks. There could be more landslides."

As they moved toward the shore, the crewmen saw the rock slide that had created the new rapids. It extended from the shore out, near the middle of the river. If they had gone against the captain's orders and rowed toward the shore to go around the rapids, they would have piled head on into the rocks. The captain had heard the water rushing over the newly fallen rockslide to starboard and knew to avoid that course. The river had warned them not to take it lightly.

Nevertheless, they still uestioned how far the captain's sharp senses extend. The crew knew the river and they knew the captain. But would the captain's senses be sharp enough to detect danger in the realm of evil spirits? For the crew was convinced that their greatest danger lay not in the river, but in the uncharted *Yin* realm.

— 21 —

There was a knock at Li Bo's door. He put down the white silk poem, wiped the tears from his eyes with the sleeve of his light blue robe, and bid Ma to enter. The dim morning light masked Li's face, but Ma felt the mood.

"Another poem?"

Li looked up. He smiled weakly, but his eyes betrayed his true feelings.

"Yes. I gather you didn't find her last night?"

"There must be some reasonable explanation. Such things do not just appear out of the evening darkness. It is a piece of silk, made by humans and written on by a human hand with manmade brush and ink."

"Let me guess. In your search last night, there were only two other human inhabitants below deck. Neither would have any reason to do this, nor any knowledge of Chen, much less her handwriting."

Ma didn't answer. He didn't have to, Li was logically correct in his assumptions.

Li leaned back against the wall and read his own poem again. As he did, he followed the graceful strokes of what had to be Chen's writing. He could sense her sadness from the way the characters were formed. There was something deeply troubling her. It made no sense. He wondered if madness was his true destination.

As Li's face moved into the light, Ma could make out the lines and taut skin around the poet's eyes.

"Come, we should have a long, deep drink to consider these things. I tell you there is an explanation for everything in this world."

Li's face lit up for a moment. "You are still young. As you grow to my age, you will find explanations become less and less useful or even relevant. I can give you many explanations of why I've been banished, some even plausible. But what difference do they make? None. Dragon Pool Sword or not, I will die in banishment. And now, I must do it without the company of friends—this is the greatest punishment."

The wine was warm and Li drained several cups as Ma and Lao-huang watched him.

"Please, you are upset. That sword will win you a commutation of the banishment order. After you present it to the Emperor . . . ."

"My path no longer involves the Court. I will fulfill my agreement with the Dream Temple Immortal and deliver the sword to whatever spirits accept it on Mount Wu."

Ma remained silent trying to understand this sudden enthusiasm for the Dream Temple quest.

"But then that filthy Blood Dragon might drain the blood out of me far before I reach Mount Wu or the tomb the Emperor has chosen. I would enjoy seeing his plans disrupted."

"Please, no Blood Dragon is going to get you as long as I am around, and you will be received at Court with that sword, whether it is unlocked at Mount Wu or not. They will accept it as a sign from Heaven of their just rule."

"Ha, you! Just like all the young aristocrats at Court!"

Ma could smell the wine on Li's breath. It was obvious that he had begun drinking much earlier. Ma just smiled.

Li laughed. "You can't even handle a shamaness, who is probably not the equal of this beast that follows me. How are you going to deal with a Blood Dragon? At a flick of her wrist, the shamaness could turn you into a butterfly, and there would be nothing you could do about it."

"You seem to know this woman rather well," observed Ma as he finished off another cup of wine.

"I know well enough that you are not her match." Li smiled and downed another cup.

"Why did you throw your Court robes overboard this morning?"

Ma let his words hang, like a fishhook. He waited to see how Li would react. Only an eye movement, a twitch, the tensing of a facial muscle; Ma knew all the signs that would reveal a man's inner feelings, for a master swordsman is able to anticipate those feelings.

Was Li too clever? Ma would later wonder. The old poet simply passed out, right on his writing table. Ma had not anticipated that response. He put out the brazier and left.

***

Chen approached the mist-drenched shore, gliding quietly across the water till she alighted on the dark stony bank. An alligator lumbered out of the river, was obscured for a moment by the mist, and returned to view in the form of Chen's uncle dressed in his dirty funeral robe.

"You must be a fast one if you've managed to bed him already," the form said in a soft feminine voice. Chen bowed and rose, keeping her distance from the tall pale figure.

"Master, he has some strange spell about him. I cannot approach him without becoming severely ill."

"Then you have failed!"

Chen was stunned. Had the monster known this would happen and simply set her up to play the role of a fool? This would suit its character. The creature enjoyed seeing humans suffer. Perhaps humans had done something to it in a past life, something so cruel that now all it thinks of is to make them suffer. Or maybe the creature, like her uncle, was just evil.

"Now it is my turn!"

"No! I can do it and I will be more effective," Chen shouted before she could catch herself.

"What!" growled the creature in a deep male voice. "You dare defy me! You nothing!"

The monster raged—flames danced in its eyes. Chen had to say something quickly, or in an instant, she would no longer exist in any realm.

"See, I have proved my point," Chen said. She raised her head and walked directly toward her uncle's form.

The Blood Dragon was taken aback; no one had ever dared address the creature in such a tone. Chen continued. "You are too quick to anger. This human will easily get you so infuriated by his stupid sentimentality that you will destroy him with the flick of your finger. Then how will you accomplish your objective?"

The monster was silent. Its eyes had returned to their normal yellow hue as it listened.

"Master," Chen threw herself down before her uncle's form. "I exist only for your greatness. If that sword will enhance your power then I will get it for you. But I cannot let you lose it by following your hatred for humans."

"You are an unusual disciple," mused the Blood Dragon. "None have ever been so frank with me. Nor have any been brave enough to confront me in such a manner."

The figure in funeral white looked closely at the prostrate form at its feet.

"I will give you an antidote to whatever talisman or other puny human contrivance he is using. It will protect you, but you must be on guard. It could be that the shamaness you mentioned has some talent. Nothing that could match my powers, but she might be able to deal with such a weak spirit as yourself."

The Blood Dragon's grating laugh shook the stones on which Chen was still kneeling.

Chen kept her head down, for she could not control the grin that spread over her lips. She had fooled the monster. Now she had to leave with the antidote without alerting it to her true intentions.

"Rise and drink this," the monster commanded, holding out a small black porcelain bottle. Chen kept her head bowed, turned from the monster, and downed the contents. It was bitter, but the thought of being able to speak with Li Bo left a sweet aftertaste.

"Now get that sword!" growled the monster.

Chen vanished before the monster could see her face.

***

Ah Wu wanted to follow Chen back to Su-lu, but could not risk too many meetings in his weakened state. His hatred for both Su-lu and his disciple, Chen, festered, but he had to avoid the monster's powers to rebuild his own—he had begun to regain some control of his internal energy—what was left of it.

He remained invisible on the ship and watched his friend from a distance. As he thought over his life with Li Bo, his wife's image appeared to him. She was hanging from the roof beam in their house. Her long red wedding scarf had been neatly double looped over the rough-hewed log that was their home's central support. The message was clear: the other loop was an invitation to be with her in death as they were in life.

With the recent loss of their sons in the T'ang army encounters with Su-lu's Turkish tribes, Ah Wu's wife had lost any interest in the *Yang* realm. She had recently talked often about meeting her sons in the *Yin* realm, seeking to comfort them and seeking the comfort of reunion. Ah Wu had little to offer her in dissuading such sentiments. Newly retired from the military, Ah

Wu had also lived for his sons. He had met the news of their draft into the Imperial Border Guards with mixed emotions. On the one hand, the pride in his own distinguished career as an Imperial Border Scout extended to his sons, yet he also shared his wife's deep sense of impending loss.

Su-lu, his old warrior nemesis, still hadn't been destroyed. His ferocious attacks continued to range up and down the Western border regions. When the news of their sons' death in an engagement with Su-lu's forces arrived, Ah Wu felt a profound sense of responsibility. He blamed himself for not being able to end Su-lu's reign of terror. A wave of resignation washed over him and he found himself wishing to leave all the suffering behind and join his family in the peace of the *Yin* realm.

Yet, he reflected, Fate seemed to have other plans. As he moved forward to mount that empty red loop next to his wife, an officer entered his home. Ah Wu moved out of the main room and into the entranceway.

Snapping to attention, not being able to see into the main room, the officer handed Ah Wu an official document. "Commander, by order of his Imperial Majesty, the Son of Heaven, you are commanded to reconstitute your Imperial Border Scout unit and report to the front. Sir, we are moving on Su-lu. He has been boxed in the Valley of the Shadows to the west of here."

There was no hesitation. Ah Wu returned the salute and called his servants. After a brief burial ceremony for his wife, Ah Wu tied on three white armbands and rode off into battle. Many of Su-lu's troops died in the following weeks, but the murderer of his family still managed to elude Ah Wu's vengeance.

Listening to the water flow past the gorge runner, Ah Wu smiled, thinking how the paths dictated by one's fate run in maddening circles. Although he turned from the *Yin* realm with his family, his path had still led there, and he was still alone facing

Su-lu—in whatever form. Yet there was still a purpose to his life; there was still his responsibility to Li Bo. And he knew that in that friendship there was great strength.

***

The day passed uneventfully as the ship had managed to wend its way through the Yellow Ox Gorge rapids. It was a boulder-strewn stretch of water that could be very dangerous when the river was low. They approached it slowly, maneuvering with both oars and reefed sail around it. yet there were still other rapids ahead, so the crew had to keep a constant sharp watch. The mist was gradual in its move down the sides of the cliffs. The captain was moving slower and had posted lookouts. Landslides were common throughout the Gorges due to the limestone and sandstone composition of the cliffs. Though they could range as high as 3,000 feet above the river, they were geologically unsound.

Li fished off the port bow. He had decided to keep away from Ma.

Ma's commitment was to "his" Emperor, not to friendship. And "his" Emperor is the one who has condemned me to this banishment—a Chinese Emperor. So it was as usual with the Chinese—friendships served political expediency. No wonder the shamaness had fled the capital; people who are sensitive to the Way are sensitive to all relationships. She transcends the simple-mindedness of the Chinese aristocratic rulers. Ma, like the rest of the Court, befouls these relationships and betrays the Way with the deceits of politics, of self-interest . . . The purity of the shamaness's character allowed the poetry to return within me, if only briefly. Perhaps there is hope. It is with her that I must associate—it is to her that I pledge my loyalty and the Dragon Pool Sword.

Li's fishing line trailed in the murky waters as the ship continued west up the Long River into the unrelenting dangers of the Gorges.

At the stern, Ma played badly at his three-string lute. While Li didn't manage a single bite all day, Ma's lute stayed out of tune. Lao-huang got into a shouting match with some of the wild monkeys roaming the shoreline. The crew found this amusing. However, when Li and Ma no lonnger appeared for any meals, the crew became upset. They were on edge, sensitive to anything out of the ordinary.

The ship also kept to its routine and anchored at night. The captain, however, added a slight change by posting a rotating armed guard on deck throughout the night. Speculation among the crew was that the captain had finally come to his wits by admitting that some sort of evil was following the ship. This, of course, was not at all the captain's thinking, for he was a much more rational man.

From where they had anchored, the Yellow Ox Gorge could still be seen. As the light faded, the cliffs and mountains, which stood row upon row like a folding fan, disappeared. Legend has it that thousands of years ago, the Yellow Ox assisted the Xia Emperor Yu in controlling the waters. It is popularly believed that the Yellow Ox, to continually remind mankind what it had accomplished, took great boulders and deposited them in the river so men would worship it at this gorge.

Li had ignored this scenic spot and settled down in his cabin. The door and porthole were locked. His dagger was next to his side, and the talisman was on a leather thong around his neck. He was at the small writing desk reading the silk poems that Chen had left when a gust of wind blew out his lamp. Once he managed to relight it, he found he was not alone. A third white silk poem was on the desk, but this one was on a long piece of silk—part of Chen's robe!

Li trembled. She was in front of him, dressed in a pure white silk gown with a soft green border.

"You! How . . . how did you get in here? Where have you been?" Li rose to take her hands.

Tears flowed from her eyes. She was trembling. "I'm sorry for leaving. I could not face the death of Ah Wu and the suffering, so I ran."

"Yes, I knew he was dead. Who can survive a Blood Dragon attack? But these poems, where did they come from? Ma searched the ship. There was no sign of you."

"That's not important now." She grasped his hands and looked deeply into his eyes. When Li looked back, hers were the green shimmering lakes that he had delighted in, the purest wine, the hidden valleys of high mountains, and her hair the sunlit golden clouds that surrounded those mountain peaks. Li forgot all his questions and even the awareness that her hands were icy cold.

"I know who you are and I made a fool of myself in front of you," she said.

Her words snapped him out of his poetry.

Li bowed his head. "I'm sorry, but I wasn't sure of your intentions."

"Yes, we must beware of strangers, and you don't understand how much your poetry means to me."

"No, only that your attraction to it is unlike anyone else's I have met . . . and maybe that's why I find myself so concerned about you."

There were more tears running down Chen's face. "Yes, I am much different from anyone else you've met. I'm honored by your concern. Your poetry is my life . . ." was all she could manage to say. She had broken down into deep sobbing.

"They are only words, and words are only powdered charcoal and water on worthless paper . . . ," Li said, amazed by her obsession for his poetry.

"There is little time for this—the Blood Dragon bears down on us."

"What?"

"You asked where I've been. I have been with the monster."

"How is that possible?"

"There is no time for all that. The sword . . . the sword is the key to defeating the Blood Dragon."

"Then we are lost," Li said, releasing her hands and sitting back down at the low writing table.

"Don't say that! During this long dark night of my present existence, your poetry has been a beacon of hope for me. Don't belittle or negate yourself now. Your powers are great, but you must have confidence in them, and in the sword, else we are lost. The author of these verses cannot be the desolate man before me!"

Li realized that Chen had truly taken his visions to heart. It was through people like her that his words would live beyond him—perhaps the only real form of immortality available to him, or anyone else. If the shamaness was his teacher in a deeper perception of the real nature of the world, then Chen was his true disciple. His poetry empowered her with life. He was deeply moved by these realizations.

Before he could say any more, she had slipped out of her robe and was sitting before him naked. The warm glow of the oil lamp played across her soft supple body. She was probably nineteen or twenty years old and, thought Li, so pure. But she seems to have suffered so much, and he wondered as to the cause of her suffering.

Before he could formulate the words to ask, she had moved to him and had begun undoing his robe; a soft red glow from the brazier shone in her face as she leaned him back onto his bed mat. The tear in Li's eye glistened in the serene light. He could hear the wind rising outside. The warm scented storm of her golden hair swept over him and the night grew warm and loving—and in their loving all questions dissolved and dreams arose.

***

Her coughing broke the spell. Chen had dressed and left the pallet. She lay on the floor, her body quaking with convulsions before each cough. Li wrapped his robe around himself and quickly moved to her.

"I don't understand it . . . . It must have worn off . . . . How can that be?" he heard her whisper.

"What's the matter? Shao-lin. Shao-lin." Li called her by her given name. "Are you ill?"

Chen Shao-lin stared at the talisman around Li's neck. The waves of nausea were intensifying. She couldn't ask him to remove the talisman without alerting him to her true nature. Would he accept the truth? It was hard to concentrate. No, not now. The sword was their most urgent problem; without it no matter how deep their affections grew the Blood Dragon would remain a deadly threat.

"The sword, we use the sword. It is the key to stopping the Blood Dragon."

"You are sick. Quick, let me get you into bed."

"No, there is nothing you can do about this. The sword is more important. Where is it?"

She began to shake and cough again. Li put his arms around her and tried to move her to the bed. She pulled away.

"Master Li, please, we must secure the sword or you will die and become the monster's slave . . . the sword, is it safe?"

Li saw he could not get her cooperation without putting her preoccupation with the sword to rest. He didn't expect his answer would make her any more comfortable, but at least the truth might bring cooperation.

"The sword cannot be released from its scabbard . . . . It is useless."

She was becoming much more ill. The nausea was so strong now she could hardly speak.

"No!"

"I am supposed to take it to Mount Wu, perhaps to find one who possesses a pure heart . . . and that purity of heart can also be . . . ."

". . . Pure *evil*, like the Blood Dragon," Chen finished Li's sentence. "Oh, Heaven!" she cried. "What are we to do now?" She could no longer hold it back. The vomit was a clear fluid. She had to leave. Gathering up all her strength, she managed to stand and move to the door.

"Where are you going?"

"Air . . . I must get some air. We must find a safe way to Mount Wu. The monster must not get it. I will return."

A gust of wind blew out the lamp. Li struggled with it for a few moments before he could get it lit. The room was empty. He secured his robe and rushed out of the cabin onto the deck.

The brightening mist obscured the sky far above; dawn was spreading. The lanterns on deck were still lit. As soon as Li reached the deck, he saw a figure moving toward him.

"Shao-lin are you . . . ?" He realized it was the watchman.

"Oh, it is you, Sir! Almost scared the Floating Ants out of me. Strange things have been happening on this voyage . . . can't be too sure," grumbled the sailor in a sleep-soaked voice.

"Did you see where she went?"

"She?" asked the sailor as he tried to wipe the sleep from his eyes. "There has been no one on this deck, except us watchmen, since everyone turned in last night, sir."

"But a woman just ran out of here. You didn't see her?" said Li Bo as he tried to make out the various forms up and down the mist-covered deck.

"Sorry sir, you're the only one who's come on deck. I must get back to my post. Be careful; strange things have been going on."

Li nodded and the sailor moved away toward the stern. Li stood there watching the mist flow over and around the ship—he was alone again. "Strange things." He recalled the sailor's words.

Yes, very strange things. The river was oddly quiet. There were few sounds from the direction of the shore.

Li moved to the railing. He listened to the mist and water. If she were in a boat, he thought, he could hear the oars. Nothing— a breeze had picked up and the river had begun a gentle lapping against the boat. Had he dreamed it all? Li walked all over the deck meeting only the guard again. Chen, if she had really been with him, had disappeared. "Strange things." He kept hearing the guard's words.

Li returned to his cabin. The third silk poem was there, ripped from her dress. And the fluid she had vomited was congealed on the floor in a small pool. Then it hadn't been a dream—she had been here. He didn't remember that he had once before seen such clear fluid in its congealed state. Instead, he realized there was only one person on this ship who could help him.

— 22 —

Li Bo knew exactly where the night watch was posted and avoided him on the way down below deck. In the darkness of the lower deck, he lit the small lantern and moved toward the cabin. The companionway was empty. At the bottom, the dim light from the lantern painted the door. Li knocked softly and waited. She must be fast asleep, but this is an emergency, he thought. Again, he tapped—nothing. As he prepared to knock a bit louder, a muffled voice rose from within.

"Help me. I have been poisoned and cannot move."

"Shamaness Luo, Shamaness Luo, can you hear me?"

"I cannot move. You must break in the door."

For a moment, Li thought the voice sounded a bit odd, then he answered. "I'm coming in!"

The door was solid, like the rest of the ship, and Li doubted he could force it. After several body slams he gave up. He swiftly surveyed its construction to find a weak spot for his dagger. There was none.

"Hurry, please." The voice rose from the other side of the door.

Who could he turn to? Not Ma. Not the crew. Then it had to be the captain. He only had a passing interest in the shamaness and might prove to be the least meddlesome, and he knew the ship. Li moved and almost collided with the dark form standing in the middle of the companionway.

His first sensation was to yell, but his instincts took over. He stood back, his arm moving toward his left sleeve. However, it stopped as soon as his eyes focused on the black-clad figure standing in front of him. There was a short sword belted to his back. He wore a broad-brimmed straw hat that covered most of his face. What little Li could see revealed that he was an albino. Li imagined his sickly pink eyes. He knew an albino eunuch at Court who was said to be a tea master. The figure in front of him, however, was no thin courtier. A metal case suspended by a leather thong hung around his thick neck. His hands, smooth and white, hung limp by his sides. Li recognized the "limpness" as a sign of the swordsman's readiness to act. Li knew he was no longer a match for such swordsmen and withdrew his hand from reaching for his knife.

"Excuse me," Li heard himself say. "I feel a bit seasick and need to go on deck to get some air—I'm not used to all this rocking." As soon as he finished, he realized how silly that must have sounded since the ship was now as steady as a mountain.

"Oh, please forgive my clumsiness, I always seem to get in the way," the swordsman said with a smile forming on his pale lips. Yet he did not move out of the way.

Li realized that these people, the one in front of him and Ma, were the same kind. Both were killers, probably hired killers, who, for a price, would force their will on others. He and the Shamaness Luo were also two of a kind, but they sought to realize the boundless freedom of the Way. This bond with Luo was precious and must be protected. Li's hand started to edge back toward the left sleeve.

"Pardon me, but are you not the famed poet, Li Bo?"

The swordsman's question startled Li. His hand froze.

"Why yes," he answered awkwardly. "And who do I have the honor of being recognized by?"

"Master Li, you were once a trusted councilor of the Emperor. Can the Court again rely on your honor?"

"What do you mean?" Li was quite startled, and a bit flattered, by the stranger's acquaintance with his background.

"Can I trust you, master Li, with a grave Imperial matter?"

"Don't you know? I've been banished by the Emperor to Yunnan?"

The swordsman moved closer. Li still couldn't see his eyes because of his hat. Li edged back, ever so slowly.

"No! This is terrible, one of the empire's greatest poets condemned to such an unfit place. It must be a mistake. I have heard nothing of this."

Li was speechless. The swordsman seemed concerned for his situation. This did not at all fit the picture Ma had drawn of his opponent.

"But then," continued the swordsman, "my duties keep me far from the capital and such news eludes me. I'm terribly sorry to hear this and insist on interceding for you with the Emperor."

Li's hands went up in front of his chest grasping each other in a gesture of politeness to thank the swordsman and refuse his courtesies. Nevertheless, the swordsman ignored him and continued. "No matter what they have cooked up against you, I will not believe that a poet as talented and loyal as you would seek to harm the empire."

"I am greatly moved by your sentiment, kind friend, but quite at a loss to understand your relationship with the Court . . . ."

"Can I trust you, master Li?"

Li still could not read the swordsman's eyes. He wanted to pull the man's hat off but knew that before he could reach it the swordsman would have cut off his arm. Could he trust this faceless man? An albino, no less! Li spoke before he could really decide.

"Yes, I am a loyal subject of the Emperor."

"I thought so. I am on a mission to capture one of the empire's most notorious bandits—Ma Ssu-ming."

Li managed to control his facial expression, but ever so slowly his foot again slid back over the rough wood flooring. He tried to put a little more space between himself and the faceless swordsman; to get out of sword-striking distance was preferable.

"What has this to do with me? How could I, a poet, possibly help you capture a bandit?" he answered with a weak laugh.

"Did you not make friends with him after you left the salt hauler in Xia-zhou? Dine with him in Xia-zhou and book a passage on this ship with him? Has he not been your constant companion since Xia-zhou?"

So we've been watched, thought Li. Now I understand why Ma put on that fish-slicing demonstration at the inn. He must have spotted this fellow and attempted to warn him away. I am no longer interested in the Court or its problems, thought Li. *I have to get rid of this fellow and help the shamaness.*

"The gentleman I have been traveling with is also named Ma Ssu-ming, but the names are surely coincidental. I am confident that the Ma Ssu-ming that I have befriended is a gentleman and no bandit."

The swordsman's attitude was beginning to annoy him. What did he know about good companionship, friendship among noble minds? What bandit could play and sing like Ma? Stupid government official . . . wait, he thought, is this man really a government official?

"I'm sorry, but the gentleman and the bandit are the same."

"What is this Ma fellow wanted for?"

"He is following the Emperor's chief shamaness to kidnap her and steal the very precious scrolls she is carrying."

"Is the Emperor not trying to force her back to Court against her will?"

"When she had first left, he had considered taking that course. But after counsel, in which I must humbly admit some involvement, he changed his mind and decided to reward her for saving his life with her complete freedom."

"Then what about this Ma Ssu-ming character?"

"We captured one of his gang and learned of his plans to impersonate an imperial agent and try to kidnap the shamaness. The Emperor would be quite distressed if any harm came to her. In addition, the scrolls she bears could be very dangerous to the dynasty if they fell into the hands of someone with occult powers equal to hers."

"What scrolls could possibly be so dangerous to the Empire?"

"Again I must trust you. These scrolls chart the celestial movements. With them someone with enough skill could see clearly into the future."

"But if the future is favorable, then . . . ."

"Ah, but who is to say? The one who possesses those scrolls has the final say. In the hands of someone set on bringing down the great Tang dynasty, it would be rather easy to predict its downfall, true or otherwise, and have numerous brigands attempt to fulfill the prediction."

Li knew the pattern quite well. It had repeated itself throughout the history of the Middle Kingdom. Could this be the danger that Shamaness Luo had alluded to? But that involved the sword. Could the scrolls and the sword be somehow tied together? He could not reveal this to the swordsman, for even if he were the Emperor, Li's first concern now was for the shamaness. Then he thought of golden-haired Chen. It seemed as if years ago he had come here for the shamaness' help and now she was dying. He had to act.

"Listen, I believe you, but what can I do?"

"I must first convince you," said the swordsman. With that, he reached into his robe. Li expected the worst and started to reach for the Damascus blade hidden in his robe sleeve.

The swordsman was quicker and a rectangular block of carved wood came out of his robe and rose above his head. Even before Li's brain could register the block's significance, he was on his knee, bowing—he knew the routine so well that it was a reflex action.

"I am the High Censor to the Son of Heaven, charged by the powers of Heaven to bring righteousness and order to the Empire."

The block disappeared back into the swordsman's tunic.

Li rose. Memories of his arrest for high treason played through his mind and then the realization that Ma had never shown him any proof of his position. This was still too fantastic. He had sung and drunk with Ma. Surely, he knew him. Who was this stranger with a block of wood and pink eyes—which he could not see?

"Now to complete your trust in me, I must ask you to come with me. I think it is time to show you something." As the swordsman turned toward the stairs leading up to the deck, he continued. "Put out that lantern and grasp the end of my scabbard to follow me out of here."

Li quickly put out the lantern and groped for the scabbard strapped to the swordsman's back. It was cold to his touch but wasn't made from metal or wood—some other material that felt like some sort of skin. They reached the steps and the gray dawn light showed the way. Li released his grip on the scabbard. Quietly they moved up. Reaching the deck, but keeping low, Li saw it.

Across the stretch of water that separated them from the stone-bound shore, a light shown; masked by the mist, it quickly disappeared. In a moment, another flash appeared and then nothing. The swordsman, his straw hat still covering most of his white features, leaned toward Li and whispered, "The sentry has gone to his cabin. Dawn is up and the crew will be coming on deck. Right now only one person, besides us, is paying any attention to this. Come, quietly."

They moved out on deck in a crouch. When they were almost below Ma's cabin, the swordsman stopped and pointed to the porthole. A light shown briefly, twice, and then the curtain was drawn.

"I must return to my cabin. I cannot allow Ma to see me—I hope you trust me. His gang is out there following us. At some point, they will be signaled to come aboard. You can see why I might need your help."

Li nodded, but his mind was preoccupied by the shamaness's condition.

"I will be in contact and shall return your trust with the Court."

Li turned to see some of the crewmen appear on deck, then turned back to the swordsman. He was gone.

"Help! Help!"

Li looked around, there was no one. The crew didn't seem to notice it. She was communicating directly to Li through his mind—it was the language of the Immortals, and only he could hear it. The Emperor and all his secret agents be damned! Li quickly stood up and ran toward the captain, who had just emerged from his cabin.

"My, for a poet you're up rather early," the captain said irritably. He clearly did not enjoy the early morning hours.

"Yes, Captain, one of the passengers is very ill, possibly near death."

"How about a drink first?"

"The sha . . . erh . . . the entertainer. Please come quick."

"We don't need another death, especially a passenger. Wait, let me get my medicine kit."

Li was already down the stairs when the captain caught up with him.

"How do you know she's ill?"

"I couldn't sleep and was up on the deck. Your watchman can verify my story, and I heard her crying out. But I cannot break in the door."

The captain smiled as he reached the shamaness's door. "Yes, she's a stout ship. My father built her, used the finest cypress. If you knew my father, you'd also know that she has her tricks."

The captain quickly drew forth an odd looking key from his robe. He inserted it in the hole in the doorjamb, just above the handle. Li had completely missed the small hole. He hooked it onto something and withdrew it. The door bolt slid back and he moved the handle. The door swung open.

Li saw the "well" character first and pushed the captain, who was just about to place his boot on it.

"Hey!" yelled the captain.

"Careful, there are hidden dangers here," said Li, pointing to the character cut in the doorsill.

"What is . . . ." The captain didn't finish, for Li had already left him and was kneeling next to the shamaness.

"Can you speak?"

Only her eyes moved, from side to side.

"Quick, she has been poisoned." Li saw the cut on her hand.

"And possibly stabbed," added the captain.

"What?"

The captain pointed to the bloodstains on the robe over her heart. He examined her hand and then placed three fingers on her wrist to determine her body's *chi* flow. As he worked, he noticed the dart imbedded in the wall behind her.

"The poison has somehow been neutralized, but its side effect, paralysis, is interfering with her breathing. Quick, heat some water on that small stove."

Li got the charcoal in the brazier heated and placed a small ceramic bowl of water on it. The captain moved over it and when the water was sufficiently heated, he sprinkled powders from several small containers into it. After simmering it for a few moments, he let the medicine cool.

Li noticed that the captain had placed one acupuncture needle in Luo's big toe and several about her neck. Li moved back to Luo. He held her head as the captain offered a small cup of his brew to her mouth. She could barely move her lips, then slowly they parted, offering just enough space for the liquid to flow. Li gently laid her head back on the simple wooden headrest.

"It was much worse when the rebellion had just started. I had to learn about treating wounds and such to keep my business on this river. Things have been getting better . . . ," said the captain. However, the grave expression on his face led Li to notice that he was looking at the dart imbedded in the wall. Must be the albino, thought Li, but I have to figure this out first; can't trust anyone, yet.

The captain turned his attention to the wound over Luo's heart. He moved the robe back from her shoulder, exposing the gentle curve of a pearl-like globe of flesh. The smooth skin of her breast was broken at one point by a scar that was oozing blood.

"This is an unusual wound for a woman," observed the captain. He noticed the quizzical look on Li's face.

"It's a sword wound, very deep, that has been cauterized. Even stranger is that although the cauterization is perfect, it is leaking. This is not normal."

"Can you stop the bleeding?" asked Li.

"I can try." The captain turned to his bag and brought out a jar of white ointment. He applied the ointment to a bandage and placed it over the wound. After he tied it all in place, he helped Li lay the shamaness back again on the wooden headrest. Both men then noticed that the ship was again in motion.

"I must leave or else we could all end up at the bottom of the river. I'll be on deck with my bag nearby. Leave the acupuncture needles in place, and this afternoon I'll come and check on her." The captain paused. "In the old days we had robberies and murders, but it's different now. I know my men . . . . I don't know my passengers. If you like, I will send down some Floating Ants wine for you."

"Ah . . . thank you, Captain, for what you've done. I will stay with her until the paralysis ends. Maybe later I'll come up and have a drink with you. No need to send any down," Li smiled as politely as he could; he preferred his wine filtered.

"Well, I just thought it would be a shame to waste the heat of such a good brazier . . . ." The captain smiled back, rose, and left, being careful not to step near the doorsill character.

~ 23 ~

Chen lay on the shore as Li's ship crawled toward the mouth of the Horse Liver Gorge. The bamboo sail was reefed, and the four oarsmen were now positioning the ship to navigate the rapids. The mist continued to enfold the craggy tops of the yellow and white limestone cliffs on both sides of the river. Higher up, the sky was overcast, ready at any moment to rain. The broken cliffs outlined strange forms. Somewhere out there was a cliff shaped like a horse's liver from which the gorge drew its name. The westward flowing *shang-feng* wind remained steady.

Chen was sick. Spasms of nausea spread out from her stomach and passed through her whole body. She knew the Blood Dragon was sure to find her. Something went wrong. The antidote hadn't held. Worst of all, Li wasn't able to release the sword. The monster would certainly catch her lie and try its own crude method of dealing with him. With Ah Wu dead and even the possibility of getting close to Li Bo gone, Chen's heart began to feel as forsaken as her body cast upon that desolate boulder-covered bank.

***

Ah Wu saw Chen flee from Li's cabin and decided to follow her. He reappeared on a cliff above the shore where she fled and was watching her. Something was amiss. What happened to her plan? Maybe now he could ask Su-lu for the antidote to Li's protective charm to verify what had happened between Li and the woman Chen. This would give him the opportunity to warn his friend.

A motion in the water interrupted his thoughts. A long dark green object had floated to the surface and glided toward the shore. The water sparkled, obscuring the form, and Su-lu's figure broke the surface. He has become a water monster, thought Ah Wu, and that is the source of his power. He lay still in the grass and concentrated on listening to their meeting.

"You have failed," said the monster as it strode onto the shore.

Chen raised her head, but did not turn round to face the creature. "No, I have slept with him. Your antidote failed."

"What! You speak to me like that? I should send you into the Void on this very spot!"

"What do I care then if you get your sword or not!"

The Blood Dragon had raised its hand to strike, but checked the blow. "Face me!" the monster growled.

Chen stood up and moved toward the form of her uncle. She looked directly into its eyes.

"Ha! So you are willing to be destroyed. What has come over you that you are now so fearless? Could it be?" It began laughing. The ground shook with the force of its laughter. Chen only continued to stare into the monster's eyes. The creature stopped laughing and looked deeper into Chen's eyes.

"Your attraction to this scholar is strong. More than that, yes, your eyes betray you. You are in love! A ghost in love with a human! What a hopeless situation and you realize your own hopelessness, don't you? That is the reason for your fearlessness!"

The Blood Dragon's eyes glowed. It turned away from Chen and paced the beach.

Chen backed away and walked to the edge of the shore. She watched the Long River on its relentless flow east. Now she knew the extent of the monster's ability to read her mind. For a brief moment, she was no longer afraid of the Blood Dragon. And in the brief moment of fearlessness, she saw not her uncle, the man who had molested her as a child, but an ugly old beast. Yet Chen knew this would not be the end. The monster would not give up. As soon as she realized this, fear's dark cloak hid her insight, and the phantom of her uncle's image returned.

"You have won." The Blood Dragon's softest human female voice intruded as it approached. Chen turned and faced the beast, but was careful not to look directly into its eyes, for now was not the time to reveal her heart.

"Won what?" asked Chen.

"I can no longer control you. Since you are willing to give everything up, I have no hold on you. You are a more pitiful creature than I."

Chen's fears were heightened, but she kept a cold face and downcast eyes to the monster.

"So now that I can no longer use you, I will take care of the human myself!"

"And you will lose the sword and defeat yourself!"

"What choice do I have? You have backed me into a corner of your own making. Foolish ghost, how can you expect to love a human?"

"It is true that I love him and I know it is hopeless. That is my affair. I can still get the sword for you and am willing if you promise to spare him."

"Ah, a compromise. Yes, his life for the sword. What can the useless life of one human mean to me in return for the Dragon Pool Sword? Agreed!" The Blood Dragon's eyes darted with flame.

"Not so quick!" Chen announced, putting her hand up as if to stop the creature's glee.

"What is this?" The Blood Dragon was not accustomed to humans telling it what to do. Its eyes narrowed. "Do not try my patience, for I could still send you and your lover to the Void—together!"

"It is a simple matter of getting close to him again, but your antidote does not work."

"Impossible!"

"It lasted for less than an evening. Could it be that this shamaness is more powerful than you expected?" Chen said with a sly smile.

"Silence!" yelled the monster as it struck Chen across the face.

Chen fell, but now the sting of the blow gave her great satisfaction. She had finally hurt the monster. How long has it been? A year? All the sweeter was Chen's satisfaction. A change had taken place. The meeting with Li Bo, like his poetry, had changed her "life," if that was what you could call her present existence. No matter, things would get better; they had to.

"If this shamaness is that skilled, then she could be a threat to my plan. Since she is the author of the charm that protects Li Bo, I will destroy her. That will end the charm's potency and eliminate any further interference." The Blood Dragon turned from Chen and moved back into the river.

Chen knew she had to act quickly. She had to find out what the monster was planning.

"What is this plan you speak of? Perhaps I might be of some further use."

The monster stopped in the water and turned, "Of further use?"

"Yes," said Chen, now standing. "Have I not brought the capabilities of this shamaness to your attention? Imagine if at a crucial moment you discovered you had underestimated her. I'm sure your plan is subtle enough that such unforeseen events could be handled, but why add unnecessary complications?"

"Do you mock me?" The monster's eyes glowed through the likeness of its human face as it tried to search Chen's mind. However, its actual powers, unknown to either ghosts or humans, in reading the thoughts of other beings were quite limited.

Chen, averting her glance, for she had rightly surmised that the monster could read the truth in one's eyes, said, "What would I gain by mocking you? The Void? The more I understand your plan, the better I might prepare to help in the retrieval of the sword. My only concern, of course, is for the safety of Li Bo. By pleasing you in my service, I am further protecting him."

"Your logic is good. I wonder if your sincerity is as constant."

"Whatever I answer, the truth still lies in my heart. So gaze upon my heart."

With that Chen stepped forward and looked long and deep into the monster's fiery heart. Chen then understood that its only desire was to become more powerful. It hated its present status as an immature, incomplete creature and longed for the power and respect that its species as Rain Dragons enjoyed. yet it also hated its species because in their fully matured form as Rain Dragons they looked down upon Blood Dragons as worthless, degraded forms of life.

"Yes," the Blood Dragon continued in its softer feminine voice, after delving into Chen's eyes. "Your love for him is deep. You are a fool to seek such a limited goal, but useful to me. Don't you understand that as a ghost you have much greater potential? Humans are weak. Your powers, once developed, would allow you to rule over them, have whatever you wanted. Why waste all this on one human?"

Chen hesitated, knowing that she could enrage the creature by pointing out that in the end, even as a Rain Dragon, it was human respect that it was ultimately seeking, for without humans what significance would Rain Dragons have? However, that tack would not serve Li Bo's cause.

"Then show me, Master, your plan and allow me to appreciate the brilliance of the Blood Dragon."

The monster moved back to the shore, its white funeral robe rippling in the river breeze and its eyes aglow as it unknowingly allowed itself to bask in Chen's "respect."

"You ask for my plan? Can you really understand such lofty concepts? I wonder. But you are an unusual servant; none has ever faced me as you." The creature smiled. "yet none has ever retained human folly as long as you have. Love. What do you understand of that? I am a creature of pure *Yin*. I lack the balance of the *Yang* force. This balance will come once I am fully matured." Its smile widened. "yet I am unlike the others. I do not seek the balance; rather, I have chosen to destroy it!" Its eyes glowed, radiantly red. "But I am only a lowly Blood Dragon and have limitations that make it nearly impossible to destroy the balance."

"Can this be done? Can the very essence of Nature, the balance of *Yin* and *Yang* be upset? Is this possible?" asked Chen.

"Now it is you who think me the fool," laughed the Blood Dragon. "Of course, I could not accomplish this through my puny force alone, but if I were to use one much more powerful, then this so-called balance could be upset."

A shiver ran through Chen. "To what purpose?"

"Evil, an unbalance in Nature, would gather an upper hand and with it the power to control one of Nature's great forces—the Long River."

Chen's eyes widened as she realized the depth of the creature's desire. "Who is powerful enough to tip the balance? Only Nature itself possesses such power."

"The Rain Goddess of Mount Wu is Nature's spiritual manifestation in this region. Everyone on that ship," the monster gestured toward Li's ship, "is being drawn toward that power. Our destinies intertwine. The outcome of this matter touches all of us. It is the Dragon Pool Sword that is the key to the power of the Rain Goddess—and so you see the sword's value. Or do you, human?"

"What do I care about this philosophical chatter, as long as Li Bo is left unharmed I will retrieve the sword for you," Chen spoke, trying to cover up her horror at the monster's ambitions.

"Yes, I thought such matters were of little interest to you. Remember, the sword for his life. Now I must attend to this meddlesome shamaness." With that, the monster plunged into the cold gray river and disappeared.

***

Ah Wu moved back from the ledge to contemplate all he had heard. He was shocked, for not only had he misjudged the woman Chen, he never suspected that Su-lu was as evil as this. He also realized that the sword and Li Bo's dream were linked to what he had just heard. The sword was the key to the success or failure of Su-lu's plan. Li Bo's dream provided the answer to the sword's role in this matter. They had to get it to the Rain Goddess on Mount Wu. Somehow, thought Ah Wu, humans always end up doing the dirty work for the spirits. But these philosophical matters were better understood by the likes of Li Bo and Ma Ssu-ming.

Ah Wu's immediate problem was to warn Li Bo about the importance of the Dragon Pool Sword. He had to tell him that it wasn't cursed, for he was afraid that Li Bo, in his grief, might get rid of the sword. It was clear that if Su-lu got his hands on it, their world would be plunged into chaos. Ah Wu pulled back to the ledge and looked for Chen. Maybe it was time to introduce his presence? A second glance over the ledge showed that the introduction would have to wait—she was gone.

***

Ma Ssu-ming had just finished stowing away his signal lamp. "Well, Lao-huang, what are we to do? You know old Li is right. No matter how much fighting skill I possess or how many young swordsmen await my command, this shamaness has powers I cannot cope with. What do you think, my drunken Immortal?"

Lao-huang responded by falling off his perch and landing on the floor in a drunken heap.

"Yes," said Ma as he scooped his partner up and put him on his bed to sleep it off. "The situation doesn't look promising. yet if we can't bring the shamaness back to Court, I bet we could bring the Dragon Pool Sword and be just as well honored. Certainly, Li Bo is no longer interested in returning." Ma then headed out on deck to look for Li and find out what his intentions were.

The ship was underway again and passing through the East Bend Rapids. Whitewater shot up from either side of the bow. The ship plunged downward then back toward the sky, but with the captain's steady hand and ample experience they made it through without a scratch. The oarsmen were now aligning the ship to cross Horse Liver Gorge.

"That damn pilot should have been waiting for us before we shot the rapids," yelled the captain to his helmsman.

"Probably drunk again," said the helmsman.

The captain laughed. "Well, he damn well better make it for the New Rapids or else we might be swimming the rest of the way."

Neither the helmsman nor the other crewmembers who heard the captain's remark laughed. They just looked at each other. The New Rapids weren't really that new. They had been around for quite a while, frequently sinking ships that tried to cross them without a native pilot. They were "new" in the sense that landslides in that section of the Horse Liver Gorge were common, due to the unstable sandstone composition of the cliffs that towered over the river at that point. A native of the region was aware of the most recent collapses and knew which areas to avoid.

The Horse Liver Gorge may well be shaped like a horse's liver, but usually, only the riverboat captains could identify it. There were other gorges, however, like the Lion's Cliff, that everyone could pick out.

Ma had too much on his mind to bother about any rock formations. He went directly to Li's cabin and found it unlocked and empty. The cabin was unkempt, unlike Li Bo's normal manner. Ma spotted the torn white silk poem on the floor. What had happened here? he wondered. He closed the door and ran out on deck. The ship was small enough that Ma knew at a glance Li wasn't on deck. He headed to the galley.

"Has master Li been in for breakfast?" Ma asked the cook, who was slowly wiping down the rough wooden table.

"None of them have been here," growled the cook, who looked upon their absence as an insult to his cooking.

"Master Ma," a voice came from behind, "if you please, a word with you."

Ma turned and smiled. "Why yes, of course, captain." He walked out of the galley and out of earshot of the cook. The captain followed to the middle of the ship and stopped. Ma watched him stare out at the rock formations that populated the ridges that hung over them.

"We are now passing below the horse's liver," he said, pointing up at a strange limestone formation that seemed to hang off the sheer wall of a cliff. Ma wondered when it would loosen and fall on a passing ship.

"Master Li is below deck in the entertainer's cabin," said the captain, who was now watching Ma with the same intensity with which he viewed that rock formation.

"Why," Ma said, a smile relaxin his face, "you do pay such warm attention to your passengers."

The captain made a short bow with his head. "Of course, master Ma, I said before that my passengers are one of the more interesting aspects of this river transport business."

"I was looking for master Li, but think it would be very impolite for me to disturb him in such circumstances. After all as Confucius said . . . ."

"Whatever he said," interrupted the captain rather hurriedly, "is of as little interest to you as it is to me. Your companion is tending to the entertainer's wounds."

"Wounds?" asked Ma, his hand clutching the hilt of his sword.

"Yes. Someone has attempted to kill her. If you know anything about sword wounds, which you probably do, then I suggest you help your friend. I have done all I can."

"Sword wounds?" Ma said, figuring it must be the eunuchs' hired assassin. What was Li doing there? The captain continued to study him.

"Thank you, I will go to him at once," Ma said, and he headed to the stairway below deck and to the shamaness's cabin.

***

Shamaness Luo opened her eyes just after the captain left. Li had moved her to the sleeping mat and covered her with a quilt.

"Thank you, master Li. Again, I'm in your debt."

"You have returned to us. Rest, this chest wound is not easy to heal."

She smiled. "It will not heal until I reach Mount Wu."

"Why?"

"I was wounded in my dreams just before I fled the capital. It was a mortal wound, but through the intervention of my guardian spirit, the Lady of the Purple Vault, my life was spared."

"But . . . ."

"Let me continue . . ."

Li nodded.

"I made a vow, a vow to serve the mistress of Mount Wu— the Rain Goddess. The power of the vow sealed the wound. Yet I have again become involved in earthly affairs, weakening the vow."

"You mean my affairs, the Blood Dragon and its ghosts."

The shamaness only smiled to affirm Li's remark.

"There is an assassin who stalks me, and the Emperor has his own agents sent to retrieve me. I am not yet free of earthly affairs. It is better that I choose my own path. Your poetry has given me much, just as it has to Miss Chen."

"You know about her!"

"Of course. She is one of the ghosts whom I have spoken to you about."

"No! How can . . . . No, why only last night . . . ."

The room was enveloped in red mist. Li jumped back to the wall next to Shamaness Luo, his Persian dagger drawn.

"Ha! You insult me with that puny weapon. Even your friend's famous crossbow bolts were no match for me. Stupid humans," growled the creature.

Li could not believe what stood before him. It was an old man in a funeral robe, white hair, white moustache and goatee . . . how could this be, he thought, it was . . . himself? Li Bo as a very old man! The searing red eyes, however, snapped him out of his shock. He made a move to attack, but the shamaness pushed him off balance, and he stumbled when he tried to stand. The monster laughed even more at what seemed to be Li's clumsiness.

It did not notice, however, the small brass mirror that the shamaness had drawn forth. With her eyes half closed, the shamaness entered a deep trance by repeating a powerful incantation transmitted to her by the Lady of the Purple Vault.

When the monster returned its attention to the wounded shamaness, it was staring into a small bronze mirror. The shamaness was holding it aloft, pointing it directly at the monster's face as she deepened the trance. A purple light shot forth, streaming from the shining metal surface. It struck the monster directly on the forehead just above the bridge of its long ugly snout. The creature screamed and tore at its head. In an instant, it vanished.

Li was just regaining his balance to attack again as he saw the beam of light hit. The shamaness fell back on her mat and passed out. Fresh blood was pooling around the medicated cloth that the captain had placed on her chest wound. His acupuncture needles had shot out of her body. Li replaced his dagger and hurried to her side. He would not let her die. He had to get the captain. Rushing to the door, he flung it open and was face to face with Ma. Li's right hand moved for his dagger.

~ 24 ~

The captain heard the thrashing water off the starboard side and moved there to look. A large alligator was furiously lashing the water. White foam was everywhere. A moment later, it plunged deep into the river. He lost sight of it as the river closed over the spot.

"Captain," the cook rushed out on deck, "what is it?"

"Some sort of fish must have got a nice fat bug." The captain had a lifetime on the river; he knew an alligator from a fish. He also knew that alligators had never been sighted this far up river—another portent to add to the others on this trip. As he moved back to the tiller, he realized that his passengers were involved in their own deadly game, one that might quickly involve him and his ship. He smiled.

***

Ah Wu was still sitting on the cliff above the beach when he saw Su-lu emerge from the river and drag himself onto the beach. He lay still for a moment. Ah Wu thought this might be his chance to kill him, but he was still not able to wield his weapons. So he lay still and watched; patience, he reminded himself, was the mark of true skill—the skill would return.

What could have possibly countered Su-lu? Hadn't he gone to attack the shamaness? Could it be possible that the shamaness was his match? He could only wait to see if Su-lu revived . . . patience.

***

"You!" said Li Bo, shocked at meeting Ma and realizing, at the same moment, that he was reaching for his dagger. He withdrew his hand, lest Ma realize he harbored suspicions.

"What happened to her?" Ma asked.

"Please come in and close the door. Maybe you are the only person on this ship who can save her. But now we have two opponents to deal with." Li actually thought three, counting Ma, but he didn't voice that thought.

Li led Ma to the shamaness's side and removed the makeshift bandage on her chest. The blood slowly pooled in the wound. Li replaced the cloth.

"It is the assassin's blade. The wound is very peculiar, for it no doubt reached her heart, but she is still alive and the bleeding is slight," said Ma. Truly, he thought, she has powers that are beyond the *Yang* realm, for no ordinary human could have survived such a blow. Old Zhou hadn't. His killer was aboard.

"Yes, she told me that it was a mortal blow delivered during a dream and thwarted only by a vow proposed by her spirit guardian. She says that only on Mount Wu will the wound heal," Li said, interrupting and confirming Ma's speculation.

"Then the swordsman that is tracking her is an assassin and the same who attacked me in my dreams."

Li reached for his dagger. "And killed my boatman. I've seen him, he's the albino in the bow compartment."

Ma pressed his hand against Li's and smiled. "Forget it. He is too powerful for you. I fought him in Xia-zhou. Leave him to me, elder brother, when the proper time comes." He released Li's hand and tended to the shamaness.

"If it bleeds at that rate, she might make it. On the other hand, if the flow increases then it is impossible for her to reach Mount Wu alive. At the rate we are sailing, it will take four days to reach the mountain."

"The flow had slowed a bit, but we were just attacked by . . . ." Li's face went pale.

"By what?" Ma looked around.

"It came right through the hull."

Ma gently touched Li's shoulder. "Who did it look like?"

"Perhaps I've had too much to drink . . . ."

"The person you fear the most?"

Li smiled, "Perhaps . . . ."

"It was the Blood Dragon. The monster takes the form of whomever you fear the most."

"Even more peculiar," said Li, "is the shamaness's power. She seems to have dealt it a near fatal blow."

Ma's face reflected his surprise and concern. "Is she the equal of a Blood Dragon?" he marveled.

"What do you know of such creatures?"

Ma's face grew taut. "Not much. Once on a mission, a group of my men and I came across such a beast. Most of them were destroyed by it." Ma paused and rubbed his face with his hand, lightly running his fingers over his moustache.

"I escaped only by being thrown into the river by the creature. By the time I came to, the river had carried me far from the battle site. When I returned there were only the drained corpses of the men in my unit. Blood Dragons are fearsome creatures and it takes something or someone with great powers to defeat them. I never found that creature."

"And what do you know about her powers?" asked Li gesturing toward the shamaness.

"I knew the Shamaness Luo was powerful, but this type of power is beyond that of an ordinary shamaness."

Both men stared at the unconscious woman. Beautiful, no doubt, but she looked so ordinary and defenseless—by what power could she be the match of a fearsome Blood Dragon?

"So what does this mean?" Li didn't understand what Ma was driving at.

"I don't know, elder brother. I am only a swordsman. Those realms beyond the human are best left to students of Daoism and those with a penchant for mists and flights of fancy." Ma's face relaxed a little; a smile flickered there for a moment. "I should be asking you that question."

"Immortals, yes. I have had a long interest in such beings, but shamanesses, Blood Dragons, and whatever—these things are areas of popular lore that I am not familiar with."

Ma turned from Li and tended the shamaness. Then, in a softer tone, moving back to Li, he said, "Elder brother, you have recently become attached to this woman."

"We are brother and sister in the ways of the Dao. I will not let her die or be tormented by some hired trash or that monster," replied Li, looking into Ma's eyes.

Ma understood Li's challenge, but unlike many of his fellow swordsmen, Ma had learned to come to terms with his ego and saw no point in a hostile response. Instead, he smiled, for he knew that he still needed Li to help him get Luo back to the capital. The Emperor wanted her back. She had saved his life, and there was little doubt that the Emperor wanted her alive and well to continue protecting him. This encounter with the Blood Dragon only increased her worth to the Emperor, for it proved that she was no mere shamaness. And of course, thought Ma, there is the Dragon Pool Sword.

"What will you do with the Dragon Pool Sword?" he asked.

"I will keep my pledge and take it to Mount Wu with the shamaness."

"And after that, perhaps to the Court?"

"I follow the Way."

"We can still cooperate," said Ma. "I must return her alive to the Court, and if a trip to Mount Wu is the only way to save her, then I pledge to aid you in this journey."

He leaned closer to Li and whispered, "She saved the life of the Son of Heaven. Do you think such a gallant act would go unrewarded?"

"Do not speak to me of Court rewards. They come and go as the seasons and are far less predictable," said Li. He contemplated the sense of tranquility he felt around the shamaness.

Ma pulled back. "There is nothing to worry about. The Emperor cannot afford to be without such a powerful guardian. Her well being is assured." A smile preceded his next remark. "Whereas the value of a man of words is certainly, at Court, subject to the whims of fashion, that would not be the same for such a magnificent Heavenly portent as the Dragon Pool."

Li knew that the shamaness's chances for survival and his own success in reaching Mount Wu would be reduced considerably if an open break with Ma occurred. He held back and simply nodded in apparent approval. Despite the odds, however, he was committed to protect the shamaness. Besides being a matter of honor, she had become his sole source of poetic inspiration.

When Li further examined his reasons for his new commitment, he realized that he had become a rebel. He was openly, or at least in his mind, breaking with the Court and all it represented. While he dared not flout the orders for his banishment, since the Court could always exact its revenge on his family, his allegiance was now to aid the shamaness in her escape. Maybe, through this action, he could find the courage to go a step further like the shamaness and openly leave worldly affairs behind. He believed that if he succeeded, the poetry would stream through him again. Furthermore, whether Ma was acting for the Court, as he claimed, or, as the albino claimed, for his own benefit as an outlaw, Ma's interests were ultimately opposed to his. For the time being, however, Li needed Ma on his side.

He turned to Ma and explained how he had found the shamaness, what had happened with the captain and the Blood

Dragon, but he neglected to mention that he had initially gone to seek her.

"So how did you come across her?" asked Ma after listening intently.

"Chen showed up at my cabin last night."

"What! Where is she?"

"She stayed the night, became ill, and vanished." That last word reminded him that the shamaness had called Chen a ghost.

"What's the matter?" Ma's hand reached out to support Li, who was beginning to pale.

"Nothing, nothing. I'm sorry. The shock of seeing Chen and then rushing out on deck to find her gone—it is coming back to me. Once out on deck, I searched for her and heard the shamaness's call for help."

"I see," Ma paused. "And Chen was nowhere to be found?"

"Yes, and what's worse, the nightwatch told me he saw no one on deck all night. How could this be? You searched the ship. Where did she come from and where did she go?"

"Did you ask her?"

"Yes, but she evaded the question." Li realized that she had not been open with him. But what did she say? She was with the Blood Dragon. Now the shamaness says that Chen is a ghost. Could it be? Did he not make love with her last night? Was that not real? Was she not warm and loving? A ghost? That made no sense—and yet how to explain recent events?

Ma studied Li's eyes as all this went through the older man's mind.

"Brother Li, you have affections for Chen. I understand how you must feel about her disappearance. The shamaness must have said something to upset you. These holy types are always calling down ghosts and spirits for every little thing. They go too far in everything, but then what can we expect—this is the only type of explanation they know. There must be a more logical way of understanding all this."

Listening to Ma's consoling words, Li understood the younger man's unspoken affection for him. He could not believe that such a person was a common bandit. Yet there were the lantern signals from his cabin. Court politics, again. A bandit gang or a unit of the palace guard . . . were they that different? And were they not under Ma's command? If they were, thought Li, then the shamaness is even in more danger, especially in her wounded condition. Li moved over to the shamaness and drew the quilt up to her neck.

"She weakened herself on my account. I am now responsible for her. I do not take such responsibility lightly."

"Elder Li, I understand and will assist."

Ma then produced a small packet from his robes and untied it. Inside were various herbs and ointments. He began to prepare a salve.

"This is a very potent ointment for sword wounds given to me by my master. While I don't expect it to heal her wound, it might help further reduce the flow of blood." As Ma applied the salve he continued to speak in a low voice. "Let us set up alternate watches. At the least, it will only take four days. We can also talk to the captain and see if he will go directly to Mount Wu and skip the scheduled stops at Guei-jhou and Ba-tung."

"Yes, excellent idea," Li said. He didn't like leaving Ma alone with the shamaness. However, he couldn't think of any alternative. His mind was numb with exhaustion.

"Do you think the captain will really depart from his scheduled stops?"

"I think if he is paid enough, the captain could be induced to depart from this realm," said Ma. His face broke into the happy-go-lucky grin that Li had enjoyed so much before the shamaness entered his life. He could hear Ah Wu lecturing him on "women" and the trouble they caused. It made him sad that his old friend could not be with him.

"Maybe so, maybe so, my young brother. Do you mind if we begin the first watch with you right now and allow me to take a moment's rest?" Li said, and made himself comfortable on the straw mat that covered the floor. Ma smiled and checked to make sure the door was secure before he leaned back against the bulkhead and took up his watch.

***

Su-lu awoke. He turned toward the river and pulled himself, hand over hand, back into the water. The river swallowed him. Ah Wu rose to his feet to see clearly. Would he drown? A confusion of bubbles broke the surface, and the green scaly back of some large creature appeared. Slowly its great tail moved back and forth, sending it out into the deeper part of the river. Farther and farther out, then it dove, its tail lashed the water and was gone. Has an alligator attacked Su-lu, Ah Wu wondered, but there are no such beasts in this region of the Long River.

When the solitude was broken, it was by the appearance of another form on the shore, but this time out of the mist that had rolled up along the river. At first Ah Wu just took it to be a denser patch of fog, but it rose on two legs and walked away from the river's edge. He remembered the mist near the Dream Temple, how it dissipated and sailed down the mountain after he had fired a crossbow bolt at it.

Chen managed to walk several steps before she fell to the ground. Ah Wu appeared before her.

"Well it seems as if we are destined to find each other in such situations," he said, and knelt down next to her.

She looked up and screamed. "You! You're dead—you're a ghost!"

Ah Wu laughed, the first time in a long time he noted, and said, "So are you."

She stopped screaming and thought for a moment.

"I have wronged you; please kill me—if that is possible." She bent her head down to the ground exposing the back of her neck.

"I don't know how to kill things, yet. Even this old crossbow," Ah Wu patted the weapon that was strapped to his back, "is useless to me. Are you all right?"

"I'd rather be dead. However, since I am, I don't know, just not this present existence," she sobbed.

"Quiet," he said gently. "Some passing spirit might hear and take you up on that wish. If you left this realm, how would you help me save Li Bo?"

She turned toward him. "You don't hate me for what I did to you?"

"I am at the mercy of my old nemesis, Su-lu. I know his power and I know you are risking your being for Li Bo. The past has been destroyed by the existence of this creature. With your help, we can make sure it doesn't destroy the future."

Chen sat up and wiped her eyes with the broad sleeves of her tunic. "That creature is not your nemesis, whatever his name may be. That is a Blood Dragon. It takes the form of the one you fear or hate the most. When I look upon it, I see my uncle. He abused me as a child after my parents died. When I was old enough, I killed him and fled to the Middle Kingdom."

Chen's words, spoken aloud for the first time in so many long years, brought back the image of her dying younger brother. Her father, a village herbalist, had tried to save him with a special drug purchased with the money she had secretly obtained by selling herself into bondage to her uncle. The drug had failed, and her father, confronted with the loss of his only son and the revelation of Chen's bondage and subsequent abuse at the hands of his own brother, committed suicide. Chen, in turn, killed her uncle with a special rat poison brewed by her father for the local farmers. A fitting death, she believed. Her escape from the region, however, was cut short when she was taken prisoner by a merchant caravan and sold into the wine houses of the Imperial capital.

Ah Wu's question brought her back to the Long River. "Then it wasn't an alligator that feasted upon him just a few moments ago!"

"No. It was the phantom's transformed body you saw dive deep into the river. As soon as it touches water it takes the form of an alligator."

"We must go to Li Bo and tell him the sword is the key to defeating the monster," said Ah Wu.

"I have told him. The problem is that it can't be released from its scabbard."

"Mount Wu," they said together and laughed. With that laugh, Ah Wu saw her in a different light. He saw her as he once saw his wife, loving and vulnerable. The wars and the loss of their sons had driven her mad and finally caused her to take her own life. He could never forgive himself for that. Yet this woman, golden-haired and green-eyed, so like his wife. . . .

"Then we shouldn't be sitting around here. We must find Li Bo," said Chen, who sensed in Ah Wu, despite his gruff exterior, the same gentleness that she associated with Li Bo's poetry and the memories of her father and brother.

Ah Wu felt his spirit rallying; Li Bo's life was in danger. "The monster has suffered a serious wound."

Chen's eyes showed her shock. Ah Wu explained what he had seen earlier and his idea that the shamaness somehow had proved to be the monster's match.

"It is probably fighting to save its own miserable existence right now," said Ah Wu. He scanned the river surface for any more signs of the Blood Dragon.

"Yes. It has gone down to the river bottom to seek a cave where it can heal its wounds. This happened once before when it attacked the Hsiang Goddess river spirit that it stupidly mistook for human, and it was seriously injured. That means we have three days to help Li Bo."

Ah Wu was very intent; this could be their only chance. "Why three days?"

"That's the time the spells and medicine that the monster must prepare need to take effect and heal it," answered Chen.

"There was something else you said." Ah Wu struggled. "My memory is not what it used to be. Something you said about it making a mistake in attacking . . . ."

"Yes, it attacked the Long River's spirit, the Hsiang Goddess while the goddess was using a human form to enjoy the river."

"Exactly, if goddesses and those sorts of beings are its undoing, then our shamaness is no simple spirit caller."

Chen was now sitting up with her legs folded under her. Her eyes were clear and as green as a forest of pines in mountain sunlight. She considered the significance of Ah Wu's observations.

"You're right. Look at the talisman she gave Li Bo. Even the monster's best elixir couldn't subdue it. And now it returns in such a condition. We must find Li Bo and assist his journey to Mount Wu. Once the sword is freed from its scabbard, the Blood Dragon can be defeated."

"But how can we get near him," Ah Wu stood up and began pacing, "if he wears that talisman?"

Chen sank down to the ground again. "I forgot. It is very powerful and we couldn't even get to shouting distance before we would be overcome with sickness."

"And I don't trust swordsman Ma, so we couldn't use him to communicate with Li. I'm sure Ma would love to have such a sword," said Ah Wu.

"Ah! It is so simple. Just write him a note telling him the situation, asking him to take off the talisman so that we can appear before him," said Chen, almost dancing with glee.

"Yes, that should work," said Ah Wu.

***

The albino swordsman was deep in his trance working the cold black orb as he roamed through the dreams on the ship. He kept searching, trying to find either the dreams of Li Bo or the shamaness.

"Cold-hearted orb, ruler of the darkness, seek out the poet or the shamaness. Show me their dreams. Open the gate and allow my poison into their hearts."

Over and over he chanted and over and over he drew only silence and emptiness. Could it be that neither of them dreams, he wondered. Certainly, he had caught her that night in the capital, but she had survived. And since that night, he hadn't been able to fix on and re-enter her dream realm. However, this poet fellow, with all the drinking he does, thought the swordsman, must be susceptible to all the dream states. Yet there was nothing, only an annoying purple haze whenever he made contact with the poet's aura. The albino continued to concentrate.

25

The rain began to fall just after darkness penetrated the Gorges. The ship was at anchor after an eventful afternoon. The native pilot never showed up, and the captain, quite drunk, decided to pilot the ship through the New Rapids himself. Actually, he had a trick up his sleeve. The river's steady rise after they entered the Horse Liver Gorge alerted him to the fact that it must be raining farther up the river. With the river on the rise, the most dangerous rocks in the New Rapids would be submerged. Of course, there was always the possibility that a new rock slide had deposited rocks that were above or near the surface of the water level, but then, he reasoned, that was what Floating Ants was for—to deal with anything unforeseen!

He had the crew use the oars to position the ship, then ordered the full sail raised. He went to the stern, lit some incense and prayed to the river spirit, the powerful Hsiang Goddess: "Let it be now, if you so desire," and he threw the incense overboard. The crew thought this a rather strange way to approach such a powerful spirit, but they knew that their captain was certainly not a "normal" man and held on tight on for the ride through the rapids.

As soon as the incense hissed into the water, a powerful following wind rushed up the Horse Liver Gorge and drove the ship forward. The captain called the crew over and they all grabbed on to the helm, following the captain's commands. "Port helm . . . starboard helm . . . quarter helm!" And while they swore he was aiming for the rocks, the ship always managed to miss them and come clear. It plunged through the foaming whitewater, sending the river's spray all over the deck. Several times the crew thought the ship would be swamped, but each time she rose up out of the water and forged ahead.

Down below, the albino swordsman remained unperturbed in his vengeful trance as he sought to enter the dreams of the shamaness and her newly found supporters. In the shamaness's room, Li and Ma were awake, trying to keep the shamaness still. The ship's diving and rolling made them wonder if they would soon be swimming upriver. Several times, they heard and felt the ship's bottom make contact with the rocks—long scraping sounds and loud jolts. Just as Li suggested they might be better off on deck rather than trapped below if the ship piled onto the rocks, it was over. The room stopped jumping around and the gentle motion of the river replaced the sound of raging water against the hull. With the activity above deck lessened and only the lapping of wavelets heard, Li and Ma knew that the ship had cleared the rapids. Once they sailed into calm water, the crew dropped the sail, threw the anchor overboard, and got raving drunk.

Later that evening, once the captain came to, Ma had been able to convince him that they should sail directly to Mount Wu and forgo the next two scheduled stops. At first, he had refused, but when Ma began placing silver pieces on the table before him, he underwent a predictable change of attitude.

"Well, at least this way I can show a profit," the captain growled between cups of Floating Ants.

Ma was now on watch with Lao-huang. Li Bo, after gathering some blankets from his cabin, was asleep on the matting in the shamaness's cabin. He was not going to leave her alone.

At first, he didn't realize he was dreaming as he felt himself rising, getting lighter, lifting from the ground. Slowly his head turned and watched his body grow smaller down below on the straw matting. Then he cleared the ship. Rising through mist and rain over the Gorges, he lost sight of the river. Higher and higher he soared. The stars were shining brightly. The world was finally free from the mist and the heavens were rushing toward him.

A purple aurora surrounded him as he walked toward a pavilion that seemed borne in space by that same light. To either side of him were vast fields of stars, but their light was also purple hued. The source of light, now directly ahead of him, was concentrated in the pavilion.

As he neared it, he could make out a woman sitting on a davenport. It was elaborately carved out of sandalwood and its fragrance filled the air. The woman, dressed in purple silk robes, was the source of the purple glow—it was radiating out of every pore of her body. She had long white hair looped on top of her head in some sort of Court fashion unfamiliar to Li. Her ample cheeks and large eyes were modestly adorned with purple accents. Her purple lips parted in a smile. She raised a fleshy hand, her fingernails further attesting to the preference for purple, and bid him join her.

In front of the seat was a table of dark polished wood covered with a variety of fruits and delicacies. Except for bunches of red, ripe litchi and some very large peaches, the rest he did not recognize.

"Please—" she seemed to speak with her luminous black eyes without moving her lips—"join me in some refreshment, for you've had a trying time."

Li sat across from her. She pointed to a peach of unusual size and it appeared in his hand. Li tasted it and felt refreshed. She smiled and continued; without moving her lips, Li heard, "You have shown much courage in protecting the Grand Shamaness. Due to your efforts, her mortal life has been extended. It is now my turn to guide her spiritual life to fruition."

She paused for a moment, allowing Li to adjust to this new communication form. She was transmitting her thoughts directly to him without using sound or graphic form.

"Li Bo, we know you are familiar with the ways of the Immortals. The Grand Shamaness will now fulfill her spiritual development. Fear not when she dies, for this is only a first step to a higher realm."

Li's mind seemed coherent again as it registered shock.

"Dies? No! I will not allow anything to harm her. She is a vehicle of the Way and must not be interfered with!"

With a flick of her horsehair flywhisk, Li found himself without the anger that had welled up within him.

"Your anger does you disservice here; save it for those who seek to harm the Grand Shamaness. We have little time for such petty emotions. Listen carefully to what I am about to explain. Even now as one evil attempts to pry into your dreams, its more dangerous *Yin* counterpart is gathering strength below the Long River for a final strike."

Li listened.

"As soon as the Grand Shamaness dies, have a coffin of simple wood fashioned for her. Have all of its cracks and crevices sealed tight against water. Place her scrolls in the coffin with her and nothing else. You must guard it closely, for her enemies would even try to desecrate her physical remains. In three days the ship will sink. Do not fear, for you and the coffin will be reunited. Just make sure you carry your *jheng* with the Dragon Pool Sword hidden in it when you leave the ship. Take only the *jheng*."

She read his mind and answered his objections before he could direct them to her. "Only those who have tried to harm the Grand Shamaness will perish in the wreck. Fear not over the loss of life. The good will survive. Once you are reunited with the coffin, do not part with it. Stay with it and you will be taken to her burial site. You will know the spot when the coffin moves no farther."

She stopped and looked deeply into his eyes. Li was transfixed by her stare. Her eyes turned into deep purple flames.

Her thoughts came again. "If any of what I have said is not followed, a great tragedy will befall this dynasty and its people. Hold no doubts about what I say, Li Bo. Follow my words and a great and wondrous event will come to pass. You must tell no one of what you have just realized."

She smiled and began to fan herself gently. Li looked closer and realized it was his fan, the gift from the Emperor, the fan that the woman in the Dream Temple dream had exchanged with him for the Dragon Pool Sword.

A blinding light seared through his eyes and seemed to set his brain on fire—it was as if the woman's words had turned to fire and been burned forever into his consciousness.

He awoke. Ma was shaking him. "Brother Li, awake! Quickly! It must be the dream assassin. You must awaken!"

"Stop! I have never been so awake," said Li. He looked around and saw Lao-huang. "It was no assassin; just ask your master."

Ma looked at Lao-huang. He was munching calmly on a peanut, certainly not his normal state when ghosts or other unwelcome guests were afoot.

"Then what or who was it?"

"Ah," Li remembered the woman's warning. "Oh, probably just some Floating Ants that are still swimming around in my stomach. I don't see how anyone can drink that stuff."

"We have to be careful, for the assassin must know we are keeping this watch and will try to attack when we sleep."

"Yes, maybe he was trying to break into my dream," Li blurted out.

"What!" Ma moved closer. "How do you know this? How did you manage to keep him out?"

"I . . . I'm not sure what happened, just a feeling, just a feeling. Anyway you jolted me too soon for me to remember all the details."

"We must be very careful . . . . There is also the Blood Dragon. We don't know the extent of its injuries. It will not give up on the Dragon Pool Sword," said Ma. His boyish smile returned.

"It is going to be a difficult three or four days. I can take over now. Why don't you get some sleep?" said Li.

"Fine, but given the situation I will sleep here as you do. We can look after each other while we take turns sleeping. If we can watch over each other and wake when he enters our dreams then I think we will be safe."

"Good idea," said Li, who was hoping Ma would hurry up and fall asleep so he could go over what the woman had just told him. The prediction of the shamaness's death had upset him.

— 26 —

At the bottom of the Long River, there are many caves. The Blood Dragon called the initiating spell to mind and was admitted to a large underground grotto. Inside, the creature transformed itself into a human female form, for it was more convenient to move this way, given the tasks now at hand.

Its forehead wound was beginning to heal in the incensed air of the grotto. It went about preparing the altar. Several oil lamps lit the grotto. Besides the central altar, there was a stone alchemical stove with a perpetual fire burning brightly. First, the necessary ingredients needed to be mixed and then cooked in the stove. Time was critical for it would take three days for them to cook to the right consistency. There could be no rushing—too soon and they would not have full potency; too late and they would be lethal.

The Blood Dragon moved quickly among the various bins of strange medicines; plants; preserved animal, human, and insect parts; and other exotica stored in the cave. Gathering the exact proportions of its secret elixir, the creature placed them all in the black iron alchemical pot to simmer for the next three days.

Once its power was restored, it intended to deal personally with those who would interfere with its quest. For the fools on that ship, it planned a most horrifying death. Now, however, its two slaves had to be taught a lesson. The monster was contemptuous of human emotions. It decided to use their emotions to punish them.

The creature walked over to one of the cave walls and pushed. A section of the wall slowly revolved and revealed on its opposite side shelves of small black urns. Each had its own special white character on it. The creature smiled and took two urns from a shelf. It moved back to the altar. Opening them, the creature poured their contents into a white ceramic bowl. The thick red liquid frothed as it filled the vessel.

Next to the altar was a small mound of earth that rose from the stone floor. The earth was white and packed hard. The creature dipped a writing brush in the white bowl and wrote on five slips of colored paper mystical symbols—symbols handed down from a time beyond mortal recall. It then placed one at each of the four compass points around the mound and the fifth on the top of the mound. It took the bowl, sipped from it, and poured its contents onto the top of the mound. The red liquid against the white earth looked as if the earth had received an ugly gash and was pouring out its life.

The creature then performed the shaman's dance of Yü around the mound. Round and round on one foot it hopped the intricate pattern that traced a journey through the Great Void. From star to star it moved, chanting the tones and harmonies that would call down the most horrific spirits.

By the time the pacing was completed, the creature was soaked with a sweet-sour sweat. It threw off its robe and walked naked to the mound. Sitting in the center, on the red liquid, it lay back with its head to the North and spread its arms and legs.

"I call to the power of the Yin force" —its voice was that of a human female— "grant this spell that I now cast."

"Speak, for your offering has found great favor," a cold, thin voice answered out of the incensed air. The creature smiled. Though it was not human, its form was that of a voluptuous woman. The creature had used that form to seduce many of its human victims. Now it would combine its mystical powers and its experience with humans to punish Ah Wu and Chen.

"For three days a great lust" —it used the words with angry contempt— "should overcome those two who defy me."

"So be it," the wind that blew out the lamps seemed to answer. The grotto grew dark as the creature's laughter drowned out the bubbling of the alchemical pot that would be imbibed three days hence.

***

In a deserted temple up on the rocky shore, Ah Wu had built a fire. He was sitting next to Chen as she prepared a fish that he had caught. Her hand twitched into contact with his. A great desire sprang from within her. She glanced away from him, thinking that he must know. Her cheeks reddened and grew hot.

At first, Ah Wu thought he had moved his hand too close to the fire. He examined it for a burn but found, instead, that his sexual appetite was growing. Strange, he thought. Such desires had long remained dormant. Ever since he had lost his wife, he had vowed celibacy to offer merit to her tortured soul. This journey with Li Bo had reinforced that vow. To keep himself fully alert, he had tried to restrain his emotions. He had been right about his forebodings—his death was confirmation enough. Now, however, his sexual desire was growing rapidly. Why? The girl! Is she a fox spirit? She must be weaving some sort of spell. He turned to watch her and found that she was curled up in a corner of the room, crying. Abandoning suspicion—to which he knew he was greatly prone—he limped to her side.

"Chen, what is the matter?"

Again, desire forced itself into his consciousness. He could feel the warmth of her body near his face as he bent close to her.

"We are being attacked," she sobbed.

Ah Wu straightened up and wheeled around.

"Where?" he shouted.

She continued to sob. "Oh, the ache!"

"What is it? What are you talking about? There is no one here."

"Don't you feel it?" she cried.

"What? Feel what?"

"The longing, the desire . . . ."

The closer he came to her the more overwhelming the passion to take her. What was this? His mind tried to pull back, to cool itself.

"Yes, yes, I don't understand . . . ," Ah Wu grunted as his hands tore at his head.

"The Blood Dragon is casting a spell over us, using our emotions to cripple us."

"I can fight this. What's there to gain if the beast makes us lose control? How could this harm us?"

"No, we cannot lose control! You don't understand . . . ," cried Chen as she tore at her clothes. Ah Wu seated himself on the other side of the fire and circulated his *chi* force in an attempt to cool down his body and regain control of his emotions.

"Why is this so dangerous?" He exhaled.

"It has our blood. It keeps a small amount of the blood of its victims to torture them for entertainment. The monster is capable of many esoteric arts. We must not mingle our sexual essences, for if we do, we will be delivered to the monster's complete control for the duration of the spell. It wants to cripple us and reach Li Bo before we can. It fears the sword. Ahh!" Chen had completely disrobed and was moving toward Ah Wu.

As he watched her smooth, warm figure approach him, his desire flared anew, shattering his concentration. He had forgotten he was now a ghost and hadn't recovered all of his mental concentration. Chen began taking his tunic off. Her body was covered with the sweat of passion, but her tear stained face showed her inner torment. Ah Wu tried to get up and leave.

However, she had reached the source of his physical desire and in a moment of passion was down upon it.

The fury of the night rain transformed the dark shadow of the Long River into a ribbon of white foam. Ah Wu and Chen were swept into a maelstrom of blinding desire and agony. An overwhelming white heat consumed them for the rest of the night and beyond.

The Blood Dragon had won the first round.

⇠ 27 ⇢

As soon as Li Bo was off watch, he headed back to his cabin. If the ship was going to sink, he'd better have the *jheng* with him. The dream made so little sense, he thought. Why does the shamaness need to die?

He entered the cabin and picked up the *jheng*. Out on deck, Li paused a moment ducking into the darker shadows that still lined the ship. The watchman was moving along the deck, and Li did not want to be spotted.

Murmuring voices caught his ear. The early morning river was perfectly calm. The rain had let up, but the mist was lingering on the cliff tops, with some strands wafting downward and over the ship. Woven into those river-level strands that wafted past him were the voices of the captain and several of the crew. There was also another voice. It spoke in high-pitched whispers. Li stayed down and peered over the lower railing that led out of the below deck quarters area.

The albino swordsman, whose skin seemed to glow in the early dawn grayness, was carrying on an intense discussion with the captain. When he pulled his censor's credentials from his robe, Li Bo knew from personal experience what he was doing to the crew. He moved over to the other side of the ship and worked his way back to his cabin.

Li was trapped. He needed to get back to the shamaness as quickly as possible, but he couldn't break in on whatever was going on at the other end of the ship. He would have to wait for the albino to finish his business with the crew. Whatever it was,

Li was sure this meeting could only bode ill for the shamaness. Should he warn Ma? Certainly, thought Li, he himself didn't have the skill to hold off the whole crew and the albino single-handedly if they tried to take the shamaness away from him. Li sat in his cabin toying with a wine cup, thinking about the present status of his relationship with Ma Ssu-ming:

Common ground now exists with Ma. Are we friends? At least, he is willing to get the shamaness to Mount Wu. Of course, he has overlooked one thing—once the shamaness is cured, her powers will be restored. Ma will be helpless against them. Could he have really overlooked this? But he has no other choice at this point. Perhaps, but I must remember Ma is no fool.

Then there is the dream. I cannot imagine her death. Can this be her destiny: to become an Immortal on Mount Wu? Why am I so sad at this prospect? Immortals . . . I only know the name; what do I really know of such fabulous creatures? Am I only a dreamer as Ah Wu liked to chide me? Ah Wu—I miss you. I will avenge your death once the Dragon Pool is unsheathed!

The sudden shuffle of feet past the cabin reminded him of the albino swordsman. That was an immediate problem. Li had no idea as to the albino's plan, but this meeting with the crew was ominous. At least Ma was a known quantity, more or less. Li knew he had to throw in with Ma against this so-called court representative. After all, smiled Li, a bandit who could drink and sing well was definitely preferable company to any pompous Court official.

***

"What are you doing with that?" asked Ma as he let Li back into the shamaness' room.

"Well, she enjoyed . . . erh." Li caught himself remembering he hadn't told Ma about his meeting with the shamaness last night on deck. "I think it might make the whole atmosphere more comfortable if there was a little music. Don't shamanesses spend most of their lives enjoying music?"

Ma gave him a strange look and shrugged his shoulders. Li set the instrument down and went to sleep.

Just after dawn, Lao-huang woke them. His chattering had alerted them to the sound of footsteps coming down the steps from above deck. Li remembered the meeting between the albino swordsman and the crew. He had forgotten to tell Ma. There was a gentle knock on the door.

"Stop," he whispered. Ma reached for the door latch. "Don't open it."

"What?" Ma was surprised that Li was awake.

"Something might be going on between your albino friend and the crew. They were having a meeting when I left for my cabin." Li looked down at the sleeping shamaness. "Sorry, it slipped my mind."

There was more tapping at the door.

"Nothing we can do about that," said Ma in a brusque tone. Ma knew it meant trouble for them. The captain was greedy and he would sell his mother's grave for more Floating Ants. Now they could only wait. Ma stood back from the door and readied his sword.

Li pulled his Persian dagger from its resting-place under his left arm. Ma looked under the door, but he could make out only two shadows. He held up one finger to Li—one man.

Ma tried to sound tired. "Yes, what is it?"

"Captain sent some breakfast down for you gentlemen."

"Fine. One moment."

Ma laid his sword near the door so it wasn't visible to the person outside but still within quick reach. Then he pulled his short dagger from its sheath in the small of his back and palmed it in his left hand. He opened the door with his right hand.

A sailor stood there with a wooden tray loaded down with breakfast dishes. Ma took it from him and quickly placed it on the floor. In one flowing movement he returned to the door, bowed, then closed and bolted it. The sailor remained outside staring at the closed door. Ma's dagger ended up in his right hand held behind his back. He turned back to Li Bo and both men smiled at each other.

"Our problem has just begun," said Ma.

"Why?"

Ma smiled and held out a dish. "Would you like the first bite?"

Just then, the shamaness's eyes opened wide and she sat up. Blood began to flow freely from her chest wound.

"My journey begins! Oh Lady of the Purple Vault, receive me!" she said and fell back on her mat. Her eyes remained open and her breathing stopped.

"No!" cried Li as he rushed to hold her.

Ma put down the plate. "She is dead. I have never seen such a death. This is no ordinary sword wound."

Li paid no attention. He held the shamaness's head and stared into her open eyes. They had become deep brown, like the earth at plowing season, but as pure and transparent as they were deep. Then he began to catch sight of something. As if it was surfacing from a clear, deep pond, the object seemed to float upward. As its outlines took shape, Li recognized the face of the woman in his purple dream. She looked directly into his eyes and smiled. Then the image faded and dissipated—only lifeless brown pools remained. Quietly, he lowered her head onto the headrest and closed her eyes.

Li and Ma didn't have time to settle the question of breakfast. They figured that once the shamaness's death was known, the albino's plans would be upset. That could give them a little more time to get closer to Mount Wu. Li Bo even naively thought that it might satisfy the albino, that he would break off and return to his masters in the capital.

They informed the captain of her death and requested that a coffin be built for the shamaness out of the spare planking on board ship. Li insisted that the finished work be completely sealed against water.

"Do you want a ship or a coffin?" the captain had complained.

"These are the sacred rules of her professional order. Would you like to chance a curse for violating them?" said Li, who had told the captain that she was a magician. This was enough to get the crew to do a very thorough job of sealing the coffin. They didn't want to offend anyone connected in anyway with the "unknown"—magicians were widely believed to have good connections in the *Yin* realm.

Ma was dismayed when Li placed the stolen Imperial scrolls in the shamaness's coffin. Nevertheless, Li would hear nothing of his arguments, especially when Ma evoked the right of the owner, the Emperor, to have them returned.

"She knows much better, where she is going, how to use those scrolls than the whole Han-lin Academy," Li scoffed. Since he had once been a member of that prestigious body of intellects attached to the imperial person, he figured that should be enough to make his point.

Ma said no more; he needed to figure out what his next move would be. At least with the scrolls sealed in the coffin, he knew where they were when it came time to retrieve them.

Down at the other end of the ship, the captain had wasted no time informing the swordsman of what had happened.

"Wait for my signal" was all the albino said to the captain.

***

The coffin was finished just after the ship anchored for the night. Li had asked that it be placed in his cabin for shelter while they made for Mount Wu. There was no room in his cabin for both the coffin and himself, so he moved in with Ma across the hall. They kept the door to Li's room locked and placed Lao-huang out in the hallway to stand guard.

"Elder brother Li, we are now only two days from Mount Wu. They will strike us tomorrow night as we come in sight of the port at Ba-tung. That way" —he took a sip of wine that had been warming— "they can get into port and claim we killed her."

"Let them come," Li said offhandedly, not really interested in what they tried. He could only think of her death. So sudden, and that face rising in her dead eyes? Would the dream be fulfilled? The Immortal said in three days, tomorrow night. And what of his poetry? Had that too died with her? He wondered if maybe it made more sense just to take Ma's offer and travel back to the Court with him and present the sword to the Emperor. There was a lot more certainty in that plan then what now faced him.

"Elder brother Li, are you listening to me?" asked Ma, well aware that the odds were not in their favor.

"Why, eh, yes, sorry but I'm still in shock over her passing. So sudden."

"Yes, strange. yet we must consider the living, and that's us. It's no longer a simple matter of how to get her back to the Court. Now we must worry how to get us all out of here—alive."

"What," said Li, sipping from his wine cup as the warm steam from the liquid wended its way upward and disappeared, "will you do regarding your responsibilities?"

Ma smiled as if it was a minor inconvenience to have lost the Emperor's favorite diviner. "There is not much I can do. I can't bring the dead back to life. Those scrolls" —a smile reappeared on his face— "would certainly make a particular august personage very happy."

"How about if you gave that certain personage a map to where they were buried?"

"Yes, and you would, of course, draw it to precise scale?"

Li smiled. "Why of course, it is the least I could do for you, dear brother."

Ma's face grew serious. "Considering where you are going, I'd think twice about this issue. Those scrolls do not belong to the shamaness and are considered by the Court to be of a most dangerous nature."

"yet if in the end, after the sword is unlocked on Mount Wu and the Blood Dragon dealt with, I returned with you to present it to Court?"

Ma was surprised that Li was still considering that course of action. "Well, of course, that route is always open to you. The Emperor would be most pleased to possess the Dragon Pool word and to have his scrolls returned. He would liberally reward such a benefactor."

"But first, I must honor the agreement with her that, if she died, I would transport her body with those scrolls to a burial on Mount Wu."

Well, that was almost what had happened, thought Li. He continued. "Now after I have done that, I will reconsider my relationship with the Court."

"Ah, a real gentleman," laughed Ma.

Li's eyes lit up at Ma's obvious sarcasm. He was being pushed too far, Ma was impugning his integrity.

"Please accept my apologies, for the wine did not allow me to resist the chance of seeing your eyes like that," said Ma. "Good idea," Ma followed up, not letting Li recover his balance. "That way we are both satisfied. Of course, you won't interfere with my retrieval of the imperial scrolls, since I am helping you keep your word."

"Yes, we both come out of it as gentlemen." Li raised his cup in mock salute. He would never let Ma or anyone else desecrate her grave, but he needed time to think his way out of this.

"All we need to figure out is how to get to Mount Wu alive," Ma said, returning the salute with his wine cup.

***

In a cave below the Long River, candles flickered to life revealing a woman in meditation upon a mound of earth. A bittersweet smell permeated the grotto and mingled with the scent of sandalwood incense. On the other side of the central altar the low sound of bubbling liquid seeped from a covered black iron alchemical pot on the stone stove. It would take another complete day before the elixir reached full potency.

The Blood Dragon came out of its trance. It was now dressed in the ceremonial robes befitting its demonic rank, which wasn't high. Rising, it moved to the altar. Lighting incense and bowing, it picked up a handful of paper-cut doll figures and a larger one made of wood. The creature placed them on the top of the white earthen mound where it had been meditating. The blood thrown there earlier had been completely absorbed and the mound had returned to its original pure white color.

Disrobing, the Blood Dragon took up a short iron sword and prick ball on a hair cord. The ball had long thorns protruding from it in every direction. The creature began singing and hopping on one foot around the mound. As it jumped, it struck its back and breasts with the prick ball and drew the sword across its thighs. As the flow of blood from the multiplying wounds increased, the Blood Dragon moved across the mound. The paper-cut dolls and wooden figure were splattered with the monster's blood. Once the figures were fully coated, the creature returned to the altar and made full body prostrations to the demonic figures on the altar.

There was movement on the mound. One by one the paper figures, then the wooden doll, began to shake. The Blood Dragon walked over to the mound and sprinkled fine incense powder over the figures.

"Ha! My little bloody ones. Drink deeply of my energy. Strengthen yourselves for the coming fight and bring me back the heads of all those on that ship!"

The creature rubbed a finger across one of its bloody wounds and drew a charm on a narrow piece of white paper. It placed the paper on its sword and raised it over the altar allowing it to touch an incense stick and catch fire. The ashes fell into a cup containing water drawn from the Long River. The Blood Dragon drank and with its mouth sprayed the contents over the mound.

"Go now and avenge me in their blood!"

A huge fireball rose from the mound and turned the grotto crimson yellow, outlining a dark female figure holding a sword high over the mound. It flew out of the cave and boiled toward the river surface.

— 28 —

The tightening of the fishing line in the water disturbed the stillness of the mist-shrouded night. The watchman at the other end of the ship never heard it or the sound of the fish being pulled out of the water. Lao-huang was not your ordinary monkey. He knew that the night had to return to its stillness before he could try for another.

Ma and Li had gone the whole day without any food. They were too busy guarding the shamaness's coffin. When they finally realized they were hungry, Ma suggested sending Lao-huang out to do some fishing. They were very happy when the monkey returned with three good-sized fish. Ma, Li, and their little fisher friend ate grilled fish and drank warm wine till late in the night.

Things on the ship had quieted down. The mist had settled from the cliff tops around the ship and the river continued to push gently past them. Li, however, couldn't help thinking about his dream, while Ma savored the food and drink.

The Purple Immortal, as Li had come to think of her, had said within three days the ship would sink. If that were correct, it would be tomorrow night. It made sense, thought Li, since we will be off Ba-tung tomorrow night. That way it would be easy to get the coffin out of the assassin's hands and on shore, where he might find some bearers or even another ship to transport it to Mount Wu. If the Purple Immortal hadn't forbidden him, Li Bo would have warned Ma about the impending disaster. Perhaps, he consoled his conscience, Ma will be deemed one who wished no harm to the shamaness and be spared.

Lao-huang had also returned with a bag of cooked rice. He raided the galley as the fish cooked and the crew slept.

"We have enough food to carry us till we reach Ba-tung," said Li.

"If we can keep the captain on course," Ma said, as he picked at the fish with his frosted slicing knife.

"You really think they will try something when we reach Ba-tung?"

"The albino is up to something. With the shamaness's death his concerns will have shifted to those scrolls and possibly a part of the shamaness."

Li stopped eating and looked up.

"What do you mean?"

"Most likely her head," Ma said. He took some rice with his fish, never glancing up at Li.

"No! Why? She is dead."

"My dear elder brother, I thought you knew the ways of the Court. This is no shock to those who have witnessed their power struggles. Much worse has been committed in the name of the will of Heaven," said Ma, throwing back a cup of wine to down the mouthful of rice he had swallowed.

"No wonder she wanted to leave it all behind; even in death they allow her no peace." Li gripped his wine cup. He took several more cups of hot wine, then looked for his *jheng* to make sure it was near. More than ever he wished for the shipwreck. He recalled the Purple Immortal's words—only those who have tried to harm the Grand Shamaness will perish.

Li didn't wish to continue the conversation. "Will you or I take the first watch?"

"I think now that there is a sealed coffin to watch over and not a life at stake, we need only let Lao-huang stay out in the corridor."

"Yes, we need our rest. Who knows what tomorrow will bring?" Li said, having a strong apprehension about the next day's events. Both men bedded down as best they could in Ma's small cabin.

Li fell asleep right away, but Ma lay on his bed mat staring at the red glow from the brazier reflected on the ceiling. They would have to be careful, he thought. The albino will be practicing his craft, tonight; he hadn't mentioned this to Li. The old fellow needs his rest. But, if I were that assassin, thought Ma—and master Li seems to regard us as the same type—finishing off opponents in their sleep saves a lot of trouble.

Of course, continued Ma to himself, killing a man in his sleep is not much of a challenge and is rather cowardly. Too bad master Li doesn't really understand that there are differences even among killers, but he is very much taken by the shamaness and isn't thinking all that clearly.

***

Outside, around the ship, the mist thickened. The Long River was calm as the captain came out of his cabin. The watchman turned and saluted him. The captain acknowledged and wandered down to the bow. He moved to the rail and watched the bow lantern's reflection in the water. An unusual pearl-frosted strand of mist moved off the river and onto the ship. It glided toward the captain and swirled around him.

He sat down on a cushion that Li and Ma had used.

"So you have come to say good-bye to me?" the captain said with a smile. The mist moved round, round the man, then flowed away from him, and began to condense. The other end of the ship, where the watchman stood, was completely engulfed by what had now turned to fog.

A form took shape from the strands of congealing mist. A woman in a mist-like green robe trimmed in cream borders with finely embroidered red silk lotuses stepped forward. She was slender, with long black hair intertwined with duckweed that flowed down past her delicate waist. There was a soft luminescence about her. Her eyes were the stars that sparkled in the Silver River high in the heavens at night, and her lips, fine like the thin kelp that grew along the shores of the Long River.

"Soon we shall be together, fear not," so faint her voice that it seemed to be like rippling water far out across a vast distance. Yet she stood there in front of him.

"I suspected," the captain whispered.

"Do not be so sad. At last, you shall be with me, forever," the voice continued.

"Yes, I have so longed for that. It's hard to believe the time has come. I am ready. There is an evil aboard that is forcing me to do things against my principles."

"Yes, I know. The *Yin* element has caused much suffering and pain. Bear with it, for soon my love, so soon, you will be freed from it all; for I am part of the balance."

The voice faded and the glow dimmed.

***

When dawn broke, the crew found the captain fast asleep with a bottle of Floating Ants next to him. An unusual blanket woven from river reed was wrapped around him. When he awoke, the captain ignored all the crew's questions and went about his duties as usual.

Once again, none of the passengers showed up for breakfast. The crew wondered if this was going to be the new routine; at least, they would have plenty to eat. While the captain's sleep on deck seemed to have been accepted as one of his drunks, they could not help speculating on their passengers' reluctance to eat.

"I don't like it. That woman dies and now those two passengers spend all their time with the coffin."

"Yes, things are getting stranger the farther we move up river."

"I tell you it has to do with Mount Wu. We are getting closer and closer to it. The power of that Rain Goddess must be increasing."

"Bah, makes no sense to me. The Rain Goddess affects the brains of those two passengers? Come on, don't you see—one of them is a swordsman. That type has little respect for the spirits. No, something else is going on here. I don't like it, but I can't figure it out either."

"And that albino government official . . . ."

"The less said about him, brother, the better for us all."

When the captain moved within sight the conversations stopped and the men went on their way. Of course, the captain knew the men were concerned. He had a good idea why Li and Ma didn't show up for breakfast. They weren't stupid. Probably they had seen him talking with that albino bastard. They knew he would pressure or buy off the captain to have at them.

The captain turned to check the river depth and found himself face to face with the pink-eyed albino.

"Have they eaten yet?" he seemed to whisper in his high-pitched hissing voice.

"No, no. They haven't come out yet. Probably too drunk."

"Or too smart. Are things ready for tonight?"

"Yes. We will anchor off Ba-tung and make your signal."

"Remember, just before you drop anchor make the signal, then you and your crew are to leave the ship. Anyone found on board will never be heard of again. Understood?" he hissed.

"Yes, yes," the captain answered, averting his eyes. When he looked up, the swordsman was gone.

The sky was still overcast as the mist had returned only to the cliff tops. A pair of falcons glided down low over the river, but the river was sullen and refused to part with its gifts. The wind, however, remained generous as the ship moved upriver toward Ba-tung, the last port of call before Mount Wu.

— 29 —

After lunching in their cabin, Li Bo and Ma Ssu-ming made an appearance on deck. They brought some cushions with them and their brazier. At the bow of the ship, they settled to some song making and wine drinking. Everything seemed normal and the crew relaxed a little. It was Li, alerted that today would be the ship's last, who first noticed the shift in the weather.

"Brother Ma, do you feel the wind?"

Ma stopped poking at the reddening coals in the brazier and looked up. The mist was now swirling above the cliff tops with much greater intensity. A cold wind came up from behind the ship and blew across the bow.

"Yes, it's cold," Ma said, moving closer to the brazier.

Whitecaps began to form on the Long River and the ship rose and fell more rapidly. Li could see the captain at the stern issuing orders to the crew. The mist cleared, revealing high-rising storm clouds. All around them the dark clouds seemed to be pushing the mist away and blotting out the sun. The world darkened. For a moment, everything was quiet.

Then the wind gusted, tearing at the sail, blowing it one way and then another. The crew lowered it and began preparing the long oars. Li and Ma broke up their nest and moved along the deck toward their cabins. They noticed the cook lighting the ship's running lanterns. Day had almost become night. It would be a long and rough pull to Ba-tung. The crew rowed slowly to conserve their energy and keep the ship under control in the whitecap-tossed river.

"Well, there's not much more we can do," said the captain, coming up behind the two friends.

"Can we outrun the storm?" asked Li.

"Not sure. If the wind settles down, we could hoist the sail and make a run for it."

Just as the captain finished speaking, the wind moved to the stern of the ship and blew steadily. He looked at the two men and shook his head. "I don't like this, even for the Three Gorges this is strange."

"Come, Captain, Nature is not so easily understood," laughed Li.

"Perhaps, but we will have to seek shelter at Ba-tung if this turns into a storm," answered the captain. He yelled to the crew. "Hoist the sail and keep someone on it if the wind comes around again."

With the sail at full height and the wind bearing down with greater intensity on the stern of the ship, they began to make good headway. The captain stayed at the bow watching for any obstacles that might abruptly end their progress. Li and Ma walked back to their cabins.

"The albino got to him. Looks like Ba-tung will be their attacking point," remarked Ma.

"Perhaps the storm will pass and the captain will surprise us," smiled Li.

"You don't really believe that do you?" said Ma. They settled in his cabin to drink and sing the afternoon away.

The river, however, was not to be soothed. It reacted to the wind's steady increase by becoming more restive. The sky continued to darken and the ship was tossed from wave to wave. Li and Ma had to extinguish the brazier and stow things away in the cabin.

Around dusk the rain hit. Without warning, it streamed from the heavens in long strings. Birds and monkeys, along the shore, called out as if startled by the sudden intensity of it all. Li and Ma thought their cabin had been hit by thousands of arrows.

Lao-huang came scampering in from the hallway. The Long River churned. It glowed white in the evening darkness—as if a white rainbow settled in it.

Li remembered the start of their river journey, out on the deck in the pouring rain. The shamaness had explained the white rainbow as the river churned pale with rage. Could the shamaness, thought Li, have been predicting her own death when she commented on the white rainbow? Whatever, the journey may be ending—an end of some sort, he thought.

"We should get ready," said Ma, who was adjusting his sword and making sure his small dagger was within easy reach.

"What do you mean?" said Li, wondering if the Purple Immortal had also visited Ma.

"I figure with all the speed we made this afternoon we should be just off Ba-tung somewhere, and the captain is probably trying to find some safe anchorage."

As if right on cue, the ship slowed and floundered.

"He's dropping the sail, trying to anchor somewhere out of the main force of the storm."

Li quickly looked around for his *jheng*. He wrapped it up and strapped it on his back. Ma gave him a strange look.

"If I get thrown into the water, the *jheng* will help me stay afloat, and the sword will stay with me," said Li, who was doing his best to act natural.

Ma thought for a moment. "Yes, that's a good idea. But the storm might be an advantage for us. It could have disrupted the albino's plans long enough that we might get away."

On deck, the captain and his crew were fighting both the storm and their passenger.

"I don't care who you are! We have to drop anchor. If we all leave the ship now, there is no telling where it will be when your men arrive," the captain shouted. The rain pelted him and his albino passenger.

"All right, but I don't want to tip off your guests. Do it now!" the swordsman hissed and moved off to the bow. He fired a small rocket high into the storm-tossed night sky. It wavered, buffeted by the winds as it climbed, and exploded. After a moment, the clouds and rain smothered its yellow light. The albino waited at the bow. The storm lashed at him, trying to drive him back down below, but he remained. From somewhere out in the dark storm a green light shone. It began to move toward the ship. The albino moved the two white lanterns from either side of the bow together over the center of the bow to give his men a fix on the ship.

Lao-huang's chirping had alerted Ma. He caught sight of the rocket's explosion. He turned from the porthole and rummaged under his bunk. Pulling one lantern out, he lit it and placed it in his window.

"Your men?" said Li calmly.

"Yes. And hope they can see it."

"Why?"

"The albino has called for his men and our faithful crew is abandoning ship."

Li's eyes widened. He had heard the anchor go over just before Lao-huang began chattering. Now he could hear something bumping at the stern of the ship. It must be the small lifeboat they towed behind them. So that was the plan, Li thought. The albino's men would replace the crew and do whatever they wanted—without witnesses. From the bow, Li heard another bump. The assassin's men were boarding.

"Time to fight!" Ma drew his sword. Li and Ma were preparing to leave the cabin and meet the boarders in the darkness of their hallway when they heard fighting.

"My men have arrived!" shouted Ma. Screams came from the bow. Ma dashed out. As Li made sure the *jheng* was securely lashed to his body, Lao-huang jumped up and down. He kept leaping at the wall behind Li, who thought the monkey had gone mad.

Then he saw what Lao-huang was trying to attack. In the seam between two of the planks a small figure of a man was wiggling to get out. The figure was flat and seemed to be carrying a spear. It pulled itself out, dropped to the floor, and thrust the spear at Lao-huang. As soon as it hit the floor, it grew into a full-sized man—with a full-sized spear aimed at Li.

Li Bo leapt to one side as the spear flew into the wall, cutting the sash that bound the *jheng* to his back. It fell to the deck, but before the man could pull the spear out, Li, freed from the awkwardness of the *jheng*, moved in with his knife and attacked. He slashed violently at the man. Each time a cut landed, Li heard the sound of paper ripping, and blood filled the cut. In a short time, he had reduced the man to a pile of shredded, bloody paper, which disappeared.

Ma rushed into the room where Li had retreated. He saw the *jheng* on the deck and the spear in the wall.

"We are under attack by another force. Some strange, armed group is destroying the albino's men. Several attacked me, and it was like cutting paper when I destroyed them."

All the while Ma was speaking, screams came from the bow.

"Well, maybe we can just hole up here and let the little paper men do the job for us," said Li.

Before Ma could answer, another had wiggled through the wall and landed on the floor. Armed with a sword, he struck at Ma, who parried and cut at the figure's head. Before he could subdue it, another had entered from the wall. Things were getting very crowded in the small cabin, so Ma moved the fight out into the hallway, leaving Li to contend with their newest visitor.

As Li fought, he thought these figures were obviously the work of some magician or shaman. There is an easier way to defeat such figures, he remembered. As soon as he had dispatched the one left in the room, he rummaged through the scroll satchel in his backpack and pulled out a copy of the *Yi-jing*.

A figure was wiggling through the porthole rim. Li faced it and made an incantation:

"O *Book of Changes*, I direct your great transforming power at these creatures to call them back to their original state." When the figure dropped to the ground, Li opened the scroll facing the figure. It collapsed into a paper cutting splattered with blood.

"It works!" was all Li could manage to say as he heard Ma yell for help. He grabbed the scroll and ran to the deck.

Ma was fighting a huge monster-like figure that brandished a large double-edged sword. The wind and rain were fierce. Li could hardly make out Ma and his opponent. He quickly recited the incantation to the scroll and ran up to the creature. It saw Li and moved on him to attack.

"Stay back. He is more than a match for you!" screamed Ma.

As the giant loomed over Li to strike, the poet was quicker. He let the scroll unfurl in the wind and fly on a gust of wind into the creature's face. Within an instant, it disappeared and a wooden doll fell at Li's feet. The scroll flew up into the wind and the darkness. They saw it move away from the ship. Lightning strikes began.

"You never cease to amaze me, elder brother," Ma laughed as the wind screamed past them. Li's smile was tired and wan—too tired to tell Ma that the "trick" with the *Book of Changes* was something he learned as a youth with his Daoist sword master.

"Let us go to the cabin," he yelled. They got as far as the hallway out of the direct fury of the storm, when Li stopped.

"My dagger. I dropped it on the deck when I unfurled the *Book of Changes*. It was a gift from my Daoist swordsmaste., I must retrieve it!" said Li. He ran out on the deck.

Ma let him go and dashed back into the cabin. He unwrapped the *jheng*, opened the end, and took out the Dragon Pool. Its red gemstone was still glowing.

"Lao-huang, here, take this to the kitchen for safe keeping." The monkey grabbed the sword and ran off into the storm. Ma replaced the end and rewrapped the *jheng*.

"I will bring it to Court for him. He is too confused and too idealistic to follow a practical course," said Ma aloud to himself. He put down the *jheng* just as Li entered the cabin.

"Got it! We must abandon the ship; the crew is gone," said Li. He went for his *jheng*, cut a strip of cloth from his old blue robe, and fashioned a new sash to tie it on his back.

"Elder brother, I must seek out the albino swordsman and finish it here. He is the Emperor's sworn enemy, and there is no telling what he will try now. His men are destroyed and he is alone."

Li tried to argue against more fighting. "With this storm you have to be crazy. We must get off the ship and to shore. Save ourselves. Now is not the time to continue the fight."

"No! Now is the best time—strike first!" yelled Ma, raising his sword.

"The Blood Dragon might be nearby," insisted Li.

"What!"

"Those puppet warriors were its spirit proxies. Their dead forms will pile up at its feet. Soon it will be on us in a rage. We must leave here for we are no match for its powers."

"Give me a few moments. If I don't return, then leave the ship without me." Before Li could protest, Ma had disappeared. Lao-huang came screeching down the hallway and ran after him. Li had to attend to the shamaness.

As Li opened the door to his cabin to check on the coffin, a great wave hit the ship. It was driven in one direction until the anchor chain pulled taunt and jerked it back. Everything in the cabin went flying. The coffin rammed into the wall smashing it. Another mountain of a wave caught the ship and drove it forward. The anchor pulled back, but this time the chain snapped.

The loud BANG! made Li think the ship had exploded. The ship, now freed, moved at incredible speed toward its death.

Li had just reached the coffin, which was on the deck, and he was trying to push it back into the cabin when the ship plowed through the rocks that loomed abruptly in its rampaging path. The impact tore out the bottom of the ship. Within a single lightning flash, it sank out of sight. The rain continued to whip the Long River as the wind and lightning drove everything before them.

— 30 —

"Chen, Chen, are you okay?"

There was no response as Ah Wu watched her naked body lying face down on the cave floor. He pressed his fingers to her jugular vein and felt a very slight pulse. She could have died, thought Ah Wu. He wasn't in much better shape, but at least he was conscious. He moved over to the small stream that flowed through the building and drank from it. He ripped a piece of cloth from his robe and soaked up water with it. Ah Wu crawled back to Chen. He turned her over and gently wiped her forehead and face with the wet rag.

Her eyelids fluttered. Ah Wu pulled her robe over her so she wouldn't awake naked. How is she going to react? he wondered. For three days, they had made uncontrollable love. yet thought Ah Wu, should I think of it as love? Since their actions had been forced on them by the evil intentions of the Blood Dragon, how could he dignify it with the word "love"? yet he could not deny that something more than hatred and anger had been within him for these three days. Their "love-making" seemed to have dissipated those negative emotions—probably not the Blood Dragon's hoped-for results! More than that, it had brought back to Ah Wu the tender feelings he once shared with his wife, feelings that after their sons' death and her subsequent suicide, he had buried deep in his heart.

Her eyes began to open. Ah Wu squeezed the remaining water from the rag onto her lips. He noticed a red glow in her cheeks that wasn't there before. Then she focused on his face and smiled. "I have grown up, haven't I?"

"What?" For the first time, he could feel his scar blush.

She laughed. "I guess I'm no longer 'that little-girl Chen.'"

"Oh, I'm sorry . . . ah . . . ."

"Yes. Well, there was not much we could do about this, was there?"

"The monster is pure evil," said Ah Wu. He turned his back so Chen could dress.

"Yes, we are like camel dung to it—something to burn for warmth. It seems the spell is over, and that means the monster will soon be on the move. Its potions are ready to be taken, and it will be revived to full strength," said Chen.

Ah Wu turned around and, for a moment, caught something in her bamboo green eyes. Yes, she had grown. There was something different. Something between the two of them, and not just the suffering they had gone through together as slaves of the monster. It was something positive. And then, there were camels. Ah Wu remembered camels; he had forgotten them! A faint smile played over his hairy face.

Chen caught Ah Wu's glance and smiled. A warm smile seemed to acknowledge Ah Wu's sense of the positive. She broke off and returned to the present problem.

"Ah Wu, enough of this romantic nonsense; we must leave. The monster will first come here to see its handiwork and finish us off."

"Oh, yes, yes, of course. We must find Li Bo and rescue the Dragon Pool Sword. It is our only chance."

"But how do we find him?" Chen wondered.

"Follow the Long River. He is certainly on it."

Chen looked worried. "To follow the river," she said, "is dangerous, for the monster will be using it to come to us. We would be in its natural habitat."

"Then we go inland and follow the river from the land?"

"That will take more time, but it is safer."

They tried to cover the traces of their three-day stay before they left. Behind the derelict temple was a mountain range that paralleled the Long River. They headed into that range and flew off toward the port city of Ba-tung and Mount Wu. Progress was slow at first, because Ah Wu hadn't completely mastered, nor was completely comfortable with, the technique of flying.

~ 31 ~

It was time. The monster understood the scents coming from the cauldron. It rose from its meditation cushion and stumbled.

"What's this?" it growled. At its feet were the cut and torn remnants of the spirit troop it had sent against Li's ship.

"They have destroyed my army! For this they will experience death and enslavement at my hands!" Its eyes burned white. Then it remembered the elixir. It rushed to the stove and dampened the flame. Pulling the iron kettle from the fire it opened the top and smelled. Was it right? The creature sniffed again. Might be slightly over-cooked, it thought, but, of course, such things cannot to be judged in a precise manner. As it waited for the potion to cool to drinking temperature, it began to plan the next move.

"First, I should take care of those useless slaves of mine. I shall send them straight to the ninth circle of Hell. Then they will see how kind I was," it said and laughed aloud. The cave shook and the river above broke out in whitecaps.

"Next," it continued, "I will visit the poet's ship and drain the blood from him and his companions one by one, as their spirits vie to tell me the location of the Dragon Pool Sword. Then I will turn on the shamaness," it said with a smile, and went into the one-legged dance of Yü.

The potion was cooled and it drank the frothy dark liquid to the last drop. The Blood Dragon grew in size. A dark glow enveloped its body. It was ready to seek revenge. The creature moved out to the underwater entrance of the cave and shot to the surface of the Long River. It swam at a frightful pace to the deserted temple where Ah Wu and Chen had been attacked by its spell.

Transformed into its human shape, it searched everywhere but found no trace of the two. Again, its eyes burned white. "Have they eluded me?" it questioned. "Impossible! They are nothing. It is Li Bo that I must have."

It shot back into the water and disappeared. Using the tunnel network that exists deep under the Long River, the Blood Dragon could cover the distance to Ba-tung much quicker than by following the river's natural course.

Surfacing off Ba-tung, it found an angry river, swept by rain and lightning. Swimming toward the shoreline, it passed several human bodies, then some full paper forms of its spirit troop. Someone used an incantation on them, it thought—must be the shamaness. But what has happened to the ship?

Then it found a small boat caught up in the weeds near shore. Changing into human form, it appeared in the boat. A man lay back against the bottom. The creature went to the man and cradled his head. It could feel the blood still pulsing through his veins, warm and inviting. First, it thought, I must find out what happened. The monster blew into the man's face and he revived.

"What have the Floating Ants done to me this time?"

"You are delirious. What has happened to your ship?" growled the monster.

"My ship?" He seemed on the verge of tears. "She is dead, her heart torn out by the albino."

"What? Your ship sank? What of Li Bo? The shamaness?"

"All dead, all dead, all blown to Mount Wu. And my ship. Dead, dead . . . ," were the captain's last words as he joined his ship.

So much for that, thought the monster as it moved to bite the man's armpit and take his blood. The scent of sweet basil permeated the air. The monster stopped. Where had it smelled that scent before? This was a warning of some sort. Then it looked beyond the stern of the boat. Floating across the storm-tossed river was a figure in light green robes moving toward it. The scent grew stronger as the figure got closer.

"This time you should make no mistake as to my identity, for I do not appear as a simple fisherwoman."

A sudden chill ran through the Blood Dragon. The Hsiang Goddess, Mistress of the Long River and Lake Dong-ting! For a moment, the thought of the recently ingested elixir buoyed its spirits.

"What concern is this of yours, that the mighty Hsiang Goddess should involve herself with this human thing?" it asked.

"Be gone, filthy one! Your elixir is dog piss to the Hsiang Goddess. It makes you no more my match than the first time."

The Blood Dragon, realizing that the Hsiang Goddess knew everything that happened in her river, was shaken. It lay the human back down and retreated overboard, diving deep into the river. Once I have the sword, it thought, I will return for her and her human.

The Goddess moved on board and summoned the dead man's spirit.

"I have come for you, my love, as I promised," she whispered. The captain's spirit form opened its eyes and smiled.

***

As the Blood Dragon continued its descent, it came across more of the paper men that it had sent against the ship, then another slip of paper. Immediately it felt uncomfortable. Looking closer, it recognized an unusual Daoist talisman. It had to be the one that the shamaness wrote for Li Bo. The monster swam away from it. So, it thought, the ship has sunk and Li Bo thrown into the water. Searching the bottom of the river, the Blood Dragon found the wreck, but Li's body wasn't among those that were feeding the fish.

Mount Wu, it thought, the human had just said. That is the only place where the Dragon Pool Sword can attain its potential. The creature rose to the surface. It was night and the storm raged on. The Blood Dragon moved calmly upriver toward Mount Wu. There was plenty of time, now, for Li Bo must be moving along the slower land route—the storm would keep all shipping off the river for a day or so.

**

Li Bo awoke to the sound of rushing water. There was a pale light all around him. He was on top of some sort of wooden object, for he could feel the rough grain of the wood against his fingers. The water was making a thudding sound. He listened. "*Wu-shan, Wu-shan, Wu-shan, Wu-shan*" it seemed to be throbbing.

"Mount Wu?" he said aloud as his eyes opened. Surely, he thought, I must be far downriver by now, taken by the Long River's eastern flow, far from Mount Wu.

Then he realized he was on top of the shamaness's coffin—it had saved him, not the *jheng*, which was still secure on his back. How? From the time the ship smashed against the rocks to this moment was a blank. So, thought Li, that is why the Purple Immortal wanted the coffin waterproofed. She wanted to save it when the ship went down.

The water hitting Li in the face made him realize that the coffin was not moving downriver away from Mount Wu. He looked ahead and saw the coffin was pushing through the waves under its own force—upriver! He was frightened. There was no sail, no oar, and no bamboo towlines—how could this be? He gripped the coffin even tighter.

Now he noticed that the water, which splashed occasionally over the front of the wooden box and hit his face, was warm. Odd, he thought. Last night the water was chilling to the touch. He moved his hand out into the river as it flowed by the sides of the coffin—warm.

The weak morning light was trying to make its way through the mist that had taken the river back from last night's fog. It was, thought Li, a wondrous mist; no longer a white frost in hue, but a radiant warm pearl-like glow. The greens on the banks of the Long River had a special softness to them. How tranquil things have become, he thought. Visibility up ahead was still limited, and even the steep limestone cliffs of the river were obscured at times. Li tried to make himself as comfortable as possible. He could hear monkeys and birds chattering along the cliff walls. He wondered if Ma and Lao-huang had made it.

After a while, he moved farther up on the coffin lid and noticed that his clothes were dry. Just as his initial fear had subsided, it returned. He dipped his sleeve into the river. When he pulled it out, he gasped, "It's not wet!"

This cannot be, he thought. Then I am dead. I am a ghost like Chen . . . maybe even under the power of the Blood Dragon. Li Bo knew that only ghosts could travel through water without being wetted. He flung his arm down on the coffin top and laid his head on it. When his face rubbed the wooden top, he felt its smoothness. He raised his head and studied the wood. The crew had used old rough knotted scraps to fashion her coffin. The wood had changed; it was smooth to the touch and becoming smoother.

Li watched in amazement as the coffin began to change, almost imperceptibly, its form. At first, the wood smoothed out, losing its imperfections and roughness. Then the shape of the coffin was transformed—rounder and sleeker. It began to take the shape of the burial container of an aristocrat. Once its shape seemed to stabilize, it picked up speed and easily equaled that of the fastest down-stream gorge-runner on a good day.

More changes. The color of the box changed, as designs, very ancient designs, formed all over it, symbolizing mystical clouds, fantastic mountains, and strange creatures. Li became increasingly uncomfortable, for those designs were those associated with the "Perfected Ones"—the Immortals, those rare, extraordinary beings that Li had devoted his life to seeking out, but had never glimpsed. At least, he reminded himself, until that night at the Dream Temple.

She was a shamaness—a great shamaness, but could it be that there is much more than this? Have I missed so much? Perhaps . . . Perhaps, I should just throw myself into the great river and save the time and suffering of reaching my appointed place of death. Is there a greater fool spending a lifetime of offering poems to those wondrous beings and then, when faced with one, not recognize her? Now the shamaness is dead, and with her my hope to regain my poetic voice. Ah! What has become of me in my old age?

The scent brought Li Bo out of his despair. It seemed to rise out of the coffin just as Li had thoughts of throwing himself into the Long River. It was frankincense, the same fragrance as at the Dream Temple. Li bent his head down near the top of the coffin and inhaled. What a wonderful scent, he thought. A purple light seemed to fill the air around him and he heard a voice:

"The twelve peaks; the twelve peaks."

He saw himself standing as he had in the dream—on a mountaintop, surrounded by the twelve peaks. His destination was clear. Overwhelmed by the fragrance and the vision, exhausted from last night's ordeal, Li laid his head on the coffin top and fell asleep as the warm fragrant waters of the Long River swirled past him.

PART THREE

THE MOUNTAIN

— 32 —

When Li awoke, it was dark. The coffin had stopped moving; around him were the sounds of the Long River flowing, the insects singing, the occasional owl hoot, and the chirping of small water frogs. He looked up and saw a campfire. His feet were on land. The coffin had beached itself.

Then, out of the darkness, he heard the cry, a long mournful cry, and he thought of Ah Wu and Old Zhou. The mournful cry filled Li Bo's heart—it was a gibbon. As he looked up, he could just make out the silhouette of the mountain against the faint light of the mist. Twelve peaks! Mount Wu was the ancient home of the Rain Goddess and her lost lover, the ancient King of Chu, who for centuries has wandered in search of his love, crying out his despair. The cry of the gibbon is said to be his ghostly voice. A light rain began to fall.

Li noticed movement around the campfire. There were four figures, each bearing a torch. They moved toward him. Four women in heavily decorated ceremonial robes stood before him. In the torchlight, he could make out that their hair was piled in a knot on top of their heads and they wore some sort of cap.

"Forgive this intrusion—" Li assumed they must be in the midst of some sort of religious ceremony—"but I've been shipwrecked and washed up on this shore." One woman remained with Li as the others went over to the coffin.

"Oh, that. It's a long story, but first I must get it to shore."

He moved back into the water and tried to move that end of the coffin out of the river. It would not budge. Strange, he thought, it was light enough to float here under its own power.

The women approached the coffin with a lifting harness and strapped it on the front and back. Then each took a position and lifted the coffin out of the water. They moved it into their camp. As Li followed them with a torch, he noticed something. They had crossed the damp shore without leaving any footprints. Ghosts, fox spirits, specters of some sort, he thought.

He stopped in his tracks. What should he do? Then the fragrance of frankincense returned. With it came the Purple Immortal's words—the coffin would only go where it was supposed to go. Li moved toward the campfire. When he arrived, they offered him food and drink. No words were spoken, but he seemed to understand their intentions. The wine! He knew it, had tasted it before. But where?

The fragrance, the color—there is something so familiar about this wine—strange, it seems the more I try to remember, the less there is to grasp—of course, the Dream Temple! This is the Dream Temple wine—but what of Ah Wu? Was he not right in warning me of the dangers of dreams? Where is he now—a ghost wandering the shores of the Long River? Has my selfishness cost his life? And Old Zhou, Chen, Ma, and the Shamaness Luo—it is as if the meaning of my existence is to cause the death of others . . . .

The more Li thought about his friends, the more he drank, and the more he drank the less he could remember. He had already forgotten Old Zhou, Chen, and Ma. His mind, emptied by the wine, was overtaken by sleep. He passed the night dreamlessly.

***

That same night, downriver in the port of Ba-tung, Ah Wu and Chen were in an inn drinking ordinary rice wine.

"Why were you at the Dream Temple?" asked Chen as she leaned closer to Ah Wu. It didn't really matter how loudly they talked, because the inn was so busy and noisy no one would have heard them.

Ah Wu explained that Li was upset by his banishment and was trying to find a way back to his Court life.

"Li Bo, the great poet of spontaneity, would desire a life at Court?" asked Chen, her eyes wide with surprise.

Ah Wu laughed. "Dreamers are like that. What they write and how they behave doesn't always add up," He took another sip from his wine cup.

"Yet it was his dreams and wild flights of imagination that kept me from falling into the void of *Yin* existence," said Chen.

"I understand now. Those same dreams kept Li Bo alive, safe from the void of *Yang* existence, but with the imprisonment and banishment, he became confused and lost sight of his true roots," said Ah Wu. He smiled and sipped his wine again. This time he held it in his mouth for a moment and let its warmth permeate his tongue. His human *Yang* feelings were returning—he owed much to Chen.

"Li Bo," he continued after another swallow, "has long suffered the fate of any outsider in a closed group like the capital aristocrats. And his brilliance in a language that is not his native tongue isolates him even more."

Chen's eyes widened. "Then, why not use his native language to express himself?"

Ah Wu smiled again and poured more wine into his cup and into Chen's.

"And who would be his audience? Writing in Chinese, he has the empire at his feet. Yet with such reputation comes jealousy and then hatred."

"The master despised by those who should be the students," said Chen.

"Life," said Ah Wu. He raised his cup in mock toast.

"Did the Dream Temple help?" Chen wondered aloud.

"We met, didn't we?" Ah Wu said. He could feel his scar redden with embarrassment.

"Even with all the suffering that you must have endured in his companionship, you still follow him . . . ." Chen's voice trailed off.

"Is this not the same with you?"

"For the dreams?"

Ah Wu did not answer. He played with the ceramic wine bottle, turning it round and round in his big hard hands.

"I guess you could put it that way, though the idea of following a dreamer never sat well with me. You see, our relationship is very simple. Li Bo saved my life. Now, in my line of work, that is nothing remarkable. I have been in many battles where my comrades have saved my life and I did the same for them. This is the way of a warrior. For us it is unremarkable. yet we do not forget such gifts."

"Then what is so special with Li Bo?" Chen asked. She moved closer.

"I had never been saved before by a dream."

"What do you mean?"

"Here, have some more to drink. You're getting too carried away with this conversation." Ah Wu poured more of the hot wine in her cup and tended to the brazier. As he poked at the coals he continued. "I had been reprimanded by one of the Chinese officers in the Imperial Guard for a remark about his mother being a camel—a fat, hairy camel, to be exact. He ordered my execution. Since it involved the Imperial Palace Guard, the Emperor was also involved. Li was at Court that day and the Emperor turned to him for advice on the nature of my execution. Thoroughly drunk, as usual, Li spun off a poem reminding the Emperor that he should not take lightly the lives of those who offer their lives to protect him."

"Heaven! He got away with that!" said Chen, spilling wine on her robe.

"Ha! The poem was so brilliant—the rhyme scheme and the deft use of classical allusions—none of these things that I understand, and done with such ease, that the Emperor pardoned me as a gesture of admiration for Li's talent. I had finally lived to see the day when the flicks of a brush, wielded by a drunk, could stand the Court on its ear! Of course, he made enemies because of his brilliance. Perhaps those who are behind his banishment are the same who were shamed by the poem that saved my life. Anyway, I prefer his company . . . ."

Ah Wu's sentence was cut off by his excited reaction to the loud conversation that passed by their table.

"Did you hear what they said?" he said to Chen.

"Yes, there's been a terrible shipwreck with a great loss of life."

"The ship," said Ah Wu, moving closer to Chen so the other guests in the inn couldn't hear their conversation, "was traveling upriver."

"Could it have been Li Bo's?" wondered Chen.

"We don't even know his ship's name. It could be anywhere on the river by this time."

Some guests started screaming. There was a great commotion and people were running for the exits. Ah Wu and Chen looked around trying to figure out what was the matter.

"A fire?" Ah Wu asked Chen. But before she could answer, a man sitting at the next table laughed aloud. Ah Wu and Chen turned toward him. Ah Wu, with his hand on his crossbow, rose from their table.

"Something funny?" he said.

"Yes, in fact." The large man with a great black beard laughed.

"What?" said Ah Wu in his old threatening tone. At the same time, he noticed that he could now handle his crossbow. Things were beginning to get back to "normal." Well, almost normal, he thought.

Chen started laughing, too, and Ah Wu looked at her.

"What is the matter with all of you?" People were still running around outside screaming.

Chen tried to stop laughing. "Sit down and get control of yourself," he told her.

Ah Wu looked down. His right leg was invisible. "What is this?"

"You're like me, friend," roared the heavily bearded man. "A new ghost who has yet to master his *Yin* existence."

"Ah Wu, concentrate! Get your leg back into the *Yang* realm."

"Sorry, haven't tried drinking and staying in this realm at the same time. The *Yin* realm is much too much a mental one for me." His face was flushed with embarrassment.

"Tell me, friend, how you recently left the *Yang* realm," asked Chen.

"Shipwreck, last night."

Ah Wu and Chen looked at each other and moved to the man's table, with their flask of wine.

"Can you tell us about it? We had a friend on board."

The man drew back for a moment. He spoke slowly. "Your friend wouldn't have been an albino swordsman?"

"No, not that bastard," said Ah Wu. "A poet, Li Bo. Thin, with a wispy white hair, likes to drink . . . ."

The sailor sat back, more at ease, with a smile on his face. "Oh, that one. Yes, he couldn't stand that shit Floating Ants wine that the captain loved. The captain pushed it on all his guests. Ah, those were the days."

Ah Wu reached out and touched the man's sleeve. "What happened to the poet?"

At first, the sailor moved back, but when he saw the anxiety in Ah Wu's eyes he leaned forward. "They were all lost. The storm snapped the anchor chain and drove us into the rocks. No one could have survived."

Ah Wu's head bent down. Chen touched his shoulder and tried to fight back her tears. The sailor reached for wine and took a long drink.

"The whole trip was cursed from the beginning. We had several deaths before we even reached Ba-tung. One of our crew, and then the female passenger. Your poet friend was chivalrous enough to have a coffin be built for her."

"A female passenger?" said Ah Wu.

"Yes, the captain said she was an entertainer of some sort."

"Thank you, sir. Please help yourself to our wine; we must leave now," said Chen. She got Ah Wu to his feet.

"What?" Ah Wu gave her a questioning look.

"We must leave. Now!" She gave him a kick and they disappeared.

Chen managed to get Ah Wu to reappear in a back alley.

"Listen, the woman must be the shamaness that wounded the Blood Dragon."

Ah Wu was still having trouble getting his right leg to fully reappear. At Chen's insistence, he stopped trying and paid attention to what she was saying.

"The shamaness is dead?" she said. "Who killed her?"

"Maybe she died of her wounds in the fight with the monster."

"Possibly, but then why would Li Bo go through the trouble of having a coffin built for her?"

"She must have been attractive," Ah Wu said offhandedly. Chen hit him. His leg reappeared.

"No. It's not that simple."

"Wait!" said Ah Wu, who, now, with all of him present in the *Yang* realm, could give his complete attention to the question. "She must be the shamaness that Ma Ssu-ming was following. She had escaped from the capital. Li was probably doing it for Ma."

"But if she was that powerful, who could have overcome her, and why would she be going upriver?"

"Mount Wu. A lot of shamans and shamanesses like to hang around there," said Ah Wu. Chen nodded in agreement.

"Aaai-yaa! I got it!" yelled Ah Wu. "It's Mount Wu. That's where Li Bo was told to go in his dream at the Dream Temple!"

"What's this have to do with the shamaness?"

"Don't know yet but Mount Wu is where they are all heading. Let's go!"

"Hold on. How do you know Li is alive?" said Chen trying to hold Ah Wu back. He stopped and turned back to her. She could see he was hesitating to give her an answer.

Ah Wu scratched his curly beard. "I would never admit this to Li Bo, but there are some dreams that I also cling to."

They rose off the ground together, turned into mist, and flew off toward Mount Wu.

***

Slowly making its way up the Long River toward Mount Wu, the Blood Dragon began to pick up a scent. It was a rare scent, but familiar. The farther upriver it swam, the stronger the scent became. It was around noon that the creature was able to match the scent with a name: "Frankincense!"

Of course, it thought, the Lady of the Purple Vault. That is her personal scent, and the ray that emanated from the shamaness's mirror was purple.

"The old bat must be the spirit guardian of that shamaness. And the source of the Dragon Pool Sword. Ha, she has finally made a fatal error to entrust such a powerful weapon to such a puny creature. They will all be doomed once I have it," the Blood Dragon said to itself. The creature reasoned that the scent must be leading directly to Mount Wu, and, somehow or other, the poet must still be with the shamaness, and with him the sword.

It dove deep into the river. The water became colder and darker. The creature's eyes glowed red, illuminating a path before it. Finally, it reached the riverbed and the entrance to the tunnel system. The Blood Dragon, having traversed the tunnels for centuries, knew the direct route to the twelve-peaked home of the Rain Goddess.

~ 33 ~

When Li awoke, he found four women dressed in the robes of high Daoist priestesses studying him. He sat up. The air was cool and fresh, but he was not cold. Behind him, the river was gone, erased by the mist. In front of him was a mountain that rose steeply into that same pearly mist—a fitting abode for the Immortals, Li thought. Beyond the staring Daoists lay the entrance to a large cave through which raged a turbulent stream. Its roar reverberated off the stonewalls.

"Good morning, kind protectors," Li said, with his finest courtly accent and bow. The four Daoists saluted him silently and escorted him to a table. He was served some sort of fruit drink and a type of breadfruit. A meal so simple, but unlike anything he had eaten before. He could feel a surge in his *chi* energy as he ate.

Right after he finished eating, the women took up the coffin harness, lit their torches, and moved toward the cave entrance. The robes they wore were extremely ornate—moreso than any he had seen in the capital. The silk garment had broad Imperial Court-length sleeves, long enough to cover the hands and touch the ground, and a high collar. The sleeves had wonderful dragons and phoenixes at play embroidered in gold and white silk.

On the back, over a light gold background, rolling waves were embroidered around the border that encircled an auburn representation of a mountain in the center. No doubt, the mountain must be this one, thought Li. On the left and right sides, dragons rose from the billowing waves. Above the dragons were the sun and moon. On top of the mountain was a palace and, over it, a golden stream of light flowed upward from the left where a man was holding the source of the light. A multi-colored rainbow shone through the palace windows.

This was strange, thought Li Bo. Outside the mountain scene, everything was standard Daoist iconography. But what of this man as a source of the golden light? And a rainbow within the palace? Li had seen many Daoist paintings and robes, but none with scenes like these.

Cold water brought him back from his journey over the seas and mountains of the robe. He was knee-high in the torrent that flooded the cave. The four Daoists and the coffin had continued—on the surface of the water. Li Bo stood there with his mouth open. Yes, he had read of such wondrous events among the Immortals, even imagined them in his poetic wanderings, but now it was happening right before his eyes.

The women stopped and one turned back to Li. Another motioned him to come forward. He took a step and the water closed over his waist. He stopped. She continued to motion. Then Li thought, a test? A test of my faith? Hadn't this type of event commonly occurred in the records of the Perfected? A potential disciple is asked to do something that no mortal could survive and, depending on his response, he gains or forfeits their companionship. The decision was easy. Li simply thought of his coming death in Yunnan and all his lost friends. He preferred clear mountain water to a lonely death among poisonous snakes and insects.

Down into the icy water he plunged. It was so cold and so deep that all his muscles knotted up. He could not move. Blackness took over his mind as he lost control. There were no memories, nothing to haunt him—only release, neither cold nor warm, neither *Yin* nor *Yang*. He let go. All his senses were bathed in a wondrous golden light—he could actually feel, hear, taste, smell, and see the light.

The mountain was extremely steep, its uppermost peaks now completely cloaked in gray clouds, but there was a path of sorts leading up from the other side of the cave. Li blinked, again. He saw the group moving up and away from him. The pearl-hued mist seemed to surround and warm him. His clothes were dry and his body relaxed. He turned and watched the mountain torrent rush past him and into the cave. He was on the other side. A dream? A release? Another realm? Li smiled; he no longer needed to figure things out. He moved up the path with the Daoists and the coffin. They had entered Mount Wu, the Realm of the Rain Goddess.

A light rain continued to fall. The smell of wet earth and foliage was so thick he could taste it. Li Bo's thoughts turned to the climb he and Ah Wu made to the Dream Temple. Those thoughts still saddened him. No doubt, he thought, this is the destination that the old woman of his dream had in mind. Perhaps he would find some connection with Ah Wu up here.

The air seemed filled with the sound of flowing water. They passed turbulent streams, their waters all white with fury; calm brooks that snaked through magnificent pine and blue-green juniper forests, their waters crystal clear; and waterfalls that seemed to hang in the air and fall from space, shattering into millions of pearl-like beads as they crashed into the jagged rocks far below.

All this water, thought Li. Mount Wu is certainly the appropriate home for a Rain Goddess. Then he noticed that the flowing water seemed to respond to their passing by increasing in volume. Could it be the drink they gave him, he speculated, or just the nature of this whole mountain—the "realm of the Immortals"? The sound of those characters intoxicated the mundane world, but here earth-bound language was somehow disagreeable. Like music played on the wrong instrument, it didn't fit.

They rested at noon, though Li doubted the Daoists needed any rest at all. He looked down the path they had followed and could just barely make out the cave far below. As he was enjoying the crashing of a nearby torrent, something emerged from the water just outside the cave. Li strained to get a clearer glimpse. It was long and dark, and crawled out onto the shore.

By this time the Daoist priestesses, who were preparing lunch for him, came over to share the view. They, probably having much better vision, Li thought, reacted with horror. He watched their eyes as they recognized whatever it was moving far below. They gathered up their things. One of them motioned to Li to finish his juice drink. Perhaps, he thought, I will need this nourishment. He drank deeply then had to move quickly to keep up with the group.

Higher and higher they climbed up toward the clouds that were between them and the twelve summits of Mount Wu. Though the pace was more than even Ah Wu could sustain, Li was not tired and kept up.

It occurred to Li Bo that if these were really Immortals, what could it be down there that frightened them? Immortals should be beyond all fear. What was it they saw? he wondered. The realization came slowly, for the higher they climbed, the more the beauty of the mountain overwhelmed him. Li could not take his eyes off the rows of mountain ridges spread out below him like the waves of the Long River. However, the closer to the cloud layer they moved, the less he could see. Finally, there were only the four torches to guide him.

His mind refocused on the question of the strange figure crawling out of the stream. What would move like that and give these women such a scare? What could threaten the shamaness?

Just as they burst through the cloud layer, Li Bo realized what it was. The twelve peaks of Mount Wu towered before him. It was the apparition in his dream at the Dream Temple.

Off to the right, mist began to flow in from a high valley formed by the slopes of two mountain peaks. To the left, on a small plateau just before the main peak, which must be Rain Goddess Peak, there was an altar of stone and behind it a cave. The mist traveled from the mouth of the valley, across the other peaks, and toward the altar. The words from the Immortal Lao-tze rose in Li's mind: *The gateway of the mysterious female is the wellspring of Heaven and Earth.*

This was it, thought Li, the *Gate of the Mysterious Female.* There on the plateau must be the burial site for the shamaness. He understood—that location would be the recipient of Mount Wu's vital energy, thus imbuing it with great transformational power.

He also understood something else—it was the Blood Dragon climbing out of the stream down below. It had come to stop the shamaness's burial in that spot of mysterious power, and the Daoists were frightened that the monster could succeed. Li suddenly realized the purpose of bringing the Dragon Pool Sword here: with it, someone of pure mind could defeat the Blood Dragon. He would probably meet that hero down below at the burial site.

He couldn't spend much more time thinking, for the pace had picked up and he needed all his attention on the narrowing stone ledge ahead. It was obvious now that they intended to make camp at the plateau before nightfall.

***

It was morning, just after Li Bo and his group had left, when Ah Wu and Miss Chen landed at the cave entrance to Mount Wu.

"It's too high; the mist will never carry us up there. This cave must be the only entrance to the mountain," said Chen. However, when they tried to use their *Yin* powers to pass through the cave, they were repulsed.

"I don't understand, I thought water, a *yin* element, would be receptive to our passing, but here we go deeper and deeper and never seem to rise," said Ah Wu, who was exhausted from the attempt.

"Yes, and we tire so easily," added Chen.

"What's the matter?"

Chen thought for a while before answering. "We're not clean."

"We're ghosts! What the camel's ass does it matter?" raged Ah Wu.

"Please! Your language is changing back to 'normal' as your memory improves. What is this thing about camels? Listen, it matters to the water spirit of that stream. This is Mount Wu, home of the Rain Goddess. If we approach the mountain from outside that cave, we have to be ritually clean."

"Sorry about the camels; too long in the Western Regions. But so what about the water spirit?" said Ah Wu.

"The realm of the Rain Goddess is pure. How should I put it delicately, beings such as ourselves who have just had relations . . . ."

"Relations! What the camel's, uh, what are you talking about?"

"She has remained pure for over a thousand years since she parted from her lover." Chen finished her sentence with a smile.

"No wonder it's so hard to get through," cracked Ah Wu, with a smile.

"Quiet! You want to get the whole mountain down on us?" hissed Chen.

"Spirits! Here we go again, just as on that Dream Temple mountain; nothing ever is what it seems. Anyway that must be the female version of the Rain Goddess's life, for it is certainly not the male version!"

"Who cares! Whatever version, we still need to purify ourselves. Let's see how many days was it since we, ah, ah," Chen was blushing as she spoke. "Yes, I think an evening of fasting and meditation should do it."

Chen then went about explaining to Ah Wu what they needed to do to gain entrance to the mountain. He grumbled a lot, especially about the fasting, but did as he was told. He was a spirit now, and Chen was his senior, as in the army, even if she was a female.

During the night, a great storm took place on Mount Wu. Ah Wu and Chen watched for most of the night and wondered if there would be anything left of the mountain by morning. Curiously, the storm did not affect areas outside the mountain.

"I don't like it," said Ah Wu, "Li Bo is in there."

"Back to our ritual," said Chen. "It's the only way we can reach him."

***

On the upper reaches of Mount Wu, darkness had enclosed Li's camp. The coffin had come to an abrupt stop just before the stone altar. The Daoists had marked off a space around it in the rocky soil and set up the altar with red spirit lamps, incense, fruits, scriptures, and other offerings. They performed some sort of ceremony that Li had never seen before. The music and their chanting were unearthly and, as the ceremony unfolded, the winds picked up and the mist got thicker.

They had set up a place for Li to rest in the cave that was directly behind the altar. It seemed that this would be the shamaness's final resting-place. In the cave, they had built a fire and provided Li with a new drink. This was obviously much stronger and seemed to be a sort of wine, possibly for use in the ceremony. Its taste hinted of various fruits, but none that he could readily identify.

The weather grew more intense. Lightning flashes and rolling thunder bursts became more frequent. Li grew tired and fell into a fitful sleep. During the night he woke to the sound of thunder that shook the earth, to incessant rain that seemed as if it would wash the whole mountain away, to the sound of trees being uprooted by the wind and flung through the air. Each time he awoke, he could only remain conscious for a few moments before the powerful fingers of sleep drew him back. He remembered feeling that Mount Wu's twelve peaks were sinking into the Long River.

~ 34 ~

When Li rose, dawn was just arriving at Rain Goddess Peak. The fire had gone out and he was alone. Out beyond the cave entrance, nine pine trees stood—three behind the altar and three on each side of it. The night before there had been no trees on the plateau.

The coffin was gone. A large square hole had taken its place. The incense and altar offerings were still intact and had been refreshed sometime during the night. Li rose and walked out of the cave.

Off in the distance, the mist was flowing in from the Gate of the Mysterious Female. It was like an artist painting with fog and mist, thought Li. As this mysterious artist dipped his brush in the valley entrance, the tops of the mountains disappeared, whole valleys were layered over by a brush of fog and mist. The excess from the brush ran down the mountain slopes and lightened the greens that were emerging from the dawn light into white shadows. As the brush became drier, the "ink" became lighter and lighter.

A hideous laugh shattered Li's poetic painting. It came from the open grave. The mist had reached the plateau and was washing everything pale white. From the grave, a red light drifted upward through the whiteness. Li drew his dagger and moved to the edge of the grave. The Blood Dragon in its monstrous natural form stood on the coffin, drinking the blood of a Daoist priestess. Three others lay strewn around the top of the coffin, their beautiful robes drenched in blood. The monster turned up toward the top of the grave, its long ugly snout smeared with blood, and smiled at Li Bo.

Li ran back from the grave. In an instant, the monster had jumped up from the bottom of the grave and crawled after him. As its mouth opened, a forked red tongue darted out from its parted rows of long white teeth.

"So, Li Bo," it said, in its sweet female human voice, "we meet again. Surprised at this form? It's this cursed mountain, forces reality upon all of us. The form matters little to me, but your shamaness is dead and I will send her into the ninth level of Hell when I destroy her remains and any chance of her rebirth as a meddlesome Immortal. Ah Wu is my slave, as is the female, Chen. But don't feel sad. You will soon join them as a fellow slave! So much for your dreams!"

It moved toward Li. He backed closer to the cave. He had to get to his *jheng*, which lay in the cave still wrapped in its waterproof cloth.

"My powers could never match those of the Rain Goddess. However, I have waited patiently for centuries. Now, thanks to your stupid human emotions, I have the chance to destroy her. Your destiny was to bring me that sword, for it holds the power of her destruction! Try, Li Bo, to act with the intelligence that your species credits you with. Moreso than that moron companion of yours . . . . I know you have the Dragon Pool Sword."

"What sword?" Li said, on purpose. He wanted the creature as angry as possible so that it wouldn't notice him moving backward to the cave.

The creature's eyes burnt white. "You stupid human, you dare taunt me! Your death will be painful."

It crawled closer and reared itself up using its tail for balance. Its full height towered over Li Bo and its hideous laugh shook the plateau, but it was cut short. Something hit the creature from behind and protruded from its chest. Li looked in amazement. It was a crossbow bolt. Before it could yell, the monster turned and received another in its left eye. It screamed and disappeared.

"Ah Wu!" Li yelled.

Out of the mist, two figures ran toward Li. The large one he knew right away. He wept as he embraced Ah Wu.

"Oh, my faithful friend, you are alive; you are alive!" Then he made out Chen's features and cried some more.

After a moment, Ah Wu spoke. "Camel's ass! Not a bad shot, eh? Been out of practice." He continued, as heloaded two more bolts into his crossbow, "Li Bo, we are in great danger. My bolts can't kill it. We must prepare for its return. Get the Dragon Pool Sword!"

It was as Ah Wu spoke that Li realized his friend was a ghost. Chen saw Li looking where Ah Wu's right leg should have been—it was still invisible.

"What does it matter?" she said to Li. "We are together. We are friends and as such the monster is our only limitation."

Yes, thought Li, friendship. He looked at Chen. She had changed. There was a sense of confidence about her that he had not been aware of before.

"We have all changed over the last few weeks. Now we face the Great Transformation—but our friendship shall overcome," said Li. "Quick, it's in the cave!"

Before they could take another step, however, the monster, bleeding a whitish fluid from its chest and lacking a left eye, appeared behind Ah Wu. It hit him with its open claw. The blow crushed Au Wu's left shoulder and arm. He dropped the crossbow, but he used the monster's force to swivel to the right, his broadsword drawn, and to slice through the creature's right arm at the elbow. Yet his own wound was too much, even for a ghost, and Ah Wu dropped to the ground, his broadsword falling from his hand.

The Blood Dragon staggered backward and let out an earth-shaking roar. Its one good eye was a searing white flame. Chen ran to Ah Wu's aid. Li had managed to inflict another cut on the Blood Dragon when it had hit Ah Wu. He ran forward, placing himself between the monster and his friend. He heard Ah Wu call out to him.

"Don't bother with me! Get the sword!"

"Yes!" yelled Li. As he turned to run, Chen screamed. The monster was on her. Li ran into the cave and ripped off the *jheng* cover, "Behold, your undoing, the great Dragon Pool Sword," he shouted. He tore at the end of the *jheng*.

The monster brushed Chen aside, moved passed Ah Wu, who was lying in pain, and came toward Li Bo in the cave. Li got the end off and turned the open end of the *jheng* downward. Nothing happened. He flipped it over and looked inside. Empty! He threw it on the ground with such force that it shattered. Chen reached his side. She realized that there was no Dragon Pool Sword and fell to the ground sobbing.

"Ha! So you don't have it! No matter. I can still destroy all of you, for the shamaness is defenseless without the sword. That alone will be worth my effort in this affair."

A roar shook the ground, but this one was different. Ah Wu, Chen, and Li looked up as a sword broke through the monster's chest, just at the point where a human's heart would be. The sword withdrew and thrust again. The monster, in a wild rage, spun around.

There stood Ma Ssu-ming, his sword held high, "A toast to the morning, eh! Old friends!" In his other hand, the Dragon Pool Sword. "Lao-huang reminded me what friendship is really about." The little yellow monkey chattered and jumped up and down. Ma threw the sword to Li Bo just as the Blood Dragon's powerful tail caught him across the chest, and flung him into the air, up and over the monster.

Li jumped up to grab it, but the monster was faster. Its scaly green claw wrapped around it a moment before Li Bo grasped it.

The green gemstone on its hilt glowed. The line from the Dream Temple tomb flashed into Li's mind, *"Only a mind so pure as the Dragon Pool, Will be its master."*

The Blood Dragon's taunt—"Ha! Pure evil!"—was cut short as Ma came down with his sword still drawn, cutting off the monster's arm, and falling into a bloody, broken heap at its feet. Li was left standing with the Dragon Pool Sword in his hand and the monster's amputated claw still grasping it. A golden light shone from around the edges of its scabbard mouth. Chen got up and shrieked, "It is free, use the sword!"

"No, impossible!" roared the Blood Dragon, "you can not be pure!"

"Perhaps, but I have turned your hand against you," Li said, as he drew the Dragon Pool Sword free from its scabbard. A blinding golden light flowed from the exposed blade. Li could hardly keep his eyes open—the light grew. He felt himself traveling through space, up and up. He stood before the seven stars of the Dipper, saw the two hidden soul stars and moved across them all. The Gate of Heaven swung open and he traveled onto the Heavenly Pivot.

Now he was back in the cave on Mount Wu. He got up and moved out of the cave, the monster retreating before him. The light shot up toward the sky and lit the whole mountaintop. High above them, it changed form, from a band of light into an animal shape. A head formed, then four legs and a tail.

"A dragon!" yelled Li Bo as he bent next to Ah Wu.

"A Light Dragon," cried Chen.

A Celestial Light Dragon formed over the Blood Dragon and opened its mouth. A purple ray shot from it and hit the monster in the head, reducing it to the size of a small lizard which scampered away, leaving a wisp of smoke and an unpleasant odor. The bearded traveler who would later tell the tale claimed it was without a doubt the odor of watery camel dung.

The Golden Light Dragon then took to the heavens, transmuting itself into the form of a golden rainbow. The earth on the shamaness's grave filled, and a blank stele appeared over it. From the Heavens a purple beam came down and inscribed the stone.

Li and Chen tried to turn their attention to Ah Wu, who was in terrible pain, but, exhausted, they fell unconscious. A light, fragrant rain fell as they slept and the welcome water washed away the dirt and pain from the three survivors.

~ 35 ~

Li Bo fell into a dream sleep. His spirit traveled high up Rain Goddess Peak and entered a palace. In one room, he found a woman in purple waiting for him.

"I know you," Li said. "You're the Purple Immortal. You came to me about the ship sinking and told me how to take care of the shamaness."

She smiled. "I am the Lady of the Purple Vault. You have done well, Li Bo, and you will be rewarded. First, I must return this to you."

Li's fan appeared in his waistband.

"Then you are also the lady I met at the Dream Temple!"

She smiled. "And I am the same adept whose journey led to the creation of the Dragon Pool Sword; a journey, with the successful release of the Dragon Pool Sword, you briefly experienced. Now listen to my instructions one more time, Li Bo, and your quest shall end successfully."

Li bowed in compliance.

"When you awake, take the black pearl in your hand between your thumb and index finger. Calm your mind and call upon the Rain Goddess of Mount Wu. Do this three times and she will appear to you. This is important. Do exactly as I have instructed."

Li felt something nudging his ear. He brushed at it, then again. He turned over and went back to sleep. The warm wine that splashed over his face got him up. Li rubbed his eyes.

"What's the idea of that, Ah Wu?" he grumbled. Then he noticed Ah Wu still on the ground, unconscious from his wounds. Chen was fast asleep next to him and Ma's bloody corpse was across from them. Li heard chattering from behind, and something landed on his shoulder. He reached for his dagger but it was gone.

"Lao-huang!" Li yelled. The monkey jumped off his shoulder, landed in front of him, and chattered wildly.

"Yes, I know. I'm sorry he's dead. He gave his life for ours—there are no greater swordsmen, no greater friends."

Lao-huang kept chattering. He had something in his hand. Li stretched out his hand and Lao-huang deposited a large black pearl in it.

"The albino swordsman?" questioned Li. Lao-huang jumped up and down.

"Ma killed him?" Lao-huang scampered around.

"And you stole this from him?" The monkey did a somersault.

Li laughed. "I suppose you are an Immortal, too. Quick, I must get to work with it and complete this journey."

Li took up a meditation position with the black pearl and followed the Lady of the Purple Vault's instructions. His body lightened. He continued to call on the Rain Goddess. Slowly at first, he felt himself rising from the ground. Above his seated body, then out above the gravesite, gaining height, he soared above the plateau as Rain Goddess Peak appeared before him. He moved to a palace on the peak; rainbows shone through its portals.

With the scent of frankincense, he found himself in a bright room. Its tatami mats were golden hued and fragrant like the fields of spring. Their borders were trimmed in dark green silk. In front of him, a woman sat amid numerous colored silk cushions that Li imagined to be clouds floating in the sky. He moved closer and recognized the face of Luo Jhu-yun, the Grand Shamaness.

"Shamaness Luo, we meet again," Li said in courtly tones.

"Yes, Li Bo, we meet again, but I am no longer the Shamaness Luo." She smiled. Li looked puzzled.

"I am *the dawn clouds and evening rain*."

Li was thunderstruck. Luo was the Rain Goddess of Mount Wu! Li bowed again, this time lower. The Rain Goddess laughed.

"Please, no courtly manners. Here our reverence is for Nature and not for shallow formalities. Rise Li Bo."

Her voice had a more measured quality to it, a soothing tone. A sign of her spiritual maturity, thought Li Bo.

"Yes, and the same spiritual maturity awaits you and your companions."

"You can read my thoughts?" Li said.

"If I choose," she said and smiled.

"Li Bo," she continued, "for the loyalty that you and your companions have shown the Rain Goddess, I can offer all of you the Path to Immortality. This means your friends, who are now ghosts, can transcend the *Yin* realm and become Immortals."

"This will be wonderful news for them, but I'm concerned for Ma Ssu-ming. Is it too late to save his spirit?"

"No. It is still within the time limit. An Immortal will appear to lead his spirit out from his body to join Ah Wu and Chen. If he so chooses, he may also become my disciple, for in the end he showed his loyalty by giving his life for a friend."

She paused a moment and looked into Li's heart.

"What about you, Li Bo? What path will you follow?"

Li looked at her for a moment, staring deep into her eyes, and smiled. "Then you know of my heart's confusion?"

"It is not confusion, Li Bo. It is wisdom, which you do not yet understand. Most of all, Li Bo, calm your heart. Like the waves of a pure mountain lake, once calmed, the depths reveal themselves. Seek its source and let it always guide you. A pure heart never falters."

"Yes, but this is where I falter. Where my heart was once excited in following the mists of countless mountains and the courses of myriad rivers, it now remains silent and barren. I have lost the voice known as Li Bo."

"Have you? Do you really believe that it was the Blood Dragon's heart that released the Dragon Pool Sword?"

***

Li awoke with Lao-huang pulling at his ear.

"Yes, yes, yes, the wine is ready, I'm coming," said Li, his eyes still closed. Everyone laughed. His eyes popped open to find Ah Wu and Chen standing around him. In front of the altar, Ma's body had been cleaned and properly arranged. Li jumped up, paid his respects to Ma's prostrate form, and told them about his dream visit to the Rain Goddess. For his own reasons, however, he left out the last part of their conversation. Ah Wu and Chen were greatly pleased.

"Li Bo," said Ah Wu, "would you mind if I became the Rain Goddess's disciple?"

Li Bo was touched by Ah Wu's faithfulness. "Ah Wu, Ah Wu, follow your heart. You and Chen belong together, and I could think of no grander association than that of Immortals," Li said, smiled, and embraced Ah Wu and Chen.

"But what of our friend here?" Li asked, sadly, as he walked over to Ma's body. "We must see that brother Ma's spirit properly joins us."

Lao-huang leaped on the altar and set three fresh incense sticks into the burner. He somersaulted through the air. What landed next to Ma's body was no longer a monkey—he was a young swordsman. He bowed to the other three, reached down and touched Ma's forehead. From it, he drew out Ma's spirit. Within an instant, Ma Ssu-ming stood before them, as real as Ah Wu and Chen.

"Ma Ssu-ming, from Ding-chou, a musician and drinker by trade and now, I understand, soon to be an Immortal. A toast to my friends, to the grand Way and its ever mysterious twists and turns!"

Li was overjoyed—they were all back together. The Immortal swordsman brought them wine and introduced himself.

"I am Lao-huang, an Immortal here on Mount Wu who was sent to enlighten swordsman Ma's protection of the Rain Goddess."

A great cheer went up as they emptied their cups. During the first evening of their celebration, Lao-huang explained that the Rain Goddess was reborn every thousand years. At first, none of the Immortals know where or who she is. Then, over the years, reports of shamanesses who seem to have extraordinary powers filter back to Mount Wu, and it is always as a shamaness that the Rain Goddess returns.

The Lady of the Purple Vault, Lao-huang continued, looks after the spiritual training of the new Rain Goddess once she is found. It is, however, only after her physical death in human form that her spiritual embryo can be fully developed. The critical period comes with interment on Mount Wu at a precise location that also changes every thousand years. Thus, explained Lao-huang, if the Blood Dragon had destroyed the coffin, the final transformation into a complete Rain Goddess would have been aborted. This would have been a cataclysm for the ruling dynasty as the Rain Goddess harmonizes the flow of the Long River. Without her, the river would quickly go out of control. Another thousand years would have to pass before another Rain Goddess came forth. All this information was inscribed on the stele that appeared over the shamaness's tomb.

The celebrations went on for another week. Ah Wu and Chen drank and took long walks together. Li had never seen his old friend so content and at peace with himself. He had even forgotten camels.

Li and Ma sang and played all night long, watching the stars and moon at night, and during the day, the dawn clouds, then the evening rain. A heavenly chorus joined their music. yet with all this merriment and celebration, both Ma and Ah Wu noticed

Li Bo was not his usual self. Ah Wu figured Li must have still been adjusting to the changes in his life. Ma, however, noticed that Li seemed particularly ill at ease when the gibbons cried late at night.

Early one morning, far enough from dawn that the Silver River was still brightly illuminating the Heavens, Li and Ma were alone on the edge of the plateau, drinking and looking out at the night sky. A gibbon's cry shattered the darkness. Ma glanced at Li. Tears were falling from his eyes. Ma put down his wine cup and moved over to Li.

"Elder brother, why so sad?"

"I am being summoned to the Realm of the Immortals, but I do not know how to answer."

The wind began to pick up and a luminescent mist covered the plateau. A gentle rain fell.

"Elder brother, we should move to the cave."

Li got up as if in a trance and moved toward the cave. The rain increased in intensity. Lit by a strange glow from the mountain and blown by the wind, the rain appeared to dance all around Li.

Ma moved away and watched. A gibbon howled again. The rain moved like the soft silk curtains in a grand palace blown by a wild wind. As Ma watched, he thought he saw a woman's form moving around Li. There was a serene expression on Li's face as he moved over to the edge of the plateau. Before Ma could realize what was about to happen, much less act, Li threw himself over the edge.

— 36 —

They had searched for several nights and days but found no trace of Li's body. Ah Wu felt that by going off with Chen, he had deserted his friend.

"No, brother, I am not convinced that it is as simple as that," said Ma.

"What do you mean?"

"The gibbons stopped crying after Li threw himself into the rain."

"And every night we have wild rainstorms," said Chen, trying to comfort Ah Wu.

The three friends decided to hold a vigil for three nights to ask the Rain Goddess for assistance. Li had given them the black pearl to contact their master. Now they sat in a circle, each touching the pearl as they chanted her name.

Every night, during the rainstorm, each one heard something different. The first night, Ah Wu heard laughter and the sound of wine cups clinking. The next night, Chen heard Li singing his poetry. Some poems were familiar, others were completely new and as beautiful as any Li had composed. During the third night, Ma was certain he heard the unique tones of Li's *jheng* pouring forth music that wove in and out of the beating rain.

On the dawn of the fourth morning, Li Bo walked back into camp.

"We missed your music and singing. What happened to your celebrations?" Li asked, with a smile.

"Li Bo!" Ah Wu rushed up and embraced him.

"Old friend, there is nothing to be so worried about. Right, brother Ma?" Li Bo said, and laughed.

"Elder brother. Then, you are leaving us?" asked Ma.

"You learn fast, younger brother. Please help Ah Wu. This path that you have chosen will not be easy, but your futures are all so bright."

"And yours, elder brother?" Chen asked tenderly.

Before he answered, Li smiled at his friends. "The Way of Li Bo is the Way of the clouds and rivers—the Way of Dreams."

***

After three more days of drinking and singing, they parted. Ah Wu, Chen, and Ma remained on Mount Wu to serve the Rain Goddess. Li Bo left and continued up the Long River. Besides the clouds, mists, mountains, and rivers—a small yellow-hued monkey that liked to drink wine joined him in his travels and listened to him compose his new poems.

THE END

EPILOGUE

History records that when Li Bo reached the Mount Wu region, he received news that the Emperor had granted him a full pardon. Li turned back down the Long River, sought out his family, and later resumed his wanderings all over China until his death.

History, however, doesn't record whether Li ever met up again with Ah Wu, Miss Chen, Ma Ssu-ming, or the Rain Goddess. There are, however, some storytellers who claim knowledge of such meetings. But then, whoever pays attention to storytellers? Ah Wu would call them dreamers, or worse.

How we got our name

. . . from *Pleasure Boat Studio*, an essay written by Ouyang Xiu, Song Dynasty poet, essayist, and scholar, on the twelfth day of the twelfth month in the renwu year (January 25, 1043):

> "I have heard of men of antiquity who fled from the world to distant rivers and lakes and refused to their dying day to return. They must have found some source of pleasure there. If one is not anxious for profit, even at the risk of danger, or is not convicted of a crime and forced to embark; rather, if one has a favorable breeze and gentle seas and is able to rest comfortably on a pillow and mat, sailing several hundred miles in a single day, then is boat travel not enjoyable? Of course, I have no time for such diversions. But since 'pleasure boat' is the designation of boats used for such pastimes, I have now adopted it as the name of my studio. Is there anything wrong with that?"

Translated by Ronald Egan

Following is a complete list of books by
Pleasure Boat Studio: A Literary Press:

Good Night, My Darling • Inger Frimansson • Trans fm Swedish
   by Laura A. Wideburg • **a caravel mystery** • $16
Falling Awake • Mary Lou Sanelli • **an aequitas book** • $14
Monique • Luisa Coelho • Trans fm Portuguese by Dolores DeLuise
   and Maria do Carmo de Vasconcelos • fiction • $14
Way Out There: Lyrical Essays • Michael Daley • **an aequitas book** • $16
The Case of Emily V. • Keith Oatley • **a caravel mystery** • $18
Against Romance • Michael Blumenthal • poetry • $14
Speak to the Mountain: The Tommie Waites Story • Dr. Bessie Blake
   an aequitas book • $18/$26
Artrage • Everett Aison • fiction • $15
Days We Would Rather Know • Michael Blumenthal • poetry • $14
Puget Sound: 15 Stories • C. C. Long • fiction • $14
Homicide My Own • Anne Argula • fiction (mystery) • $16
Craving Water • Mary Lou Sanelli • poetry • $15
When the Tiger Weeps • Mike O'Connor • poetry and prose • $15
Wagner, Descending: The Wrath of the Salmon Queen • Irving Warner
   fiction • $16
Concentricity • Sheila E. Murphy • poetry • $13.95
Schilling, from a study in lost time • Terrell Guillory • fiction • $16
Rumours: A Memoir of a British POW in WWII • Chas Mayhead
   nonfiction • $16
The Immigrant's Table • Mary Lou Sanelli • poetry and recipes • $13.95
The Enduring Vision of Norman Mailer • Dr. Barry H. Leeds • criticism • $18
Women in the Garden • Mary Lou Sanelli • $14
Pronoun Music • Richard Cohen • short stories • $16
If You Were With Me Everything Would Be All Right • Ken Harvey
   short stories • $16
The 8th Day of the Week • Al Kessler • fiction • $16
Another Life, and Other Stories • Edwin Weihe • short stories • $16
Saying the Necessary • Edward Harkness • poetry • $14
Nature Lovers • Charles Potts • poetry • $10
In Memory of Hawks, & Other Stories from Alaska • Irving Warner
   fiction • $15
The Politics of My Heart • William Slaughter • poetry • $13
The Rape Poems • Frances Driscoll • poetry • $13
When History Enters the House: Essays from Central Europe
   Michael Blumenthal • nonfiction • $15
Setting Out: The Education of Li-li • Tung Nien • Trans fm Chinese by
   Mike O'Connor • fiction • $15

Our Chapbook Series:

No. 1: *The Handful of Seeds: Three and a Half Essays* • Andrew Schelling nonfiction • $7

No. 2: *Original Sin* • Michael Daley • poetry • $8

No. 3: *Too Small to Hold You* • Kate Reavey • poetry • $8

No. 4: *The Light on Our Faces: A Therapy Dialogue* • Lee Miriam Whitman-Raymond • poetry • $9

No. 5: *Selected New Poems of Rainer Maria Rilke* • Trans fm German by Alice Derry • poetry • $10

No. 6: *Through High Still Air: A Season at Sourdough Mountain* Tim McNulty • poetry and prose • $9

No. 7: *Sight Progress* • Zhang Er, Trans fm Chinese by Rachel Levitsky prose-poems • $9

No. 8: *The Perfect Hour* • Blas Falconer • poetry • $9

From our backlist (in limited editions, from Empty Bowl Press, unless otherwise marked):

Desire • Jody Aliesan • poetry • $14

Deams of the Hand • Susan Goldwitz • poetry • $14

Lineage • Mary Lou Sanelli • poetry • $14

The Basin: Poems from a Chinese Province • Mike O'Connor poetry • $14

The Straits • Michael Daley • poetry • $14

In Our Hearts and Minds: The Northwest and Central America Ed. Michael Daley • poetry/prose • $14

The Rainshadow • Mike O'Connor • poetry • $14

Untold Stories • William Slaughter • poetry • $14

In Blue Mountain Dusk • Tim McNulty • poetry (a Broken Moon book) $14

Orders: Pleasure Boat Studio books are available by order from your favorite bookstore, directly from PBS (at the email below), or through the following:

SPD (Small Press Distribution) Tel. 800-869-7553, Fax 510-524-0852
Partners/West Tel. 425-227-8486, Fax 425-204-2448
Baker & Taylor Tel. 800-775-1100, Fax 800-775-7480
Ingram Tel. 615-793-5000, Fax 615-287-5429
amazon.com or barnesandnoble.com

Pleasure Boat Studio: A Literary Press
201 West 89th Street
New York, NY 10024
Tel: 212-362-8563/Fax: 888-810-5308
www.pleasureboatstudio.com/pleasboat@nyc.rr.com